RULE OF TWELVE

BOOK 2

I0561734

CONVERGENCE

BRADLEY ALLEN

First published in Ireland 2022.

This second edition published in Ireland in 2024.

Published by TPAssist LIMITED.

ISBN 978-1-0686295-3-2

[1]

TPAssist LIMITED
14 Penrose Wharf
Cork, T23 W440, Ireland

www.tpassist.com

This book is dedicated to my wonderful children.

This is for your future.

Chapter 1 – New surrounds

1

Dukk put the news aside, closed his eyes and focused on the creed. He recited it in his head. "Focus on that which is real in the heart. Create the space so that the process can emerge. Honour that which serves you well. Engage in the journey as it unfolds."

When he opened his eyes, the others were still at the table, staring at him.

At the other end of the long table, was Mentor.

Mentor hid his forty-nine years well. He was tall, muscular and of dark brown complexion, with cool undertones. He had dark brown eyes and short black hair with wisps of grey.

Mentor had joined Dukk's crew one month earlier at the start of the adventure that saw the end of Dukk's beloved Dinatha. Mentor was taken on as a generalist, owing to his experience with all aspects of keeping inter-galactic rigs moving. He also had medical qualifications. These skills had already been put to good use.

Dukk had just learnt that Mentor was acting as a double agent. That news went a long way to explaining Mentor's odd behaviour over the last month. However, it wasn't enough. Mentor was still very much a mystery to Dukk.

"That is about to change!" Dukk thought to himself.

On Mentor's left was Bazzer. He was a stout and fit man in his late forties. He had fair complexion, dark green eyes and unkept long red hair that was often secured in a low ponytail.

Bazzer was Dukk's mentor and someone he had known since his first day as an apprentice haulier, fifteen years earlier.

Bazzer was a rig engineer, and the best Dukk had ever known. It was Bazzer's skill that kept the space craft's complex array of systems humming.

Bazzer had been instrumental in building Dukk's skill and confidence as a haulier. He had helped Dukk get to the position of captain well ahead of what was typical.

Next to Bazzer, was Trence, the one remaining observer. There had been two, but circumstances had got in the way.

"Hopefully, that would be rectified soon," Dukk reflected to himself.

Trence was of medium height, slim build, and warm brown complexion. Otherwise, typical for an observer.

Until recently, Dukk had given Trence a wide birth. Observers weren't Dukk's cup of tea. Not surprising considering the observers were the overlords who scrutinised Dukk's every action, ruled with an iron fist and, as far as Dukk could tell, squandered their time. However, they had been necessary to have on board in Dukk's line of work. Without an observer on board, Dukk wouldn't have the authorisation codes needed to bring his rig back into the Earth's citadels. And these citadels had been where he had secured the contracts to haul the highly sort after fresh produce.

Now Dukk saw Trence as just another fellow human being, struggling with the toil and trying to stay sane.

On Dukk's right was Annee, a short, but strong and muscular woman in her late twenties. She had a sharp tongue and a cheeky grin. Her brown complexion with cool undertones, gave her a certain poise and style.

Annee was the backbone of his crew. She was the chief mate. Her skill in managing the day-to-day operations of the rig was second to none. She was more politically savvy than him, a useful skill in keeping everyone happy.

Dukk had known Annee for several years. She was his confidant. She had taught him plenty as he had her.

Opposite Bazzer was Bognath, an outsider in many ways.

He had started as a passenger one month before. He was now a de facto member of the crew. And that was not just because he had been put on the rig by the contracting agent to help with external security. Bognath was also spending lots of time with the rig's apprentice.

Bognath's complexion was warm brown with orange-red undertones. He was slightly taller than average, had short black hair and brown eyes. In his mid-twenties, his look was tough and hard. A look that went well with his chosen profession.

Next to Bognath was Luna, the apprentice.

She was in her early twenties, of average height, with brown hair and eyes that matched her brown complexion, which had warm, orange-red undertones. She was slim but strong and incredibly agile.

"She might be only one month into learning the haulier ways, but she is far more capable than most. Also, the love she has for that sniper rifle is quite frightening, if I am honest," Dukk thought to himself.

Next to Luna, was Marr, Luna's mentor, and friend. Dukk felt he knew Marr the best of all the new crew that joined one month ago. He was also hoping to continue that trend.

Marr was two years his junior. She was of average height and medium build. She was toned and strong. She had fair complexion, with a tint of olive. Her hair was dark brown, and her eyes were light blue.

Dukk wouldn't have typically considered her for his crew. She had tremendous technical qualifications and planet side pilot certificates, but no space time. He had been looking for a strong co-pilot who could already handle the demands of space. However, he was given no choice by the contracting agent. He was now glad of that.

As Dukk looked at her now, he observed her attractiveness. It was subtle. It was in the way her eyes smiled before her mouth.

Marr had been looking around the table at the others also. But mostly, she had been observing Dukk. She watched him as he looked at each of the others. Their eyes now locked.

"There is something new," Marr thought to herself.

It wasn't in his physical appearance. He still looked all his thirty-three years. His wide shoulders and big chest combined with his average height, gave him a stocky look. But she knew from the time in the gym together, that he was all muscle. And there was still that warm smile with a touch of seriousness, that Marr found very appealing.

"It is in his eyes," Marr concluded to herself.

His petrol hazel eyes that looked brown against his hair, held something new. A weight. An inner turmoil.

"Not surprising," she thought. "Less than four hours ago, you were the captain of the Dinatha. An inter-galactic long hauler. Now, you are assuming captaincy of the weaponised rig sent to destroy the Dinatha and kill us all. Perhaps you are also in conflict over the demise of the previous crew. While it was not by your hand, you might feel responsible for their deaths."

"The turmoil I feel won't be going to go away anytime soon," Dukk thought to himself as he looked at Marr. "It is time. The self-reflection will have to wait."

"Right," Dukk announced, standing up. "I need rest before I can process this further. Before that, I am going to have a look around. Annee, do you want to update the chore rota and watch roster?"

"Yep, on it, captain," Annee replied instantly.

"Mentor, do you know these rigs?" Dukk added.

"Somewhat," Mentor answered.

"Good, you take the conn while the rest of us get orientated."

"Sound."

"Annee, I'm going to do a walk around and then collect my things from the container. Since you are still chief mate, will you sort out the cabin allocations so I can take a shower."

"Of course," Annee replied.

"Bazzer, I want to know the state of the rig as soon as possible."

"Already running diagnostics. Next stop is the engine room to take a closer look," Bazzer replied.

"Luna, I am assuming based on your choice of weapons that you might find it interesting to research this rig's weapon systems?"

"Absolutely, after seeing the engines with Bazzer," replied Luna with a smile.

"Of course, and I am sure Mentor can help direct you. Just don't blow us up. We've all had enough excitement for now," Dukk added in a jovial tone.

Mentor nodded and the others smiled.

"Ok, Marr do you want to join me for a look around?"

"Absolutely," replied Marr eagerly.

That got an even bigger smile from the others.

"Let's start back in the cockpit. I want to cover every inch," Dukk suggested to Marr as they left the crew mess via the forward door.

"Is this the type of luxury you'd imagined when you shared your plans for the future?" Marr asked as they passed through the open space that included a lounge area to the right and passenger seating to their left.

"Yes, it is something else, isn't it," Dukk answered as he opened the cockpit door.

The cockpit had two rows of seats. Two seats in the first row and in the second row, two sets of two on either side. Six in total.

"I like this layout, with comms and med systems on the right there for Annee and Mentor, rig systems on the left for Bazzer and Luna, and you and I in the front," Marr commented as she made her way to the front row.

"Yep, it definitely has a good feel to it," Dukk answered as he closed the door.

"Good visibility too," Marr said as she peered out of the windshield. The view was of the featureless rock planet they were now orbiting.

Turning back from the windshield, she collided with Dukk. He wasn't looking at the view outside.

He smiled.

"May I?" Dukk asked as he leaned in.

"Of course," Marr replied as she accepted his lips.

Their second kiss was gentle and long.

Their arms wrapped around each other as they kissed. Their bodies pressed against each other.

Eventually they pulled apart slightly.

"I am glad," Dukk said softly.

"For what?" Marr replied.

"That the kiss after we crashed in through the port door, wasn't just a once off."

"Me too," Marr smiled as she lent in again.

When they separated the second time, Dukk said warmly, "I owe you, my gratitude!"

"What for?"

"Saving my life," Dukk answered. "When the Dinatha exploded."

"You are very welcome, Dukk," Marr said sincerely as she kissed him again.

When they separated for the third time, Dukk said, "Should we inspect the rig?"

"Yes," Marr replied. "We'd better get going. We've only eight hours until the next traverse!"

Dukk raised his eyebrows and smiled. He then turned to look at the back of the cockpit.

"I guess the other door must be the ladder shaft," Dukk said.

"Let's find out."

Marr and Dukk made their way down the ladder to the level below.

They exited the ladder shaft and found themselves in a corridor.

In the middle of the corridor was a landing that served two flights of stairs. The aft flight went up and the forward flight of stairs went down.

Dukk recalled that the door to their left was the port airlock door that he and Marr had crashed through.

They turned right and opened the first door on their left. It had a three-bed med bay.

The next door led to a room with spare g-suits and E.V.A. propulsion and bio system backpacks.

The final door on the starboard side of the corridor led to the starboard transport pod bay. The bay was long and narrow. Three five-person transport pods were parked nose to end. A large door at the forward end of the space was clearly the opening for launching the pods.

They backed out of the bay and explored the port end of the corridor.

The first door on their right after the stairs led to a large lounge with a big screen.

As well as the port airlock door, the port side of the corridor had another room full of spare g-suits and E.V.A. backpacks. There was also a door to the port transport pod bay. The first pod was the only surviving pod from the Dinatha. Two more newer looking pods were parked behind it.

Dukk was about to close the door when Marr stopped him.

"There is a door back there," she said.

"Lead the way," Dukk replied.

The door at the aft end of the transport pod bay led into a ladder shaft. It too had spare g-suits.

"Down?" Dukk suggested.

"After you," Marr replied.

3

The aft ladder gave them access to the lower level. There were three doors at the bottom of the ladder shaft. One forward, one aft and one on the inner side of the small space. They opened the inner door. It led into the hold. Within was the large robotic container they brought across from the Dinatha before it blew up. The container held their personal effects and all the supplies they managed to salvage.

The aft end of the hold had two large doors. One was open.

Marr and Dukk peered in. It was the engine room.

Bazzer and Luna were already there.

Remembering their first rig tour together, a month earlier, Marr and Dukk smiled at each other. They stood still and listened.

"Wow, three TLM series ten reactors. Did you know, that, series ten reactors are slightly smaller than the Dinatha's, but more powerful. Having three makes slow running more efficient," Bazzer could be heard saying.

"Are those engines all dual mode?" Luna asked.

"Should be. Let's have a closer look?" Bazzer said as he looked at the console. "Propulsion is delivered via three TLM TH8 quad core, twenty-six-gauge hard burner thrusters. Once more, they are slightly smaller than the Dinatha's, but they deliver much greater thrust. This bird is going to move fast when we need it to."

"Vertical lift?"

"Looks like four vertical, eleven-gauge dual mode burner thrusters."

"What about directional control?"

"Eight five-gauge dual mode thrusters. Like the Dinatha, just more modern, more powerful, and more efficient. Hey, look at those power readings. We clearly have loads of batteries. I haven't seen them yet. Did you come across them?"

"Yep, some are in the wing sections and also up there along the ceiling."

Bazzer looked up. "Oh, cool. Now, what else do we have here," Bazzer said as he looked around. "Well, well!"

"What?" asked Luna.

"That is an unlocked industrial printer!"

"By unlocked, you mean we can print parts that are restricted by the overlords, like computational units?"

"Not only computational units, but with the right materials, weapons and ammunition."

"That can't be allowed!"

"Nope. It isn't. We'd be disappeared at once if the observers ever found one of these on our rig!"

"Interesting times!"

"Yes, it is. Imagine having one of these on the Dinatha. We'd have been able to fix the heat shield locks the moment they broke, not have to pay over the odds for Citadel approved computational parts. We would have had the old bird singing an even sweeter tune!"

"Are you going to continue comparing everything to the Dinatha?"

"Probably for a bit. Well, at least for the next five years," Bazzer laughed. It wasn't a full laugh. There was a touch of sadness in it.

Marr looked over at Dukk. A tear had formed in the corner of his eye. She reached over and wiped it gently from his cheek. He smiled at her.

It took them a moment of enjoying looking at each other to realise Bazzer and Luna had stopped talking.

Marr and Dukk looked around. Bazzer and Luna were standing nearby grinning at them.

"How is the rig looking?" Dukk commented to deflect the attention.

"Looking fine, captain. How is your inspection coming along?" Bazzer replied, giving a provocative emphasis to the word, 'inspection.'

Both Marr and Dukk raised their eyebrows and laughed.

Just as Dukk turned to leave the engine room, he noticed five large canisters secured to the wall.

"What are those?" he asked.

"We found them in the hold," Luna replied. "We had to move them to make space for the robo container. Bognath suggests they hold composite mesh. He said it can be traded in many places. No questions asked. Mentor said that was probably part payment for the contract to take us out,"

"Are they full?"

"Yep."

"If that is composite mesh, it is worth a small fortune."

"So, we are rich now?"

"Well, we are going to need it seeing as our previous means of generating credit just blew up," Dukk replied apprehensively.

"We'd better get on with the inspection," Marr interrupted.

"Yep, good idea," Dukk replied as he headed into the hold.

Marr and Dukk opened the container and retrieved their lockers. They helped each other lift them down and then made their way forward along the side of the container.

The far end of the narrow hold had two large doors. They passed through them into a storage space. It had several robotic crates.

A door on the other side of the storage space led into a corridor that was like the one on the level above.

The door on their immediate right was the bottom of the forward ladder shaft.

"Let's leave our lockers in here and have a quick look around the rest of this level. We can then use the conveyor in the ladder shaft, to lift them to the upper level," Dukk suggested.

"Good plan," Marr answered.

From the ladder shaft door, they turned to the starboard side. The first door on the left was a small cabin. It had a small desk and two bunks, stacked. It also had an en suite bathroom.

Moving aft, they came across a console and then a kitchenette and dining space for fourteen.

"Wow, this rig must be fitted for troops," Marr announced.

"I guess so," Dukk observed.

There was a door beyond the dining space. They went through it. It opened into a narrow room. Inside were three stacked sets of bunks. There were g-suits lining the walls and a small desk. At the end of the room was a bathroom. It had two toilets and two showers.

"Very compact," Marr commented.

"It is, and look this door leads to another ladder shaft. I guess it mirrors the one on the port side," Dukk observed as he opened a door at the back of the bathroom.

"Must be. Let's check."

4

They passed through the ladder shaft space, back into the aft end of the hold and across to the port aft ladder shaft.

This time they went through the forward door. As they suspected, it led to a mirrored bathroom and then set of bunks.

The space beyond the accommodation had consoles and sofas.

They were now back in the corridor near the bottom of the forward ladder shaft.

On the port side of the corridor, they also found a laundry room and a large gym with multiple treadmills, exercise bikes and other various pieces of training equipment.

"This rig is definitely fitted to accommodate troops. I now understand why there are nineteen g-seats in the passenger area upstairs," Marr commented as they found themselves back at the door to the forward ladder shaft.

"There is one more door, it must lead to the stairs."

"Let's see."

The door opposite to the ladder shaft opened to a corridor. At the end, was the bottom of the flight of stairs they had seen on the level above.

"This looks like an airlock," Marr said as she opened a door opposite the stairs.

Within was another corridor. At the starboard end was a hatch in the floor. At the port end, there was another airlock door.

They ventured over to the port door and peered through the portal window.

"It looks like a self-contained ramp hatch?" Dukk suggested.

"Is this the access ramp that we saw them using to get on and off the rig in Mayfield?"

"I guess so. It is very compact."

"Yep, and practical. No waiting for port authorities to provide access stairs."

"Absolutely. Let's get back up top."

"After you."

They traced their way back to the ladder shaft, where they connected their lockers to the conveyor and headed back to the upper level.

The top of the ladder shaft had two doors. One led back to the cockpit. They took the other one. It brought them through the lounge and passenger seating area. In the middle of the space was the top of the stairwell that led to the lower levels.

They made their way to the back of the passenger area. A small bathroom was on their left and the door to their right was open. Dukk stopped and looked in. It was a large cabin. There was a double birth near the window and a long lounge near the door that looked like it could be converted to a single bunk. It also had a small dining table, small couch, kitchenette and en suite.

"Guest suite?" Marr asked as she looked in too.

"Yep, looks well appointed," Dukk answered. "I guess it could also double for observers as it is not within the crew area."

"That room is for Trence. Keep going, captain," Annee announced from behind them.

They turned around. Trence and Bognath were with her. They were dragging lockers.

Marr pushed past Dukk and opened the door that took them back into the crew mess.

A series of doors ran down either side of the open space they had used for their earlier debrief. Between the doors were floor to ceiling interactive screens. Most were currently showing a view of the planet they now orbited. In the middle of the room was the fourteen-seater table. On the right was a couch with a console next to it. Mentor was sitting there interacting with a series of panels. He looked up and smiled.

"This first cabin on the starboard side is yours, Dukk. A double with en suite. The captain's suite," Annee said. "Luna and Bognath kindly sent the previous occupant's belongings towards the planet before we traversed. Though, you might want to give it a once over at some point. Also, we brought fresh bedding from the Dinatha. Marr you can have the next one on the starboard side. Mentor is in the last cabin on that side. The port side will be me first, then Luna and finally Bazzer. Bognath is setting up in the small cabin on the lower level. We also have two aft ladder shafts, one on the port side and one on the starboard side. You can use them to get straight to the transport pods, hold, engine room and lower-level accommodation."

"As we discovered," Marr commented. "Very convenient."

"Yes, this rig is definitely well laid out," Annee replied. "Also, there are two bathrooms aft, one on the port side and one on the starboard side. Back there, you'll also find the kitchenette, laundry, and the airlock with the roof hatch," Annee said pointing towards the doors beyond the table."

"Did you see all the cabins are doubles?" Luna said cheerfully, as she appeared from the bathroom in a robe. She headed towards her cabin. "And the automated showers are nearly as good as the real ones back on Earth."

"Can't wait," Marr replied.

"Did you see the gym?" Luna added from her cabin doorway. "It is huge."

"We did," Marr answered as she made for her cabin door.

"That is, of course, if you need other forms of exercise," Luna said with a giggle and a wink, before closing her door.

Marr laughed nervously.

"Ann, What's the plan for watches?" Dukk asked from the middle of the room.

"Mentor made a suggestion that I agree with. We are exposed in this system. Others may have known the flight plan. Until we traverse again, we need to be on high alert. Also, since Mentor is really the only one that knows how to use the weapons properly, he needs to be on watch. So, we'll do a hybrid watch roster until the traverse in eight hours. Mentor on and one of us with him. I suggest everyone else gets some rest. I'll take the first two hours. Then Luna the next two. Bazzer the two after that. Marr, and you can take the last two as it will run up to the traverse."

"That sounds reasonable," Dukk replied. "Thank you, Mentor."

"No problem, Dukk," Mentor said getting up from the console. "I'm going to get setup in the cockpit. It will be less disruptive. We can put the rig in night mode for a bit."

"I'm going back to the container. I'd best keep busy for now," Annee said as she disappeared through the door to the port aft ladder shaft.

Dukk looked over at Marr. She was standing in the doorway to her cabin.

"Six hours?" Dukk said suggestively.

"Yep, one could achieve a lot in that time. Shower. Sleep. Get better acquainted," Marr answered in a provocative tone.

Dukk smiled and put out his hand.

Marr pushed her lockers into her cabin and closed the door on them. She walked over and took Dukk's hand.

5

The alarm in Dukk's implants woke him. It was time to get up for watch.

He felt Marr in his arms. She was warm. Her breathing was soft.

"Hey," she said softly as he opened his eyes.

"Hi," Dukk replied warmly, looking at her.

"That time already?"

"Yep. Well, perhaps we have a few more moments before we need to get going," Dukk answered with a smile.

A short while later, Dukk and Marr were showered and suited up. Marr tentatively opened the door of Dukk's cabin.

"About time," came a voice from the middle of the crew mess. It was Luna.

Bazzer and Luna were having something to eat. They were sitting on the same side of the table looking directly at Dukk's cabin door. They were smiling.

Marr laughed as she gave up trying to hide and walked towards the table.

"So, Marr, what is the verdict?" Luna asked.

"We are not having this conversation, Luna!" Marr answered with a laugh.

"What conversation?" Dukk asked as he joined them.

"The conversation relating to what sex is like in near zero-g?" Luna replied.

Dukk laughed. "Got to love your spirit, Luna!"

Luna laughed heartily. As did Bazzer.

"By the way," Bazzer said, after composing himself. "Mentor wants to see you two in the med bay. He has some new toys for you. Says it must be done before our big chin wag."

Marr and Dukk left the crew mess and used the stairs to drop down to the middle level.

They entered the med bay.

Mentor was interacting with a compact console against a wall. He was using one of the beds as a seat. Dukk noticed that he didn't have his bracelet on.

"There you two are. I hope you got some rest," Mentor said as they entered. "Take a bed each. I've got an upgrade for you."

"Upgrade of what?" Marr asked.

"Your implants," Mentor answered.

"Come again?" Dukk stated.

"I used the printer to make some replacement components. I've also got a software upgrade to apply."

"What for?" Marr asked. "By the way, why aren't you wearing your bracelet?"

"I don't need it, neither will you after I have upgraded your implants. Now, on the beds. Lie on your stomach. Face down. I need to apply some local anaesthetic. This isn't a big job, but I am sure you won't appreciate me slicing into the soft tissue behind your ears without numbing the area first."

Marr climbed up on a bed. Dukk did the same.

Mentor jabbed them both, behind each ear.

"Now, while that kicks in, I'll talk you through what is going on."

"That would be appreciated," Dukk said.

16

Mentor smiled. "The implants you have are standard. They give you access to comms and are your interface to other systems. Dukk, as you also discovered recently, the implants track your movements, and record and broadcast everything you hear and say. With the right equipment, observers can monitor your every move. A month ago, Dukk, you gained access to a digital bracelet like we all wear. As you know, when active, it temporarily obscures the broadcast capability by inserting background noise. This upgrade will give you the ability to obscure the broadcast capability without the need for the bracelet. You will also be able to run interference to the implants of those around you."

"Cool," Dukk said. "Who else has these upgrades?"

"Elites, level seven observers and those in the know and with sufficient means."

"By in the know you mean, the resistance," Marr asked.

"Yes."

"Like Ileadees," Dukk commented.

"Ileadees. No, the port commissioner of the Maple Tower hub isn't resistance," Mentor answered. "But yes, he has upgraded implants."

"He acts as he is resistance."

"Money talks. No, Ileadees is an opportunist. Which is useful at times. Now stay still, this might be a little uncomfortable."

Twenty minutes later the procedure was complete.

"Sit up and let's try them out," Mentor said to them both.

They sat up and swung their legs off the bed.

"Sense the implants and tell me what is new?"

"Okay," Dukk said as he gave his focus to the implants. "I can sense my regular channels. Nothing new."

"Me neither," added Marr.

"Focus harder. Focus beyond the channels."

"There is something else there," Marr replied. "A toggle."

"Yep, I sense that now too," Dukk added.

17

"Right, that is the obscure mode. The function of your bracelet. Try your bracelet."

Dukk and Marr activated their bracelets.

"Now go back to focusing on the toggle," Mentor instructed.

"I see," Marr said. "It has changed."

Dukk nodded.

"Good," Mentor replied. "Now focus on changing it."

Marr did that. As did Dukk. When he focused on the toggle, it changed.

"Ok, that works," Dukk said smiling. "What else?"

"Marr, can you try something for me and let's see what Dukk notices. Focus on the toggle to turn it on, but when it activates hold your focus longer. At the same time, Dukk I want you to keep checking on your toggle, but don't change it. Dukk, tell us what happens as Marr holds."

After a moment, Dukk spoke. "It just turned on."

"Now, Marr turn your toggle off but as before stay on it. Dukk monitor yours."

After a moment, Dukk spoke. "It just turned off again. Wait, does that mean Marr can activate or deactivate my obscure mode remotely?"

"Actually, it did mine too. It isn't specific. It simply triggers obscure mode in all implants in the immediate vicinity."

"So, we can obscure conversations in others at the same time."

"Exactly."

"What if we forget to turn it off and the other person walks away?"

"The obscure capability times out after a few minutes if the activating party is no longer nearby."

"Wow, that will come in handy. Why have the bracelet then?"

"Optics. It's best that most don't know about these capabilities."

"Ileadees wasn't bothered."

"He is a show off and that attitude might come unstuck. I'd suggest keeping the bracelet on hand for when you are interacting with those that know what you knew up until this morning."

"That makes sense." Dukk reflected aloud.

"What else can these do?" Marr asked.

"Let me show you," Mentor replied. "Dukk, come over to this console. Activate it."

Dukk went over to the console and put his hands near it. It came to life. The console showed all the panels he had access to as the captain of the rig. Which was everything.

"Done, looks normal."

"Good. Now step away so that the console locks again."

Dukk did that.

"Now focus on the obscure mode toggle. Then look further. Look beyond it."

Dukk focused.

"Nothing. Oh, wait," he said after a moment. "There is something there. Another toggle."

"Toggle it and then go back to the console."

Dukk did that and then went over to the console. He put his hands up. Instead of his usual full access, the console now showed a big red sign. It read, 'Err.'

"Wait, what is going on?"

"The upgraded implant has biometric impersonation. It sends signals and interference to biometric systems and video capture equipment, in the immediate vicinity. That toggle is empty now, so the console's biometric sensors came up blank. Focus hard beyond the blank space you just found."

Dukk did that.

"Wow, there is another blank space," Dukk stated.

"Do you mean I can have two additional IDs?" Marr asked.

"Actually, those implants support four. Once configured you can impersonate four other personas to get into consoles and through doors and ID gateways in the ports, hubs, and citadels. You can now change who you want them to think you are."

"But we can't just make up IDs. Can we?"

"No, that is correct. We need to buy them and the backstory in the systems needs to match, particularly when moving around ports, hubs and entering citadels."

"Where do we buy them?" Marr asked.

"Ileadees can help source IDs that work in most places outside Earth. I can help with those needed to get in and out of the citadels."

"Anything else these can do?" Dukk asked.

"I'll upgrade your wrist wraps now and you can find out for yourselves."

Chapter 2 – Awareness

1

Marr and Dukk made their way up the stairs, through the passenger seating area and into the cockpit.

They took their seats. Dukk on the left and Marr on the right.

Dukk took a long look at the controls. The first time, seven hours earlier, had been very rushed. It had been in the early hours of the morning. The DMD, an AI driven machine embedded into the structure of the rig, had nearly completed its twelve-hour long calculations. Those calculations were to find a safe path through the dark matter. The process was called a traverse. It would bring them from the orbit of the planet in one system to the orbit of the target planet in another system, light years away. His priority at the time was getting the rig to full power. His focus had also been to get the crew hooked up to the med control system. A system, connected from the back of the seat to a fitting at the top of their spines. A system that would send a cocktail of drugs into the bloodstream to ensure they didn't go into cardiac arrest as the rig traversed. Earlier, Dukk didn't have the time to really get familiar with the controls. He had time now.

The flight controls consisted of two identical consoles. Each console had a vertical wrap around screen that sat just below the windshield, and a horizontal screen that sat just above the knees. Both screens were interactive and fully customisable. From here one could control every aspect of the rig. Joysticks sat on either side of the seats. And each seat had its own holographical projector. In the centre console and in the ceiling above the two seats, were further interactive screens with gauges, switches, and indicators for critical system components.

On her console, Marr opened the traverse controls and projected the count down.

"We've got sixty minutes until the traverse. What's the plan?" Marr asked.

"Let's do a full set of system diagnostics and then run some traverse simulations," Dukk replied. "It might be good to get familiar with evasive manoeuvres protocols too."

"Good plan."

"I'll do the checking. Do you want to find the checklists and walk us through them?"

"Already got the checklists open," Marr replied grinning.

"I might as well go back to bed," Dukk laughed.

"I'd have to keep you company, and then who would be left here to run the diagnostics," Marr answered cheekily.

"So, co-pilot, what is first on the list?" Dukk said grinning, bringing focus back to the task at hand.

Marr smiled back before returning her focus to her console. She was happy to take Dukk's direction on refocusing.

"Biosystems are first," Marr said after a moment. "Verify the last recalibration and compare remaining time against contingent flight plan."

"On it. Let me see. Where are the biosystem panels. Found them. Calibration is using the last six hours. At current depletion rates we have twenty-two days. Given we have no flight plan, I can't complete the last check."

"That seems like a lot of capacity."

"I guess that would reduce if we had a full complement of passengers. What's next."

"Battery load and emergency running."

"Ok, let me see. Found the controls. It looks like a load test was executed two hours ago. I guess we are shadowing Bazzer. The results suggest we have fifty-three hours emergency backup. That feels adequate. What's next."

"Hull integrity."

"I bet Bazzer has already been there too. Let's see. Yep, full diagnostics completed ninety minutes ago. Only warning is a slight fluctuation on the roof hatch. I gather it was forced open when Mentor, Luna and Bognath crept on board earlier."

"What do we do about that?"

"Let's see if Bazzer has created a job jar in the system logs. Yep, there is a note here. He has flagged it for inspection after the next traverse. I guess he'll get out for a walk. We'll get the drones out too and do a proper survey. What's next on the checklists?"

"Fuel. Starting with mixed mode. We need to check tank levels, balancing and projected range."

"Cool. Lots to look at on these fuel panels. Let's see. We have four hybrid fuel tanks for the thrusters. Two tanks on the starboard side and two on the port side. They have been balanced recently. Bazzer is on the ball. Overall, we are ninety percent full. These tanks look sizable. Plenty of capacity."

"What does the range look like?"

"Let's see. Using the consumption rates to hold orbit over the last six hours, it looks like we have sufficient fuel to stay up here for a further thirteen days."

"That feels a little low if they refuelled before leaving Mayfield yesterday."

"Yes, it does," Dukk answered.

"Perhaps they didn't take a full load of fuel."

"Perhaps. I guess we'll need to monitor it."

"What about hub manoeuvres?"

"There doesn't appear to be any data for that at the moment. I guess things were reset when we reset the conn this morning. The Dinatha consumed the equivalent of twelve hours of orbit adjustment for thirty minutes of loaded thrust. This rig should be more efficient, so I'd say we have plenty of margin."

"Cool. Next, we have hard fuel checks. We need to verify the tank levels, balancing and launch readiness."

"Right. Hard fuel. Got it. Three tanks. One for each hard burner thruster. Levels are showing as at seventy percent. Are there any notes against the checklist?"

"Yes, it says we have thirty minutes of hard burn at maximum load when correctly calibrated."

"Cool. That means we have capacity for at least one fully loaded launch. That's much better efficiency than the Dinatha. What's next."

"Reactors. Running time and fuel dilution percentage."

"What are the recommended parameters?"

"The checklist says three thousand hours for partial service and refuel. Six thousand hours for full service. Refuel should also be done if dilution goes above eighty percent."

"Let's see what we have. Ok, the running time clocks show an average of two thousand hours. And fuel dilution is at an average of forty five percent. I also see that they were running at least one at full power last night. Odd."

"Why would they do that?"

"Not sure. Perhaps we'll find out further into the checklists. What is next?"

"Extinguishers, and the materials and compounds for the printer."

"Most are showing as full. We are a little low on graphite oxide. I guess Mentor's activities building upgraded implants used some of it. What's left on the checklists."

"That's it for core systems. There is a section on weapon systems. Also, the extended list covers housekeeping and provisions."

"No point doing the weapon system checklist until we know more about them. It might be worth having Mentor give us a walk through after this evening's chat. Let's leave the housekeeping and provisions for Ann. In fact, I bet she has already done a full inventory."

"So, onto the traverse simulation?" Marr asked.

"Yes, let's run the simulation from the fifteen-minute warning," Dukk replied.

"Right. First task is to check with the crew. We need to get a status update from engineering. We need all three reactors powered up."

"Check. I'll power up the reactors in the simulator."

"I see this rig has fixed position solar panels. They are integrated into the heat shields in the underside of the rig. That makes things easier."

"Yes, no risk of them catching as they are retracted, as was the case on the Dinatha."

"Cool. So, continuing the checklist. Next, we check in with the chief mate for the status of passenger and rig preparation."

"Let's walk through that as if we are short crew."

"First, we'd have to visit each passenger or guest and ensure they are in or getting into their g-suits. While they complete that and make their way up to the passenger seating area, we do a walk-through of the rig. We secure movable objects, seal the doors, and look for anything that looks out of place. We finish the walk around in the passenger area and help the passengers fit their helmets, belt in, and connect to the g-juice supply."

"Let's take that as done."

"Right, now we check for other vessels in the area and also any reason to abort the traverse."

"Checked. All clear."

"Next, we double check the traverse instructions against the flight plan."

"Checked. Coordinates match."

"Next, we broadcast to the relay in the system. We give them an update on our flight plan and sign-out of the system. I guess that doesn't apply since we are hiding in an unmonitored system."

"Agreed. It is something we are going to have to get used to."

"Looks like it."

"What's next on the checklist."

"That is, it for preparation. Now we wait for the other crew to check-in and join us in the cockpit."

"Great," Dukk said. "I'll fast forward the simulation to the point that we are all seated and hooked into the med system. Let's pick up the simulation from the four-minute mark."

"Right," Marr replied. "First is a broadcast to the passengers and crew to remind them of the plan."

"Do you want to practice the steps from here?"

"Sure," Marr replied. She then cleared her throat.

"Good morning, all," Marr said a little reluctantly before relaxing into the role play. "I hope you made good use of the last eleven hours. This process might be a little uncomfortable for those experiencing it for the first time. Please rest assured that we have done all the necessary preparations and will be on hand after to help you. Please relax and allow the system to take you under as we traverse."

Dukk laughed. Marr had mimicked what Dukk had said one month earlier, when Marr was about to experience the traverse for the first time.

Marr grinned, giggled and then continued.

"Four minutes, unmuting crew comms so we are live to each other through the traverse. Status check. Med vitals first."

"I'll play the part of chief mate and also chief engineer," Dukk answered. "All stable. Medical calibration is near one hundred percent."

"Systems status?"

"All doors shut. Integrity is showing as at one hundred percent. Reactors are at full power. All systems showing green lights."

"Great. Crew check-in?"

"Ready, ready, ready, ready, and ready," Dukk answered laughing as he mimicked the presence of the rest of the crew and how they would be responding.

"Excellent. We are committed. Three minutes. Load up the passengers and guests."

"Juice is running", Dukk said as he interacted with the simulation. "Heart rates dropping."

"All stable," Dukk added after a short pause.

"Taking back med control," Marr said as she watched the simulation count down.

At the thirty second mark, Marr spoke the count down in ten second intervals.

"Running the juice to the crew. See you on the other side," she said at the ten second mark. She looked over at Dukk and smiled.

Dukk smiled back. He had adopted the 'See you on the other side' statement, as his signature piece before putting the crew under for the traverse.

"Excellent stuff," Dukk said. "Let's continue the simulation from the point after the DMD has taken us into the target system and we have woken from the short, induced coma. Do you want to continue as lead?"

"Sure," Marr answered. "Status?"

"Back, back, back, back and back," Dukk laughed.

"Glad we are using an experienced crew for this simulation and not inexperienced hauliers like a month ago. At this point, the combination of nausea, shortness of breath and dizziness would be overwhelming them, and they'd be trying not to vomit."

"Yep," Dukk laughed.

"Ok, so assuming we are all good, first up is an update on vitals."

"Take it as read that everyone is stable."

"So, next we check the rig integrity and systems."

"Yep, all good."

"Then we check that we have arrived in a safe orbit that is clear of obstructions."

"No alarms. We are good. What's next."

"We bring the DMD back online, load it up with our next traverse destination and get an estimated time of departure."

"Great. Let's skip that part for now. What's next."

"The checklist has a section on stealth mode. What do you want to do with that?"

"What does it say?"

"It says keep one reactor at one hundred percent before engaging stealth mode. It also says we need to check the hybrid fuel levels as thruster bursts occur more often when stealth mode is engaged."

"Interesting. That would explain why they were running a reactor at one hundred percent overnight. It also perhaps explains why the hybrid fuel level is lower than I would have expected for this stage of the journey."

"This information feels important."

"Yep, it does. What is next on the checklist."

"We put the rig into slow running mode."

"Talk us through the protocol for this rig."

"It says when not using stealth mode, we cycle down two of the reactors and run the third at twenty five percent."

"Done."

"Next, we enable the 'track the sun' setting in the autopilot to maximise the solar panel exposure."

"Done."

"And that is it. Do we have time to practice the protocols relating to evasive manoeuvres?"

"Do you want to have a look at those on your own? I want to do a walk around. I also want to have a closer look at the engine room."

"Yes, sounds good. I'd like to have another look around too. I'll go when you get back."

"Perfect."

Dukk turned to get out of his seat. Marr was looking at him. She was smiling.

"What?" Dukk asked.

"Just checking you out," Marr replied in a cheeky tone.

Dukk smiled and raised his eyebrows.

He then reached over towards her hand. She turned her hand and accepted his.

The tingle ran through them both instantly. The warmth swelled. They smiled. After a moment Dukk broke the silence.

"I'd better get moving before we lose track of the task at hand."

"Yep, that might be a good idea," Marr replied grinning.

Dukk took a deep breath. He let go of Marr's hand, stood up and headed for the cockpit door.

Dukk made his way into the crew mess. It was empty but for Mentor.

Mentor was sitting on the couch opposite the console. His hands were resting on his knees and his eyes were closed.

The console was showing a series of panels. The panels on the left were what Dukk knew to be radar and other systems for detecting the presence of others sharing the orbit. There was no activity. The panels on the right were unfamiliar to Dukk. He assumed they were the controls for the weapon systems.

"Everything okay?" Mentor said as Dukk stood looking at the console.

Dukk turned to Mentor.

"I'd like to know more about Tieanna?" Dukk said bluntly.

"I am sure you do," Mentor answered as he opened his eyes. "I'd like to tell you more about your mother. I suggest we wait, though, until after we figure out the plans for the next few days. There will be plenty of opportunities to explore the past once we have clarified our immediate future."

"It is refreshing that your answers are no longer monosyllabic. However, it is frustrating that you are still talking in riddles."

"My gut tells me that what I know of your mother is for you and Marr to hear, together at the same time. I also feel it is not for the others. Therefore, it would be better that I answer their questions first. The three of us need to find a suitable moment alone to talk about things of this nature."

"That sounds fair. Although, I am now even more curious."

Mentor smiled.

"Anything to concern us?" Dukk said nodding at the console.

"Nope, all quiet, thankfully. I would have expected company by now if the plans of the previous crew were known to others."

"Good to know. What about our flight plan? I see the coordinates of the next traverse put us further away from Mayfield, not closer to it. If we are to rescue the girls, shouldn't we be heading towards it?"

"As we will explore later this evening with the others, we have to do some preparations first."

"New digital IDs?"

"Yes, and we need to give this rig a new identity."

"Maple Tower. Is that the direction we are now headed?"

"Yes, Ileadees can help us get what we need."

Dukk nodded and headed for the port aft ladder shaft door.

Dukk made his way to the lower level. He passed directly from the ladder shaft to the engine room.

The reactors filled the lower part of the space. The outer casings of the thruster burners filled the upper regions. The generators for the DMD sat vertically in the middle of the room. They ran all the way to the ceiling.

Dukk found a spot in the middle of the floor and lay down.

He closed his eyes and focused on clearing his mind.

He pushed away all his thoughts and feelings.

He listened. He focused on the sounds. He tried to isolate each unique vibration and hum. He observed the rhythms in those sounds and vibrations.

Dukk knew from the system checks done just now with Marr, that the rig was in full working order. He wanted to get to know what that sounded and felt like.

He continued that for as long as his mind could stay free of the questions. It wasn't long. He sighed. He would need to return to this another time.

Dukk sat up and looked around again. The moments of disconnection had heightened his senses and awareness.

He saw double doors in the engine room wall. He hadn't noticed them earlier. He got up and went over to the starboard side. He activated the panel and opened the doors.

The doors gave him access to the inside of the starboard wing. He had to duck down to get into the tight space.

Within he saw the usual array of tanks and casings. He could also see tube like structures that were unfamiliar to him. He assumed they were part of the weapon systems.

"How's it looking?" came a voice from behind him.

Dukk jumped. He banged his head on the ceiling in the process. He turned around.

"Ann," Dukk laughed. "You startled me, and the gym isn't in here!"

Annee was standing in the doorway. She was wearing a sports bra and yoga pants.

"Sorry," she laughed. "On my way there. But I wanted to see how you were getting on. We haven't spoken much since things went to shit. Marr said I'd find you down here."

"I am fine. Let's get out of here. I am on a walk around. We can walk and talk."

Annee smiled as she backed out of the tight space.

"How are you getting on?" Dukk asked as they moved out of the engine room and into the hold.

"I am pretty shaken up," Annee answered. "So much has happened. Losing the Dinatha, our home. The things Mentor shared about the Rule of Twelve. The broken sleep. The planned rescue. I am all over the place. I am not sure what any of this means. I can only imagine where you are at."

"Yes, things are pretty mental," Dukk laughed as they passed through the storage area and stopped in the lower forward corridor.

"You seem jovial about it all?"

"In a way. I guess. It is all so surreal and yet it feels like it is meant to be. Perhaps I am just following the creed."

"Remind me of it. Perhaps that will help calm me down too."

"Sure, Ann. Focus on that which is real in the heart. Create the space so that the process can emerge. Honour that which serves you well. Engage in the journey as it unfolds."

"I am going to give that all some more thought. Perhaps on the treadmill. We've got about forty-five minutes before the traverse."

Dukk smiled as Annee disappeared into the gym.

4

An hour later the rig was out of the traverse. They were now orbiting another featureless rock. It looked very much like the one in the system they had just left. Dukk had given the DMD a set of coordinates for another deserted system. It was another system that Mentor had suggested. It wasn't a system or track that Dukk knew of. However, he had no new reason to distrust Mentor.

With the rig in slow running, Dukk removed his helmet and turned around in his seat to look at his crew.

"So, Ann are we starting the standard watch rotation?" he asked.

"Yes, Dukk, that is what I suggest," Annee replied. "Four-hour rotation. Let's go with Utopiam time as we have no better reference point. It is nearly four p.m., so Bazzer and Luna have another two hours. It will then be yourself and Marr until ten p.m. Myself and Mentor will take over until two a.m. Then, it will be Bazzer and Luna for the graveyard shift. Does that work for everyone?"

"What about Bognath?" Luna asked.

"Good question, I guess that he is practically crew now. Anyone got any ideas?" Annee replied.

"Luna, why don't you take him under your wing. Show him the ropes, so to speak?" Dukk suggested sincerely.

"I take it that we are still talking about running the rig," Marr laughed. "There is hardly anything more Luna could teach him otherwise."

Luna could be heard blowing a raspberry in Marr's direction.

"That is a good idea," Bazzer said. "He is basically around us most of the time anyway. Might as well put him to good use."

"Great, that is settled. Luna, will you let him know," Annee said smiling over at Luna.

"I will."

"What about Trence?" Marr asked.

"I have a suggestion," Mentor answered. "The observer won't be interested in giving up sleep in the late hours. However, there are many things that need answering. I suggest that you and I take Trence under our wing for the daytime watch. It will take time for the observer to come to terms with this new reality. Learning the day to day running of this rig will help in that process."

"Good idea, Mentor. Anyone got a problem with that?" Dukk asked.

No one did.

"Right, let's get into the crew mess for our big chat. Does ten minutes work for everyone?" Dukk asked.

There was general agreement.

Ten minutes later they were all seated in the crew mess.

Dukk had purposely got to the table first and sat in the middle. He didn't want to sit at either end. He didn't want to be seen as the authority. For now.

Mentor had a similar idea. He had got to the table just after Dukk. He sat on the other side, but not opposite.

The others had sat around them. Marr sat on Dukk's right. Annee was on his left. Trence sat next to Annee. Bazzer was opposite Dukk, sitting to the right of Mentor. Luna sat on Bazzer's right. Bognath sat next to Luna.

There had been a little banter as they had entered the crew mess, but now with everyone seated, silence fell. All eyes were on Dukk.

"If you don't mind," Dukk said softly. "I would like to set the scene and propose the guardrails for this open discussion."

Nods and smiles met his suggestion.

"We are here to get answers and to plan our next course of action. I have asked each of you individually and you are all in. You have until we reach the hub to change your mind. After that, you will be committed. We are led to believe that at least four girls are at risk and need our help. The last that we heard, was that they were in one of the penthouses in the resort in Mayfield. They had been trafficked there by a group thought to be led by Craig Atesoughton the second. Over the last month, Mentor has been using the beef contract, we had been servicing, as cover. He orchestrated the assassination of Craig in an attempt to dismantle the trafficking ring. That appears to have failed. The group appears to be still operating. Also, someone betrayed you, Mentor, and our primary observer, Kimince got caught up in it. It isn't clear who was behind that. So, in addition to helping the girls, we need to get Kimince away from there too. We also know that the order to assassinate Craig came from his father. The reasons are unknown to you, Mentor. However, it fitted in with your attempts to tackle the trafficking, so you accepted the contract. You knew of the trafficking because of your activities within the resistance movement. However, you couldn't openly disrupt the trafficking because it would

34

compromise your cover. Anyone feel I have missed any of the immediate context?"

"Yes, what about the Dinatha?" Annee stated rhetorically. "It got blown-up in the process."

"Yes, there is that too."

"And we are now assumed dead and possibly marked if we ever surface again."

"Yes, Ann, and that."

"And we have no means to support ourselves."

"Yes, perhaps."

"We have a stash of composite mesh, that will help. Won't it?" Luna interjected.

Dukk smiled. "Anything else?"

No one spoke up.

"Ok then," Dukk said firmly. "I'd suggest that to keep things on track, for now, we focus purely on understanding the context and plan to rescue Kimince and the girls."

More smiles and nods.

Dukk brought his gaze to Mentor.

"Mentor, I would like you to get us started," Dukk said as he looked directly at Mentor. "I'd like to know what you know about all of this before we get onto the plan."

"Of course," Mentor said pleasantly holding Dukk's stare. "Where do you want me to start?"

"Where do you suggest?"

"I suggest we talk about trafficking. To do that, I need to fill you in."

"Great idea. Go for it."

"Craig came to my attention because of work I was already doing for the resistance."

"Can I stop you there," Trence blurted.

Mentor turned to look at Trence. He nodded.

"What is the resistance?" Trence asked.

"It is a game b movement." Mentor replied.

"What is game b?"

"Game b is what happens next. If the status quo is game a, then game b is what comes after. The movement is formed on the principles of being self-organising, network-oriented, decentralised, emerging, and oriented towards human flourishing. It looks to build on what works to address what doesn't."

"And how do you do that?" Trence asked.

"Good question, Trence," Mentor replied calmly. "One way is to build and maintain hope."

"By shooting sentinels and assassinating elites?"

"Yes, we do what we can to reduce that which stifles or snuffs out hope. Sabotage of unjustified and brutal activities is certainly one method. We also educate in the ways of old. It is all done in a manner that doesn't cause overreach. It takes surgical precision. We step out too far and the repercussions are severe. Do too little and people continue to lack the willingness to try, to do something different, to innovate, to grow, to strive for something better, to support each other and to stand-up to those that seek to abuse or destroy."

"For what ends?"

"To get somewhere better than where we are now. It isn't our desire to destabilise or destroy that which is productive and aids in building and maintaining hope. Taking out an authoritarian regime just leaves a void for another to fill. No, we want to bring people back together, not turn them further away from one another."

"And building hope achieves that?"

"We think so. One of the major challenges we face is people disappearing. Losing contact with people you care about, definitely has the potential to snuff out hope. The sentinels are fast and efficient. If someone gets compromised or puts a foot wrong, they simply disappear. There is no defence or opportunity to make amends for one's mistakes. A word is given from on high and they are picked up and disposed of. Even as a level seven observer I have little say in that. Trafficking is also particularly good at destroying hope. Obviously for those that are the subject of the trafficking. It is also hard on those that get drawn in. Staff, security, pilots, and the like. Most don't know what they are involved in, until it is too late. Once in, it is hard to get out."

"What do you mean by disposed of?" Annee asked.

"Compost incinerators are the most common means. In with the organic waste."

"But what happens to the ash?"

Mentor paused. Stared. Said nothing.

There was a collective 'ugh' from the room.

"How horrid," cried Trence.

"Will I continue?" Mentor asked.

Annee nodded.

"So, part of my work was to keep an eye on citadel monitoring activities. I would give our people warning if I got wind of a plan to disappear someone. We would try to get to them first. We'd take them to our camps outside the citadel. We'd red pill them and help them rebuild.

"Part of the challenge we faced was knowing if someone disappeared. Through that work, I got access to people records. Well not the full detail. It is hidden well. But I could see headcount via the population control measures. I could see the pregnancy completion rates. I could see details of deaths. Industrial accidents, suicide, and that type of thing. I could use the gap in the counts to calculate the disappearance rates. It allowed us to see if we were having a positive impact."

"You have confused me again," Trence interrupted. "What do you mean by pregnancy completion rates?"

"I could see when incubation centres were allowed to see a pregnancy complete and when they were not."

"This morning you said the incubators are mostly a lie. That while there were plans initially to manufacture people in laboratories, it never really worked. You said that the results were terrifying. That the same was true of the early attempts to genetically modify the entire population. You said things went back to being done the old fashion way. Women are impregnated and then they give birth. The babies are raised in the incubation centres. What do you mean by not complete?"

"Some pregnancies are terminated early."

"What happens then?"

"The unborn child dies."

"I don't understand. If the aim is to keep the population at a certain level, why allow the pregnancy in the first place?"

"The concubines are not sterilised like most. They can get pregnant at any time."

"Wait, now you've lost me," Annee interrupted. "What do you mean by not sterilised like most?"

"The test," Mentor answered.

"That doesn't make sense," Annee said. "The test at the age of ten is to figure out if you will continue education and become an observer. Most, however, are deemed unsuitable, designated as unprivileged and start the labour rotation."

"Not totally correct," Mentor replied. "Yes, the test does put you on a certain track. But not all become observers or labourers. The day after the test, potential observers only make up a small proportion of those that don't wake up in the dorms with the labourers."

"What happens to the others?"

"Some are disappeared at once. If their personality traits are seen as a threat. But for the most part, the boys are shaped into sentinels."

"And the girls?" Marr asked.

"They are trained as hostesses and eventually will be put into service as a concubine for the elites. These girls are not sterilised. This is where our population comes from."

"I thought that capability was engineered out of our DNA because it was too dangerous. Do you mean we could all have children if it weren't for the test?" Luna asked.

"As mentioned, this morning, the DNA engineering story is a lie. So, yes, if observers, sentinels, and labourers weren't sterilised at the age of ten, they could have children."

"How do we not know this?"

"Steps are taken to intervene with the process of conception for most. It is well hidden as to not raise suspicion or alarm."

"What do you mean by that?"

"Concubines don't know they are any different. I understand this strategy is to enable uninhibited engagement. It ensures they willingly submit to the elites."

"Do all hostesses become concubines?" Marr asked.

"No, not all. Some get roles within elite households."

"But they aren't sterilised, so they could get pregnant if they have sex with elites."

"Yes and no."

"What do you mean?"

"There are ways to sterilize temporarily. Their meds can be modified so they don't get pregnant."

"Do they know their meds are modified?"

"Not usually."

"This is doing my head in," Annee said in shock. "If I am not then mistaken, we are all children of the elite men?"

"Yes, that is how it is," Mentor answered.

An eerie silence filled the room.

After a few moments, Annee spoke again.

"So, what you are saying is that many girls, like those we aim to rescue, are designated as concubines from the age of ten. Their purpose, once trained, is simply to be sex toys for the elites."

"Yes, until they become pregnant," Mentor answered.

"What happens then?"

"Do you mean if the pregnancy goes ahead or if it does not?"

"Tell us about both."

"Okay, I guess this is a time of truth sharing. So, it depends. There are two possibilities if the pregnancy goes ahead. Firstly, and very rarely, the elite family raises the child. But mostly, the new-born is put into the incubation centre to be raised in a pod of twelve."

"And the mother?"

"It will depend on the choices of the elites involved. Some girls are returned to work as a concubine. But most are discarded."

"Disappeared?"

"Yes."

"What the F!" exclaimed Luna.

"I fear to ask," Marr said. "But I am going to anyway. What happens when the pregnancy doesn't go ahead?"

"Same answer as for mothers that give birth."

Silence filled the room, again.

Chapter 3 – The plan

1

Dukk broke the silence.

"This is quite disturbing and while perhaps important, we should probably stay focused, or we'll be here to the end of time. Mentor, I think you were telling us about how Craig came to your attention."

"Yes, Dukk. I was. So, in looking at the gap in the counts to see if our efforts were having a positive impact, another anomaly appeared. The anomaly was within the hostesses. We knew exactly who was being recruited for the resistance and the type of activities they were put into. We purposely kept those under eighteen out of harms way. So, we knew our activities wouldn't have impact for those in this age group. However, a gap was showing in female counts. We found the discrepancy when we looked at the number of concubines and the number designated as hostesses at the age of ten. Girls were simply disappearing.

"After lots of careful investigation we found the reason. Trainee hostesses often socialised with the elites in their parties and gatherings. That was typical for their training. What wasn't typical was for some not to return to their dorms. We explored further and found a culture of competition within the young hostesses. They considered it an accomplishment to get taken on trips off Earth to party. It had become quite widespread practice. While most returned, some didn't.

"Some level of reprieve was achieved by tightening of the gateway ID procedures. That needed some very carefully managed influence using my level seven designation. It was in the elites' own interest that only they could come and go as they pleased. The new procedures helped reduce the practice of encouraging girls to leave on elite cruisers to party. However, it didn't stop the disappearances. It simply pushed things underground. The power of the elites is strong. People were paid off and the practice of taking girls away to party continued. Just not using the elites' own cruisers. They started using mercenaries. That made it harder to identify who wasn't playing by the rules. In hindsight clamping down on IDs might have been a mistake. I guess that made it all more personal."

"That is why you personally took the assassination contract?" Luna asked.

"Yes, eventually," Mentor replied.

"What do you mean?"

"So, with the elites hidden behind mercenaries, we had to go back to the drawing board. We looked at those elites who were involved initially. Those using their own cruisers before we clamped down on the IDs. That is where Craig's name showed up. However, getting to him and stopping it wasn't straight-forward. He was too well connected. The Atesoughtons are immensely powerful. So, we started looking at the mercenaries. We looked for activities that were suspicious."

"Like the anomaly we found in the relay in Mayfield?" Marr asked.

"Exactly. We looked at times when the number of persons showing up in orbit didn't match the numbers at ID checks when the cruisers departed or landed."

"So, you found Craig's new operation?" Annee asked.

"Not right away. The comings and goings of elites is largely untraced. They don't want their movements tracked. They see it as a violation of their individual rights. So, mercenaries under contract to elites got similar treatment. But, yes, eventually we found a pattern and linked a cruiser registered under Craig's son's name. It was moving between Mayfield and Earth on regular intervals. It typically used main routes inbound and then went via less travelled hubs on the return to Mayfield."

"Hubs like Maple Tower."

"Exactly."

"Wait, so Craig Atesoughton the third is involved too?" Luna interrupted.

"No, I am pretty sure Craig junior had just lent that cruiser to his father. It is known that Craig the second doesn't get on with his father. The old man. Junior's grandfather. There was some kind of falling out when Craig was in his late twenties. A year or two before junior arrived. When junior was born, the old man disowned Craig. The old man is setting up his grandson to be his heir. He will skip a generation."

"So, the late Craig Atesoughton the second wasn't flush and had been taking handouts because there was bad blood. That might explain why the old man put the assassination contract out on his son."

"Yes, that is a strong possibility."

There was a pause as everyone processed this latest disclosure.

"Why didn't you just take out those mercenaries?" Trence asked.

"Because well paid work is hard to find. Others would readily step in?" Annee suggested.

"Exactly, Ann," Mentor replied. "Besides, we didn't have proof. We only had anecdotal evidence."

"But we found it, when we got involved in giving the girls a lift from Maple Tower?" Annee prompted.

"That is correct."

"Were you behind the cruiser breaking down in Maple Tower?" Dukk asked.

"Yes, when the assassination contract came to light, I got help to delay the cruiser in Maple Tower. It was important that we were the ones who picked up those girls. I needed to see first-hand what happened when the girls arrived in Mayfield. I wanted to see who collected them."

"So, I gather you were also behind Wallace's insistence that we went via Maple Tower instead of the more popular Kaytom Beach hub?"

"Yes, I was behind that too."

"The huge contract signing bonus Wallace provided. The incentive to ensure I took you, Marr and Luna on as crew. Where you behind that too?"

"Yes, Dukk, that was me too."

"That is why Ileadees gave it to us in Maple Tower. You have a black-market wallet there. You transferred it to Ileadees, and he transferred it to us to keep your role in it hidden. I bet he took a cut too."

Mentor smiled.

"And Bognath, you joined us for that first leg out of Utopiam because the cruiser was broken down," Annee noted.

"Yes, that's right," Bognath answered. "Carltor and I got the order to get ourselves there on the first available rig. That same morning a posting went up showing that the Dinatha was leaving Utopiam that evening. The destination was Maple Tower. We couldn't believe our luck. We made sure we were on it by offering to pay well above the odds."

2

"The penny drops," Annee said. "Everything is connected. Although, it concerns me that you were aware of what was going on, Bognath."

"Yes, Ann. It is something that I am not proud of. I won't try to offer any excuse or claim victimhood. I regret my involvement and want to make amends for my poor choices."

"By helping to kill these bastards!" Luna said in a raised voice.

"First we rescue the girls," Mentor answered. "We get them out of harm's way."

"Then we find those involved in this and we take them out," Luna added.

"That might not be enough."

"Do you mean there are more trafficking rings?" Marr asked.

"Absolutely, and other things," Mentor replied. "But also, something happened during this operation. I was betrayed. We need to find out who was behind that."

"What do you mean by other things?"

"There are unofficial incubators, some of the disappeared end up there. Their children are born and raised," Mentor said in a quieter tone.

"What is the problem with that?"

"Let us just say, teenage girls aren't the only ones that are facing harm. Young children too. I haven't seen it with my own eyes, but I hear stories. The odd person has escaped. Tried to tell their story. The story doesn't get far before the escapee will be disappeared too."

"This is ghastly. Where are the unofficial incubators?"

"I am not sure. There is evidence of them on Earth. It makes sense they are elsewhere too."

"Why are you unsure? Wouldn't you know as level seven?"

"The observer's domain is the middle and outer rings. We have some access to the inner ring of the citadels, but much is hidden. Equally, we have little access to the inner areas of elite compounds in other systems."

"Wait a minute," Dukk interjected. "Aren't we getting a little ahead of ourselves?"

"What do you suggest, Dukk, turn a blind eye again?" Annee said rudely as she slammed the table and turned to face Dukk.

Dukk sat back and looked at Annee. He frowned.

"Might be time for a break," Bazzer said to break the tension. "We have just heard some pretty heavy stuff. Perhaps a fresh round of coffee might be in order."

"Yes, Bazzer," Annee responded. "You are right. Sorry for my outburst, Dukk. I'll make the coffee. Who's in the need?"

"That is okay, Ann," Dukk said kindly. "This is all difficult to take on board. I'm definitely in need of coffee. Let's do it together."

Dukk and Annee pushed back their seats and got up together.

The others acknowledged the offer and put in their orders.

"Do you really think we can make a difference?" Dukk asked as he helped Annee make the drinks.

"I think we can, Dukk," Annee replied. "All the years of suspecting what was happening, and we finally know we were right. And we are now in the company of some very capable people and in the command of an amazing rig. Why not?"

"We are a small band with a small stolen ship against a galaxy of elites and their resources. Are we getting ahead of ourselves?"

"Didn't you hear Mentor? All we need to do is help build hope by reducing where it is being destroyed."

"That is, it though, isn't it? Where does this end? Mentor also mentioned there are plenty more trafficking rings. And whatever else."

"Good point."

"Can I help?" Marr asked. She was standing at the door to the kitchen.

"With building hope or making the coffee?" Dukk asked, smiling.

"Both?" Marr laughed.

"You can start by helping take these drinks to the table," Annee replied, smiling.

With the refreshments sorted, everyone gathered at the table again.

Dukk waited for the banter to die down.

"Mentor, if that is sufficient background, I'd suggest we talk about what we are going to do to get Kimince and the girls out of harm's way?"

"Yes, I think that is the general context we need for now," Mentor answered. "I am sure other topics will emerge. We can cover them when that happens."

"Great, so let's get onto the plan. Let's start by hearing more of what you know of Mayfield and what we might be up against."

"I might suggest Bognath start us off. He will have more detail than me on the layout of the resort."

"Bognath?" Dukk prompted.

Bognath nodded.

"The penthouse used by Craig is in one of the original top floor apartments. They are in a dull building at the back of the resort. The girls were kept in rooms of that penthouse. As mentioned earlier, in the corner of the room with all the bondage apparatus, there is an elevator lift. The lift goes to a disused basement. This basement connects to the tunnels used during construction. Those tunnels connect to the old port. There are tunnels from there to the new port. The girls would be brought to the penthouse via the tunnels and that lift. They typically wouldn't be allowed to leave the penthouse. So, they should still be there."

"What about security?" Marr asked.

"Craig had a half dozen security personnel assigned to him. He had access to a much larger contingent, through his son."

"That is how you got involved?"

"Yes, I was based in Utopiam escorting staff for the Atesoughton family. Carltor and I got assigned to Craig when the cruiser broke down in Maple Tower."

"So, six if he replaced you?"

"Yep."

"Now, it is more likely to be three or four," Mentor said.

"Why?" Annee asked.

"The assassination took out a couple."

"What about Craig's fellow abusers?" Marr asked. "Don't they have their own security?"

47

"They might have them elsewhere, but from what I understand, they always came to the penthouse without any."

"Plausible deniability," Trence blurted. On seeing the expressions of the others, he blushed and sat back into his chair.

"What about the building security?" Marr asked.

"The building has external and entrance monitoring. No internal cameras. There are no cameras in the tunnels or lift. They like their privacy."

"So," Marr said sitting forward. "No internal cameras and perhaps only four security people to worry about. That doesn't sound too hard. Any other staff to consider?"

"Perhaps cleaning staff. They'd have to be on the take to keep quiet."

"So, they can be bribed. We could find them and get more information. Perhaps even take their uniforms and use their access IDs to get into the rooms unnoticed. Then take the girls out via the lift and tunnels."

Bognath nodded.

Silence filled the room again.

3

Dukk had enjoyed watching Marr step up and take the lead.

Marr paused as she realised that she had taken a lead role in the conversation. She looked at Dukk. He smiled warmly. She looked at Mentor. He nodded. So, she continued.

"How will we get the girls to the rig unnoticed? And what about Kimince?"

Bognath shrugged his shoulders.

"I have an idea for Kimince," Mentor said.

"Let's hear it," Marr answered. She was enjoying being in charge.

"I use my privilege. We advertise ourselves as a merchant cruiser bringing a level seven observer to Mayfield. I pull rank at the staff village lock-up and simply bring Kimince out. I will need an entourage for it to be realistic. Trence, you will play yourself as my subordinate. And Bognath, you are the right height for the security role. Perhaps a hood and mask might be needed as you might get recognised otherwise. It will be a small entourage, but that might still work."

"But you don't look like an observer, they will know," Trence said.

"That is true now with no make-up, but you didn't recognise me from your disciplinary hearing."

"Oh, yes, that is true."

"So, while that charade is going on, we get the girls out of the resort and onto the rig?" Marr suggested.

Mentor smiled.

"What about the surveillance in the port?" Luna asked.

"We print a video scrambler," Bazzer said. "We can use it to disrupt their video feeds. Before they realise something is up, we can be making for orbit."

"It is a good distance between the port and the resort via the tunnels," Bognath said. "It would take a few hours to walk."

"Carts?" Luna suggested.

"Yes, that is how they would have got there in the first place."

"So, we get a cart."

"We might need more than one cart. I've heard there could be as many as twelve girls."

Sighs filled the room again.

Marr gave everyone a moment and then continued.

"We'll need to work out some of the details later. For now, yes, we'll get carts. Dukk and Annee, you'll oversee getting them and driving through to the resort. Bazzer runs the video scrambler, looks after the rig, and gets it refuelled. Mentor, Trence and Bognath go to the lock-up to get Kimince. Luna and I will get into the penthouse and secure

49

the girls. We'll bring them down the lift to meet Dukk and Annee. Anything else?"

Dukk laughed.

"What?" Marr responded.

"It all sounds so simple when you lay it out like that."

"Complexity leads to complexity," Marr said in a jovial tone.

"Nice work, Marr," Mentor added. "We are going to need disguises. We will also need new IDs for ourselves and the rig."

"What about a rig name?" Luna asked. "Surely, we can't go landing in Mayfield with Ukendt plastered on the hull?"

"Yes, Luna, we need to register a new name with the new bogus ID and then get the hull re-painted."

"Maple Tower?" Dukk suggested.

"Yes, when the right monetary incentive is offered, Ileadees can be quite accommodating."

"What shall we call the rig?" Luna asked.

"I have a suggestion," Mentor said.

"Let's hear it," Dukk responded in an unsurprised manner.

"'Imhullu'", Mentor said. "It means divine wind weapon."

"I like it," Luna replied.

Dukk smiled. Marr did too. The others followed.

"I guess Imhullu it is then," Dukk said. "You are now the crew of the Imhullu."

"And you are the captain," Luna said enthusiastically.

Dukk smiled.

After a moment of checking everyone's demeanour, Dukk continued.

"So, we make for Maple Tower, get the IDs sorted and then head to Mayfield. We follow the plan Marr just outlined and hopefully be there before the party starts. It will be tight."

"We could take some short cuts," Mentor said. "We could traverse through unmonitored systems. From where we are now, we'd only need two more traverses and we'd be in the Maple Tower system. We could apply a similar strategy to then get to Mayfield. We'd get there in plenty of time. It would have the added benefit of staying hidden."

"I agree that we want to keep our path hidden where we can. I am happy with that approach if everyone else wants to take that risk."

Everyone nodded.

"Right then, we have what we need to update the flight plan. Anything else in the plan that needs discussing right now?"

"Yes," Bazzer replied. "We won't want to go gallivanting about the galaxy with a load of composite mesh. We'll just put an even bigger target on our backs."

"Good point, any ideas?" Dukk asked.

"We hide it," Mentor replied.

"We create a pirate's hoard?" Luna suggested.

"Yes, instead of traversing directly to the Maple Tower hub we visit the asteroid belt of the system. We find a suitable rock and stash it there using the empty container."

"That sounds challenging," Marr commented.

"Yes," Dukk said as he looked over at Bazzer. "It would need the knowledge from someone who has worked the belts."

Bazzer laughed, "yes, it would require a strong knowledge of rock hopping."

"You've worked the belts?" Luna asked.

"Yes, when I was young and stupid. About your age, Luna."

"Hold up old man. Are you implying something about my intelligence?" laughed Luna.

Bazzer laughed again.

"Is it plausible?" Dukk asked.

"Yes, I think so," Bazzer answered. "We'd need to exit the traverse at a low speed, clear of dangers but close enough to a suitable rock. We don't want to spend the next year navigating to it. Navigating the belt wouldn't be our only concern. We'd need a rock of minimum mass and therefore gravity to worry about, but big enough to have caves of the size needed to stash the container. We also need to prepare the container so that it can be secured easily to the inside of a cave. We wouldn't want it getting dislodged and floating away. We'd never find it again. We are going to need up to date charts of the field. And we'd want to stay clear of any mining activity."

"I have the charts for that field," Mentor replied. "It includes accurate details of current activity."

"Great," Bazzer answered. "So, we have what we need to pull this off. Between now and the traverse this evening, we can scan the field and pick a medium size rock."

"How much time are we talking? Can we afford the side excursion?" Dukk asked.

"If we get the waypoint and exit speed spot on, and don't have any issues inserting the container into the rock, it will only be a quick traverse hop back to the hub. I'd say it will add four hours. Six tops."

"Perfect," Dukk said.

"Pirates, with a hoard. Love it," Luna blurted. "Will we put a big white 'X' on the charts so we can find it again?"

Marr, Bazzer and Mentor laughed. The others grinned as to not feel left out of the joke.

"Have you never read any of the pirate classics?" Luna offered on seeing her joke hadn't landed with everyone.

Dukk smiled. "Marr, it looks like we have our plan for this evening's watch. We are reviewing charts and practicing rock hopping. Anything else?"

"What about getting into Maple Tower?" Marr asked. "Won't we show up on the relay with the current rig ID?"

"Mentor?" Dukk prompted.

"Yes, I have an idea for that," Mentor replied smiling. "We drop into the system and enable stealth mode. We then use an anonymous broadcast message. I have the format Ileadees uses. He will see the message and will then organise things, so our approach and arrival are discreet and go unnoticed."

"What about moving about in the hub with our current digital IDs?"

"Marr, good point. We'll need to hang tight in the rig until Ileadees supplies the new digital IDs. That reminds me. Unfortunately, we are all supposed to be dead. We need to keep it that way until we uncover who is behind the double cross. That means we can't interact with messages using our current digital IDs. We can't make contact in anyway with those that we knew. For now."

"So, we keep those that care about us thinking we are dead? When will that change?" Annee asked as she sat forward.

"When we talk to those that Craig left behind. I am hoping they will know more about what happened."

"So, we can't make contact until we secure the girls and find the other perpetrators?"

"Yes."

Annee sat back in her seat. Her manner showed disappointment but acceptance. The others had similar demeanours.

"Anything else?" Dukk said to break the tension.

"We need new patches for our jackets," Bazzer said tapping the patch on his jacket. The patch had the word 'Dinatha' on it.

"Yes, Bazzer, perhaps we can print them?" Dukk said has he sat back.

"I'll look into it."

"What about adding a rig emblem?" Luna asked.

"What would it look like?" Annee asked.

"Not sure. Just provided it doesn't look anything like the Veneficans' motif. We don't want to be mistaken for them. Or do we?"

"That reminds me," Trence blurted. "I ran into a Venefica. The afternoon we landed in Mayfield. She was on the Hyperloop. She asked all manner of questions about Kimince and I. She asked about the rig, and the crew, the passengers, the type of cargo, all sorts."

"Did you answer?" Annee asked.

"Of course, why wouldn't I have?"

"This is an interesting development," Mentor said.

"Why?" Dukk asked.

"It is interesting in that I know little of them or why they would be so interested in our activities. We'd better be wary of them until we know more."

"Have I done something wrong?" Trence asked.

"Not at all," Mentor answered. "You were just being yourself. That matters most above everything else."

"I have a couple of other questions that I'd like answered while we are all together," Dukk said in attempt to rebuild momentum.

4

Dukk gathered his thoughts. He didn't want to upset the momentum, but he was keen to clear the air.

"Mentor," Dukk said. "I am guessing you might know more about Wallace and Thumpol."

Mentor smiled.

"Wallace said it was Thumpol's plan to take out me and the crew. The suggestion was that I was difficult to corrupt. Is that true?"

"What is true?" Mentor replied. "That you are difficult to corrupt or Thumpol planned to take you out?"

Dukk raised his eyebrows.

"Point taken," Mentor laughed. "I understand Thumpol had plans to take you out."

"Perhaps those plans only surfaced when it looked like I was exploring other options? Perhaps he got wind of my midnight trip to Utopiam?"

"They are unrelated. Yes, I think he did get wind of the change of plan. Hence the situation with the stabilizers and the presence of Joantyi and Larony. However, I understand that his mind was made up well before any of that. For the reasons Wallace shared."

"Okay, I can accept that," Dukk stated. "I have another question."

Mentor nodded.

"On our most recent arrival into the Mayfield system, we got pushed up the landing queue. Did you have something to do with that?"

"Yes," Mentor replied. "I contacted the handlers for Craig Atesoughton the first. I said the delay would jeopardise the plan."

"That fits," Dukk said.

"My next question relates to our arrival into Utopiam during the entanglement with the robin hood raiders."

Mentor smiled. Marr sat up. Luna did too.

"The lead raider's behaviour was odd. While perched on the rig nose, as we sped towards the citadel, she took a moment to look harder at both you, Mentor, and you Marr. What was that about?"

Mentor looked over at Marr. He nodded.

"She recognised us from our resistance activities," Marr answered. "I couldn't see her face for her mask, but I suspect we'd met in one of the underground bases near Utopiam."

"What do you mean by underground bases?" Annee asked.

"The resistance has many bases," Marr answered. "Some are close to the citadels. Some are in other places."

"And that is where raiders and the like live?"

"More so in the remote bases. The bases close to the citadels do have some permanent residents, but most of these bases are used as day centres. We'd return to the citadel at night to protect our cover."

"Cover?"

"Luna and I were keepers. Our job was to mend the fences and monitoring equipment in the orchards, vineyards and grazing lands that surround the citadels."

"And you would also do work for the resistance?"

"Yes. Maintaining the equipment didn't take much of our time. We'd make it look like it did for the benefit of the observers. But mostly we'd spend our time training and doing our job."

"What do you mean by job?"

"Occasionally we would help with the raids. But our main responsibility was to keep watch on the port. Our job was to alert the raiders when a valuable load was on its way in."

"You'd better explain what you mean," Dukk interrupted.

"We'd sit up in the hills outside the citadel and watch the port activities. Me with my binoculars and Luna with her sniper rifle. The presence of a sentinel squad before a rig arrived would indicate the inbound load was valuable. We'd alert the raiders, and they'd drop in on the rig after it connected with the maglev track."

"You mean you were complicit in the disruption to our arrival and downtime?"

Marr grinned sheepishly.

"Not to mention our safety," Annee added.

"Yes, Ann. We did what we thought was needed," Marr answered sincerely.

"Thinking like that is going to take some adjustment," Dukk reflected aloud.

Annee nodded.

"What do the raiders do with the things they take?" Trence asked.

The question caused everyone to look around. The interruption also broke the tension.

"It would be used, sold or traded," Marr replied. "The raids fund the resistance."

"But why are they called robin hood raiders? Why not just resistance raiders. What is the robin hood thing about?"

"Robin hood was an outlaw who robbed from the rich and gave to the poor. He lived in a forest. The use of the title takes the focus away from the resistance. Most wrongly assume the raiders are the wild people."

"Oh," Trence replied. "I need to think about that some more."

"I have one final question," Dukk said. "It is for anyone that cares to share."

He looked around before continuing.

"How did you all get weapons on board the Dinatha? You all came through the ID gateway when you joined the rig. Everything, including yourselves, was scanned."

"The beef containers," Luna blurted. "My rifle still smells of dead cow!"

"But the containers were sealed!" Trence said.

"Oh, I'd forgotten about that! Mentor gave me my weapons during the first leg out of Earth. I hadn't questioned it."

They all looked at Mentor.

"Level sevens can break and reseal containers," Mentor said sheepishly.

"Handy," Dukk laughed.

"Wait," Trence interjected again. "Luna, you are a sniper! And you and Marr worked in the hills! The attack on the Bluilda. The sentinel exploding. Me getting demoted and joining this rig! You did that!"

"Yes, Trence," Luna answered with empathy.

"Well, I guess it is done and I have a new and perhaps much more exciting life ahead."

Luna nodded. "No hard feelings?"

"Well, no. I am not sure I am there yet," Trence answered quietly.

Dukk gave the moment a little space before resuming.

"But what about you, Bognath?" he asked.

"I picked up a weapon in Maple Tower," Bognath replied. "You'd be surprised what you can pick-up there with sufficient credit."

"That is good to know. Well, that does it for me. If there aren't any more questions for now, I'd suggest we get on with getting into the rescuing business. Besides, I am hungry. Anyone up for an early dinner?"

"Definitely," Marr replied. "Who's turn is it to cook?"

"That joke is getting old," Luna laughed. "Dukk's sense of humour is rubbing off on you. Unless, of course, this rig has a hidden kitchen with a stash of real food. That also assumes someone here actually knows how to cook."

"Not to my knowledge," Marr laughed. "Nope, the only thing on the menu is rehydration packs of the usual variety."

A little later the gang were back at the table, ready to enjoy a meal together.

"Let's start by giving thanks," Dukk said to get everyone's attention.

"May I," asked Trence cautiously. "I've been practicing with Mentor."

"Of course," Dukk answered in surprise.

Everyone stopped. They sat up straight and looked over at Trence.

Trence looked about, nervously. The observer's eyes came to rest on Mentor.

"You have got this," Mentor mouthed.

After a pause, Trence sat up straight and looked blankly towards the middle of the table.

"I express gratitude for all that was, is and yet to be," Trence said slowly and hesitantly.

The observer then stopped and looked over at Mentor.

Mentor nodded and smiled.

Trence continued, "may my new friends help me continue to learn of the reality of things. May we find what is needed within ourselves to rescue Kimince and the girls. Thanks, I give."

"Thanks, I give," they all replied compassionately.

With that Trence burst into tears. Tears of joy.

The others found it hard not to join in.

"Did I do alright," Trence muttered between sobs.

"Yes, Trence, it was perfect," Dukk answered sincerely.

As the crew meal ended, Dukk asked if there was any housekeeping that needed addressing.

"Yes," Bazzer answered. "That hatch up on the roof isn't sealing properly. The seal motor was damaged when we took the rig this morning. I have already printed the replacement parts. I'd like to fix it when we come out of the next traverse. Which, I see, will be near midnight. I'd also like to deploy the drones and scan the outer hull. We'd need the DMD off. It should only take thirty minutes. Can we accommodate the delay?"

"Yes, I think that should be alright," Dukk replied.

"Perfect. So, it will be a two-person job. I'd like someone to help me?"

"I'll help," Mentor responded. "After all, I did the damage."

"That is sorted then," Bazzer replied.

"Anything else?" Dukk asked.

Dukk waited a moment for any comments before continuing.

"Great, it is time to try the gym," Dukk answered.

He turned to look at Marr. She nodded and smiled.

"Well, enjoy that," Annee said jovially. "I for one am going to sleep. It is five hours before my next watch, and I intend to enjoy every bit of that time with my eyes shut."

"Me too," Mentor added.

"Looks like me and you are doing the dishes, Lunes," Bazzer stated.

"That's not my name, Bazz! And, it is your turn," Luna answered with a cheeky grin.

5

Ten minutes later, Marr and Dukk were making their way through the rig. Their destination was the gym on the lower level.

Dukk was wearing his usual gym gear; Skin-tight shorts, a sleeveless skin-tight top and runners designed for use in near zero gravity. Marr was similarly attired in shorts and a crop top.

Marr was leading. She stopped as they entered the gym. She turned to face him. She smiled.

Dukk approached her. He took her in his arms. Their bodies pressed against each other. They kissed deeply.

"I am not sure if it will be easier or harder to exercise alongside you now," Marr said when the kiss finished.

"Harder. Definitely," Dukk answered.

"I can tell," Marr whispered as she kissed him again.

"Woohoo, I won't tell if you don't," came a voice from the doorway.

Marr and Dukk stopped kissing and looked over.

It was Trence.

They smiled, separated, and went to explore the equipment.

"How are you getting on?" Marr asked Trence as the three of them paced it out on the line of treadmills.

"I am feeling hopeful," Trence replied. "I miss Kimince's company, and I feel broken inside after what I learnt today. However, Mentor has given me a minute-by-minute plan to help me. It includes exercise, sleep, eating, reading, things to look at and chats with him. He also said I must try to speak with everyone else on this rig. He feels getting to know you all better will also help me find myself again."

"It gets easier."

"You've been through this too?"

"In a way. I was younger than you are, so I suspect it was easier."

"How old were you?"

"I was eighteen when I learned of the resistance and its efforts. However, unknown to me, I had been recruited during the labour rotation. I was already primed to receive the truth."

"What do you mean by primed to receive the truth?"

"During the eight years of labour rotation I was given access to contraband material: books; films; music; art. It is eye opening to learn about the past and see the magnificent, complex, and beautiful creations of our ancestors. By the time I turned eighteen I was ready to see and hear things that didn't fit in with what was visible."

"But we looked for that type of thing. It was part of what I did in security. We checked what people were reading, watching, and listening to. We'd alert our superiors if we found any of the banned material showing up?"

"It wasn't an issue for the first two years. Then at twelve when I got the comms implants and med-lines, I was shown ways to access the material covertly. Films and music were the hardest to consume. But not impossible. A lot of it had subtext. I also learnt to read sheet music. I could get a sense of the tune and melody of the music and film soundtracks. Eventually I got hold of a bracelet and that made it even easier."

"What is an example of something that you learnt?"

"Okay, let me think."

Marr paused and gave her mind space to answer the question.

"I know," she said after a moment. "There is the idea of realistic optimism. I can't recall where I first came across this. Anyway, the idea is that when you go into a jungle, you should take a spear. Hoping for the best but ignoring the dangers will only get you eaten."

"How horrid," Trence said. "That doesn't sound optimistic."

"I haven't finished. The idea is that you must put yourself in the neighbourhood of danger on a regular basis if you want to have a rich and engaging life. Never going into the jungle for fear of finding a sticky and uncomfortable end, holds you back from being your true self. However, that doesn't mean you can avoid every danger or pitfall armed solely with a cheerful outlook."

"I don't get it."

"Let me elaborate. There is this story about a man's experience of travelling to a foreign city. The man went jogging through an old walled section. That part of the city had lots of narrow, winding streets, which the man found fun to explore as he ran. He got increasingly confident as he dashed about the streets, the vehicles, and the people. That is when he came unstuck. He forgot where he was. He stopped considering that he was in unfamiliar surrounds. As he went to run past a streetside coffee stand, a small dog dashed out and nipped him on the ankle. It shocked him and he wanted to kick it and defend himself, until he realized that he was in the wrong place, not the dog. This small dog was the property of the stall owner. The man was invading the dog's space by running in fast without any warning. The dog's reaction was defensive, protecting his owner. The man had gone into the jungle with his eyes wide shut."

"But that wasn't a jungle."

"Yes, of course. Jungle is a metaphor for daily life. Which inevitably involves dealing with challenging situations, typically involving other people but also our own doubts and fears. We need to equip ourselves appropriately."

"I am confused."

"Let me share more. Another way to look at this, when facing an adversary, is to 'Hope for the best, plan for the worst.' At times that is simply a matter of sizing up your opponents and looking for their weaknesses. At other times, you must enlist help from you network to gain access to the arsenal necessary to prevail."

"This is something about preparation?"

"It is. But also, it is about taking responsibility for the actions one takes. It is about being accountable not just after the fact but ahead too. When you simultaneously strive to move forward while looking positively at who you are and what you want, you are being a realistic optimist. Let me finish with this passage from one of the many books that I've read on this subject. 'Life is a wonderful experience when I venture into the jungle. To survive the jungle, I need to prepare myself without over-cooking it. Half the fun is the frantic search for a tree to climb when the spear breaks.'"

"Wow. This is wonderful."

"It is, isn't it. It speaks to the creed."

"Can you remind me of the creed?"

"Of course. 'Focus on that which is real in the heart. Create the space so that the process can emerge. Honour that which serves you well. Engage in the journey as it unfolds.'"

"Amazing. I'd like to have a look at these books."

"I can help you get access to the hidden archives if you like?"

"Thank you, I'd appreciate that."

"Count me in," Dukk said. "I'd also like to learn how to access these hidden archives."

Chapter 4 – Reframing

1

Just before six p.m. Dukk was leaving his cabin. He was showered and changed into his g-suit. He was ready for the start of the four-hour watch.

"Looking good, captain?" Luna said from her chair at the console in the crew mess. She was swinging the chair back and forth.

"Thanks," Dukk answered. "Did we win?"

Dukk pointed to the console screens. The console was configured with the weapons system controls. The console screen showed a paused simulation scene. In the image was a planet and a load of wreckage.

"Of course, I am kicking butt with the tools on this bird. I blew the bejesus out of that pirate vessel."

"I am not sure if that gives me comfort or concern," laughed Dukk.

Luna grinned and laughed.

"By the way," she said. "Bazzer said he will hang on a bit to go over the charts for the astro field. He is in the cockpit."

"Excellent," Dukk replied. After a pause he added, "how are you getting on?"

"Going with the flow."

"Any ideas yet for the Imhullu's motif?"

"Nope," Luna replied smiling. "I'd forgotten about it. I'll give it some thought when I get onto the treadmill."

Dukk smiled. "Any sign of Marr?"

"She is just out of the shower. She's getting dressed. I'm waiting for her to have a chat."

"Anything I can help you with?"

"Nope, girl's stuff."

"Cool. I'll head into the cockpit. Will you tell her that we'll do the suit cross check in there."

"Roger, captain," Luna said as she gave him a salute.

"Looks like we'll have plenty of options," Dukk said as he entered the cockpit.

Bazzer was sitting in his seat in the second row. The cockpit projector was illuminating a large area of the Maple 13 asteroid field.

"Too many, in fact," Bazzer replied. "I am about to overlay the recent mining activity. It should narrow down our options."

Dukk sat in the seat opposite and surveyed the projection.

"What are the yellow dots?"

"Records of encounters with pirates for the last ten years," Bazzer replied as he continued to interact with the console. "It will give us a sense of potential locations of other hoards. We want to stay clear of them too. Right, I have it."

The projection changed. Blue dots now appeared in small clusters across the projection.

"Still looks like we have plenty of options."

"Yes," laughed Bazzer. "Now we pick one."

"How?"

"Luck."

Dukk laughed.

"Why don't we wait for Marr to join us?" Bazzer suggested. "She can have the honours."

"Good idea."

Dukk stared at the projection. It was immense. The scale of things still caught him off guard.

"How are you getting on?" Bazzer asked in an empathetic tone.

Dukk looked over. He smiled.

"I am doing okay," he said. "Things are mental and with every answer I find a load of new questions. But I still get the sense that this is all as it is meant to be."

"What type of questions?" Bazzer asked.

"How long have you been part of the resistance?" Dukk asked with a smile.

Dukk had been reflecting on why only Bazzer, Marr and Mentor laughed at Luna's attempted joke about putting a big 'X' on the charts. After hearing Marr talk about the hidden archives it dawned on him that perhaps there was more to Bazzer also.

"Good question," Bazzer laughed. "For as long as I can remember."

"You never let on. Why?"

"I felt it best that you find your own path. Besides, I didn't exactly keep it all to myself."

"By that do you mean the concepts you have shared with me and skills you insisted that I learn?"

"Yep," Bazzer said with a smile.

Dukk returned to looking at the projection. He had another question.

"Mentor is known to you, isn't he?" Dukk asked.

"Yes," Bazzer answered sincerely.

"When I asked you about the comments Ileadees made about him, you said he and Ileadees have history. That was a deflection, wasn't it?"

"In a way," Bazzer answered with a grin.

"You and Mentor have history too?"

Bazzer nodded.

"And did you know of Mentor's plans for us this last month?" Dukk asked.

"No. I had no knowledge of his immediate plans," Bazzer answered sincerely. "I was genuinely surprised to see him join the rig as crew. We had not had any interactions in years."

"Can you tell me more about those interactions?"

Meanwhile, Marr had found Luna waiting for her in the crew mess.

Marr sensed something was on her mind.

Luna's expression made that clear. It was subtle but not for Marr. Spending nearly every waking moment with someone for three years did that.

"Hey, are you okay?" Marr asked as she sat on the couch opposite her.

"Something happened during the planning chat. It got me thinking," Luna said with a smile.

"What happened?"

"You took charge."

"I did," replied Marr.

"Mentor was always in charge. For as long as I've known you both, he always directed you and me. I was under your wing, and you were under his."

"And?"

"I recalled Teacher's question. The one she has been asking me of late."

"'What occurs to you at this moment in your journey?'" Marr said.

"Yes, that question."

"What about it?"

"I get it now. I had thought my place was in the fields and doing jobs for the resistance. When this gig came along, I thought it was just a mission and we'd be back in the fields when done. I was looking forward to getting back. Then I got into the swing of it. The life of the haulier. I grew fond of it. Then it all changed last night. The Dinatha was no more. During today's chat, I realised I was grieving. But when I quietened my mind, asked, and listened for the answer, I didn't get back anything about the fields and life on Earth. I got this life. The haulier life. That was what I was grieving. That is when I recalled Teacher's question. I realised something."

"What did you realise?"

"Joining the Dinatha was never about a mission."

Marr nodded.

"The events last night," Luna continued. "This new rig. You taking charge of the planning. Sure, Mentor has a hand in it, but he can't have planned every detail about where we are now. There were no specific orders to follow. Things just unfolded."

Marr smiled.

"This is the journey that Teacher was referring to," Luna said. "The three years in the fields was just one part of that journey. As was the last month. And now there is something new. It all joins up. It is my path."

"Yes, that is what I believe," Marr said. "Are you okay with that?"

"Yes, I think I am," Luna replied smiling.

2

Marr and Luna looked at each other. There was a softness to the exchange. They enjoyed the moment. Then Luna broke the silence.

"You and Dukk?"

Marr grinned.

"Is he? You know? Was it worth the wait?" Luna asked in a provocative tone.

Marr giggled.

"Not willing to share the details," Luna said. "At least you are consistent. You know the DMD will be off for a time after the next traverse. And you and Dukk won't be on watch. You won't get many opportunities like that for time together in zero-g."

Marr laughed and raised her eyebrows.

"I'd better get to the cockpit," Marr said as she stood up. "We are picking the location for the hoard."

"Yeah, okay," Luna laughed. "Have fun."

As Marr opened the cockpit door, Dukk and Bazzer turned around to look at her.

"Later," Bazzer said to Dukk. "We've got a rock hop to plan."

"Is that the asteroid field?" Marr asked as she moved to the centre of the cockpit. She stood in the middle of the projection and looked about.

"Yep, Marr. We need to pick a suitable rock," Bazzer replied. "Do you want to have the honours?"

"Of course. What should I take into consideration?"

"We want to avoid the activities of others. It needs to be a size like this rock," Bazzer said as he pointed to an object floating in the air between them.

"Then what?"

"You and Dukk runs simulations. Once you are happy that we can get right on top of it safely and out again, lock it into the flight plan."

"Piece of cake," Marr laughed. "Anything else to think about?"

"Yes, you will want to have put some contingencies in place should Ileadees be operating a patrol in the region?"

"Patrolling for what?"

"Pirates or scavengers."

"What are the chances that we encounter a patrol?"

"None unless they are in the same region of the field and doing DMD probing."

"What do you mean by that?"

"So, you know that the process of initiating a traverse between systems can take up to twelve hours. However, the traverse is instant if the destination is nearby, say the moon of the planet we are orbiting or across the same region of an asteroid belt."

"What about the safety?"

"Yes, to provide time for the traverse juice to be administered, the DMD has a safety. Usually about thirty seconds. So, to jump to the moon we'd suit up, hook up the med lines and then insert the destination into the DMD. Thirty seconds later we'd traverse."

"Yes, I understand that. So, what is DMD probing?"

"Okay, so the DMD is highly accurate and self-preserving. It won't traverse to a location if there is an obstacle at the destination. It will adjust the arrival point slightly. It will make allowances for obstacles or other craft to move out of the way. That adjustment takes more time. For a local jump it would be a fraction of a millisecond. Unnoticeable for us, but measurable all the same. Probing involves an automated process. The process feeds the DMD with predefined nearby locations. Locations that should be free of obstacles. If the DMD sets a traverse time that doesn't match the safety exactly, you can assume something else is near the destination. Something that shouldn't be there. Like us plugging a container into a rock. If the time is exact, the automated process aborts the traverse and puts in another location."

"What happens if there is a slight variation?"

"The patrol crew allow the traverse to take place, and then investigate."

"We can work through these scenarios using the simulator," Dukk added.

"Exactly. And if there are no other questions for me, I'm off to the gym. Leave you to it," Bazzer said as he rose.

Marr stepped aside to let him pass.

In the third hour of the watch, Dukk was sitting quietly in the cockpit.

He and Marr had completed the simulations and planning. Marr was on a routine walk around to check the rig.

Mentor opened the door of the cockpit.

Dukk looked up.

"Perhaps it is time to have that chat that I have promised you?" Mentor said.

"Yes, that's a good idea."

"I ran into Marr on the way in here. I suggested we chat together, and we do that somewhere that we won't get interrupted. She has gone down to the lounge on the middle level. You can send the conn to the console there."

Dukk nodded.

"Marr, are you in the lounge?" Dukk said into his comms link.

"Yep, it's all ours," Marr replied instantly.

"Sending you the conn."

Mentor turned and opened the cockpit door. He held it for Dukk. Together they used the stairs to drop to the middle level and enter the lounge.

Marr was already sitting on a couch.

Dukk joined her.

Mentor sat opposite them and smiled.

3

"Mentor, I'd like to know more about my mother. Will you share what you know?"

"I will. I will do that by sharing my story as it relates to her. I have some other knowledge of her life, but it is better that she tells you about that herself."

"That's sounds fair."

"So, our story starts when we were young. In Utopiam. We were in the incubation centre at the same time. We weren't in the same pod, but we mingled and played together with all the other children. It wasn't until after the test that we really got to know one another."

"So, she is an observer too?"

"No, she was training to be a hostess, but she went a different direction."

"What is she now?"

"Let's come back to that question."

"Okay, so you are the same age and passed the test together. That allowed you to continue your studies and not start the labour rotation like myself, Marr and most?"

"Yes, for all intents and purposes we are the same age. Though, I am older by 4 months. And yes, we were selected for privilege."

"What happened after the test?"

"We were in the same study classes. We learnt about the Rule of Twelve and what was ahead of us. She had a great love of learning.

More than me. I enjoyed her company, so I went along with it. By the age of twelve we had consumed every piece of information in the standard curriculum. She went searching for more and she found it. She got access to the restricted material in the archives. The archives gave us access to history before the reset."

"Weren't you monitored? How did the teachers not know what you were doing?"

"Some of the teachers were red pilled already. They were part of the resistance. They gave us bracelets which we used whenever we were reading or talking about the material. I suspect those teachers are how Tieanna got access to the material in the first place, but I haven't been able to confirm it. At the time it didn't matter to us. We just couldn't get enough. Over the course of the next four years, we consumed mountains of material."

"That makes you sixteen. Why didn't you continue studying? You would have had two more years as students."

"Shortly after her sixteenth birthday, Tieanna abruptly disappeared. I was devastated. At the time I figured she got caught with the banned material and was disappeared. It was her disappearance that cemented my resolve to join the resistance. It was then that I signed up to the plan of achieving level seven so I could use that level of access to further the plans of the resistance. For the next four years I did all that I could to gain favour with the observers. I was promoted faster than my peers and was at level ten by the time I turned twenty. Then everything changed, again."

"What happened?"

"I received a message from your mother. She was about to take up a new role with the Atesoughton family. She was leaving Earth and she needed my help. She needed me to come to Kuedia."

"That must have been a shock," Marr observed.

"It was, Marr," Mentor replied.

"Wait! Oh shit!" Dukk interrupted.

"What?" Marr asked.

"The age. If Tieanna is the same age as you, Mentor, she is forty-nine now. That meant I was born when she was sixteen. She left Utopiam when she became pregnant with me. She went to Kuedia to have and then raise me. And then she left Earth when she was twenty. I would have been four. That is why I can remember her being around when I was young. It explains how she was suddenly gone."

"Yes, Dukk, that is correct," Mentor replied.

"What did she need you to do?" Dukk started to ask before stopping himself.

A tear welled in his eye. After a pause, Dukk continued.

"I know what she asked of you. She asked you to look out for me. That is why you are so familiar to me. You went to Kuedia. You were there with me in the incubation centre after Tieanna left?"

"Yes, Dukk," Mentor said in a manner that indicated a huge weight had just been lifted. "I requested and then got transfer to Kuedia shortly after I got her message."

Marr stared with her mouth open.

After a moment, Dukk spoke again. "Did you see her before she left Earth?"

"Briefly. For a few weeks only," Mentor replied. His demeanour changed slightly. Marr noticed it.

"Where you two companions?" Marr asked gently.

Mentor was taken aback by the question. He looked at Marr for a moment and then turned to look at Dukk again.

"I'd like to know the truth, please," Dukk said honestly.

"Yes, when we met again in Kuedia, we were. I guess, we still are," Mentor replied.

That piece of information took a time to sink in. Eventually Dukk spoke again.

"Why?" he asked.

"Why what?" Mentor replied.

"Why did she go to Kuedia? Why did she leave to work for the Atesoughtons? And what of my father?"

"Those are questions for your mother. I have an idea, but she doesn't speak to me of those times. It is best that you ask her yourself. All I know for certain is that at the time, she was working in the incubation centre in Kuedia."

"Okay, so what else can you tell me of her? What happened after that?"

"For her, I have bits and pieces. She worked for the Atesoughton family. She was the nanny for Craig Atesoughton the third. She raised him. After that she became a sort of advisor for Craig. She moved in his circles. She became a member of his staff. But a member with influence and privilege."

"What about you?" Dukk asked.

"I focused on getting promoted and I kept an eye on you. It wasn't easy but I did my best. Then at twenty-five I reached level seven. After that I could go where I pleased."

"I would have been nine. Just about to take the test?" Dukk noted.

"Yes, that is true."

4

Suddenly Dukk leaned forward. His hands went to his face. Marr and Mentor sat up.

"Are you ok?" Marr asked immediately.

Dukk sat back up. He sighed. "It was true!"

"What was true?" Marr asked.

"The test. You were there!" Dukk stated as he looked up at Mentor.

"I was," Mentor said quietly as he sat back. "What do you remember?"

"I was taken to a medical room. I remember lots of questions. They also told me things. I clearly remember being told this was for my own good. It would protect me from a life of pain and hardship. Then they injected me with something. It made me drowsy. I was told to close my eyes and go to sleep. I closed my eyes. Then I heard noises. I tried to open my eyes. I was sleepy so it wasn't easy. There was another person in the room. And I was sure there was a struggle. Then I woke up. I was in my own bed, in my dorm. Half the beds were empty. Those that passed the test were gone. And my testicles were sore. I had a slit either side. The carers said I must not touch the cuts, but I had to let them know if there was any bleeding or pus. Over breakfast those of us that were left behind, shared stories of the test. We all had slits either side of our testicles. We were all sore. But when I told them about the other person in the room and the struggle, they laughed. They made fun of me; said I was going mad. The carer overheard and scolded me. I was told not to ever speak of it. So, I pushed it aside. I buried the memory. I never spoke of it until now. You were that other person. You were in the room. What happened?"

"All I can tell you is that I prevented a great travesty. I can't speak any more of it, yet. I made a promise to keep the events of that night from you. It isn't time for you to know."

"Who did you make that promise to."

"That I cannot say, yet."

Marr had been watching the exchange in awe. Her thoughts had drifted to her own story. It was dawning on her. She knew so little of these things. Perhaps she too had hidden memories of a similar nature.

Dukk had let this news sit for a moment. He felt anger and frustration. The mysteries would do him in. He put it aside. He cleared his mind. He would allow things to unfold. Then another memory hit him. He sat up again.

"What now?" Marr asked.

"I have another memory after the struggle," Dukk answered. "You spoke to me before the drugs put me under."

Mentor smiled.

"You said something like 'You have been saved because you are special. Listen to The Light. Follow your inner voice. When the time comes you will choose to be known as Dukk."

Mentor nodded.

"And, let me guess," Dukk laughed. "Tieanna put you up to it so that when I came to choose the name, I would use the name Dukk as it was already planted in my mind. And I should ask her about all of that?"

Mentor smiled again.

"You might as well continue. We are on a roll. This can't get any weirder. What happened after the test?"

"You did the labour rotation and I carried out another promise I made to your mother."

"Which was?"

"To steer you towards seeing more than the inside of the Citadels. I used my influence to make sure the labour roles had something to do with the port, rigs, and hauling. Even when you were on the dish washing rotation, I made sure you were in a place that had a window that overlooked the port or the maglev."

Dukk laughed and shook his head.

Mentor smiled again.

"What about after the labour rotation," Dukk asked when he stopped laughing. "What about when I turned eighteen and joined a rig as an apprentice?"

"I left you in someone else's capable hands. Someone to watch over you. Someone to train you. To keep my promise to Tieanna."

"Bazzer!" Dukk said with a smile.

Mentor nodded.

"So, you were done with me until these recent events?"

"Pretty much. I kept in touch with Bazzer and helped where it was needed. Besides, I had a new mission to attend to. A new challenge back in Utopiam."

Dukk sat back. He thought about that. Then he turned his head and looked at Marr. Mentor followed.

"Me?" Marr said in surprise.

Mentor smiled.

"You returned to Utopiam to mentor me?"

"Yes, you were sixteen and your interest in the past ways was exceeding the patience of those around you. I was called back to help channel that energy."

Marr laughed. "Looks like we've both been played, Dukk. Who would have thought!"

"Yep, so it seems," laughed Dukk.

Marr and Dukk enjoyed a moment before Marr moved her gaze back to Mentor.

"I was sixteen when you returned to Utopiam, but we didn't meet until I was eighteen," Marr said.

"I was in the background, initially," Mentor answered. "I helped direct activities. Put the right things in your way. I also had to free up my time and hand over a lot of my responsibilities. I knew I would need to give you my full attention the moment you turned eighteen. The moment you got into the fields and got a taste of autonomy. Too much time and effort had been put into your development. It was important that your energy and enthusiasm be kept in check."

"What do you mean?"

"The grander plans for you."

"Which are?"

Mentor smiled.

"Let me guess, you can't say. Or is it you don't know?"

"Bit of both," Mentor answered.

"Who does know?"

Mentor smiled again.

"So, answer me this then. Who gives you your resistance related orders? Tieanna?"

"No, not Tieanna."

"Who then?"

Mentor paused. "I suspect you know the answer to that."

"Teacher?"

Mentor nodded.

"So, it is her I need to speak with to get some answers."

Mentor nodded again.

After a period of silence, Mentor sat up.

"Time for me to get ready for watch," he said. "I suggest we leave any other questions for another time."

"Yes, that works," Dukk replied. "I need time to process all of this."

"Me too," added Marr.

Marr and Dukk watched Mentor leave, then turned back to look at each other.

There was only a moment of hesitation before they both smiled.

In unison they moved towards each other and kissed deeply.

Time paused. For a moment. A squawk in their comms brought them back.

5

"Dukk and Marr, I'm at the console in the crew mess if you want to send the conn here," Annee announced into Marr and Dukk's comms. "Mentor mentioned you were chatting and might need a moment."

Marr and Dukk fell back onto the couch laughing.

"On it," Dukk replied in the comms.

After collecting himself, Dukk stood up and walked over to the console in the corner of the lounge. He sat down, activated it, and directed the conn to the crew mess. He waited for Annee to accept the transfer.

"Having consoles in so many locations, makes life easier. The Dinatha was a little backward only having the three locations," Dukk said as he swung back and forth on the seat.

"Definitely allows for more flexibility," Marr added.

An alert on the console indicated the conn was now with Annee.

"Right," Dukk announced as he turned back to look at Marr. "It is ten now. The next traverse is just after mid-night. Two hours."

"I think I need some time alone to process all of this," Marr said.

"Yes, me too. Time on the treadmill listening to Radio Birdman is what I need."

"More of that retro stuff," Marr laughed.

"Yes, absolutely. After that I want to do more simulations for tomorrow's rock hop."

"I want to get some more practice in too. With you, Mentor and Bazzer driving transport pods to move the container. And, with Annee flying the drones for visibility, I'll be on flight control on my own!"

"Nervous?"

"A little."

"You'll be fine. I've seen how you respond under pressure. If something goes wrong, you'll manage it."

"Thanks. Although I don't know I responded that well when you and Luna had the E.V.A. accident."

"There have been plenty of other moments since then. You've come a long way in four weeks."

Marr smiled. "I guess. Besides, I'll have Luna to keep me company."

"No, she will be with me. I have a special job for Luna."

"Do tell."

"Nope, it is a surprise," Dukk said with a smile.

Two and a half hours later, a familiar chime sounded throughout the rig. Moments later a familiar tingle washed over them.

"Shit!" Dukk exclaimed.

Marr gasped as the DMD came back to life and the near zero-g came into effect.

They crashed back on to the bed. They giggled as they did their best to untangle their naked bodies.

"All done, captain," Bazzer announced into the crew comms. "The roof hatch is repaired, and we are slow running ahead of the traverse into the astro belt in eight hours."

"Oh, good, Bazzer. Glad to hear it," Dukk answered on the shared comms link.

"Didn't disturb you, I hope," Luna giggled on the comms. "What's the verdict?"

"You will keep, Luna," Marr answered with a chuckle as she reached for the bed covers.

Once snuggled into each other under the bed clothes, Marr said, "That was good." She emphasised the word good.

"Absolutely," Dukk answered warmly.

"It almost feels like they coordinated things, so we'd have this time together."

Dukk laughed.

"What?" Marr asked.

"That hatch repair could have waited until Maple Tower. Bazzer planned it for now so the DMD would be down for a time. They orchestrated the opportunity for us. It is kind of a haulier tradition."

"Here was me thinking it all unfolded as it was meant to be."

"Can't that be true too?"

"Yes, I guess it can," Marr replied as she yawned.

"Time for some rest. We have a busy day ahead."

"Absolutely," Marr said in a sleepy tone.

When Dukk woke, he was alone. He checked the time. He had fifteen minutes before the start of watch.

"Wow," he said aloud.

"I can't remember sleeping so soundly," he reflected to himself.

He sat up and swung his legs off the bed.

There was a message scribbled on the pad he kept on the nightstand.

It read, "I need a long shower, see you for the suit cross check. M. xxx"

Dukk smiled as he did some basic stretches.

Marr had enjoyed the shower. The cyclone-based technology in the shower system was efficient but surprisingly refreshing.

When she left her cabin, just before six a.m., she found the crew mess still dark, but not empty.

Luna was sitting at the console in the corner.

"Hey Marr," Luna announced to the room.

"Good morning, Luna," Marr replied. "How are things?"

"All quiet out there, but busy in here." Luna replied as she waved her hands at the projected image of the system and then to the floor below.

"Busy?" Marr enquired.

"We have been printing equipment and making modifications to the container. The printing and modifications are done. We just need to get the equipment into the transport pods."

"We can do that if you want to get some rest," Dukk said at his cabin door.

He was suited up and looking refreshed.

"Yes, that is why I am here in the crew mess. I came up here to suggest that you two do the final preparations while we get some downtime. We've got ninety minutes before the traverse."

"Perfect. Marr do you want to take over the conn and I'll go down to check-in with Bazzer."

"Yep, that works," Marr replied. "Suit cross check first, though."

Marr smiled over at Dukk.

"Leave it out you two," Luna laughed.

With the suit check done, Dukk used the starboard aft ladder shaft to drop down to the lower level.

He found Bazzer and Mentor in the hold. They were loading four of the five canisters into the container.

"Hey captain," Bazzer said on seeing Dukk. "Did you get some rest?"

"I did, thanks Bazzer," Dukk laughed.

"Good to hear it."

"Are you and Mentor enjoying working together again? Perhaps you've also been discussing how your plans for me have worked out?"

Bazzer stopped what he was doing and looked over at Dukk.

Mentor did the same.

"I guessed it, when talking with Mentor," Dukk said. "He asked you to look after me."

Bazzer looked at Mentor.

Mentor smiled and nodded.

"Yes, however it was more about looking out for you than looking after you," Bazzer said. "When you joined me as my apprentice, you were already more switched on than most."

Dukk smiled.

"Are we good?"

"Yes, just wanted to clear the air," Dukk replied.

"Clear air is what we need," Annee said as she appeared from the side of the container.

Bognath was with her.

Dukk smiled at them both.

"That's the drones prepared. They are in the port airlock, ready to deploy," Annee said. "They needed to be re-configured to work properly in caves."

"By the sounds of it, you have all made great use of the wee hours," Dukk said.

"Haven't we all," Bazzer said in a provocative tone.

Dukk laughed.

"Let me know what's left to be done. You all better get some rest. It will be busy once we reach the Maple 13 system."

"Yep, that is the plan," Bazzer said as he turned and looked towards the engine room.

"Those two rock bolt guns need to be put into the back of transport pods," Bazzer said as he pointed towards the floor near the industrial printer. "One in each of the first pods on the starboard and port sides. Also, these brackets. Mentor and I will each take a pod. We will go ahead and get these brackets in place. You and Luna take another transport pod, extract the container from the hold and bring it in to the cave. Bognath will stay in the hold and help hook up the container to save us some time."

"Anything else?"

"Yes, we haven't done the checklists for the transport pods. That needs to be done too. They should be fully charged by now, but we want to make sure they are fully functional. Especially the search lights. We will need them to illuminate the cave."

Dukk helped Bazzer close the container doors. He then watched as Bazzer, and the others disappeared into the ladder shaft.

Dukk opened his comms to Marr.

"Marr, this all looks straight-forward. I'll complete the jobs down here if you want to keep an eye on the rig systems and logs."

"Perfect, will do," Marr replied.

Chapter 5 – Rock hopping

1

Dukk moved the rock bolt guns and brackets from the floor of the engine room, into the starboard aft ladder shaft.

He unfolded the basket at the bottom of the vertical conveyor that ran up the side of the shaft. He put the equipment into the basket and then climbed the ladder to the middle level. Once off the ladder, he activated the conveyor to lift the equipment.

With the equipment out of the basket, he opened the door to the starboard transport pod bay. He moved the equipment into the space next to the third pod and then closed the door.

Dukk then walked to the second pod and interacted with a small control panel embedded in the pod's outer hull. Immediately, the pod's canopy opened slightly and then slid out of the way. A section of the pod side wall slid down giving Dukk access to the seating. The pod had five seats. Two rows of two and a single seat that sat in the back between the bio systems. It was a tight fit, but adequate.

Dukk sat in and interacted with the controls. The small craft came to life. After starting the self-diagnostics, he moved to the first pod and did the same. With the starboard pods in hand, he used the forward door to cross over to the port bay. He repeated the process in the first pod.

While waiting for the diagnostics to complete, he had a closer look at the pods.

The insignia on the side of the pods had been changed. It now read 'Imhullu' instead of 'Ukendt'. Even the older pod they had brought across from the Dinatha, had 'Imhullu' imprinted on the sides. The older pod was also now at the back of the bay. Dukk assumed they were moved earlier in the morning when the DMD was offline to fix the roof hatch.

An alert caught Dukk's attention. He returned to the controls of the pod. The diagnostics were complete. The tanks were full. The battery load test was positive. The micro-reactor was working properly. The bio-systems were in good order.

Before shutting down the pod, Dukk use the controls to move the front seats back and lower the seats in the back. The plan was to wear E.V.A. backpacks, so the front seats needed to be adjusted to make more room. The space in the back was needed for the equipment. Dukk then returned to the starboard bay and repeated the process with the other two pods.

With that done, he retrieved the rock bolt guns and brackets and secured them into the back of each of the first pod on each side.

"Looks like you are having fun," came a squawk on Dukk's comms. It was Marr.

Dukk smiled.

"Are you spying on me?" he said into his comms.

"Not spying," Marr giggled into the comms.

"If we didn't need someone at a console, I'd insist you come down and help me inspect the pods," Dukk said in a provocative tone.

"Insist?" Marr replied in an equally provocative tone.

Dukk smiled up at the camera in the ceiling above him.

Five minutes shy of the traverse into the Maple 13 system, the crew were seated in the cockpit. Helmets on. Bazzer was the last to take his seat. He had been in the engine room monitoring the reactors as they all came back to life.

"Let's go over this slowly," Dukk said into the comms. "It's the first time with new protocols and our first venture into a monitored system since we went underground."

"Right you are, captain," Luna said cheerfully.

Dukk enabled broadcast mode. "Bognath and Trence, I'm including you on the crew comms for this traverse. It will give you a sense of what is happening in here. Please just listen in for now."

"Will do, captain," Trence answered.

"Ok, four minutes," Dukk said on the comms. "We stay live now. Status check. Vitals, Mentor?"

"All stable. Calibration is at ninety seven percent," Mentor answered.

"Engines, integrity and biosystems, Bazzer?"

"Indicators are all green. Integrity at one hundred percent. Good to go," Bazzer replied.

"External comms, scanners, Ann?"

"All clear, we are out here alone," Annee replied.

"Stealth tech, weapons and defences, Luna?"

"Stealth ready to be enabled after the traverse. Weapons fully loaded and on standby," Luna replied quickly.

"Defensive only, right?" Dukk asked.

"Yes, boss, we don't fire first," Luna replied in a disappointed tone.

"Good," laughed Dukk. "Marr, flight control?"

"All set, captain," Marr answered smiling over at Dukk.

"Check-in," Dukk said smiling back at Marr.

"Ready," was the response from all in quick succession.

"Ready too. Deep and full breaths everyone. We are committed. Three minutes. Load up Bognath and Trence," Dukk said firmly.

"Juice running. Heart rates dropping," Mentor replied.

They all waited. A minute later Mentor added, "All stable."

"I am taking back med control," Dukk said as he interacted with his console. He then watched the countdown.

"Thirty seconds," he announced.

"Twenty seconds."

"Ten seconds."

"Running the juice. See you on the other side," Dukk said as he hit the button. Seconds later, the cocktail hit his blood stream. His consciousness faded.

2

A moment later, Dukk was awake again. He fought back the traverse sickness. He counted backwards. He quietened his mind and relaxed his body. He brought his heart rate back down.

"Status," he croaked into the crew comms as he opened his eyes.

He looked up. Above them outside, was a black object with a red glow on the rim. The asteroid. They configured the traverse to bring them to the dark side of the rock. They would cast no shadow. They now shared the asteroid's orbit within the asteroid belt. Relative to the asteroid, it appeared they were stationery.

The crew acknowledged they were back.

"Right, med control back with you, Mentor. Vitals?" Dukk said into the comms.

"All stabilising, captain."

"Any neighbours, Ann?"

"Nope, all clear," Annee replied.

"Great, let's leave the stealth off for now. No point chewing fuel unnecessarily."

"Systems, Bazzer?"

"All green," came the reply.

"Right then, Marr, do you want to scan the surface. Let's see if we can find a suitable cave?"

"Done," Marr said as an image appeared in the space between them.

"Any potential locations?"

"Overlaying the size calibrations now," Marr replied.

The image changed slightly. Red shaded shapes appeared across the image.

"Nope, all the openings are too small for the container."

"That's inconvenient," Dukk answered. "Looks like we are going to go around. Hold tight everyone."

Dukk interacted with the controls. He provided a new waypoint and hit execute. The rig shook as the thrusters engaged to bring the rig on a loop around the asteroid.

"Luna, bring on the stealth. We might as well."

"On it," Luna replied.

"Ann, anything?"

"Nope, still no sign of other craft," Annee replied.

Ten minutes later the rig was on the other side of the asteroid. The belly was facing the red dwarf sun. They could look up, out of the cockpit and clearly see the surface of the rock. They could also see their shadow.

"How does it look now?" Dukk asked when the rig stopped moving relative to the asteroid.

"Better," replied Marr.

The image projected in the middle of the cockpit now showed the surface with a handful of green shaded shapes on the image.

"Let's go for this medium size one," Marr said as a circle appeared in the projection.

"Perfect," Dukk said. "Let's stay running hot for now. We might need to get busy if we get any company."

"The rig is yours, co-pilot," Dukk said as he removed his helmet and unbelted.

"I will take great care of it, captain," Marr answered with a smile.

"Team, let's get ready to move while Marr brings us in closer."

Marr smiled as she interacted with the controls.

The rig responded and gently moved closer to the surface of the rock.

Dukk got up, clicked his boots into the floor and headed towards the cockpit door.

"Dukk, I assume you don't mind if I take your seat for this exercise," Annee said.

"Not at all, Ann," Dukk replied as he opened the cockpit door. "Trence, you might want to hang in here with Marr and Ann."

"Yes, that is what we planned," Trence said confidently.

Trence entered the cockpit and sat behind Annee.

"Wow, I should get in here more often," the observer said once settled.

Marr turned and smiled briefly before returning to making the orbit adjustments to bring the rig closer to the cave entrance.

"You should," Annee said dismissively before returning to configuring the panels so she could fly the drones.

"I have a question," Trence asked, oblivious to the brush off from both Marr and Annee. "Dukk mentioned he was engaging the stealth tech. If the stealth tech stops other vessels from detecting this rig, what happens if another craft out here, is also using stealth? They can't see us. We can't see them. What stops us from crashing into each other?"

"Passive proximity scanners," Marr said casually without taking her eyes off the controls.

"Passive what?"

"Passive proximity scanners. They are built into the stealth system," Annee answered.

"How do they work?"

"They look for obstacles in our path or objects approaching us," Marr commented. "They have a wider range than normal proximity scanners. With the auto pilot active the system can take evasive action, if something else gets too close."

"Won't the thruster burst make us visible again?"

Marr laughed. "Your knowledge is growing. You'll be up here flying this rig in no time. Yes, but only for a moment. The system alters direction during the manoeuvre, so it is difficult to track where the vessel went."

"Oh, that works," Trence replied.

Meanwhile, Dukk had led Bazzer, Mentor, Luna and Bognath down the stairs to the middle level.

At the landing, they all entered the g-suit room on the starboard side.

Luna and Bognath got straight into getting into their backpacks. Dukk was aware they had been getting some E.V.A. practice together, however he hadn't observed them since the accident three weeks ago. He watched them out of the corner of his eye as he got organised.

They first attach their gloves and helmet to thigh clips. Then they bent their knees slightly and backed up to their packs. When in position they inserted their arms into the straps and reached between their legs to find the groin straps. With the straps connected they put their hands up over their shoulders and grabbed the shoulder apparatus. They pulled it up and over their heads. Dukk heard the click as the frame connected to the 'neck v' in their suits. With that done they lifted the packs off the racks and turned to face each other. They did a cross check and then fitted their helmets and gloves.

Luna looked around at Dukk. She grinned. She had noticed him watching them.

Dukk was now ready too. He connected the comms.

"Looking good gang," he said. "Luna and Bognath look sorted. Bazzer, I'll check your suit, you check Mentor and Mentor you can check me."

"Roger," Bazzer replied.

With the checks complete, Dukk led Bazzer and Luna into the starboard transport pod bay. Mentor headed to the bay on the port side. Bognath used the ladder shaft to drop down to the lower level.

Within the transport pod bay, Dukk and Luna sat into the second pod. Dukk started the pod and then closed the side panel and canopy.

"You ready?" Dukk asked Luna.

"Absolutely, captain," Luna answered. "Though you still haven't shared why I am here."

"All in good time."

"Luna and I are ready," Dukk said into the crew comms.

"Me too," Bazzer added almost immediately.

"Ready," Mentor said.

"I am in the hold and ready," Bognath said.

"The rig is in position," Marr stated.

"Excellent. Let's do this," Dukk replied.

"Deploying the drones," Annee added. "The video feed is now live. You can follow them in."

"Depressurising the bays and hold," Marr added.

3

"Dukk, Bazzer and Mentor, I am opening the bay doors," Marr said moments later. "You are good to go. Bognath stand clear. I am lowering the hold platform."

Dukk and Luna watched as the pod in front of them slid sideways on the runners that now extended out of the bay door.

Once clear, Bazzer engaged the pod's thrusters and it disappeared.

Immediately, Dukk and Luna's pod started moving forward on rollers. With a jerk, the pod then slid sideways out the door.

Dukk pushed the joysticks to the right and the pod lifted off the runners and swung up and away from the side of the rig.

Dukk pulled the joystick around and the pod turned to face the rig.

They watched as the hold loading platform dropped from the belly of the rig. The container sat on the platform.

Bognath was holding on to the side of the container.

Beyond the rig they could see Bazzer and Mentor's pods heading towards the cave.

"The platform is down," Marr said into the comms. "The container is all yours."

"Thanks, Marr," Dukk answered. "Let's get it hooked up."

Dukk interacted with the controls and the pod dropped below the rig.

Bognath had swung out two towing arms. One on each side of the back of the container.

Dukk reversed the thrusters and backed the pod into the towing arms.

With the pod in position, Bognath came over and connected the arms to the back of the pod. He then moved out of the way.

"All secure, you are good to go," Bognath said into the comms.

Luna waved at Bognath as Dukk engaged the pod's thrusters to float the container free of the platform.

"Let's get this into the cave," Dukk said as the pod and container moved away from the rig.

"Follow the drone beacons," Bazzer said into the comms. "Ann has found a suitable nook."

Marr was enjoying calling the shots. She was in her seat in the cockpit. Video feeds filled her view. She could see the goings on below the rig and the view from each of the pods.

Annee was next to her driving the drones. She had zoomed around the cave, took measurements, and found a suitable place to secure the container.

"Bognath, I am raising the hold platform," Marr said into the comms.

"Right you are," Bognath said as he locked his boots into the floor of the platform.

"Good luck guys," Marr said moments later into the comms. "We are locking down and will wait for your return."

The video feed showed the pod and container heading towards the cave. Marr double checked all doors were closed and that the stealth systems were engaged.

Marr then sat back in her seat. She took a couple of deep breaths.

"You did great," Annee said as she looked over.

"Thanks," Marr replied with a smile.

"Now we wait."

"And that is my cue," Trence said. "All this has worn me out. I am going for a nap."

Marr laughed quietly to herself as she and Annee watched Trence leave.

Marr looked back at the video feeds. One showed the inside of Dukk and Luna's pod. She could see they were talking, but they had gone local on their comms.

Marr turned back to Annee.

"I see you and Dukk are close."

"Yes," Annee replied. "He has been the second constant in my life for the last seven years."

"Second?"

"Hauling is the first."

"Of course," Marr laughed.

"You and Dukk look to be getting on well," Annee said as she raised her eyebrows.

"Yes," Marr giggled. "I am growing fond of him. He seems very balanced."

Annee laughed.

"What?" Marr asked.

"He has his moments."

"Don't we all."

"What have you noticed?" Annee asked.

"He needs his own space. He thinks about things deeply and likes to do that alone."

"Until he reaches a conclusion," Annee laughed.

"Yes," Marr laughed. "Then you can't shut him up."

"Sounds like you have him down pat already."

Marr laughed nervously.

"He is solid," Annee said sincerely. "One of the good ones."

Marr smiled.

"What about you?" Annee asked. "Any 'moments'?"

Marr smiled.

"Well?"

"I guess I tend to over think things," Marr answered. "And I want all the detail. And I have high expectations of myself and others."

Annee laughed. "Dukk is pretty used to that having had me in his ear for years."

Marr laughed as she turned back to the video feeds.

After a moment, Marr looked up again.

"What about making companionship work out here? The tight quarters and working together constantly is new territory for me."

"Yes, companionship is challenging for a haulier," Annee answered. "You either opt for being alone most of the time, with the flings when in port, or with a passenger, or you try to make it work with one of the crew. Both approaches have advantages and disadvantages. Most of which are obvious."

"Yes, I am getting a sense of the advantages," Marr giggled. "I also sense the disadvantages."

Annee smiled too.

"You maintained companionship for a time, with the previous captain, Rachelle. Any tips on what works?"

"Boundaries. It is easy out here to make assumptions, get notions and slip into the same old routine. That leads to losing respect for each other. Yes, boundaries are key. Also, keep talking about what is and isn't working. Dukk is clued in. So, talking about it shouldn't be an issue. He helped me with my relationship with Rachelle. He helped me appreciate the three Cs. I understand the concepts came via Bazzer. But I suspect it goes back further. And now that I know Bazzer and Mentor have history, I guess you are familiar with the concepts too?"

Marr looked over with a quizzical expression. She wasn't sure about how to tread as she had only learnt of the history last night.

"I don't have the details," Annee grinned. "I just overhead Dukk earlier this morning. I am drawing conclusions."

"That might be a topic of conversation to have with Dukk directly. And, yes, I am familiar with the three Cs. I will bring it up with Dukk, now that I know he appreciates the concept."

Annee smiled.

4

Meanwhile, Dukk and Luna were taking it handy. They were cautiously towing the container towards the cave opening.

"It feels like an age since you and I talked," Luna said casually as she watched the cave opening getting larger.

"I guess it has got crazy of late," Dukk replied as he made miniscule adjustments to the trajectory.

"Yes, lots has changed too."

"Sure has. What is your take on this all now? You were somewhat less sure about the life of a haulier when we spoke after the E.V.A. sabotage."

"I am getting used to it. Well, quite fond of it, if I am honest. And it is meeting my needs."

"What are those?"

"Adventure, excitement and risk."

"We've had plenty of that of late, but hauling isn't really that kind of life. In fact, it is quite the opposite. Except for the risk. That is a constant. Out here, the hours are long, repetitive, and lonely. There must be something else if you have become fond of it."

"Yes, I guess I need validation, purpose and a sense of where I fit in."

"You come across as very confident. I find it hard to believe you need validation or don't feel you fit in."

"Façade," Luna answered nervously. "But that is changing."

"You are feeling more validated and that you fit in?"

"Yes."

"More so than three weeks ago?"

"Yes, exactly," Luna answered as she looked over at Dukk.

"Can I ask you something?" Luna said when she returned her gaze back to the cave opening.

"Sure."

"How do you stop an intimate rig relationship from going stale?"

"What do you mean?"

"Well, being out here for weeks on end. The same scene, same space, same activities. I do fear that it will weigh on companionship."

"Do you mean making it work with Bognath?" Dukk asked cheekily.

"Yes, it feels as if the excitement is waning."

"The novelty is less or gone?"

"Yes, exactly. How do you be with someone when the novelty is dissipating?"

"Can I answer that indirectly by asking you something else?"

"Sure."

"What worked over the last month to keep you in a good place?"

"Well, a lot has been happening. Learning about keeping the rig going. Learning in general. The stop overs. The drinks and dancing. The emergencies. Having fun with Bognath. Learning about having sex out here. There has been lots to keep me busy and distracted."

"What about the many hours in between? What helped keep you from going crazy in the long quiet hours. The hours when you were alone, on watch, in the middle of the night, for example."

"Shit, that is a good question," Luna asked and then paused.

"I guess quietness," Luna replied after a moment. "Emptying the mind. Allowing my mind to go anywhere but nowhere at the same time. Taking time to just be."

"What happened in that place?"

"I became calm. I felt centred. I even found things I hadn't seen. Things around me. Things about me. Things about others. It renewed me."

"OK, and so perhaps that can work also when you are in the very intimate company of another?"

"You mean quiet time, naked with someone, in addition to time spent having sex or sleeping."

"Exactly."

"Interesting. That is something I will need to pay attention to."

"Speaking of paying attention," Dukk said. "We are coming up on the cave."

As Dukk and Luna entered the cave they could see lights off to the right.

Dukk adjusted the trajectory and moved them towards the lights.

As they got closer, they could see the two pods floating near a cavity in the cave wall.

Beyond the pods they could just make out Bazzer and Mentor on opposite sides of the cavity. They were operating the rock bolt guns.

"How are we looking?" Dukk said into the comms.

"We have nearly got the brackets in place," Bazzer answered. "Swing the container past the cavity. Come to a dead stop and then detach. We'll use the propulsion in our packs to move it into position."

"On it," Dukk replied.

After detaching from the container, Dukk stopped the pod near the cavity.

"Ok, Luna, time for a walk. Let's pressurise the suits and open the canopy."

"I'm driving myself this time," Luna laughed.

"Of course," Dukk chuckled.

Dukk and Luna moved themselves away from the pod and into the mouth of the cavity.

"Let's swing it and then back it in," Bazzer announced as he joined them.

Between the four of them they gently nudged the container into position.

Bazzer then interacted with the panel on the container and then pushed back. Large arms appeared from the sides and tops of the robotic container. The arms extended to the walls of the cavity and found the brackets.

"That should do it. Now to cripple the power supply," Bazzer said as he pulled a large box out from the side of the container.

"What is stopping someone else coming along and stealing the whole thing?" Luna asked.

"This," Bazzer answered. He was pointing to a rectangular object on the door. "Once you lock it, any attempts to open it or dislodge it will blow the container and this rock to kingdom come."

"How will they know that this is a bomb?"

"Believe me, anyone who goes poking about looking for other people's hoards, knows what a booby trap looks like."

"Ok. Wait! What do you mean by 'you lock it'?"

"Luna, that is why you are here," Dukk answered.

"It is tradition that the apprentice of the crew is the key holder for the hoard. The one with the least influence and experience. The one least likely to be able to get back here on her own and take it for herself."

Luna laughed.

No one said anything.

"Wait, you are serious?"

"Yep, go over to that panel and use your biometrics. Then we are out of here."

With the container locked, they returned to their pods.

Dukk was closing the canopy when there was a squawk on the comms.

"We have a problem," Marr said.

Marr had been watching the video feeds of Dukk and the others returning to their pods.

"Shit," Annee blurted.

"What?" Marr asked.

"We have company. Look," Annee said pointing to the radar projection.

The projection showed a vessel transponder on the other side of the rock.

"Perhaps a patrol doing DMD probing," Marr answered. "We need to get out of here. We are casting a shadow."

"Absolutely."

Marr opened the comms to the others. "We have a problem. We have company. We are moving away so we don't cast a shadow. You will have to sit tight. We couldn't see the lights from out here, so they won't either."

"Roger," Dukk replied.

"It is best that we power down the pods," Bazzer added. "They might still pick us up on scanners if we are powered up. We can sit it out in our backpacks. They won't detect them."

"We must go dark too," Mentor added. "No comms. Marr, we'll wait for your signal that we are in the clear."

Marr interacted with the controls and the rig responded.

She moved the rig away from the rock so there was no longer a shadow. She then killed the autopilot and let the rig drift.

"How are you on weapons?" Marr asked Annee.

"Clueless."

"Me too. Perhaps an oversight in our plans."

The cockpit door opened. It was Bognath.

"Need any help?"

"How is your weapons knowledge?" Marr asked.

"Coming along. I've been doing some of the simulations with Luna."

"Right, take a seat. It might be time to do it for real."

Marr, Annee and Bognath watched the radar as the vessel manoeuvred around to their side of the rock.

At one point they got a glimpse of it in the distance. It was a small craft. Perhaps room for a two-person crew.

It held a consistent arced trajectory as it passed by and then disappeared again.

"It has stopped on the other side of the rock," Annee observed. "Perhaps it is aligning with the belt's orbit again. Looks like it didn't notice us."

"Let's hope so," Marr added. "How much air supply do you think the others have in the backpacks?"

"It should be enough," Annee replied. Her tone didn't give across confidence.

They had to wait another hour before the patrol vessel traversed again.

Marr opened the comms.

"We are all clear," she said. "We are moving back towards the cave."

They waited.

There was no response.

"What's happened? Where are they?" Marr said nervously after a couple of minutes.

Annee looked over at Marr. Her expression was blank.

"We'd better get a pod ready. In case we need to go in and retrieve them," Marr said cautiously.

"Yes, good idea," Annee replied solemnly as she undid her belt.

"Imhullu, Marr," came a voice in the comms. "On our way."

It was Luna.

"Thank goodness," Marr answered into the comms. "What happened?"

"We had to divert backpack comms power into the bio systems. We got your message, but we had to restart the pods before we could respond. We are approaching the cave opening now."

"You had us worried."

"You were worried! How do you imagine it felt in here sitting in pitch black, scrambling to avoid suffocation? Got bloody cold too. Nearly froze my tits off," Luna laughed.

"At least you still have your sense of humour," Annee added. "How is everyone else?"

"All in a day's pirating," Bazzer added.

"Opening the pod bay outer doors," Marr said as she hit the button and collapsed back into her seat.

With the transport pod bay doors shut, Marr secured the rig and then brought the DMD back online. She loaded the coordinates for the Maple Tower hub and hit the autopilot button.

"Rig secured. Fifty-five minutes until traverse," she said into crew comms.

"You can pass over the conn now if you want to go down to the pod bay. Mentor and I are on watch now anyway," Annee said to Marr.

"Thanks, Ann," Marr blurted as she threw off her belt and dashed for the ladder shaft.

Dukk removed his helmet as the pod's canopy opened. Luna did the same.

"Well, there is your dose of excitement for today," Dukk laughed.

"Yep, quiet time is all that is needed now to make it a perfect day," Luna said with a wink.

They exited the pod and were about to move towards the door when they were nearly bowled over.

Marr had tried to grab them both in a bear hug. It hadn't worked because of the E.V.A. backpacks.

Dukk laughed.

Marr stood back and grinned.

"Let's get these off," Dukk said warmly.

Marr led the way out of the bay.

Bognath was at the door. He smiled at Luna. She grinned back warmly.

"An hour until traverse. Did I hear that correctly?" Luna said when the E.V.A. backpacks were re-installed into the racks.

"Yep," Marr answered.

"Annee and Mentor are on watch."

"Yep," Marr replied.

"Bognath, let's go," Luna said as she grabbed his hand.

Dukk and Marr giggled.

Bazzer and Mentor looked on in amusement.

"Do you think one can have too much sex?" Marr asked forty minutes later.

Marr and Dukk were in Dukk's bed, in each other's arms.

"Too much good sex or too much bad sex?" Dukk laughed.

"Is there such a thing as bad sex?"

"I've heard others speak of it," Dukk said with a giggle.

"You are deflecting."

"Perhaps it isn't a fair question."

"Deflection again."

"No, I don't believe you can have too much good sex."

Marr tightened her arms around Dukk.

"Hey!" Dukk yelped at the playful squeeze.

"You qualified that answer," Marr said cheekily. "That is also a deflection."

"Ok," Dukk laughed. "Yes, you can have too much sex."

"Explain."

"You can have too much sex if it is based on novelty. It isn't realistic. It doesn't have longevity."

"It goes stale?"

"Yes."

"What else?"

"This feels like a trap."

Marr laughed.

"But I will answer," Dukk said with a grin. "Sex doesn't work when one starts making assumptions and stops being honest about one's needs."

"And?"

"See, it was a trap."

Marr laughed again.

At that moment, a gentle chime rang out in their comms and the air around them. It stopped and then repeated slightly louder.

"Saved by the bell," Dukk laughed. "It is time to prep the rig for the traverse to Maple Tower."

"Race you to the shower!" Marr said with a giggle as she jumped out of the bed.

Chapter 6 – Rebadging

1

Near half twelve, thirty-six hours after the attack, the rig exited the traverse to bring them back into range of civilization. They were now in the vicinity of the Maple Tower hub.

"Ileadees' handlers have replied," Annee said to the crew. "Dukk, I am sending you the approach plan."

They were all waiting patiently in the cockpit.

A few moments earlier, Annee had fed a coded message onto the broadcast channel. She had used the format Mentor had supplied.

"Got it," Dukk replied. "Looks like we are getting special treatment again. The flight plan puts us into a hanger."

"There are hangers here?" Marr questioned. "I thought docking was all external at this old hub."

"News to me too. Let's have a closer look."

Dukk projected the flight plan to the air before them. He then zoomed into the hub.

"Looks like it is within the old industrial complex. The disused refinery."

"You'd miss the hanger if you didn't know it was there," Marr laughed.

"Mentor, it looks like you were right about how helpful Ileadees can be."

Mentor nodded.

"What's the approach look like?" Marr asked.

"Slowing down will only take two and a half hours. Coming via the belt got us closer to the required orbit. Getting into the hanger will take twenty minutes. So, we should be docked just before half three. Anything else on the message?"

"No, just the flight plan," Annee replied.

"I guess we'll keep the stealth capabilities engaged for now. Mentor?"

"Yes, I'd think that will be a good idea," Mentor replied. "We want to stay off other craft's radar as well as the traffic control within the hub. It will make it easier for Ileadees to keep our arrival under wraps."

"Perfect. Hold tight as I start the slow down."

The rig groaned as the thrusters pivoted the rig one hundred and eighty degrees. A momentary rumble could be felt as the thrusters engaged for a short hard burst.

They were all pushed back in their seats, momentarily, as the deceleration sequence was initiated.

"Looking good," Dukk said as he checked the systems. "We are back in our seats at three p.m. for the docking."

"Right, ninety minutes until watch. I'm going to bed," Bazzer said as he unbelted.

"Me too," Luna added. "I'm wrecked."

"Ann, the conn is yours," Dukk said as he got up. "Marr, I saw the wall ball from the Dinatha in the storeroom. Do you want to see how the now empty hold works as a court?"

"Keen to end your losing streak?" Marr laughed.

"Absolutely," Dukk replied.

"Dukk, you are full of energy and in good spirits," Annee observed.

"Well, near death experiences, on consecutive days puts things into perspective."

"Is that the only reason?" Annee asked in a provocative tone.

Dukk winked and smiled at her as he headed towards the door.

Dukk waited for Marr and held the cockpit door open.

He followed her through the passenger seating area.

106

"A quick change of clothes, and I'll be ready to beat you again," Marr said as they entered the crew mess.

"I hope that just because you got me into bed, you won't change how you dress when playing wall ball against me."

"What do you mean?" Marr said as she turned back to him. She raised her eyebrows.

"I hope you will still wear the hot pants and that ultra-brief crop top."

"Is it not distracting? Don't you want to win."

"Of course, I want to win. But, playing alongside you looking so hot is a great consolation prize."

"Well then, I shall dress to distract," Marr said grinning.

"See you in a minute," Dukk replied as he opened his cabin door.

"It looks like you had fun?" Annee said as Dukk and Marr arrived back in the crew mess after their match. They were looking hot and sweaty.

"Absolutely," Marr replied. "The space is similar in size to the court I'd be used to on Earth. It makes for a completely different type of match than the small space of the hold airlock on the Dinatha."

"How did you find it, Dukk?" Annee asked.

"Challenging!" Dukk laughed. "I am definitely not used to that size court."

"I gather Marr won again."

"Yep, back to the drawing board," Dukk replied. "I need a new strategy."

Marr smiled.

"Hey, you two," Luna announced from her doorway. "Wow, you are sweaty. Was it just wall ball you were doing in the hold?"

"Bigger court!" Dukk answered.

"That doesn't answer my question," Luna replied.

Dukk shrugged his shoulders.

"I did try to watch how the match was going. When I got up from my nap. The video feed was playing up."

Dukk and Marr looked surprised.

"Oh, that was me," Bazzer said from the door to the port aft shaft. "The core components for the video scrambler were just printed. I was trying them out. Looks like it works."

"Convenient story," Luna laughed in a sarcastic tone.

Dukk laughed as he headed towards his cabin.

Marr laughed and shook her head. She made for her cabin.

"Ready for watch, Luna?" Bazzer added.

"Yep."

"Anything of note, Ann?"

"Nope, all quiet on the approach. There isn't any other rig in the vicinity. I gather Ileadees has organised a clear path."

2

One hour later they were all back in their seats ready for docking. The DMD had been powered down and they were weightless again.

"All set everyone," Dukk said rhetorically. "Let's commence the docking sequence."

"There is much better visibility of the hub in this rig than the Dinatha," Luna commented. She was looking up through the windshield. The underbelly of the hub now filled their view. They could see the chaotic array of solar panels, radiation shields and DMD units.

Dukk approved the autopilot request to proceed with docking.

The rig pivoted ninety degrees as it passed to the left of the hub.

Before them was an opening in the side of the hub. Orange lights could be seen flashing inside the opening.

The rig's thrusters engaged again to swing the rig into the opening.

"I hope Ileadees got our dimensions correct," Marr commented. "That opening looks pretty tight."

"It does," Dukk said. "The flight plan didn't include any pause points. The autopilot is going to take us right in and put us down. If he got it wrong, we are going to know about it any moment now."

The rig passed nose first into the hanger and came to a stop.

The rig vibrated slightly as the thrusters held it in place.

There was a slight thud as the rig's jacks dropped down.

Then the rig moved again, coming to rest on the hanger floor.

Behind them the hanger doors closed.

Moments later the orange lights stopped flashing. They were replaced by bright spotlights.

Marr and Dukk looked around.

"This looks tight," Marr observed.

"Yep," Dukk commented. "Bazzer, let's go to slow running."

"On it," Bazzer replied.

Dukk then removed his belt so he could stand up and peer down the nose to the front of the hanger. Marr did the same.

A door was opening.

Out of the door came two armed personnel. Followed by a large, bald, and middle-aged man. Clear was the man's pasty white skin tones and bushy, wild and long grey beard. Behind him were two further security personnel.

"Looks like Ileadees has his usual entourage," Marr commented.

"Yep, let's get the ramp down and see what's what. Who's coming?" Dukk said as he turned away from the windshield.

"Count me in," Marr blurted. "I have been dying to use the ramp."

Dukk laughed as he headed for the cockpit door. Marr wasn't far behind.

They used the stairs to drop to the lower level and into the forward passageway.

On arrival at the ramp airlock door, Dukk interacted with the panel.

The door opened exposing the narrow space with the ramp and integrated stairs.

A panel near the door had the controls for the ramp.

Dukk hit the button to lower the ramp. The ramp broke the seal and started to swing down to the hanger floor.

Marr had pushed in beside him.

"I saw in the rig manuals that the ramps can be either flat or have steps," Marr observed. "Can you see how to expose the stairs?"

"Sure. I bet it is this button that looks like a staircase," Dukk said laughing.

Dukk clicked the button. As the ramp unfolded, steps appeared in the surface.

"Cool", Marr said.

"After you," Dukk said once the ramp was extended.

"Absolutely not. The honour must be yours as captain."

Dukk laughed.

"Besides, if they start shooting, I need you as cover," Marr said with a grin.

Dukk lent in, gave Marr a gentle kiss, then headed down the ramp.

"Well look at this! Dukk has risen from the dead," Ileadees boomed from the hanger floor. He was standing just back from the ramp. His security detail had their guns raised. "And Marr, and I gather the rest of the Dinatha's last crew are here too."

Dukk smiled.

"What can I do for you?" Ileadees asked.

"We need not to be here, and while we are not here, we are in the need of some of your special services."

"My specialities don't come cheap. Why should I entertain your request?"

"Blackmail!" Mentor said as he stepped into view from behind Dukk and Marr. "You know I have information that you don't want known."

"Ah, yes, Mentor, welcome," Ileadees said cautiously. "I see you haven't changed. But perhaps what I stand to lose in that regard outweighs the risk in this regard. This rig looks surprisingly like the Ukendt. It even has the same name plastered on the side. It was also reported missing at the same time as the Dinatha disappeared. I gather you don't have the old crew tucked away in there somewhere?"

"Nope," Mentor replied from behind Dukk.

"I see," Ileadees said before pausing and looking hard at Mentor. After a moment, he continued. "So, I am guessing you need a new rig ID, registration papers and a paint job?"

"You are guessing right," Dukk answered.

"Perhaps new digital IDs for you lot?"

"Yes, two each. With full bogus history."

"How many people are we talking about?"

"We need two sets of IDs for twenty-five people?" Mentor interjected.

Dukk quickly did the numbers. More than he would think. Perhaps there is more to this than Mentor was letting on. He did his best to hide his confusion.

"We scanned you on arrival, there are eight of you. Are you planning on picking up a few strays or are we creating IDs for ghosts?"

Mentor said nothing. His expression was blank. Ileadees took the hint.

"These are significant demands from people who are dead and perhaps disconnected from their lines of credit. How will you pay?"

"The line of credit associated with the 'dead' persons may be inaccessible right now, but that isn't our only source of payment," Dukk said.

"I am listening," Ileadees said.

"For keeping this under the radar, the rig re-badge, the new digital IDs, resupply, and refuel, we can give you a half canister of composite mesh."

"You have composite mesh?"

Dukk smiled.

"Ill-gotten gains perhaps. What happened to the other half?"

"We have a full canister."

"What is stopping me coming on board and taking the lot?"

Marr put her hand to the hilt of her knife and smiled at Ileadees.

"Marr, Mentor's apprentice," Ileadees laughed. "What will you do with the other half?"

"We'd like to exchange it for credits. Can you facilitate that?"

"Laundering. Of course. Less a small fee."

"I wouldn't expect anything less," Dukk said with a smile.

"When will I get said canister?"

"The minute you agree our terms."

"Before I deliver?"

"You know this rig is weaponised, right?"

"Dukk, are Mentor's methods rubbing off on you?" laughed Ileadees. "Done. Flick my colleague your biometrics, and the sex, general age and profiles of the ghosts, and the new rig name. She will get a team onto it right away."

"I'll help with that," Mentor added.

"Thank you, Ileadees", Dukk said before he enabled his comms. "Annee, you can lower the platform."

A crack and a hiss echoed above them and around the hanger, as the platform dropped to the floor. Bazzer was standing on the platform with Luna. Her rifle was raised. The canister was between them.

3

"Are we all good?" Bazzer asked as the platform stopped moving.

"Yep," Dukk answered as he stepped onto the platform and helped Bazzer lift the canister to the hanger floor.

"All yours," Dukk said as he walked back over to the bottom of the ramp.

Ileadees waved a hand at two of his security personnel. They immediately moved towards the canister and started muttering orders into their comms. It was clear this wasn't the first time they had been in this situation.

"Now let's seal this deal over a drink and some food!" Ileadees said as he turned back towards the ramp.

"Our IDs are still the old ones," Marr blurted. "Won't we show up when we leave the rig?"

"Yes, my lady. And this isn't my first rodeo," Ileadees said as he clapped his hands loudly, twice.

Out of the internal hanger door appeared a group of servers pushing carts.

"We will celebrate here, on your rig," Ileadees said with a smile. "Assuming you will invite me and my team to your table?"

"Of course," Dukk answered.

"Thank you," Ileadees said tilting his head.

They watched as the servers lifted the mobile banquet onto the platform. One was carrying a large bottle of clear liquid. The bottle was brought over to Ileadees.

Ileadees lifted the five-litre bottle and handed it to Dukk.

"Vodka?" Dukk asked as he took the bottle in both hands.

"Of course. The French method. The finest credit can buy."

"You are too kind."

Ileadees laughed. "But it is I who should be thanking you. Unlike last time, this fine liquor and food will be going on your tab. I know you are good for it."

Ileadees grinned at them.

Dukk laughed, "Mentor, will you lead the way."

Mentor turned and headed back towards the ramp. Marr followed.

Ileadees swiftly shuffled in behind Marr.

"I see the events of late haven't taken from your magnificence," Ileadees said to Marr as they climbed.

Marr laughed nervously.

"By the way, what are you now calling this interceptor?"

"Imhullu," Marr replied.

"Divine wind weapon! That is interesting," Ileadees laughed as they entered the corridor and started to climb the stairs to the middle level.

Marr looked back at Ileadees and then to Dukk.

Dukk shrugged his shoulders.

"This is a fine rig," Ileadees commented as they passed through the passenger seating area on the upper level. "A far cry from a G5 rigs like the Dinatha."

"Yes, it has more comforts," Marr replied.

"But less character," Dukk said as he followed them into the crew mess.

Ileadees laughed.

"You all have your own cabins?" Ileadees asked, grinning at Marr. He waved his hands around as if to inquire as to which was hers.

Marr nodded nervously.

"Sit, please," Dukk said nodding at the head of the table. He was still carrying the large bottle of vodka.

"I am sure your servers will be up in no time," Dukk said as he placed the bottle on the table.

Dukk was right. The starboard door to the aft ladder shaft opened.

Bazzer held the door as the servers wheeled in the carts. Luna came in behind them.

The servers immediately went about preparing the table. They had everything from a white tablecloth to fine glasses to silver cutlery. The food was hot and cold hors d'oeuvre. The drinks included wine and other spirits in addition to the large bottle of vodka, which was sat in a large free-standing decanter.

By the time everything was set, Annee, Luna, Bognath, Trence and five of Ileadees' colleagues had joined them.

"Please," Ileadees said beckoning to Dukk as he stood near the head of the table. "You are captain of this rig; I couldn't sit at the head. I'll sit on your right."

Dukk smiled and moved over to near the head of the table.

Marr quickly moved to his left to avoid sitting next to Ileadees.

Mentor moved to stand next to Marr and the others gathered around.

With everyone in place Dukk went to sit.

"Wait," Ileadees commanded. "Drinks!"

The servers hustled in with shot glasses filled with vodka.

With the drinks in hand, Ileadees raised his glass and said, "To the Imhullu, its captain and its fine crew, may thanks be given for many a year. Thanks, I give!"

"Thanks, I give," they all said in response.

With that they all drank.

Dukk paused to treasure the moment. The burn of the vodka not taking from his sense of joy.

Marr too took a moment to pause. For the first time she truly felt she was part of something important.

Before long, the noise was near deafening, as the crew drank, ate, relaxed, put their confusion and concerns aside, and competed to share their take on the events of the last two days.

Four drinks later, Marr had lost her ability to manage her amygdala. Her curiosity got the better of her.

"Ileadees, you know the meaning of Imhullu?" she blurted in a gap in the conversation.

"Yes, I have heard of the word," Ileadees answered. "The word has ancient origins. It comes from the Mesopotamian story of creation, Enuma Elish. The weapon was used to banish evil. What evil are you planning on banishing?"

"Don't worry. We are not banishing the kind of evil that is you or I, for now," Mentor interjected loudly. "Who's turn is it to pour the vodka?"

Ileadees laughed loudly.

Marr grinned. She knew much of Mentor, but not everything. She did, however, know the tone of his reply. The tone told her to leave these subjects for now.

4

Three hours later, the meal was done. The conversation was now being driven by Ileadees as he shared stories. While highly entertaining, the stories were mostly about himself and greatly exaggerated. Seated still with Ileadees were Annee, Luna, Bognath, Mentor, Trence and two of Ileadees' colleagues. The others had quietly slipped away.

Marr and Dukk were at this moment sitting together on condenser units in a dark corner of the hanger. They were watching Ileadees' people replace the rig name. The lettering was splashed across the mid-section of the rig. The repaint job was painstakingly slow. Owing mostly to the need to keep the stealth capabilities intact. It involved multiple people dangling from the ceiling of the hanger and working with handheld etching guns.

"How much longer do you think before they are done?" Marr asked absently.

"At the rate they are going, I'd guess another six hours," Dukk replied.

"Can we depart straight after it is complete?"

"I gather that will be the case. It is part of the reason the process is so slow."

They paused talking as they spotted Bazzer at the bottom of the ramp. He passed the two security personnel and then walked towards the wings. He briefly checked the resupply hoses and then returned to the ramp.

"Does he really need to do that now if we have six hours?" Marr asked quietly.

"I gather he is just keeping himself busy, so he doesn't have to endure Ileadees."

"What happened between them?"

"Bazzer hasn't told you?"

"No, he has deflected me both times I tried to raise the subject."

"I guess that is how he wants it for now."

After a further period of silence, Dukk spoke.

"Did you notice how Mentor appeared to be tuned into conversations at both ends of the table?"

"Yes, I did."

"He interjected and deflected the conversation, the moment it got close to what really happened with him and the assassination or our plans to rescue Kimince and the girls."

"Yes, I noticed that too."

"What do you think of that?"

"I guess he knows Ileadees better than us, and perhaps more of the risks we face. I figure that he was protecting us and ensuring Ileadees, and his colleagues know as little as possible."

"Yes, I figured the same. At least we now know the narrative."

"What do you mean?" Marr asked.

"I overheard some of his colleagues telling Trence about what they got from the news channels."

"What's the narrative?"

"That Kimince was Craig's lover, got overprotective and killed him with poison so that no-one else could be with Craig."

Marr went to laugh out loud but caught herself when she realised it would give their position away and put an end to their temporary escape.

"That is ludicrous. How did Trence take it?" she said quietly with a giggle.

"He went to debunk the story. Mentor interjected and changed the subject."

"That figures," Marr added.

A commotion at the bottom of the ramp caused them to pause once more.

"Give the captain my regards," Ileadees said loudly. "I gather like me; he has other pressing matters to attend to."

Ileadees and the remaining colleagues dropped out of the rig and started to walk towards the hanger door. The two remaining security personnel followed closely.

Mentor stepped off the ramp and stood there watching them leave.

"Ileadees, I am here," Dukk said as he and Marr stepped out of the shadows. "We have been admiring the skill of your people."

"Ah, yes, talented aren't they," Ileadees said with a slur as he stopped, turned, and looked up at the side of the rig. "As I was saying to the others, I have pressing matters to attend to."

"Of course," Dukk answered.

"The IDs should be with you by now. Did you get them?"

"Yes, we received them not that long ago."

"Great, now I must leave you to it. Safe travels," Ileadees said as he put out his hand.

"Thank you," Dukk said as he shook the big man's hand.

"Mentor," Ileadees said as he nodded back towards the ramp.

Mentor nodded back.

"It was a pleasure to be in your company once more, Marr," Ileadees said before continuing towards the door.

Marr smiled.

When he got to the door of the hanger, he turned back towards Dukk and Marr.

"Don't look to depart until three or four a.m. It would be best to slip away when most are crashed out."

"Will do."

With that he passed through the door.

His voice carried as the group disappeared into the hub.

"'Ileadees, champion of the resistance' has a nice ring to it. Don't you think?" he could be heard saying to his entourage.

Marr chuckled.

Dukk smiled.

"He thinks he is resistance now," Dukk said as he and Marr joined Mentor at the bottom of the ramp.

"It would appear so," Mentor answered with a smile. "Will I take over out here?"

"Actually, it is quite peaceful watching the painters," Marr answered. "You must be exhausted."

"What makes you think that?"

"All that deflecting of the conversation whenever anything of the assassination or our plans got mentioned."

Mentor laughed. "I've known Ileadees long enough to know the least he knows the better. But yes, I could do with some rest. It has been a long day."

"Great, you head back in," Dukk said. "And tell the others that they can get some rest too."

Mentor smiled, then turned and climbed the ramp.

5

Just on ten p.m. Annee appeared at the bottom of the ramp. She looked around. She smiled and started walking towards Dukk and Marr.

"You might be more comfortable in your bed?" Annee said softly when she reached them.

Dukk grinned.

Dukk was sitting against the wall with his arms wrapped around Marr. They were sharing a blanket. She was snoring gently.

"Getting there," Annee said as she looked up at the side of the rig.

"Yep, another hour or so, I'd think," Dukk answered.

"Hi Ann," Marr said as she opened her eyes. "Come to enjoy the view?"

"Yep," Annee laughed. "Mentor and I are on watch now, so you can head in for a bit if you want?"

"Sounds good. You might want to keep this blanket; it isn't that well heated in this hanger."

"Perfect," Annee replied as she helped them up. "By the way, there is another communication from Ileadees' people. It includes the hanger clearance protocols and flight plan. They have us cleared to leave the hanger at three thirty."

"Perfect. That's when Bazzer and Luna will be back on watch. Marr and I can help them get the rig out and preparing for traverse if you and Mentor want to sleep on?"

"Sound, I'll let him know."

Marr and Dukk made their way back inside the rig and up to the top level.

"You look tired," Marr said as they reached the crew mess.

"Yep, it's been a long day," Dukk answered.

"Do you want your bed to yourself?"

"I do need sleep, but I am happy to do that together if that works for you?"

"Perfect."

Near three a.m. Dukk left his cabin. He was showered and, in his g-suit. The shower had helped but he was still feeling groggy after the broken sleep and vodka.

Bazzer was alone at the console in the corner of the crew mess.

The panels showed various rig systems dials and gauges.

"How are we looking?" Dukk asked as he reached Bazzer.

"We are looking good, captain," Bazzer answered as he swung the chair around. "Just finished system checks. Luna is at the hanger door seeing that everything is ready for our departure."

"Great, I'll go down and do a quick external check then we'll raise the ramp and seal the doors."

"Perfect. Remind Luna to head to the engine room. I'll meet her there and we'll fire up this bird."

Dukk turned and headed towards the door.

"Wait for me," said a voice behind him. It was Marr.

Dukk smiled as he held the door.

"You were snoring soundly when I woke so I headed to my cabin and did some organising. The cleaners did a great job, but they moved stuff about."

Dukk laughed.

"What?"

"Tad OCD, are we?"

"You can talk, mister triple check everything," Marr teased as she passed through the door.

Dukk grinned as he watched Marr head towards the stairs.

Marr led the way down the stairs and ramp.

"Clockwise?" she suggested when they reach the hanger floor.

"Yep, but let's find Luna first," Dukk answered.

They looked around. Luna came skipping towards them from the direction of the internal door. An impressive feat since she was carrying a large box.

"You are full of energy," Marr observed.

"Yep," Luna replied. "I am excited about getting moving again."

"What's in the box?" Dukk asked.

"The toys and ammo that Marr organised," Luna replied. "Ileadees got them for us."

"He got it all?" Marr asked.

"Yep, all here. It has gone on the tab."

"Toys? Ammo?" Dukk asked abruptly after taking a moment to process what had just been shared.

"Nano drones. Tranquilizer guns and darts. Inoculation gas pellets and glass melting long range bullets," Marr replied.

Dukk took a further moment to process all of that.

"I guess I am not up to date on the details of the rescue."

"Nope, you aren't," Marr said with a cheeky grin. "We'll go over it when we review the plan later."

"Right then. Are we all set at the door, Luna?" Dukk asked.

"Yep, the remaining security personnel will lock the access door once we give them the signal that we are sealed and pressurised. They will then depressurise the hanger and open the outer doors."

"Signal?"

"Just a wave from the cockpit. They don't want us using comms to air traffic control, seeing as we aren't supposed to be here."

"All very hush hush," Dukk commented.

"Yep, very James Bond," Luna replied.

"Very what?" Dukk asked in a confused manner.

Luna laughed as she stepped onto the ramp.

"Bazzer said to meet him in the engine room," Dukk called out as Luna disappeared into the rig.

"Shall we?" Marr said pointing in the direction of the starboard wing.

"After you," Dukk replied. "This is déjà vu."

"Just don't think you can trip me over like the first time we did a predeparture inspection at Maple Tower," Marr laughed.

With the inspection done, Marr and Dukk paused and took a selfie before heading back up the ramp. They raised it behind them.

"I'll start the depressurization and integrity checks from here," Dukk said as he interacted with a mini console near the airlock.

"Great. I'll head up to the cockpit and start the pre-departure checks." Marr said as she disappeared back up the stairs.

Dukk smiled.

A chime rang out as the rig pressurised and the integrity checks completed.

Dukk popped his ears a couple of times to balance the pressure.

Once satisfied the rig was all sealed up, he opened the comms to Bazzer.

"Locked and loaded. Let's go hot," Dukk said as he headed for the stairs.

"On it," came the reply.

Before taking his seat on arriving in the cockpit, Dukk looked down at the access door and waved at the security personnel.

They waved back and disappeared into the hub, closing the door as they went.

Moments later orange lights started flashing in the ceiling of the hanger.

"How are we looking?" Dukk asked as he took his seat next to Marr.

"Checklists are complete. Launch plan has been loaded into the autopilot. It is ready for authorization."

"Perfect. Let's get a view on the hanger doors," Dukk answered as he flicked the tail cameras into the air before them.

They watched as the doors disappeared into the walls. When the doors were fully open, green lights lit up around the opening.

"I gather green means go," Marr said.

"I guess so."

"Reactors are hot, and systems are green," Bazzer announced into their comms.

"Great, let's get out of here," Dukk said as he authorised the autopilot.

Chapter 7 – Refining

1

The rig trembled as the thrusters lifted the rig off the hanger floor.

Further vibrations could be felt as the jacks were retracted.

Then the rig started moving slowly backwards.

Marr and Dukk looked around as the rig left the hanger.

Once clear, the rig turned ninety degrees and started to drop below the hub.

"Looks like we have several minutes at this pace to get clear of the hub," Marr commented as she reviewed the instructions given to the autopilot.

"Great, that will give us time to update the flight plan," Dukk replied.

"Didn't Mentor already provide the detail?"

"Yep, we just need to enter it. He appears to be quite knowledgeable of the unmonitored systems. I would have typically headed for Maple 15 from here."

"What did he suggest?"

"Here, I'll send it to you. Do you want to enter the details into the flight plan, and I'll check it?"

"Love to. Is that a promotion?"

Dukk laughed. "Getting ahead of yourself co-pilot. No, you aren't captain yet."

Marr smiled as she interacted with the console.

"Ok, so first we head to Maple 16, 4.8 parsecs."

"That looks right."

"Aren't you supposed to say 'check', once you have verified that I entered it correctly into the flight plan?" Marr said cheekily.

"Ok, yes that is the correct procedure. Check," Dukk said with a giggle.

"Next, is Finch 8, 9.1 parsecs."

"Check."

"Then we go to Finch 19, 7.2 parsecs."

"Check."

"Next is WZR15, 6.1 parsecs."

"Check."

"And then WZR18, 7.7 parsecs. Wait, WZR18 that's the system for Mayfield."

"Yep."

"So, five traverses instead of the usual six for a leg like this."

"Yep, and no intermediary inspection if we want to arrive before the party starts."

"If we were using the typical track with the twelve-hour average preparation interval between traverses, we'd be a day or so late. This track will be risky and won't have the usual inflight maintenance. Are you truly okay with that?"

Dukk laughed. "You are getting to know me. Yes, I'll bury my concerns for the greater good."

Marr smiled as she returned to the console.

"That's all in," she said.

"What does the timing look like?"

"If the intervals average between eight and nine hours as it was on our approach to the asteroid field here, for today the traverses will occur roughly at midday and eight thirty p.m. Then five a.m. and one thirty p.m. tomorrow. With, the final traverse into WZR18 occurring at roughly twelve thirty a.m. the day after tomorrow. That last traverse preparation time being longer because the destination is a normal trade route."

"That means that we will arrive in orbit during the early hours. We should have the approach into the port to ourselves. Assuming we can wake up air traffic control."

"That'll be to our advantage if we are to pull off this planned rescue."

"This is where my expertise comes up short."

"Don't worry, not mine," Marr said with a wink.

"Good to know."

Marr smiled. After a moment of contemplation, she continued. "Only two of the five traverses occur during our normal watch. That will mean broken sleep or disruption to normal downtime. That will take some getting used to."

"Let's add it to the list of things that have changed," laughed Dukk.

At that moment, the autopilot chimed. They were clear of the hub.

"Let's get the first waypoint into the DMD and see what our wait time looks like," Dukk said.

Moments later Dukk continued. "Nine hours. Exactly as you predicted. There is no doubt that crossing the galaxy using unmonitored and deserted systems saves some time."

Marr smiled.

Dukk opened his comms. "Bazzer, the DMD is indicating we need some hard acceleration for fifteen minutes. We'll stay hot until after that."

"Perfect," came the reply.

Dukk and Marr sat back in their seats as the rig's engines engaged.

Fifteen minutes later, the rig was stabilised and in slow running.

"I've got it from here, captain," Luna announced as she entered the cockpit. "See you in an hour for the start of your watch."

"Right, the conn is yours, Luna," Dukk said as he rose from his seat.

"How's the DMD dance looking," Luna replied as she plonked herself down in her seat in the middle row. She interacted with the console.

The flight plan appeared in the air between the seats. The three-dimensional representation of the flight plan showed the systems they would be traversing through. A miniature red coloured, fireworks like display could be seen in the bottom section of the image.

"Looks like we have a way to go before the DMD finds a safe path for the traverse," Marr commented as she walked through the image.

"Yep," Luna replied solemnly.

"Back to sleep?" Dukk suggested as he and Marr passed through the passenger seating area.

"I am wide awake now," Marr replied.

"Me too," Dukk said cheekily.

Marr giggled.

A little while later, Dukk and Marr were lying together in Dukk's cabin.

"Your memory of the test has been on my mind. I sense there is something there for me too."

"Like what?" Dukk replied.

"Mentor planted the name in your head that you chose when you started the labour rotation. A name he got from Tieanna."

"So it would seem."

"And before that? Did you have a nickname?"

"Yes, Fiver."

"Let me guess. Your sequence number in the incubation centre was five?"

"Gee, how did you know."

Marr laughed.

"What about you? What was your sequence number?" Dukk asked.

"Eight."

"Nick name?"

"Boss Girl or just Boss."

"Really," Dukk laughed. "Did that have something to do with your manner?"

"I guess it must have," Marr laughed. "I suppose I did take the lead in games more often than not."

"What about Marr? Where did that name come from?"

"I am not sure. I just knew it had to be that."

"Well, we know it wasn't Mentor. He wasn't anywhere near Utopiam when you were ten."

"No, it wasn't Mentor."

"But you sense there was someone there."

"Yes, Dukk, I do."

"Any ideas who it was?"

"No, the memory is very fuzzy. Like you I was drugged up."

Dukk nodded. "It is not long before we are back on watch. Do you want to get some breakfast?"

"Yep, good plan," Marr replied.

2

Thirty minutes later, Dukk and Marr were alone in the cockpit.

"What are your thoughts on what Mentor shared and the rescue plan?" Marr asked.

"That feels like a loaded question. Why don't you start. What are your thoughts?"

Marr laughed. "To be honest, I was just making conversation. My mind is somewhere else."

"Go on."

"I was thinking of us. I was wondering if time together changes things. What if this goes wrong? What if there is bad blood?"

"How so?"

"If things unfold and don't work out?"

"Nothing is certain, but I think that is unlikely."

"Why?"

"From what I can determine, we've got the three Cs right."

Marr grinned. "Did Bazzer share them with you?"

"He did."

"Mentor?"

"Teacher."

"What did she teach you about them?"

"Did you just deflect?"

Dukk grinned.

"Ok then, since I started the conversation."

Dukk laughed.

"So, to succeed, companionship must involve attention to the three Cs," Marr said. "They are chemistry, cognitive alignment, and context. Without attention to these three aspects, companionship falters and drains both parties' energy. Chemistry is obvious, but often neglected. For it to work, both must truly lust for each other. That doesn't always happen. Perhaps there is a degree of desperation, perhaps there is something about the intimacy that is new and exciting, perhaps their ego is telling them they will look good together. Unfortunately, a compromise here will be fatal later. While perhaps neglected, chemistry is the easiest to get right. The test is simple. One simply needs to ask if they are totally attracted to this person when they are at their worst, physically? That lust must be there when they meet at the end of an exhausting day, stressed and preoccupied. If that happens the chemistry is solid. If they are only physically attracted to them when they are at their best, things aren't how they should be. It's true that over time one might get a little too comfortable and take less care of oneself than one should. Nevertheless, even as one grows old, becomes less firm, gains or loses hair and gets a little more rounded, the core of the beauty will remain and that's what creates the chemistry. Without the chemistry they are just pretending."

Marr paused.

"Yep, that is how I know it," Dukk said. "What of Cognitive alignment?"

"Cognitive alignment is crucial for longevity, but not so important in casual companionship. Cognitive alignment includes aspects of personality and how we interact with the world. For longevity, companions need to have alignment in sense of humour, similar levels of emotional intelligence, similar core values, some similar interests, and a degree of alignment of ideologies and other life philosophies. Sense of humour is the most important of all these aspects and is likely to be aligned from the start. This is, of course, if one is being honest and not just letting primal urges drive laughter even when they don't get the other person's humour. Life is hard but it will become unbearable if one is not sharing laughter at oneself and the world. A similar level of emotional intelligence is important, so they relate properly. Emotional intelligence is something one grows. It's not fixed, but companionship must start at a similar level. This is so that one isn't having to educate or bring the other person along. Having a teacher-and-student dynamic can be fun in aspects of a companionship, but it gets tiresome if it's one-sided all the time. Being the basis of decisions, and beliefs and behaviours, core values will shape who one is and how one grows. A big gap here will get in the way of the companionship developing properly. Similar interests create opportunities for shared experiences. It's during those shared experiences that laughter is found, and learning takes place. Finally, having some degree of alignment in ideologies and other life philosophies ensures violence doesn't break out on the first encounter. Alignment here ensures companions have things to share that they are passionate about, but not so different that they simply have nothing to engage on together.

"Sound," Dukk commented. "And context?"

"Context is the facts that exist at the start of a companionship. These will include habits and routines, physical condition, mental condition, commitments to others, financial flexibility, baggage, and skills in managing complexity. There is always context, no matter the stage of life. This context will both enable and get in the way of a strong and lasting companionship. Lack of flexibility in many of these aspects will prevent meeting the right companion. When a meeting does take place, inflexibility makes it harder to experience each other fully. It just isn't realistic that one will be able to keep everything the same after they meet someone. They must make changes. They might need to spend less time with those they care about, to make room for the new person. They might need to change some of their routines and habits to fit better with the other's availability. They might need to invite them into their existing activities and share them with them.

They might need to work on their physical condition so that they can have better sex. They might need to seek help to remove more of the baggage. They might need to reduce their financial security somewhat, so that they have the means to engage fully in new and shared experiences. An unwillingness to share and integrate new people into existing routines, experiences, and friendships keeps others out."

"That is what I understand them to be."

"Excellent. What do you think is the most important?" Marr asked.

"Of the three Cs, while all are necessary, cognitive alignment is the most important. Having the ability to connect with each other on similar emotional and intellectual levels enables us to learn about each other's needs, our individual contexts, and is required to create the new and shared conditions necessary for rich and lasting companionship."

"So, you think that is the case?"

"As far as I can determine."

"And what of chemistry?"

Dukk laughed. "That isn't a serious question. Considering what we've been through over the last month, clearly, we've seen each other at our worst."

Marr laughed. "Yes, true."

"It is my turn for a walk around," Dukk said as he stood up.

"It is. Enjoy."

3

The rest of the morning had been more alike the typical haulier routine than any time over the last two days.

Marr and Dukk had completed their watch, then spent time in the gym. Their conversation had slipped into the typical rhythm of frivolous banter and operational updates.

Things progressed as normal for the first traverse on the path towards Mayfield and the big rescue.

With the rig in slow running and the DMD configured for the next traverse, the crew had agreed on a lunch together.

After eating and some sharing of stories relating to the previous evening with Ileadees, the conversation turned back to the rescue planning.

"Right, if it is ok with everyone, I suggest we start with a typical crew circle-up. Then move onto other topics like where we are at and the plans for the rescue," Dukk said to get everyone's attention.

There was general agreement with the suggestion.

Dukk flicked the projection of the flight plan into the air in the middle of the table.

"So, we are now here in Maple 16. Our next traverse will take us to Finch 8. Then we go to Finch 19 followed by WZR15. From there we are into WZR18. This is the system for Mayfield. The next three systems are unmonitored so we should move through each traverse in about nine hours. That puts us into orbit of Mayfield near twelve thirty tomorrow night. Any questions on the flight plan?"

"Do we run stealth tech?" Luna asked.

"Great question, Luna. I suggest we see how we get on. If we are alone, it might be wise to save fuel and leave it off. What does everyone think?"

No one saw a problem with that suggestion.

"Any other questions?"

"What about rig operations and circle-ups?" Annee asked.

"I suggest we operate as we would normally. We still need to stay alive. So, we give attention to the normal procedures and routines."

"Chores?" Luna asked.

"Yes, of course. We don't want the rig going to pot."

"What about an intermediary inspection?" Annee asked.

"Time is of the essence, so I suggest we skip that routine on this leg. What do you think, Bazzer?"

"Yep, agreed," Bazzer replied. "Besides, we are already in good shape."

"Perfect," Dukk said before continuing.

"For the circle-ups. I suggest we have another circle-up tomorrow afternoon. We have it after the traverse into WZR15. Perhaps we have a meal at that time too. The evening might be busy as we prep for the final traverse and then the rescue."

"We can do a final briefing of the rescue plan at that time too," Marr added.

"Good idea. Anything else of an operational nature?" Dukk asked.

No one spoke up.

"Great. So, now general questions," Dukk said.

After a pause to see if anyone took the lead, he said, "I have one to start. Mentor, why did we buy twenty-five sets of IDs from Ileadees?"

"It is contingency," Mentor answered. "Nothing more."

"So, it is not related to a curve ball that we don't know of?"

"Nope, just contingency. That's all."

"The number also matches the capacity of the rig," Annee noted.

Dukk laughed.

He then added, "that sounds obvious now that I think about it."

Mentor smiled.

"What else? Anyone else got a question?" Dukk asked.

"I haven't as much a question," Annee said. "But I am confused about something."

"What is that?"

"Mentor, with all your knowledge, experience, and influence, how is it that you were surprised that taking out Craig Atesoughton the second, didn't stop the party."

"Why do you think I was surprised about that?" Mentor asked.

"Your manner when you shared the message from Tieanna. The message that said something along the lines of it is a hydra and you've only cut off one of the heads. Surely you knew that might be the case?"

"Yes, I knew that might be the case. It wasn't that which alarmed me in the message."

"What alarmed you?"

"Two things. Firstly, Tieanna expressed concern about the girls coming to harm. With Craig out of the way, Tieanna thought her influence would ensure the girls were safe. It was odd that she expressed concern."

"And the second thing?"

"Her parting words."

"'They know!'?"

"Yes."

"What troubled you about it specifically?"

"I don't know who 'they' are."

"But surely it is either one of the two sources of power. The elites or the observers?"

"Granted, the emphasis she put on the word 'they' gives me the impression that 'they' have power. However, as we already established, elites run the show. The observers are bureaucrats. Please don't take it personally, Trence, but they don't have any real power or make any real contribution for that matter. Things would run just fine without them. They are just lackies to keep those in the citadels, compliant."

"So, the elites are the 'they' in Tieanna's statement. And the main elites in this part of the galaxy are the Atesoughtons?"

"Unlikely."

"Why?"

"Tieanna knew of the assassination order. In fact, she brought it to my attention. It would be odd if 'they' were the Atesoughtons because they already knew. And I knew that she knew. Her statement wouldn't have made sense if 'they' were the Atesoughtons."

"Could it be a new internal powerplay. Perhaps grandson against grandfather?"

"Maybe. It is something to explore."

"Another elite family?"

"Perhaps, but unlikely."

"Why?"

"Elites from other families do certainly make use of Mayfield and there are plenty of disagreements and minor scuffles from time to time. But messing around like this is an act of war. That wouldn't be a good idea."

"Why not?"

"The Atesoughtons are well armed. It wouldn't make sense that another family was in Mayfield looking to upset things."

"But still possible."

"Yes."

"Why not just ask Tieanna?" Trence blurted.

Everyone sat up.

Dukk shook himself and sat forward.

"How did I miss it? No one had asked about Tieanna," he thought to himself.

The others appeared to be coming to the same conclusion.

"She is missing," Mentor said quietly.

"What do you mean?" Marr asked.

"The transmission that I shared was the last communication from her. I replied and got nothing back."

"But you said you got the message before things got crazy on the Dinatha. We have been avoiding contacting others since. You said we weren't to contact others for now."

"I haven't been sending any messages since the Dinatha blew up. I received the message well before that."

"When did you get it?"

"I got the message that evening."

"What evening?"

"When we were still in Mayfield."

"The evening of the assassination?"

"Yes."

Dukk sighed and sat back in his chair.

After a moment he spoke. "So, when the security personnel arrived at the Dinatha at seven a.m. in the morning you already knew something was up. That is why you insisted we get out of there?"

"Exactly."

"Dammit, Mentor. I thought we were past the lies and half-truths."

"We are. I overlooked it too."

"If you knew something was up that evening, why didn't you try to find her? Wasn't she in Mayfield?" Annee asked.

"I wasn't sure if she was. She comes and goes. She typically moves about with Craig junior. Besides, her mention of 'they' had spooked me. I didn't know if leaving the Dinatha to look for her would put us all in danger. My instinct told me that we needed to get away fast."

"We need to talk to the girls and those men," Marr stated firmly.

"Yes, we do, Marr," Mentor replied softly.

4

"What about the Veneficans?" Luna asked after the silence got too much.

"What about them?" Marr replied.

"They were there at the time too. Can they be the 'they' Tieanna mentioned?"

"Mentor?"

"They are powerful, both in terms of muscle from what we saw and influence from what I have heard. However, the Atesoughtons out gun them. They wouldn't want to go head-to-head. Unless they had some sort of leverage."

"What about their presence that evening?" Luna asked.

"That is confusing me too. Yes, I had thought about their presence. It lines up with Tieanna's disappearance."

Mentor abruptly stopped talking.

"What?" Luna asked.

"They are a sect of women," Marr interjected. "Granted their intention and purpose is unclear. But they are women."

"Exactly," Mentor stated.

"So, you are suggesting that because they are women, they would be in favour of protecting girls. They wouldn't get in the way of attempts to get them out of harm's way?" Luna suggested.

"Yes, that is my thinking," Mentor replied.

"So not them?" Luna asked.

"That isn't clear."

"Can I ask something," Trence asked.

"Of course," Dukk replied.

"I am finding all this not only confusing but disturbing. I can only imagine how hard it will be for Kimince."

Dukk looked over at Mentor. Dukk felt the reply wasn't in his area of expertise.

"Trence, yes, it will be hard for Kimince as it is for you," Mentor answered. "Perhaps even harder for Kimince. It is going to need all your strength to gently bring Kimince into awareness."

"Me!" Trence said in surprise.

"Yes, Kimince trusts you. It must be you. We will work on a plan together. I will be there to help you, every step of the way."

"As will I," Annee added.

"Me too," Luna said.

The others followed suit.

"Thank you," Trence said quietly. A tear formed in the observer's eye.

"If that is the end of the broader questions," Dukk said rhetorically to refocus everyone's attention. "I suggest we do a rescue plan check-in. Marr?"

Marr nodded and then projected an image to the middle of the table.

"This is the resort layout. We bought the maps from Ileadees."

"I guess it went on the tab," Dukk stated.

"It did," Marr answered with a grin. "You can see the building where the girls should be."

Marr pointed to the location on the map.

"Luna and I think it would be better if we enter from the back and not via the hyperloop and resort. We don't try to find the staff and bribe our way in. Instead, we just come at them quietly. It is more our style. We go in unnoticed and leave that way. No one knows we were even there."

"That is why you got the specialised ammo and other stuff from Ileadees?"

"Exactly. We don't want anyone getting hurt unnecessarily. And we want the men alive so we can understand who got in the way of Mentor's plan. The tranquilizers are for anyone that is in the wrong place at the wrong time. The gas pellets give us options for the same reason. Luna can use the glass melting bullets to give me access points for the nano drones. Which, will be used to get eyes on the inside before we go in."

"What do you mean by 'enter by the back'?"

"We come in via the woods. This area here," Marr said pointing to a section of woods that ran from the fence line to the back of the building.

"How will you get up there?"

"We fly in."

"You had better explain what you mean," Dukk said in a surprised tone.

"We use wingsuits and glide through the valley."

"Wingsuits? What haulier has a wingsuit?"

"A haulier who wasn't always a haulier."

"Point taken," Dukk laughed. "Gliding? Gliding from where?"

"The back of the rig during final approach."

"Seriously? It will be moving extremely fast and shaking around like nobody's business."

"Not during the final approach towards the landing pad. The rig will be pointed up at forty-five degrees as the vertical and main burner thrusters slow the descent speed and keep it airborne. That angle will also reduce the air pressure at the upper hatch. That will allow us to get out and clamber to the tail. When the rig reaches a safe speed for wingsuits, we simply jump off the back."

"Have you done this before?"

"Have we jumped off the back of an interceptor on final approach to a distant planet's space port? No, but it is still within the limits of what Luna, and I are capable of."

Dukk shook his head. "Where will you land?"

"Up here, beyond the fence."

"But you'll be on the wrong side of the fence."

"I've seen those fences up close. The first time you took me snowboarding. The fences can be scaled easily with ropes and Kevlar blankets for the razor wire at the top."

"What if someone sees you."

"Unlikely. It will be dark. But if someone does see us and gets an idea of where we landed, by the time they get up there, we'll be long gone. We won't leave a trace. There will be nothing for them to find or follow."

"What about the indigenous creatures? As you pointed out, it will be dark. The day-mode lights won't be on at that point. And, when you land, as we've already established, you will be on the wrong side of the fence."

"We'll have the ski suits with us. They are designed for this terrain. We'll be invisible to everyone and everything."

Dukk shook his head. "This sounds nuts. There must be a way to do this that doesn't involve launching yourselves off the back of a perfectly good rig. Am I on my own in these concerns?"

"No Dukk. This plan concerns me too," Annee said.

"Guys," Marr replied sincerely. "I understand your concerns. But we've been doing mad stuff like this for years. It is what we are here for. To give the team an added edge."

"Bazzer, what is your take on this?" Dukk asked.

"Dukk, I agree with Marr," Bazzer replied. "It is their domain. Let them be what they are."

Dukk looked around the table. He sat back in his seat and looked at Marr. "Tell me what you need my help with."

"I will," Marr answered with a smile.

With that Dukk stood up.

"Unless there is anything else pressing, I suggest we finish things there as it appears we have work to do. Is that ok with everyone?"

"Definitely, my brain is toast," Bazzer stated as he stood.

"That might be the vodka last night, more so than the planning," Luna laughed.

Bazzer grinned.

5

The next twenty-four hours passed very quickly. The three traverses progressed as normal. The crew operated the rig. Preparation and rest were the priorities. There was a little exercise and fun too. The conversations were mostly operational. Little time was spent focused on the grander what ifs.

As Dukk had suggested the day before, the crew gathered for a meal after the fourth traverse since leaving Maple Tower. It was near four p.m.

"How is everyone holding up?" Dukk asked as they ate. "Any questions or new concerns?"

"Yes," Annee said. "How do we get into the Mayfield space port in the early hours? They, like most smaller settlements, don't typically entertain out of hours landings or launches."

"Mentor has that covered. Mentor?" Dukk replied.

"We will make a standard request and when they queue us until the morning, I will contact them directly and change their minds."

"How?" Annee asked.

"You will see," Mentor grinned.

"Ok," Annee answered in a curious tone.

"What else?" Dukk asked as he looked around.

"What happens when we land? What is the timing and all that?" Annee asked.

"Marr has a plan laid out," Dukk replied. "She will share it with us when we have finished eating."

Dukk waited for further questions.

"Well, I have a question of my own," Dukk said when no one else spoke. "What happens when we have the girls on board?"

Dukk looked around the table and stopped at Mentor.

Mentor smiled.

"We help them move forward with their lives?" he said.

"How?"

"It is a multi-stage approach. First, we need to assess the damage done and viable options."

"What do you mean by that?"

"They have been groomed to be nothing more than subservient sex toys. The beliefs they have and the reality they exist in, will need to be undone and replaced with something better."

"Like what?"

"A belief in their own potential, for a start. But also, alignment with their natural abilities, and a sense of purpose and usefulness."

"That doesn't sound dissimilar to what we all need."

"Exactly."

"So, how is the grooming undone?"

"Slowly and gently. Marr and I have the skills to start the assessment process. That will be the first step in deciding what path could work and therefore be put before them. We also need to start sowing the seeds."

"What do you mean by path?"

"Something useful for what needs to happen next."

"Like help with the resistance?"

"Yes."

"Like warriors?"

"Yes, but also growers, makers, movers, innovators, builders, educators, creators, and carers."

"So, you said you and Marr have the skills to start the assessment. Where does the assessment finish?"

"Back on Earth, with others."

"What others?"

"That will be clear when we get back there."

"Okay, so what do you mean by sowing seeds?"

"We need to help them see that there might be something more than what they have been led to believe?"

"How is that done?"

"By experiencing something different. By seeing us doing what we do. By seeing other ways of having relations with each other."

"What do you mean by other ways of having relations?"

"By being around us, but specifically being around you and Marr, and Luna and Bognath. It will help for them to see how people who care about each other, engage. That will be a significant start."

That statement caused them all to stop and pause. Marr, Dukk, Luna and Bognath blushed and looked awkwardly around at each other and the others.

After a moment, Dukk continued.

"So, we get the girls on board and head back to Earth. During the journey they get a sense of how things are?"

"Yes, that is what I suggest. However, going directly to Earth might not be long enough."

"What do you mean?"

"Ten days, even with all the hours waiting to traverse, is a brief time when it comes to dealing with undoing the damage of this kind."

"So, if we don't go direct, where do we go?"

"We see a little more of the galaxy and create some space for the conversations. I am sure even as a haulier, you've seen little outside the typical routes."

"Yes, that is so true. I am curious if I am honest. Would we go to the edges?"

"Perhaps, I think that will serve the purpose of creating the space. It will also serve another purpose?"

"What is that?"

"It will keep us away from things. Allow things to settle a little. To give space for the heat to die down."

"The sabotage of the assassination?"

"Yes."

"So, we go into hiding?"

"In a manner. But we do it in a way that creates space to grow, but also rest and play."

"I like the sound of that last part," Luna blurted.

"Do you have any specifics on the path we should take back to Earth?" Dukk asked Mentor.

"Yes, I suggest that with Kimince and the girls on board, we head to the edge of the Atesoughton cluster and cut across to the Asimov cluster. We then make our way back to Earth from there."

"That brings us back into Earth via Tau Ceti 5. Is that right?" Marr noted.

"Yes, it does," Dukk replied. "Mentor, there isn't a lot between the Atesoughton cluster and the Asimov cluster."

"No, there isn't," Mentor said. "But it is still a single traverse from one edge to the edge of the other."

"True."

"Isn't there a planet orbiting a yellow dwarf like the Solar System in the Asimov cluster?" Marr asked.

"Yes, Newterratwo," Dukk replied.

"That is an odd name," Luna said.

"Not if you break it down and say it slowly."

Luna paused and then said, "New, terra, two. So, new Earth two? As in the second new Earth?"

"Yep," Dukk said with a chuckle. "However, the name is misleading as it was with the first new Earth. Neither are anywhere near as inhabitable as Earth."

"Why not?" Luna asked.

"Gravity and the effect of the sun is similar. They have similar atmospheres too. However, the weather systems make it near impossible to inhabit."

"Weather systems?"

"Yes, massive storms. It is thought that Newterratwo was hit by a large asteroid, relatively recently."

"Recently?"

"In the last thousand years or so. Recent in astronomical terms."

"Right," Luna laughed. "It would still be cool to visit the system and see another yellow dwarf star."

"It would," Dukk answered with a smile.

"Anyone have any issues with this path back to Earth?" Dukk asked.

Everyone either shrugged their shoulders or shook their head.

"Great. This evening Marr and I can look at the shortest path to the edge of the Atesoughton cluster. We can have the first traverse coordinates ready to load once we are back in orbit out of Mayfield. We can work out the rest of the flight plan later."

Dukk then stood up. "On that note, I suggest we clear the table and get onto the detail of the rescue plan."

Chapter 8 – Rescuing

1

When everyone had returned to the table, Dukk looked over at Marr and smiled.

"So," Marr said as she sat forward. "As already established, Mentor has a plan that will ensure we get into the port soon after reaching orbit. Luna and I will use the wingsuits to get to the back of the resort. We think it will take about forty-five minutes for us to get in position and be ready to breach the building. Meanwhile, you will land and park as per normal. Then you get two, eight-seater carts."

"I have a suggestion," Mentor added rhetorically. "Why not request that the carts be provided. They offer a valet service in Mayfield like most elite settlements. You can place the order when requesting landing permission."

"Why not order the refuel too?" Bazzer added. "We don't do it when hauling because it costs more, and we have plenty of time with unloading and loading. It will give us a quicker turn-around."

"Good ideas," Dukk commented. "And we have the credit linked to this rig to do it."

"I guess that works," Marr said hesitantly. "However, we have to make sure we don't get ahead of ourselves."

"How so?" Dukk asked.

"We need to minimise drawing attention. That means we need to use Bazzer's video scrambler as little as possible. Mentor and the entourage don't need to go unnoticed. However, the carts moving to and from the old tunnels do. We should keep the scrambler off otherwise. We also don't want to have anyone near the rig while the carts are away. That will draw attention too."

"So, we do that. What else to we need to consider?"

"We have some unknowns in relation to timing. We don't know how long it will take to free Kimince from the lock-up or get the girls down to the basement. We can calculate most other aspects, like the gliding time, coming down the hill from the fence, fuelling the rig, drop offs in the port, the hyperloop trips, and driving between the port and the basement. And what we don't want is Mentor, Bognath, Trence and Kimince arriving back at the port when the carts are not ready to collect them. That will draw attention."

"We can delay in the village to make the timing work," Mentor interjected. "I anticipated this timing issue, so we've got that covered."

"Great," Marr replied. "We also want to minimise raising suspicion from using our comms. If we use encrypted channels someone might notice and investigate. We must use normal operational exchanges. They won't give us away. Also, those that aren't where they would be expected to be, will need to be on receive only. That would include Dukk, Annee, Luna and I."

"We need some other way to coordinate timing," Dukk observed.

"Which means Bazzer and I," Bognath interjected. "We will share operational chatter about the readiness of the rig for departure. Which will be code for the fact that you all, and the girls, are safely on the rig. When Bazzer says the rig is ready, we can depart the village."

"Perfect," Marr replied. "Great idea. So, let me lay it out as I see it. The carts and fuel tanker are waiting for your landing. Bazzer will supervise resupply while Dukk and Annee drive Mentor and the entourage to the hyperloop. They then return to the rig and park the carts behind it. Out of the clear view of the main thoroughfare. When the tanker leaves, Bazzer runs the scrambler and Dukk and Annee head off to the entrance to the tunnels to the old port. Meanwhile, Luna and I will land, get to the penthouse, and bring the girls to the basement. We all drive back through the tunnels and Bazzer reactivates the scrambler as we reach the port. With the girls safely on the rig, Bazzer makes the call to Bognath."

"How will Bazzer know when to run the scrambler again?" Annee asked.

"Oh, yes, good question," Marr replied.

"You could use a motion detector," Luna suggested. "Dukk and you could drop it off in the old tunnel entrance as you go towards the old port. It will then trigger on the return. Bazzer would have the receiver."

"Nice idea," Bazzer said smiling at Luna.

"Do we have a motion detector?" Annee asked.

"I can modify a rig proximity scanner," Bazzer said. "We have spares already. No need to print them."

"Excellent," Marr stated.

"Anything else?" Marr asked after a moment.

"IDs!" Luna asked.

"What about them?"

"I gather we all have to now use the new aliases we got from Ileadees?"

"Yes," Mentor replied. "From now on we must use them when we are out and about."

"What is the story with the names?" Annee asked. "They are a little odd."

"They are derived from famous jazz artists," Luna stated.

No one responded.

"What is wrong with you guys?" Luna laughed. "You need to get up to speed on the classics. Look, my new alias is Viredd as in Vi Redd. Yours, Ann, is Cabley as in Carla Bley. Marr's is Maldana as in Melissa Aldana. Dukk is Dellington as in Duke Ellington."

"Clearly, I need to learn more about the past," Annee laughed.

"I have another question," Annee then added. "What is the point of the IDs we brought from Ileadees if we still need to scramble their video feeds?"

They all looked at Mentor.

He sat up and spoke.

"The modifications made to your implants do send signals and interference to biometric systems and video capture equipment in the immediate vicinity. This does mislead the tracking systems which no longer trust your features and mannerisms as a reliable means to identify you. The ease at which plastic surgery and augmentation can change the physical appearance made video recognition redundant. The systems no longer have the capability to do that. Besides, most elites can't be bothered with the make-up and wigs like the observers, and they don't want their movements tracked. However, the digital ID interference tech doesn't stop the naked eye from identifying you. It is that which the video scramblers must account for."

"So, if the operator, like most, is lazy and just lets the system do the work, we are fine. However, without the scramblers and if they take the time to look at the video recordings, we are toast," Luna added.

"Exactly," Mentor replied.

"Oh," Annee answered.

"What else?" Marr asked after giving that latest information time to sink in.

"How will you get the girls down to the basement?" Annee asked. "It will be the middle of the night. You two will be dressed in ski gear with weapons attached, I assume. Won't they freak out?"

"If what we suspect is true, they will be sleepy and likely smashed," Marr answered. "We use that to our advantage."

"How?"

"We come in shouting. We tell them that indigenous creatures are loose in the resort. We order them to get some clothes on and dash for the lift."

"Wait! So, they come to the rig with what they can scramble to put on in a smashed and panicked state? What about their personal effects?"

"Hostesses are trained to avoid attachment. Less said about that the better. So, they won't have much. Mainly make-up. Which they won't need for a while. However, for toiletries, underwear, and the like, I will bring some ultralight carryalls. While Luna chases the girls to the lift, I will grab what I can."

"The things you have thought about blow my mind," Annee said laughing.

2

"I have another question," Annee said. "Won't Kimince be in some state. What happens when Trence appears. Kimince will surely have heard about the Dinatha. How will that be handled?"

"Mentor and I have devised a cunning plan," Trence blurted.

Most, except Bognath and Mentor, looked at Trence with a curious expression.

"Will we show them what we came up with?" Trence asked looking over at Mentor.

Mentor nodded.

"Great, who wants to help me practice my lines. Bognath and Mentor, you will play yourselves. I need someone to play Kimi?"

"I'll do it," Bazzer said.

"Great, Bazzer. Let's all stand up," Trence said. "Over here near the kitchen. Come on."

Bazzer, Mentor and Bognath reluctantly got up and followed Trence.

The others giggled and adjusted their seats ready for the show.

With the four of them standing awkwardly near the kitchen, Trence continued.

"So, this starts with you, Kimince. Picture yourself there in the lock-up. Seeing me for the first time. Just be natural."

"Got it," Bazzer replied with a smile.

"When you are ready, go for it," Trence said.

Bazzer immediately started jumping up and down, flapping his arms hysterically.

"Oh, my goodness! Oh, my goodness! Tren, you are alive," Bazzer screamed in a high pitch voice.

Everyone burst into laughter.

"Brilliant, Bazzer," Trence squealed before pausing and looking serious. "Wait, are you making fun of Kimince. And me for that matter?"

"A little, but I wanted to be realistic," Bazzer laughed with a wink.

"Oh, yes, of course," Trence replied with an awkward smile.

Bazzer continued to grin.

"Right, my turn," Trence blurted having put aside the confusion. "Yes, Kimi, I am alive, I am alive."

"But weren't you on the Dinatha? I heard that it had exploded?" Bazzer squealed.

Trence paused for a moment to remember the lines, then continued. "No, no, I didn't go with them. I stayed here to look for help getting you free. They wouldn't let me see you, so I focused on sending messages to our superiors. Thankfully they sent someone to rescue us."

"Oh, thank goodness. How wonderful. How will I ever repay you!" Bazzer squealed reaching out and pretending to offer an embrace.

That brought more laughter from the rest of the crew.

"Let's get out of here," Trence said in a slightly stilted tone. "Back to the rig!"

There was a pause. Trence looked over at Bognath.

"Bognath, that is your cue," Trence said politely.

"Oh, of course," Bognath said reluctantly before adding in a dry tone, "The rig isn't ready to leave."

"Mentor?" Trence then prompted.

"Let's get a drink to celebrate," Mentor said calmly. "I know a place. This way."

"How was it?" Trence asked with a smile looking at the seated crew members.

"Brilliant," Annee laughed as she stood and clapped.

The others joined in.

When they had all got their seats again, Annee took the lead.

"Trence that is very brave. You'll be lying to Kimince. That takes courage."

"Yes, I will be lying," Trence replied. "But I accept Mentor's advice that we need to bring Kimince into awareness of what happened gradually. That process can only start when we are away from Mayfield. The lie is needed to get Kimi on the rig. Mentor says it might anger Kimince, but it is the best option we have."

Annee nodded.

At that moment, an alarm sounded.

Dukk dashed over to the console in the corner.

"Shit," he said. "We've got company. Stations everyone."

Dukk dashed out of the crew mess and into the cockpit. Marr was right behind him. As were Annee and Luna.

Dukk jumped into his seat and started interacting with the console. Marr did the same.

"What have we got?" Dukk said as he tried to take stock of the situation.

"I have it," Marr stated. "The craft's transponder is suggesting that the vessel is an elite patrol. It appears to be an arrow."

"Great," Dukk uttered sarcastically.

"An arrow?" Luna blurted.

"Weaponised but no cargo capacity. Like an interceptor just on a smaller scale."

"They have missile locked us," Annee blurted.

"I guess our transponder is active, if they can get a missile lock," Marr said.

"I guess so," Dukk replied. "We aren't using our stealth tech. That might have been a mistake. Luna, get our weapons online."

"Dukk, we are being hailed," Annee said.

"Accept it," Dukk started to say.

"Wait," came a voice from the cockpit door. It was Mentor.

Dukk spun around.

3

"It might be time to start the charade," Mentor said. "Those weapons aren't going to be of any use if you and Luna aren't practiced. Taking on an experienced player is more than just firing back. It requires precision manoeuvres too."

"Another oversight," Dukk replied in a defeated tone.

"Dukk, I am sending you my observer identification. Tell them we are on urgent business. This rig has the capability to add dynamic interference on the video feeds. Enable it before you accept the hail so they can't ID you. Tell them you are under a confidentiality agreement. If needed, we'll share our destination and suggest we are using unmonitored systems to avoid traffic and save time. Being close to the truth is always the best policy when lying."

"Ann, do what Mentor said about the interference mode and accept the hail," Dukk said calmly as he watched Mentor leave the cockpit and close the door.

Moments later an image appeared in the air above the front console.

The image showed the inside of a cockpit. It looked like their own, except smaller. Four people were seated in view. They were dressed in grey g-suits. The image also showed Dukk and his crew in the bottom right corner. Their faces were blurred.

"Identify and state your business in this system," a surly voice demanded.

"Imhullu, merchant cruiser on charter to a level seven observer," Dukk answered in a dry and emotionless tone.

"Your video feed isn't clear," the patrol leader stated.

"Confidentiality agreement," Dukk answered.

"Observer details!"

Dukk looked at the details Mentor had just sent him. He paused before reading them.

"Thosmas. Observer level seven. Assigned to Utopiam."

"Send over the credentials."

Dukk shared the credentials.

"Please wait," the patrol leader said as the image blurred.

Five minutes later the image came back into view.

"We need visual confirmation from the observer and your flight plan."

"Give me a moment," Dukk said as he muted the video call.

"Mentor," Dukk said into the crew comms. "They want visual confirmation and our flight plan."

"Dukk," Mentor answered on the comms. "Share the flight plan. It might work to our advantage. Then bring me into the call. Leave the interference setting off for my camera. I am at the console in the upstairs lounge."

"Marr, can you share the flight plan," Dukk asked.

"On it," Marr replied.

Dukk unmuted the video call.

"The flight plan is on its way. Visual confirmation also. I am patching in the observer."

Dukk nodded towards Annee.

The video call image changed as it split to include the rig's lounge.

Sitting squarely in the middle of the lounge was a hooded figure, with the face just visible. The face was covered in roughly applied makeup. It was chaotic and colourful. Purple strands of hair protruded from inside the hood.

"Identify yourself and justify the meaning of this intrusion?" the hooded figure shouted into the video. The voice was mostly Mentor's. But it was rougher and had a touch of malice in it.

"Atesoughton patrol officer. Identification number AGTA72. Seeking confirmation of charter of the Imhullu, merchant cruiser."

"Of course, I confirm this," Mentor shouted back. "I have urgent business in Mayfield and have no time for queuing on the main routes or any of this nonsense for that matter."

"Thank you, observer. Sorry to inconvenience you."

"Wait!" Mentor said in a more congenial tone. "What are you doing here in this unmonitored system?"

"We are investigating an attack on a G5 rig, observer. Three days ago. In an adjacent system."

"I heard about that. The Dinatha. What has that got to do with us and this system?"

"There is talk of pirates and we are looking for a missing rig, observer."

"Missing rig?"

"An interceptor called the Ukendt. It went missing at the same time. Analysis of the debris suggests it wasn't part of the explosion that destroyed the Dinatha."

"You are looking for an interceptor like the one I am sitting in right now?"

"Yes, observer."

"I see," Mentor said in a raised tone. "Have you got visuals on my rig? Have you got the transponder and registration details?"

"Yes, observer."

"And what does all that tell you about the rig I am currently sitting in?" Mentor said in a malicious tone.

"The rig you are in is called the Imhullu, observer."

"Not the rig you are looking for! Right?"

"No, observer."

"Well then stop wasting my time and stay out of my way," Mentor shouted.

Mentor waved his hands and the video feed switched back to just the view of the cockpit of the arrow.

"That is all. Goodbye," the patrol leader said awkwardly before disconnecting the call.

"The missile lock is gone," Annee said.

Dukk broke into laughter as he leapt out of his seat. He raced into the lounge.

Mentor was sitting on the couch. He had pulled off the hood and wig. He was grinning.

"Well, Dukk, I guess there are no secrets now," Mentor said as the others filed into the lounge too.

"No, I guess we've seen everything now," Dukk answered.

"You have poor tastes," Luna joked. "That wig is atrocious."

"What!" Trence said in a serious tone. "I think it suits Mentor's skin tones."

Trence was standing in the hall to the crew mess.

Bazzer and Bognath were there too. They were laughing.

4

The interactions with the elite patrol had achieved two things. It had refocused their attention and it had also strengthened their belief in their ability to prevail. The crew got on with preparations, operating the rig and getting a little rest.

Just after twelve thirty a.m. the rig was orbiting Mayfield. The crew were still in the cockpit after the traverse.

"As expected, we got pushed back," Marr announced. "They have us holding until five a.m. Then it will be the usual three-hours long deorbiting and landing sequence."

"Mentor and Trence, you are up," Dukk said.

"Right," Mentor said has he got up and disappeared out of the cockpit.

Ten minutes later Mentor was back on the comms.

"We are ready in the upper lounge. As before, bring us into the call. Blur your images."

Annee initiated an urgent hail to the Mayfield port control.

"Sharing your designation," Annee said. "The call has been accepted. Mentor, bringing you into the call now too."

The video projection appeared in the middle of the cockpit. In one panel was the port control operator, looking sleepy and confused. Another panel showed Mentor and Trence sitting together in the lounge. They were wearing make-up, wigs and were dressed in the brightly coloured and chaotic outfits typical for an observer.

"Hello?" said the confused operator.

"Excuse me!" Mentor said firmly. "I understand that my designation has been shared with you."

The operator looked away. A moment later she sat up straight. Her expression changed from confusion to horror.

"My apologies, observer. How can I serve you?" the operator said.

"Apology accepted. My captain just informed me that we are in a holding pattern. Is that correct?"

"Yes, we can't receive incoming craft until eight a.m. We run a skeleton crew during the night. You are first on the list."

"This is not acceptable. I haven't come all this way to sit idle up here because of your shift management choices. I am instructing my captain to commence deorbit immediately. Please accommodate our descent."

"With all due respect, I can't do that as I have no crews to drive the AMPs."

"I am not interested in your excuses! Just make it happen," Mentor shouted. His tone was angry and threatening.

The operator just stared with her mouth open.

"That's better," Mentor said in a condescending but calmer tone. "I will have the captain share my direct comms link with you now. If anyone else wants to question my authority in this matter, I suggest they hail me directly. Just be warned, I do not respond well to being questioned on anything. Those that have, found themselves in a position where they were no longer able to ask any questions."

The operator continued to stare.

"Any further questions?" Mentor said with a sarcastic tone.

The operator said nothing.

"Good! My captain has some additional instructions," Mentor said as he waved his hands to disconnect himself and Trence from the call.

"What can I help you with?" the observer said reluctantly when the call was just her and the blurred view of the cockpit.

"I need two eight-seater carts and a refuelling truck waiting on the pad for our arrival. I am sharing a purchase order and credit access. Also, I want to request clearance to relaunch. We won't be on the ground for more than two hours."

"Anything else?" the observer asked in a timid manner.

"Yes. No one comes near the rig once refuelling is done. That's it."

"Copy. Out."

The video call ended.

"Oh shit, Mentor," Luna blurted onto the comms. "I'm nearly wetting myself. I can't imagine how that operator is feeling right now."

"What now?" Marr asked.

"We wait," Dukk replied.

Dukk sat back in his chair. He was as stunned as everyone else at Mentor's second performance.

"Got it," Marr said moments later. "Full authorisation to commence approach."

"What does it look like?" Dukk asked.

"From our current position it will take us about thirty minutes to reach the correct place to break orbit. Then we have the usual ninety-minute descent into the main port."

"Perfect. So, we'll assume usual positions to break orbit and start the descent. After that, Annee you'll take over from Marr so she and Luna can get set for the jump. Everyone clear?"

Acknowledgement came from the crew.

159

Just short of two hours later, the rig was racing towards the landing pad. The pad was halfway up a mountain that sat in the valley adjacent to the resort and staff village.

The rig was pointed up at forty-five degrees as it plunged into the valley.

Marr and Luna were suited up and waiting in the airlock at the back of the crew mess.

"Marr, we are approaching the jump point," Dukk said into the comms.

"Perfect," Marr replied as she opened the hatch.

The wind whipped at her as she crawled out of the hatch and made her way to the tail.

"Luna, you good?" Marr asked when she was in position. She couldn't see Luna as she was on the opposite side of the tail wing.

"All set," Luna replied.

"Ready, Dukk. Let us know when we drop below one hundred and fifty kilometres per hour."

"Getting there," Dukk replied. "Counting you in."

Dukk started reading out the airspeed as the combined efforts of the vertical and main hard burners kept the rig airborne as it approached the landing pad.

"Good luck," Dukk said just before reading out that the airspeed was at one hundred and fifty kilometres per hour.

"Thanks," Marr replied. "Going to radio silence. See you in the basement."

Dukk and the others in the cockpit watched the rear cameras.

They only saw a blur as Marr and Luna folded into balls and disappeared off the back of the rig.

Dukk changed the view to the underside cameras.

Marr and Luna were already only tiny specs on the video feed as they shot down towards the valley.

At that moment alarms sounded as the rig went near vertical. The full set of thrusters engaged, in conjunction with the main hard burners. They all pushed against gravity. Moments later, the rig came to a complete stop. Then before toppling over, the thrusters reversed to bring it back horizontal once more.

The rig was now hovering just above the pad.

As the rig touched down, huge doors in the cliff face before them started to retract. A single AMP, a heavily armed exoskeleton, with its driver appeared in the opening.

"Dukk, we have clearance to proceed to Pad R5," Annee said into the comms.

Dukk interacted with the controls and then gripped the joysticks on either side of his seat.

The vertical thrusters roared as the rig lifted off once more.

Dukk nudged the joysticks and the rig moved forward gently in the direction of the opening as the AMP moved to the edge of the pad and out of the way.

Within the hanger, Dukk steered the rig to the right. Further down the long narrow hanger they could see a fuel tanker and two carts sitting just clear of an empty pad.

5

Fifty minutes later, Marr was interacting with the nano drone controls.

She was crouched near a small cluster of bushes just inside the tree line at the back of the resort.

Luna was further up the hill. A few minutes earlier Luna had used her sniper rifle and the glass melting bullets. She had made holes in the rear windows of the penthouse apartments at the top of the building.

"There is nothing there," Marr muttered.

She interacted with the controls again causing the drones to do another sweep of the entire upper floor.

Then she stood, turned around and looked up the hill to where she knew Luna was positioned. She raised her hand in the air with the fist closed. Then she swung it around twice before pointing to the ground.

She then packed away the controls and waited.

Five minutes later, Luna slid down through the trees and landed on her feet just next to Marr.

"What's going on?" she asked immediately.

"There is nothing," Marr replied quietly. "No girls. No security people. Even the room on the top floor is empty. The odd apparatus and stuff are gone."

"What the hell! Where are they?"

"Good question. We'd better get into the tunnels and see if Dukk and Annee are okay."

"Absolutely. How?"

"We go via the lift in the upper room. As we planned. There isn't anyone in there anyway."

"Right. Let's go."

Marr and Luna made their way to the back of the building. They gained access and headed up to the penthouse.

Meanwhile, Dukk and Annee had just arrived at the end of the tunnels from the old port. Everything had gone smoothly. As per the plan.

"That must be it over there," Dukk said to Annee as they got out of the carts.

He was referring to some metal doors in the corner of the dusty open space at the end of the tunnel.

They headed over to the doors and listened quietly.

"I hear something," Annee said. "The lift is moving."

"Let's get into the shadows, just in case," Dukk answered as they moved away from the doors.

The doors opened. Luna burst out and rolled on the floor. Marr hung tight against the side wall of the lift. Luna pointed her gun at the carts and looked around.

"Don't shoot," Annee laughed from the shadows.

"Are you ok?" Marr asked.

"Yes," Dukk called out.

"Are you alone?"

"Yes! What is going on?"

"They are gone," Marr answered as she stepped out of the lift.

"Who are gone?" Dukk asked as he and Annee walked over to them.

"The girls. There is nothing up there."

"Shit," Dukk said. "Any ideas?"

"I guess they have been moved."

"Perhaps taken to another part of the resort?" Annee prompted.

"Maybe. Either way, they must have used the tunnels. Look at all these tracks."

Marr was shining a light on the floor.

"Unless you two were doing donuts while you waited," Luna said in jest.

"What do we do?" Dukk asked ignoring Luna's attempt to lighten the situation.

"We need someone we can trust that knows the port and can get us access to video archives," Marr answered.

"Suzzona," Annee said quietly.

"Can we trust her?"

"She should trust me."

"You'd have to make contact using your Annee ID. That will expose you and us all possibly."

"What choice to we have?" Dukk asked.

There was silence.

"Let's do it," Annee said after a moment. "What should I say?"

"Keep it casual," Marr answered. "Be informal. Say nothing about anything that has happened or what we need from her."

Annee stepped away from the group and interacted with her comms, adding the others to listen in.

"Hi," she said after a moment.

"Ann! What the hell! Your signal ID suggests you are here on Mayfield. I thought you were dead."

"Listen, I can't talk on this link. Can we meet at your place?"

"Well, that might be a problem."

"Why?"

"I am at the port. I'll explain in person. Where are you?"

"Two secs."

Annee muted the link and looked over at the others.

"We need somewhere we can get to right now and somewhere hidden but open enough should we need to get creative," Marr answered.

"The old port. We'll be there well before her. It is only ten minutes' drive from here?" Dukk suggested.

"Yes, that would work. Tell her that."

Annee unmuted and repeated the suggestion.

"When?" Suzzona asked.

"As soon as possible."

"Give me five minutes."

"See you there."

The call disconnected.

"What do you think?" Marr asked. "Is she on the level?"

"I am not sure," Annee replied. "It is early to be in the port. But I guess she might have something to resolve in the load clearance zone like at the time of the assassination."

"What then?"

"Her tone was a little odd."

"She isn't in the port," Dukk commented. "It took us twenty minutes to get to the old port."

"We'd better get there right now," Marr stated. "Annee and Dukk, you take one of the carts and go ahead. Luna and I will follow you and park a little way off. We'll cover you just in case."

Chapter 9 – Correcting

1

Five minutes later Dukk and Annee drove their cart into the dark but open space in the middle of the old port hanger.

A figure waved at them from the shadows.

They drove closer and got out.

Before them was a woman in her mid-thirties. She was of average height and well proportioned. She looked fit and strong. She had fair complexion and short brown hair. Even in the dim light her brown eyes spoke of strong awareness of the reality of things.

"Ann, great to see you are safe," Suzzona said as she stepped over and hugged Annee.

Annee returned the hug with a hint of caution.

"Why are you dressed as a haulier?" Annee asked.

"Long story. The short of it is that I am leaving. I am looking for a ride out of here. I am dressed like this to blend in with you lot."

"Why are you leaving?"

"It is only a matter of time before I get arrested."

"What for?"

Suzzona grinned.

Annee said nothing.

"Fine," Suzzona said eventually. "The shit hit the fan the day after the assassination. Every elite and his pet were in town, and they all messed around with the incoming shipments. Whole containers were traded and whisked away. That included one of the beef containers you brought in. That meant the onwards shipments needed to be re-organised. In the process they found discrepancies between what was arriving on rigs like the Dinatha, and what was reaching the resort or leaving for elsewhere."

"Discrepancies?"

"Yes, someone has been skimming the shipments and selling the produce onto restaurants in the staff village."

"You?"

Suzzona grinned.

"So?" Dukk prompted.

"A friend in port control, messaged me a couple of hours ago. Said an interceptor with a level seven observer was muscling their way into the port. Observers at that level rarely come here. And when they do show up, it is because something is about to go down. We know they track everything but largely ignore the black-market. Every so often they turn up and disappear a few to make sure everyone remembers who is in charge. I figured that might be me this time and decided to scarper before that could happen."

Annee smiled half-heartedly.

"Wait!" Suzzona stated abruptly. "How did you get in here? Why are you coming from the back of the resort? Are you with the level seven on that interceptor? Shit!"

Suzzona went to bolt. Marr appeared from nowhere and grabbed her.

"No, Suzzona," Dukk said firmly. "Your shenanigans have nothing to do with why we are here. But we do need your help."

"What do you need," she answered as she relaxed against Marr's grip.

"Access to port video feeds from five days ago."

"What do you need that for?"

"We are looking for a group of girls. Perhaps as many as twelve. They are likely dressed in full length and hooded black cloaks."

"Like the ones that came off your rig, three weeks ago?"

"Yes. You know about that?"

"It is in my interest to know exactly who comes and goes at this port. For self-preservation reasons as you might appreciate. Besides, Ann mentioned it."

"Well, we need to see the footage so we can find out what happened to them."

"You don't need the video footage."

"Why?

"Because I know what happened to them. Well, I know about their departure. I don't know what happened to them after that."

"Tell us what happened to them," Marr demanded.

"Wait, so you aren't here to arrest anyone."

"No," Dukk answered.

"But you are up to shenanigans of your own. Perhaps we can help each other. I've had my fill of this place. Also, it is only a matter of time before the authorities cop onto my operation and either shut it down or demand a cut. None of that works out well for me. So, I need a lift."

"You want to come with us?" Annee asked hesitantly.

"Sure, why not."

Annee looked at Dukk.

Dukk looked at Annee and then at Marr.

Marr nodded.

"I think we can accommodate that," Dukk said confidently.

"Great, when are we leaving?"

"It depends on what you tell us about the girls?"

"Oh, that is easy. They left the day after the assassination. On a medium size cruiser. All twelve of them. Accompanied by three security guards and two flight crew."

"Do you know the details of the cruiser."

"Of course. The Blue Weekender."

"Destination?"

"New Montana was on the launch request. They may have changed that after reaching orbit. But it is a start."

"You seem pretty clear on the details," Marr said in a suspicious tone. "There must be lots of comings and goings here?"

Suzzona turned to face Marr. She raised her eyebrows.

"Twelve girls arriving in carts via the tunnels from the old port," Suzzona said in a dismissive tone. "Dressed in next to nothing. They weren't exactly wearing those cloaks properly. It isn't something you hardly notice. Then all boarding a skanky cruiser with security guards. It makes a mark on the memory."

"Fair enough", Marr said awkwardly. "Sorry for doubting you."

"No problem," Suzzona said with a genuine smile.

"Let's get out of here," Dukk said.

"Wait, do you have hold space?" Suzzona asked.

"Yes."

"Room for a robo container?"

"Yes."

"Great, who's driving," Suzzona said as she stepped over to the cart and jumped into the passenger seat.

"Where are we going?" Annee asked.

"To get my travel lockers and my container."

"Wait! What are you on about?" Dukk asked.

"My travel lockers with my stuff in it. I'm already packed. I have it in a disused storage space near the main port. You get to it from the old tunnels. We can go there on the way."

"What did you say about a container?"

"Yes, and I have a container too. Full to the brim of fresh produce. No point in leaving it behind and it going to waste."

Dukk cracked up as Marr signalled to Luna.

2

"I assume you were the ones with the video scrambler," Suzzona said casually as they watched Luna drive over to them.

"What are you talking about?" Dukk asked.

"My contact in port control, messaged me thirty minutes ago. Said a video scrambler was being used."

"Yes, it is us," Dukk admitted.

"Great, so how about you go fire it up while Ann and I get the lockers and container. Also, you'll need to lower the platform on your interceptor."

"Luna, you go with them," Marr ordered. "Watch our backs."

Luna nodded as she jumped out of her cart. She grabbed her rifle and backpack and walked over to the other cart.

"Wow! That is a big gun," Suzzona said in jest. "I assume you know how to use it."

"Yep," Luna replied as she sat sideways into the last row of the cart.

"What have you got yourself into this time, Suzzona? Will you ever learn!" Suzzona said aloud bringing a laugh from Ann.

Marr walked over to the other cart.

"I'll ride shotgun," Marr said as she got into the passenger seat.

"I'm thinking that is literal," Dukk joked as he got into the driver's seat.

Marr grinned as she looked ahead.

"How did the jump go?" Dukk asked as he steered the cart towards the tunnel entrance.

"It was amazing," Marr replied. "Zooming into the valley above the buildings and resort. Then charging up the mountain at the other side. We only had to use two of the boosters. It was such a rush. I am still in the adrenalin haze."

"Back up! Boosters?"

"Single use, miniature solid fuel rockets. We use them to extend the glide, adjust and slow down."

"Hold it. You had pyrotechnics strapped to your backs?"

"Not strapped," Marr laughed. "They are integrated into the suits."

"If I had known that I would have," Dukk started to say before stopping.

"If you had known, you would have what?" Marr asked with her eyebrows raised.

"I would have been even more concerned," Dukk laughed.

Marr grinned.

Bazzer was standing near the bottom of the ramp as Marr and Dukk drove up.

Bazzer frowned as he realised that they were alone. He walked over to them as they parked behind the rig.

"Things didn't go quite to plan I gather," Bazzer said when he got to them.

"No," Dukk replied. "The girls are gone. But we know where they might be. Signal Bognath. We are leaving."

Dukk dashed past Bazzer and ran up the ramp.

"Wait," Bazzer added in a nervous tone. "Ann? Luna?"

"They are fine," Marr said as she watched Dukk disappear. "They are on their way. We need to get the platform down. We are not leaving entirely empty handed."

The platform had just reached the hanger floor when the other cart came flying in.

Suzzona was driving.

"Ann needs some driving lessons. She is way too slow," Suzzona said as she jumped out of the cart and dashed onto the loading platform. She lifted a cradle out of the floor and fitted the robotic container's wireless lead into the frame. She then stepped away and looked out into the darkness of the long hanger.

Annee released her hands from the handles beside her seat. Her hands were white from gripping so hard. She was laughing.

Luna was sprawled across the back seat.

"Do not, under any circumstances allow that woman near the flight controls of the rig," Luna laughed as she untangled herself.

Moments later the robotic container appeared out of the darkness. It slowed at the front of the rig, turned, swung under the wings, and then drove straight onto the ramp. It came to a dead stop millimetres away from the cradled wireless lead.

Dukk had been watching from the bottom of the ramp. He turned and walked back into the rig to retract the platform.

The others watched as the container disappeared into the hold.

"Right, let's go," Dukk said as he returned down the ramp. "Bazzer, kill the scrambler, lock in that container, and then fire us up. Marr, start the pre-launch checks. Also, we need to calculate the fastest track to New Montana. Luna, watch the ramp. Ann, let's take the carts and wait for the others at the hyperloop."

"Will I make myself at home?" Suzzona asked cheekily.

Dukk stopped and looked over at Suzzona.

"Luna, keep your eyes on her," Dukk grinned. "As you suggest, we don't want her near the flight controls."

3

Twenty minutes later, Dukk and Annee stepped out of their carts where they had been waiting near the door to the hyperloop station.

Mentor, Bognath, Trence and Kimince had just exited the station.

Kimince and Trence were being held up by Bognath. One in each arm.

Mentor, in his full observer garb, walked out in front of them. He held his head high. His facial expression was that of disgust. He walked over to the first cart and got into the back.

Dukk and Annee rushed over to help Bognath bring the observers to the other cart.

"What happened?" Annee asked as they lay each observer across a set of seats.

"Trence did ok for a bit but couldn't hold up the pretence," Bognath answered as he swung himself into the passenger seat. "One drink in and the story started to slip. Mentor spiked their drinks. Knocked them out."

Annee rushed to the first cart and headed off with Mentor.

Dukk sat in with Bognath and followed.

"Otherwise?" Dukk asked as they made their way towards the rig.

"Straight-forward," Bognath answered. "The lock-up had a skeleton staff. They barely checked Mentor's credentials. They didn't care a less what happened to Kimince."

"Other than being dosed up, how is Kimince?"

"Whingy and vocal about the suffering. So, being locked up for five days had no impact," Bognath said with a laugh.

"Sorry I didn't help at the hyperloop station with Kimince and Trence," Mentor said as they got the observers to the top of the ramp. "I had to keep up appearances."

The others were there waiting.

"No problem," Dukk answered. "I am sure you've had a hard time of it. Did Ann get you up to speed on the situation with the girls?"

"She did. I gather from the rumble of the rig we are launching immediately."

"Yes," Dukk replied.

"Before we do though, let's run the video scrambler for five minutes. We need a cover story if anyone comes looking for Thosmas."

"Do you mean Thosmas is not coming with us?"

"Yes, and everyone needs to have the same story."

"What should the story be?"

"Keep it close to the truth. That Thosmas delivered Kimince to the rig and then disappeared. Thosmas has been very visible here. It is better if Thosmas does not leave Mayfield on the Imhullu. It might get more difficult for us if that was thought to be the case."

Dukk nodded.

"Doing it now," Bazzer said.

"Ann and Luna are you good to help Mentor and Bognath get these two suited up and strapped in," Dukk asked. "I want to walk the rig before I raise the ramp."

Luna and Annee nodded.

"Bazzer, run the scrambler until just after the ramp starts to get raised," Mentor added.

"Yep, good idea," came Bazzer's reply.

"What about me," Suzzona said as she stepped aside for the group to pass up the stairs.

"Wait here," Dukk said. "You aren't authorised on this rig yet. I need to put your ID into the system."

A few minutes later, Dukk was back at the top of the ramp.

He interacted with the controls and raised the ramp.

"Come over here and scan your biometrics," Dukk instructed as he interacted with the console. "I have created a new crew member profile. It will give you permission to move about in the rig. That will be it for now."

"Does this rig have a real kitchen?" Suzzona asked casually as she waited at the console.

"Nope, just the rehydration units," Dukk answered absently before engaging the crew comms. "Sealed, commencing integrity checks. Let's do the pre-launch circle up in the cockpit. Two minutes."

Dukk then turned and headed for the stairs that would take them to the middle level.

"This rig must have a printer," Suzzona observed as she followed him up the stairs.

"It does," Dukk answered.

"Great. We can print the equipment I don't have in the container."

Dukk turned around when they reached the landing. He was perplexed at the nature of the conversation.

Suzzona smiled innocently.

"Do you have a g-suit?" Dukk asked.

"Ah, no. I hadn't got around to sourcing that piece of haulier attire."

"Helmet?"

Suzzona grinned sheepishly.

"Follow me," Dukk said as he escorted her into the g-suit room near the transport pods.

Dukk turned his back on Suzzona as he opened the cabinets containing the helmets.

"What size helmet?" Dukk said as he turned around holding a medium size helmet.

He stumbled and tried to shift his gaze.

Suzzona was standing in the middle of the room, stark naked.

"Got any fresh inner layers in these cabinets?" Suzzona said unashamedly. "There is no way I am going to launch after all this time in this flimsy underwear."

In her hands she was holding bright red lingerie.

Dukk pointed at the cabinets behind her.

"Don't worry, I won't bite," Suzzona laughed as she turned to look in the cabinet.

Dukk went to a cabinet containing g-suits.

"Are you small?" he asked as he extracted a small g-suit.

"What? These? Are you serious?" Suzzona giggled.

Dukk turned around. She was standing there cupping her breasts.

Dukk shook his head. "I'm going to leave you to it. Head upstairs and take a seat when you are ready."

Moments later Dukk reached the top of the stairs on the upper level.

Annee and Mentor were clicking Trence and Kimince into their seats and connecting the med-lines. The observers were half awake and smiling absently.

"How are we looking?" Dukk asked as he approached them.

"Nearly there," Annee answered. "Everything sorted down there?"

"Pretty much," Dukk answered. "You might want to check on Suzzona after the circle-up. She is getting suited up in the port side g-suit room."

"I will," Annee replied as she finished with the two observers.

4

Dukk continued to the cockpit. Marr was in her seat. As were Luna and Bazzer. Bognath was standing near the shaft ladder door.

"Everything in order?" Dukk said as he sat down and started flicking panels.

"Yep, launch checks complete," Marr answered. "We have launch clearance and I've loaded the flight plan into the autopilot. You just need to do the cross-checks. I've also determined we can get to New Montana in two traverses. I used the usual trade routes charts as I didn't have any other charts at hand. However, the historic records show traverses taking nine and ten and a half hours respectively, so it isn't that much difference to using unmonitored systems."

"That makes sense to me," Dukk replied. "Let's check with the others in a moment. Bazzer, systems?"

"All green. We are good to go."

"Did we miss anything," Annee asked as she and Mentor filed into the cockpit.

"Not really," Dukk answered. "We are just going over the pre-launch checks."

"So, what is the plan?"

"By now, you will all know the girls aren't here," Dukk answered. "And, that Suzzona has suggested they were last seen leaving on a rig bound for New Montana. Marr tells me that we can get there in two traverses using normal trade routes. We should be there in about twenty hours. Any thoughts?"

"What are we going to do when we get there?" Annee asked.

"Look for the rig, I guess," Dukk offered. "Mentor?"

"Yes, that is what I would suggest," Mentor answered.

"I guess we can work out the details over the next twenty hours?" Marr observed.

Dukk nodded.

"So, if no one has anything else to clarify or reason not to launch, I suggest we get suited up and on our way?"

"Do we have time for showers?" Bazzer joked as he waved his hand to his nose as he looked at Luna.

"Cheek of you," Luna replied as she poked him in the chest. "You try jumping off the back of a rig and see what you smell like!"

Dukk shook his head. "We will have plenty of time for that, once we are in orbit waiting for the first traverse."

"I have something to check before we get changed," Annee said.

Dukk smiled over at her.

"Suzzona. I guess she can grab a bunk in the six birth rooms on the lower level. At least until we locate the girls."

"She can put her stuff in with me," Bognath said. "There is a spare bunk, plenty of storage space and an ensuite. Besides, I'm hardly there."

Luna looked over at him and smiled.

"That will work," Annee said.

Twenty minutes later the rig was resting on the pad just outside the port hanger doors.

"We have a green light," Marr shared on the comms.

"Authorising the launch sequence," Dukk said as he enabled the autopilot.

The rig trembled as the vertical thrusters engaged to lift the rig gently away from the pad.

Further noises were followed by gentle thuds that indicated the rig's jacks were stowed.

The rig gently gained height and distance away from the port entrance.

The acceleration was noticeable but not uncomfortable as the rig reached the velocity required to generate lift. When it did, the vertical thrusters slowed, and the main engine took over to propel the rig away from the settlement.

Dukk relaxed into his seat as he looked up at the reddish skies and twinkling of the brightest stars. It was a view he never tired of.

Ten minutes into the flight, a bell sounded in their comms as the autopilot engaged the hard burn. The sound of the bell was quickly drowned out by the noise of the engines and air being pushed out of the way.

The rig vibrated as the trajectory and speed changed dramatically as it raced towards the upper atmosphere.

Dukk and the crew in the cockpit were pushed hard into their seats. A gravity sickness suppressant administered moments earlier and the structure of their suits, helped spread the g-force and reduce the strain they were now undergoing. That still didn't make for a pleasant experience.

For the passengers, the cocktail they had been given would keep them unaware of the strain their bodies were experiencing as the rig blasted away from the surface of the planet.

Six minutes later the engines faded out. The noise and vibration of the rig was replaced by silence and calm as the rig levelled out. They were now in orbit and weightless.

Dukk waited a further minute before commencing the post-launch protocols.

"Vitals, Mentor?" Dukk said gently into the crew comms.

"Cockpit, all stable. Passengers are coming around. Stable," was the immediate response from Mentor.

"Thanks, Mentor. Bazzer, integrity and systems?"

"All in the green zones," Bazzer replied. "Hardly a rattle on the way up. This bird is a fine thing."

"Excellent to hear," Dukk replied as he removed his helmet. "Let's get the DMD online."

A slight shiver ran through them all as the DMD came back to life.

Moments later Dukk was back on the comms.

"The DMD is responding. A little over nine hours until we make the first of two traverses on our way to New Montana. It is time that we debrief the last few hours. However, I am thinking you all, like me, are hungry and in the need of a shower. So, let us debrief over breakfast. Thirty minutes."

5

As the others made their way out of the cockpit, Dukk turned and spoke to Marr directly.

"It is just on six a.m. and therefore the start of our watch. One of us can cover the conn so we can both get a shower before breakfast. Do you want to go first?"

"Why don't you go," Marr said. "I need to take a long shower. Once you are done, I will know how much time I have left before the debrief."

"The upsides of doing what you do," Dukk laughed.

"Yep, the joys," Marr replied.

Five minutes later, Dukk sat back into his seat in the cockpit as Marr headed for the shower.

He went over the system logs and then checked the autopilot. Everything was in order. The skies were a little busier than six hours earlier. The radar showed other rigs dropping out of traverse ready to deliver their loads to the surface.

Dukk checked the details. All G5 rigs. He wasn't surprised. He reflected how hauliers all used G5 rigs. It was over sixty years since the fifth generation TLM rig first made its appearance. With the G5, TLM got the balance right between performance and capacity. That balance had yet to be match by newer models. Dukk was aware that most had upgrades of various nature, using more recent technology, but the overall platform of the G5 still dominated the medium distance hauling market. He had once heard someone suggest they were like the 747s of the twentieth century. He still hadn't got to the bottom of what that meant. Perhaps with the access to the hidden archives he might be able to answer that question, he thought.

His mind drifted to the multitude of trips made in G5 rigs.

Dukk's daydreaming was interrupted by Marr on the comms. She was showered and at the console in the crew mess ready for breakfast and the debrief. He moved the conn and headed there.

On entering the crew mess, Dukk's attention was drawn to a commotion in the kitchen.

Marr rolled her eyes when they exchanged glances.

Dukk made his way towards the back of the crew mess and entered the kitchen.

Suzzona was standing in the middle of the space. She was dressed in a skin-tight tank top and a very brief pair of shorts. Her fit body showed the evidence of exertion. She was watching Bazzer. Well, part of him. He was kneeling on a worktop near one of the rehydration units. His top half was hidden inside the back of the unit.

"That should do it," Bazzer said as he backed out of the tight space.

"Hi, captain," Suzzona said cheerfully. "We are nearly ready to make breakfast."

Dukk made a puzzled expression.

Suzzona chuckled.

"Here help me with this," she said pointing to a grill unit on the floor.

Dukk moved to one side of the long grill. He helped Suzzona lift it onto the counter.

Bazzer then jumped back up on the countertop again and married a cable on the grill to an electrical plug dangling out of the back of the rehydration unit. He then got down and used a bolt gun to secure the grill to the countertop.

"Bazzer you are brilliant," Suzzona said as she admired the grill. "On my own, I would never have been able to hook up the electricity and extractor vent in that short amount of time."

"No probs. Oh and Dukk is here. Great, another easy target," Bazzer stated as he smiled at Dukk. "She'll explain. I need a shower."

Bazzer disappeared out the door.

"Where is everyone else?" Dukk asked Suzzona as she turned on the grill.

"Ann is getting things for me. Mentor is with the observers. Luna and Bognath scarpered when I said I was looking for volunteers to help with breakfast. Marr said she was on the conn. That leaves you."

Dukk smiled nervously.

"Coming through," a voice announced from the doorway. It was Annee. She was dressed in a similar scant fashion to Suzzona and showing signs of exertion. She was carrying a stack of dinner plates. "I found some in the storage area in the nose section. Not a lot of call for these usually."

"Great," Suzzona announced. Will you clean them and watch the grill? It is warming up."

"Yep," Annee replied cheerfully.

"Dukk, follow me," Suzzona said as she made for the door.

Dukk followed Suzzona down the aft starboard ladder shaft to the lower level.

Once off the ladder, Suzzona unhooked the basket at the bottom of the vertical conveyor and carried it into the hold. She then lifted the basket into the back of the open container and climbed up.

"Coming?" she asked as she disappeared.

Dukk climbed up after her.

Contained within were numerous crates and storage boxes. Dukk also recognised refrigeration and freezer units. He figured they must have been patched into the containers power supply. In turn the container would have tapped into the rig's power when it was loaded earlier.

"Catch," Suzzona shouted from the depths.

Dukk only just reacted in time to catch packets of meat. He dropped them into the basket.

"Back rasher bacon," Suzzona said when she re-appeared having noticed Dukk's puzzled expression.

Suzzona placed bags of bright red tomatoes and huge mushrooms into the basket, then disappeared again.

"That will do it," she said moments later after placing cartons of eggs on top of the other items.

"Great," Dukk said. "Can I ask you something?"

"Sure?"

"What is going on with you? You seem relaxed about all of this?"

"By that do you mean the assassination, the trafficking, the Dinatha exploding, taking over the attacker's rig, Maple Tower, the rescue, and Mentor's true identity?" Suzzona answered with a grin.

"Yes, all of that," Dukk laughed.

"I've got some questions still, but I got enough from what Ann summarised to keep my mind at ease for now. I've seen a lot, and even though this is the craziest by far, I am still good."

"Okay," Dukk said.

"Hungry?"

"Yep."

"Good, then help me get the basket down from the container."

A few minutes later, Dukk and Suzzona re-entered the crew mess, carrying the basket between them.

The others were gathered near the table.

"I have no warmer, so this is going from grill to plate to mouth. Line up," Suzzona shouted as she and Dukk entered the kitchen.

Thirty minutes later, everyone was feeling rather full. The conversation had been free flowing and light such that by the end of the meal everyone was up to speed on the events of the last few hours.

"I cannot ever remember having such an amazing breakfast on any rig, planet side or not," Bazzer concluded as he sat back in his seat rubbing his stomach.

"I am not sure I've ever eaten food as fresh as that," Luna said with glee.

There was general agreement around the table.

Marr checked her emotions. The way things were unfolding was hard to believe.

Dukk smiled too. He was thinking how lucky he felt at that moment.

"Having a cook on the crew and access to fresh food certainly has its advantages," Mentor added.

"I'll have you know that I am a qualified chef, not just a cook!" Suzzona blurted. "And my services don't come for free. I will expect a full share of all the spoils of whatever this endeavour is all about."

Everyone laughed.

"Fine by me," Dukk said. "And talking of endeavours, we'd better get onto talking about what we do next."

Chapter 10 – Consequences

1

With the table cleared the crew got down to the planning for the next twenty-four hours.

"What is our cover story this time?" Annee asked to get things started.

"Mentor, do you have a suggestion?" Dukk asked.

"I'd suggest something simple and easy to remember. We need to be able to get in and move about without drawing attention."

"Like we are hauliers looking for new clients and work?" Annee asked.

"Exactly, but also draw on the backstory that we purchase from Ileadees. This rig isn't a G5 after all."

"What is the back story?" Suzzona asked.

"That we've been working the fringes moving high value loads, the occasional V.I.P. and protecting elite convoys," Dukk replied.

"The story also had an indication that we do it no questions asked for the right price," Marr added.

"So, apart from the protection side of things, the cover story is basically our normal story," Bazzer joked.

Mentor nodded.

"How will we find the girls?" Annee asked when she sensed it was the right time to ask.

Mentor said nothing. Marr took the hint.

"First, we will casually look for the cruiser. Finding it will confirm the girls came there or at the very least give us others to interrogate. If we can't find it or if we learn nothing from the crew, we'll need to find someone we can bribe to get access to port records and video feeds."

"That reminds me," Dukk noted. "Our credit line is running low. We blew most of what we exchanged for half the canister with getting what we needed for the rescue attempt. And the refuelling here. Can we afford the time for another trip to Maple Tower to retrieve and convert another canister?"

"Let's cross that bridge when we come to it," Mentor said. "I have some hidden reserves if we need it."

"What about the system relay?" Annee asked. "Can we hack it to find the Blue Weekender's movements? Like we did before to uncover the evidence of the trafficking?"

"Already tried," Marr answered. "The debug capability has been disabled. They must have noticed my last efforts."

After a moment, Luna looked over at Dukk.

"What time are we expecting to be in the port in New Montana?"

Dukk flicked the flight plan to the air in the middle of the table.

He interacted with it and times were displayed against the traverse waypoints.

"We should reach orbit of New Montana near half one in the morning. Unlike Mayfield, their port runs around the clock. However, we will still be subject to queuing and the usual descent protocols. Best case if there is no queue, is half four in the morning. After that who knows."

"It is bigger than Mayfield then?" Luna asked.

"Yes, much bigger. The planet is closer in size to Earth and there are multiple settlements."

"How many people there?"

"I'd say quarter of a million at this stage," Dukk answered. "New Montana is one of the main planets in the Atesoughton cluster."

"Apart from being of similar size to Earth, what drew them there?"

"Stable climate. Air composition is at levels like that of Earth. Indigenous creatures are controllable, and it has an abundance of natural resources. Materials like Earth's ores and fossil fuels. With that they have been able to build massive structures. The abundance of readily accessible fuels also makes easy of the job to power the bio systems, synthetic food production, artificial daylight, and the defences. They only need to import fine foods and drink."

"Don't forget the view," Annee added.

"View?" Luna asked.

"The position of the system and the planet within it gives a spectacular view of the galaxy."

After a moment, Annee spoke again.

"How are Kimince and Trence?"

"Dosed up and sleeping," Mentor said.

"What happens when they sober up?"

"I'm going to keep them dosed up. At least for the next twenty-four hours. They will have a fine hangover later, but it might be best they stay oblivious to what is going on until we have a better sense of what we are facing."

With that the conversation faded as the full bellies and fatigue came into play.

The next two hours wasn't easy for Marr and Dukk. They were tired but still had to keep an eye on the rig systems while everyone else got some rest. Frequent walk arounds helped keep them both from nodding off. Marr also used the time to clean her weapons. She laid them out on the table in the crew mess and worked away. Dukk had enjoyed sitting opposite her quietly, just watching as she meticulously took the weapons apart, cleaned each piece and reassembled them. Marr enjoyed him being there too. With the watch over, they crashed into Dukk's bed and slept solidly until it was time to prepare for the first traverse.

The period after that first traverse passed quickly but with a growing sense of dread. Even with the rest, the crew were starting to see the possibility that they had failed. The enthusiasm and level of hope experienced since leaving Maple Tower had waned. Marr and Dukk still found moments of joy together having felt more rested. They also got to the gym. But as with the rest of the crew, they mainly spent time alone in reflection. There wasn't even any further circle up or briefing ahead of the traverse into New Montana's system.

2

"Air traffic control has shared the deorbit and approach plan. We've got immediate clearance," Marr said aloud.

The crew were sitting in the cockpit having exited the last traverse a few minutes earlier. New Montana could be seen racing below. Patches of brightness shone through the purple tinted clouds."

"That's great news. What does the plan look like?" Dukk asked.

"From our current position, it will take sixty minutes to reach the deorbit point and then two hours in managed descent. We will be on the pad near half four."

"Do you want to load the plan into the autopilot, and I'll authorise it."

"Will do," Marr replied.

"We are getting the royal treatment again," Annee noted.

"Yes, we are," Dukk replied as he authorised the autopilot.

"Any of your doing, Mentor?" Annee asked.

"Nope. I am done with meddling for now," Mentor said smiling over at Annee.

"Right, let's get organised. Annee and Mentor, the conn is yours," Dukk said as he removed his helmet. "Let's regroup in forty-five minutes for the commencement of deorbiting protocols."

Three hours later the rig was on its final approach to the main port. The port was situated in a valley adjacent to the largest settlement.

New Montana had spared no expense with any piece of infrastructure. The port was no different.

Unlike many settlements in colonized planets, the port wasn't built into the side of a mountain or hill side for protection from the elements. Instead, the port here was spread over a wide area with a central taxi way. Large dome shaped hangers dotted down either side of the taxi way. Glass tunnels linked each hanger. The odd cart or robotic container could be seen moving within these. The tunnels all linked back to a large building. Hyperloop tubes protruded out of the building and disappeared into the side of the adjacent hill side in the direction of the settlement.

Positioned adjacent to the taxi way were three landing and launch zones. Each consisted of a circular pit with high concrete walls. A vessel could land or depart under full power with having very little or no impact on the buildings around it. The port also used automated low loaders like the Citadels back on Earth. These low loaders would move space craft around the port quickly and efficiently. This negated the need for air wash barriers that were typical in other ports and space hubs.

The rig's thrusters and main engines worked hard to bring the rig safely into the middle of the pit.

As the rig touch down, three automated low loaders drove into position around each of the rig's three jacks. The low loaders grabbed the jacks and lifted the whole rig in unison.

The low loaders then transported the rig through large doors in the side of the pit, and onto the taxi way.

The rig was taxied past several hangers and then came to a stop outside a large hanger at the far end of the space port.

The crew watched and waited for the large hanger doors to open.

With the doors open the low loaders moved the rig inside.

The hanger was large. It had room for a dozen rigs of size like their own. However, it was empty but for a single cruiser sitting in the far corner.

"Why are we being stuck way back here, at the back of the port?" Annee asked. "I just checked the port arrivals and departures board. This place is half empty."

"Oh shit", Marr exclaimed. She had been enjoying watching their entrance to the hanger.

"What?" Dukk said looking up from the controls.

Dukk stared out at what had got Marr's attention.

The cruiser in the far corner had the words 'The Blue Weekender' written on its side.

The low loaders drove to a pad just inside the door. They then turned the rig around, so it was facing out and then stopped. The low loaders placed the rig onto the hanger floor, before disappearing towards the hanger doors. Which had already started to close. The crew now had an unobstructed view of the cruiser.

"There are security guards beside the ramp," Marr commented.

"Bognath, come in here," Luna blurted into the comms. "We need to ID someone."

Moments later Bognath joined the others in the cockpit. They were all at the front of the cockpit looking over at the cruiser.

"What's going on?" Bognath asked.

"Come over here and have a look," Luna said as she moved out of the way to give Bognath a clear view.

"Do you recognise those security guards?" she asked.

"Yep, definitely part of the security detail for the late Craig Atesoughton", Bognath replied.

"Why do they need people standing guard at half four in the morning?" Annee asked.

"Look at the portholes," Marr said. "The blinds are drawn but it is clear the lights are all on. There are people in there doing something."

"The party," Dukk said in a sober tone.

"What do we do?" Annee asked.

"We get our guns," Luna said as she turned to leave.

"Wait," Marr said coolly. "This doesn't feel right. It is almost as if someone knew we were coming and why we are here,"

"I agree," Dukk said. "Putting us in this hanger with only one other old cruiser isn't efficient use of resources."

"We'd better take it slowly," Marr said.

"What if the girls are being harmed right now," Annee said bluntly. "We can't wait any longer."

"I agree," Mentor said quietly. "The time for stealth is over. I suggest we hit them now and hit them hard."

Mentor then turned to look at Marr.

3

Marr looked around. Everyone was now looking at her.

After a moment of hesitation, she stood up and moved to the middle of the cockpit.

"Luna, top hatch. Get ready to take down those two guards. I will give the word. Tranquilizers only. We may need to talk to them."

"Copy," Luna said as she pushed out of the group and bolted for the cockpit door.

"We need eyes inside," Marr said. "Ann, your drone flying skills are uncanny, let's get you the nano drones. We'll have them ready to fly up that ramp the moment Luna takes down the two guards. We'll fit the gas canisters just in case."

"I know where they are," Annee said as she got up and headed for the door.

"Suzzona, we have a job to do," she added as she passed through the passenger seating area.

"Bognath," Marr said as she reached the cockpit door. "You will be on cover, once the guards are down. We don't want any surprises. Use tranquilizers where possible. The moment those two guards drop, get out in the hanger, do a quick wide sweep but keep your head down."

"Got it," Bognath said as he turned and followed the others.

"Bazzer, we want your video scrambler running just before Luna fires."

"I'll be ready," Bazzer said.

"Dukk?" Marr asked rhetorically as she turned back towards the front of the cockpit.

"I suggest we need him in there," Mentor said. "After we have it secured, we might need to make some hard calls."

Marr nodded.

"We need someone watching the rig," Dukk said. "We are still running hot and subject to normal post landing shutdown protocols."

"Bazzer?" Marr asked.

Bazzer nodded.

"Perfect, and perhaps Annee and Suzzona can help after running the drones," Dukk replied. "I'll wait up here until I get the word to come over."

"Good," Marr replied. "Mentor, let's get our weapons."

"Are we there yet?" Trence slurred as Marr and Mentor passed through the passenger area.

"Let's get you to your cabin," Mentor said. "I am sure that landing has worn you out. A rest is what the doctor orders."

"Goody," Kimince slurred.

Ten minutes later, Marr, Mentor and Bognath were standing at the top of the ramp. They had changed into the blue uniforms of the haulier. Their weapons were concealed.

"Set?" Marr prompted into the comms.

"Check," Luna replied immediately.

"Check," came the reply from Annee.

Marr and Mentor walked down the ramp. They stopped briefly before making a b-line towards the cruiser. Their pace was intentional but unrushed.

Marr kept her eyes on the two guards. It was clear they were watching their approach. She wasn't worried about that. Nor was she concerned about them using their weapons. She knew Luna would have that covered from her spot at the upper hatch. Instead, Marr was looking for the slightest indication that they were going to alert whomever else might be in the cruiser.

Thirty metres out she saw the sign.

"Now", Marr said into the comms.

Things then happened very quickly.

The two guards dropped to the ground at the same moment as two dull rifle cracks echoed throughout the hanger.

Marr and Mentor erupted into a sprint.

Immediately their comms filled with coded chatter from the dozen nano drones. Annee had got the drones near the cruiser's ramp and activated them the moment she heard Marr give the signal. They had flown up the ramp and started streaming data. They quickly found their way through open doors and vents. Marr and Mentor already knew there was another guard at the top of the ramp and that there were no people on the lower level. The coded messages also gave other information like the number of rooms and directions to staircases.

Marr slowed her sprint slightly to signal to Mentor that he should go first. He would take out the guard at the top of the ramp.

Just shy of the bottom of the ramp, Mentor went to his knees and in the same motion fired three rounds up the ramp.

Marr launched over him and hit the ramp halfway up. She bounded up the ramp and then jumped over the slumped body of the third guard.

Ignoring the lower level, she made for the stairs.

The information from the nano drones had continued such that by the time Marr reached the middle level, she knew that it was the only level where she would find others.

Marr slowed her pace once she reached the top of the stairs.

Before her was a corridor with doors running down either side.

Mentor came up behind her.

They looked at each other and nodded. They knew the first room to their right was the best bet. The nano drones had reported that room as having the greatest cluster of larger persons. Most likely the men not the girls.

Marr interacted with the door panel. Her highly specialised technical skills finally coming to good use. The panel blue screened, and the door immediately swung open.

Mentor dashed into the room guns blazing. Marr followed.

4

The room was a large bedroom. On the bed, two girls huddled together against the bedhead. They were naked and sobbing. A third girl was kneeling on the floor near the bed. In the room also, were three overweight men in their late fifties or early sixties. They too were naked.

"Come on bitch, make it look like you want it, or I will hit you again," one of the men could be heard saying as Marr rushed in.

"Back against the wall," Marr screamed at the startled men.

The men stood back. The girl on the floor jumped up and joined the other two.

"Face the wall, hands behind your back," Marr shouted.

One of the men looked down to the coffee table near the bed. Two handguns were sitting on the top of the table.

"Go on! Give me a reason!" Marr said aggressively.

The man turned and joined the others facing the wall.

Mentor rushed up behind the men and secured their hands with zip ties. He then pushed them each onto the ground.

They groaned as he forced them to sit against the wall so he could secure their legs.

"What the hell is going on? Do you know who we are?" shouted one of the men.

"Shut it," Mentor shouted as he jammed his elbow into the man's leg.

The man squealed with pain.

"Are there any others?" Marr said firmly towards the girls.

The girls pointed towards the door.

"Where is Zarra?" one of the girls wept.

"What do you mean?" Marr asked.

"They hurt her. They took her away."

"How many of you are there," Marr asked anxiously.

"There were twelve," another girl said between sobs.

"Are there any other men?"

"The three guards," the girl said.

"Pilots?"

"They left when we got here."

"Mentor, I'm going to look in the other rooms," Marr said as she left.

Marr opened the two other rooms that she knew contained people. She found eight more girls. All naked. All distressed.

"Dukk, you are up," Marr said into the comms when she stepped back into the corridor. "Luna, get over here now too. Annee and Suzzona grab twelve sets of clothes and join us. Straight up the ramp. Stairs to the second level. Bognath, hold the perimeter."

Marr stood in the corridor and took several deep breaths. She was struggling but she knew she needed to hold it together.

She returned to the room with the men.

"Girls, go and join the others," Marr said in a firm but kind tone.

The girls jumped up and dashed out.

Marr walked over to the men and kicked the first one hard in the stomach. He screamed in agony.

She then crouched down closer to the second man.

"Where is the twelfth girl?" Marr said quietly to the man.

"She got what she deserved. Find her yourself, bitch," was the snide response.

Marr swung her elbow into the man's face and stood up as the man cried out.

Marr looked at Mentor. His expression was blank. She knew he was getting in state for what was needed next.

"Marr?" Dukk called as he reached the corridor.

"First room on the right," Marr replied.

"Oh shit," Dukk said when he entered. "Are the girls here?"

"Yes, across the corridor," Marr replied. "I'm going to search the rest of the cruiser. You need to help Mentor talk to these animals."

"What's the lay?" Luna announced as she appeared at the door.

Marr waved her in.

"We have a missing girl. You go up. I'll go down."

"On it," Luna said as she dashed out.

Marr followed her.

"What's the approach here?" Dukk asked after a moment of finding the silence deafening.

"We decide who we pity most", Mentor said in a serious tone. "They will die first and not have to watch what is coming."

"What do you want?" one of the men blurted.

"What happened in Mayfield?" Mentor said in a harsh tone.

"What are you talking about?" the man asked in reply.

"Around the time of the assassination. Why did you leave?"

"They ordered us to take the girls and get out of there. Then Craig goes and gets himself assassinated by that flaky observer," the man answered.

"Shut up you idiot," another man blurted. "We owe these nut jobs nothing."

Mentor stepped back and looked at Dukk.

Dukk looked over and frowned.

"We are not animals, Mentor," Dukk said in his mind. He hoped Mentor was reading his signals.

Meanwhile, Marr had found a small hold on the lower level. It contained several storage crates.

She paused and took a deep breath as she opened the first crate.

"Empty," she said aloud as she breathed out.

She opened three more crates. All empty.

By the time she got to the fifth crate she was feeling hopeful.

The sight as she opened the crate caught her off guard and she had to force back a vomit.

"Nothing up top! Anything down here?" Luna announced as she dashed into the hold.

Luna came over and looked over Marr's shoulder. She then nearly fell over. She had to brace herself against Marr to stop herself toppling into the crate on top of the broken body of the young woman.

"Bastards," Luna yelled as she turned and ran towards the door.

"Wait," Marr screamed as she ran after her.

Marr only just kept up with Luna, but she didn't catch her.

Marr sensed the anger. Things appeared to slow down as they reached the door to the cabin with the men.

Dukk and Mentor were standing near the bed and were also caught off guard by Luna's speed.

She dashed to the coffee table, collected a gun as she spun around.

She fired two clean shots right between the eyes of two of the men. Then she grabbed the head of the third and pushed it back. She shoved the gun into his mouth and pulled the trigger. She then dropped the gun and stood back.

"Oh crap, Luna," Marr said with frustration as she reached the middle of the room.

Marr gave it a moment.

"Did you get any information?" she then said quietly as they looked at the pile of bodies.

"Not really," Dukk answered. "What now?"

"They again," Mentor muttered in a defeated tone before adding. "Who are they?"

Marr and Dukk looked over at Mentor.

"We need to find Tieanna," he muttered.

"How do we do that?" Dukk asked in an empathetic tone.

Mentor said nothing. Instead, he pulled out a knife and went over to the men. He cut the ties on the men's legs. Then he nudged them so he could cut the ties on their hands. He then used a cloth from his pocket to pick up the gun. He wiped the gun thoroughly before putting it in the last man's right hand. He then helped the dead man fire two further shots into the chests of the other two men.

"What the hell, Mentor?" Dukk exclaimed.

"He is making it look like a murder suicide," Marr said quietly.

"Marr, we need the video feeds on this cruiser disappeared," Mentor said as he headed for the door.

"Yep, I'll overrun the buffers now. In thirty minutes, it will be only static in the storage," Marr answered as she followed him out the door.

Dukk stood there in the middle of the room. Luna was still looking down at the men.

"Luna, are you okay?" Dukk asked after a few moments of silence.

"No, not really," she replied as she turned and walked out the door.

Dukk headed to the corridor. He closed the door behind him.

Annee and Suzzona came along the corridor towards him.

"We heard more shooting," Annee said as she reached him. "And Luna just brushed past us on the stairs. She looked odd."

"In here," Marr said from a nearby room.

Dukk followed Marr's voice.

"Oh, I'll leave you to it," Dukk said as he looked in the door at the girls on the bed.

Annee and Suzzona brushed past him.

Dukk stood back into the corridor and waited. He wasn't sure what to do next.

After a few minutes, Marr appeared at the doorway.

"Dukk, will you help Mentor? He is on the lower level in the hold. Take these."

Marr handed Dukk a pile of sheets.

Dukk found his way to the lower level and went looking for the storage hold.

He found it just off the hall that served the external door.

Within Mentor and Bognath were lifting one of the security guards into a crate.

"What happens when he wakes up?" Dukk asked as he reached them.

"He won't be waking up. Luna made sure of that as she left," Bognath said.

Taking a second glance, Dukk realised the stupidity of his question. The guard's neck was clearly broken.

Dukk looked around. The bodies of the two other guards were also in crates.

Then he saw the girl. He gagged as he forced back a vomit.

Mentor put a hand on Dukk shoulder.

"Let's lay the sheets on the floor. We'll wrap the girl in them. We can't leave her here. We will take her with us and give her a proper burial."

Together they lifted Zarra from the crate and rolled her in the sheets.

"I'll carry her over," Bognath said when they were done. "I feel responsible for this mess."

Dukk and Mentor helped Bognath lift the wrapped body onto his shoulder.

They watched him leave and then returned upstairs.

Marr was alone in the corridor. She was looking despondent.

Dukk came over to her and wrapped his arms around her. She hugged him back and breathed deeply.

"Are the girls sorted?" Dukk asked.

"Yes, Annee and Suzzona have taken them back to the Imhullu."

"You did good, Marr," Mentor said as he watched them.

"Not for Zarra," Marr replied as she released the hug with Dukk and looked at Mentor.

"We couldn't have got here in time for her," Mentor said. "This is not on you."

"We didn't get the information we needed."

"It is what it is," Mentor replied.

"Will we get out of here?" Dukk asked. "Make for Earth?"

"Did you see the state of those girls," Marr replied. "They aren't well. The launch could kill them."

"We'll have to sit tight for a few days," Mentor said.

"What about the mess in there? Won't it draw attention?" Dukk asked.

"We'll lock the cruiser doors and hope no one comes near it. It is out here for a reason."

"Yes, I am wondering about that," Dukk answered.

"Let's go," Marr said.

"Yep," Dukk replied.

Dukk opened his comms as he followed Marr to the lower level.

"Bazzer, let's go to slow running. We'll need to hang here for a few days."

There was no reply.

"Bazzer?" Dukk said again into the comms.

Marr stopped at the landing and looked back at Dukk.

She then drew her gun and turned towards the top of the ramp.

She approached the ramp and ducked her head to look out.

"Put the guns down and keep your hands where we can see them," came a voice from the hanger floor.

Chapter 11 – Unearthing

1

Marr looked at Mentor. He pulled out his gun and put it on the rig floor.

Marr nodded and did the same and then slowly headed down.

Mentor followed Marr.

Dukk made his way down last.

Several armed personnel stood just back from the ramp. All with their weapons raised.

"Dellington, captain of the Imhullu, you need to come with us," one of the men shouted.

Dukk paused before remembering his alias.

"What for?" Dukk shouted back.

"Because I say so and I've got a big gun," said the man with a sarcastic smile.

Dukk paused.

"You two as well," the man said as he waved his gun at Marr and Mentor.

The leader stepped back and pointed towards carts sitting in the middle of the hanger.

Across the hanger they could see the Imhullu. A group of armed guards were there too.

"Don't worry about them," the leader said on noticing where Dukk was looking. "Behave and they will be unharmed."

Marr, Dukk and Mentor walked to the first cart and got in. Guards got in behind them and the leader got in to the front next to the driver.

The cart drove across the hanger, away from the main doors. As they approached the wall of the hanger, an opening appeared. They passed through and found themselves in the glass tunnels they saw on approach.

The cart took them to the large building in the central part of the port. Within this building they were driven over to the ID gateway in front of the hyperloop station. There were a few people moving about, but overall, it was very quiet.

The leader and the guards then escorted Marr, Dukk and Mentor through some side doors thus bypassing the ID gateway. The doors gave them access to the hyperloop platform.

They all got onto the first hyperloop carriage and took seats.

The hyperloop carriage doors shut and it started to accelerate away from the port and towards the hillside.

The passage through the hillside took only a few minutes. On the other side they were thrust into an array of glass and metal medium height buildings. The buildings sparkled and shone, even in the low intensity of the system's red dwarf sun. The wealth on clear display.

The hyperloop took them to a tall building in the centre of the settlement.

When the doors of the hyperloop carriage opened, Marr, Dukk and Mentor were escorted to a single door on the side of a large reception area and security checkpoint.

On the other side of the door were doors to an elevator lift.

The lift doors were already open. The doors closed behind them as they entered, and the lift started to ascend.

When the lift doors opened, they were looking at a large office.

More security guards were standing near a large desk in the middle of the room. At the desk was a man with fair complexion, light blue eyes, and dark brown hair. He looked a little younger than Dukk.

He waved at them to come over.

"Sit, please," the man said as they reached the desk.

The man was pointing to three seats lined up next to each other opposite the desk.

Dukk led the group over to the chairs but didn't sit. He looked at the man. He looked familiar in an odd sort of way. Dukk couldn't place it. The man did the same. Both noticed the other.

"Have we met before?" the man asked Dukk after a moment.

"I don't think so," Dukk answered. "Who are you?"

The man laughed as he flicked up the profiles of Dukk, Marr and Mentor.

"Dellington, nope never heard of you. You are clearly new to this part of the galaxy if you don't know who I am."

"I know who you are," Mentor said.

"Who am I then, Themonk?" the man said smiling at Mentor.

"Craig Atesoughton, the third," Mentor said calmly not missing a step on hearing his new alias.

Craig smiled.

"Enough of this. Please sit," Craig said as he swiped away the profiles.

They took seats. Dukk in the middle. Marr on his left. Mentor on his right.

Craig sat forward and continued to speak.

"I need to find the level seven observer, Thosmas. I understand you brought Thosmas to Mayfield. Thosmas is hard to reach at the best of times and seemingly impossible in recent days. Where is Thosmas now? And don't say, Imhullu. We just searched it."

"I don't know," Dukk answered. "Our job is done in that regard."

"And yet here you are. You have business of some sort with those men and girls. And the observer accused of my father's assassination is on your fine rig. Drugged up too I might add. Which is also a curious thing. Anyway, I need to find Thosmas. I think you can help me. Besides, it is in your interest."

"What interest?"

"Breathing."

"Perhaps if I was to know more of what is it that you need, I might be able to help," Dukk said in a polite manner.

"Let's cut the crap, Dellington. Thosmas sent you to deal with the men and these girls. What else do you know about all of this. And think carefully before you answer."

Dukk said nothing. Partly because he wasn't used to his new alias. But mostly because he felt the statement didn't need a response.

Then Mentor spoke.

"Thosmas was acting on your grandfather's behalf to have your father assassinated."

Craig looked shocked. After a moment he spoke in a suspicious tone.

"Who are you? Have we met? How do you know this? Thosmas is discreet. There is no way you could know that."

"I am the assassin that Thosmas gave the contract to."

Craig sat back and his guards stepped forward.

"So, assassin, what name do you go by?" Craig asked cautiously.

"Most know me as Mentor."

2

Craig's expression changed. There was a touch of amusement in it.

"So, the rumours are true. The legend is real. Well, I never. I heard the name floating about. Even the port logs showed a 'Mentor' on that G5 rig Kimince was on. But I wasn't sure. It was how you got in and out of Mayfield. That makes sense now. So, Mentor what else do you know."

"How about you tell me? Now you know I am real and if the legendary stories are as you suggest, you are in grave danger. Your security people here won't be enough!" Mentor said calmly.

Four more security guards rushed in.

Craig waved at them to stand down, and then sat back in his seat.

"The assassination was meant to look like suicide done with assistance of his team," Craig said with a grin. "It went bad. You slipped up. The observer got caught up in it. The girls got moved. Now you and Thosmas are trying to cover your tracks. How you crafted your own disappearance is baffling."

"I don't slip up," Mentor replied calmly.

"But you dropped blindly into my net here this morning?"

"Don't be so sure about that. Like I said, I don't slip up. Those men arriving here had nothing to do with you. You simply took advantage of their arrival. Perhaps it is you who fell into my trap!"

Craig looked puzzled. Dukk too was getting a sense that he was late to the party again.

"Rubbish," Craig said half heartily, doing his best to deflect Mentor's insinuation that he knew about the trap.

Mentor said nothing.

After a moment of silence, Craig laughed.

"You aren't here to rescue the girls," he said. "You are here to talk to my father's friends. You are trying to figure out who got in your way."

Mentor said nothing for a moment, then he spoke.

"We are here to protect the girls."

"Why?"

"Keeping the girls out of harm's way was a specific part of the plan."

"That wasn't in the instructions I gave."

"But you didn't give the instructions to Thosmas. Did you? Someone else delivered your grandfather's instructions to Thosmas."

Craig looked concerned. He then sat forward.

"Taking out Tieanna was never part of the deal! What have you done with her?"

This time Mentor sat up. His demeanour changed slightly. There was a hint of concern. He said nothing.

Craig looked puzzled for a moment. He then sat back.

"You don't know where she is either?"

Mentor said nothing.

Craig looked towards the glass windows that circled the office. The night sky was clearly visible even with the lights from the buildings below.

After a moment of looking out he spoke again whilst still gazing towards the night sky.

"She stopped answering messages the evening of the assassination. We searched the usual places. Then there was that accident with the G5 rig. It looked connected. However, there was no trace. I feared she was either on that rig or had been dumped out there somewhere. Then Thosmas shows up in Mayfield. And a day later, you show up here and start blowing people's heads off."

Mentor stared.

Marr was watching the exchange. There was something else in Mentor's usually expressionless demeanour. He was showing signs of fear.

Marr looked back at Craig. He looked intrigued.

"Perhaps he sees it too," Marr thought.

Craig's expression then changed. His face lit up as if a great insight had just been realised. He turned back to Mentor.

"You are Septemo!" Craig said quietly.

Mentor sat back in his seat.

"Mentor is Septemo," Craig continued with a giggle. "Holy shit. That is why you know things that you shouldn't. It also explains lots of things that confused me over the years. That is why this has interest to you. You aren't here to find out what happened, kill those men or deal with those girls. You are here to find Tieanna. You thought I had done something to her?"

Mentor said nothing.

Marr stared at Mentor.

His expression had changed again. There was a clear sign of concern. Dukk looked on too. He was confused.

"More mysteries," Dukk thought to himself.

Craig looked at them all. His expression went from amusement to intrigue.

"That is interesting," Craig said after a moment. "Septemo, your colleagues here don't appear to be up to speed. Will I or will you, tell them who Septemo is to Tieanna?"

"They know the relationship," Mentor said as he turned to face Marr and Dukk. "It was my nick name in the incubation centre. The name Mentor came after that. Tieanna continued to use Septemo privately. And clearly, she shared stories of those times with those she trusted and cared about."

Mentor turned back towards Craig as he said the last sentence.

Craig blushed.

"So, Craig," Mentor said after a moment. His tone carried a more authoritative nature than the last exchange. "You have been tracking us. You put is in the hanger with The Blue Weekender. You had hoped it would draw us in and in doing so shed light on what happened to Tieanna. That hasn't exactly worked out how you'd hoped."

"Neither for you from what I hear about the state of those men in the rig," Craig added smugly.

"Not necessarily. We got what we needed."

"So where is Tieanna?"

"We are working on it, but it will take a little more time."

"My resources are at your disposal."

"I have my own resources. But I do need some help with a couple of things."

"Fine, but I assume you will ensure those girls never surface again. You'll disappear them. That was the agreement."

Marr and Dukk sat up and looked shocked.

"No," Mentor answered firmly. "That wasn't the agreement I was working under."

"Are you breaking the contract?"

"Your father is out of the way. His parties will be no more. That was the agreement."

"Fine."

"So, I expect payment in full."

"Yep, the legend is real. Fine!"

After answering, Craig flicked some panels into the air before them.

"Where will I send the credits?" Craig asked.

"To the rig. To the captain here. It will be shared out from there."

Craig nodded at Dukk.

Dukk lifted his wrist to catch the virtual transfer as Craig flicked it into the air.

Dukk gasped as he opened the message. The message showed a hundred million credits.

Craig laughed on seeing Dukk's reaction.

"You had no idea who was in your midst young captain. The best doesn't come cheap."

Marr looked on in surprise too.

3

"So, Septemo, you said you need help with a couple of things," Craig said casually as he sat back.

"Yes, I need your intel relating to the events around the time of the assassination."

"It won't do you any good. We went through it thoroughly. You aren't the only ones using scramblers it would appear."

"Perhaps a second set of eyes might see something you have missed."

"Fine. I'll organise it. Where are you bound now? Back to Earth?"

"Eventually, but we need to figure out whose hand is in this."

"You said a couple of things?"

"I did. The other thing that is needed, is for 'Mentor' to disappear while I figure out the next step in finding Tieanna. I need your help with that."

"How?"

"Allow rumours to circulate that the real 'Mentor' was on the G5 rig and is dead. It won't be hard as many suspected that I was on that rig. Help make everyone think that I am dead."

"That could come back to me, if it is thought one of the best assassins in the galaxy was around Mayfield at the time of the assassination. With the observer being freed people will talk. That could bring heat."

"You can handle it. It is necessary if we want to find Tieanna. I need to be free to move about. I don't want to be watching my back."

"Fine, now get those girls away from here," Craig said as he stood up. "I think we are done."

Marr stood up. She looked cross.

"These girls are dehydrated and exhausted. They are not up to a launch. It could kill them. They need wholesome food and rest."

Craig looked at Marr. He sighed.

"So, sit tight in the rig until they are well enough for launch."

"Tieanna would have given them a place to recover," Mentor said firmly. "Somewhere safe, but away from the maddening crowd and prying eyes."

Craig sighed again. "How long?"

"Maybe a week," Mentor answered.

"For fecks sake," Craig replied as he sat down. "How many of you?"

"Twenty-one," Mentor replied.

Craig waved his hands in front of him. A head appeared in the air.

"Are any of the large retreats free for the next seven days?" Craig said to the head.

"No, all occupied," was the reply.

"Where am I scheduled to be?"

"Emerald Valley."

"Change my plans. I'll stay here. I have guests that are in the need of some quiet time. Contact housekeeping and let them know to make ready for a large group for seven nights. They will use the entire retreat. Clear any other bookings."

Craig took his gaze away from the video call and looked directly at the three of them.

"Do you want the staff there?"

"No, we can manage on our own," Mentor replied.

"Fresh or rehydratable food?"

"Fresh food?"

"You can cook?"

"We have that covered."

"Fine," Craig said as he turned back to the face hovering above his desk.

"Ensure the fridges and larders are fully stocked. Then, tell the staff to take the week off. Send access codes and instructions to the captain of the Imhullu. Also, get onto air traffic control. Organise a flight plan for the Imhullu. Immediate clearance."

Craig looked up as he flicked away the image.

"There is a hanger up there. I take it that the girls are up for a twenty-minute flight?"

Mentor nodded.

"Good. So, the resort is yours for the next seven days. Use and take what you need, then be gone. Goodbye," Craig said as he rose for the second time.

The security people stepped in, beside the desk. It was clearly an indication that Marr, Dukk and Mentor were now leaving.

Marr paused. A burning question consumed her. There was also something oddly familiar about Craig.

212

"I have a question," she blurted firmly.

Craig said nothing.

"If it isn't too bold," she added on seeing his lack of response.

Craig still said nothing.

"Why did your grandfather want your father assassinated?" she asked more gently than the tone she used initially.

Craig looked on in a puzzled expression. Then he answered.

"Same reason as always?"

"Which is?"

"Isn't that obvious. He didn't keep his sordid activities under the radar."

"What do you mean by always?"

"That is too bold," Craig laughed.

Marr kept a blank expression and stood her ground.

Craig sighed. "It started years ago, before I was born. They fell out when Granddad first found out about my father's taste for hurting young girls. Now, I suggest you get out of my sight before I decide to resolve this mess directly."

Mentor stood and moved away from the desk. Dukk followed.

Marr sensed Craig was bluffing. So, she continued to hold his stare, but softened her expression slightly.

His expression changed slightly too. It had a hint of gratitude. A sign that he was glad to have been able to share without feeling judged.

Marr felt she almost saw a slight smile.

After a brief pause, she smiled warmly, then turned and followed Mentor and Dukk.

4

Their return to the rig happened in reverse. Except once at the port, the security people put them into an auto taxi cart, handed them their weapons and waved them off. Dukk sat in the back, leaving the front seats for Marr and Mentor.

As the cart pulled away, Marr turned to Mentor.

"Did you know Craig planned to trap us?"

"No."

"You were bluffing."

Mentor nodded.

"What now?" Marr asked.

"What do you mean?" Mentor replied.

"The men are dead. We got nothing. We don't know who 'they' are?"

"Not at all. We know lots more."

"Like what?"

"We know junior isn't behind the sabotage. It could still be a new internal powerplay, but not Craig directly."

"What else?"

"We also know that whomever they are, they spoke to the men before the assassination. For what reason we don't know. But it sounds like moving the girls was unrelated to the assassination. And we know those men weren't from around here."

"How?"

"If they were connected to the Atesoughton family, Craig would have delt with it himself. No one would question his authority around here. He didn't. He used us."

"But that was to trap us. He wanted to get to Thosmas."

"If that is all he wanted, he could have just put us in a normal hanger and took us when we tried to go through the ID gateway."

"So, we need to find out who the men were."

"Yes."

"How?"

Mentor opened his wrists and flicked up some images. It was the faces of the three men after being shot.

"Suzzona might have seen them around Mayfield," Mentor said looking at the images. "Failing that, there are others we can ask."

"So, we should get onto that as soon as possible."

"Maybe."

"Aren't you worried Tieanna is in danger?"

"Yes, but if she was to be killed, she would be dead already. And, if not, they need her for something. We need to find out what that is before we go ruffling too many feathers."

"So, what do we do now?" Marr asked.

"The week here will be crucial in bringing the girls back from the brink. They won't need to be red pilled as all their previous beliefs and concepts of what is real have just been shattered. However, they will need to build a new set of beliefs before they spiral too far into the abyss of hopelessness."

"What are you thinking?" Marr asked.

"We follow the typical formula."

"A non-mandatory, opt-in program of silent reflection, structured lessons, storytelling, physical training, and shared meals. That type of thing?"

"Exactly. I would like you to lead the program."

"Lead, no way. I have only ever been a mentor."

"You are ready. I will be here to guide you. And Luna is ready to step up to mentoring. Besides, I am going to have my hands full with Kimince and Trence."

"Who will do the story sessions? The program leaders always brought the students to Teacher."

"I will fulfil that role for now. At least until we are back on Earth. I will be doing story telling sessions for the observers anyway. Annee, Dukk, Bognath and Suzzona will benefit from joining those sessions too. It makes sense to combine everyone in the same space."

"How do we get started?"

"You know the format of the program. What do you think will work to get started?"

"We start as we intend to proceed?"

"Yes, but how?"

"I guess we have a meal together, everyone, as soon as possible. At the end of the meal, I set out what will be available to them for the week if they want to come along."

"Which will be?"

"Early start, silent daily gratefulness and intentions practice, breakfast together, morning story circle, structured training, group freeform activity, afternoon story circle, light exercise, evening group meal together, open sharing and then rest."

"Good. The free form activity in the middle of the day will also provide the space to do chores. It will be important that the girls get familiar immediately with pulling their own weight."

"That is why you suggested no staff."

"Yes, but also we want to be free to talk openly."

"How will we get the girls to sign up to the chores?" Marr asked.

"Dukk?" Mentor asked. He was aware that Dukk was listening.

"Let's run it like the rig," Dukk answered. "I will suggest to Annee that she create a rota."

"Cool," Marr answered. "What about security?"

"Let's see what the site is like," Mentor said.

The cart dropped them in the middle of the hanger.

As they watched the cart leave, a loud crack drew their attention. The hanger doors were opening. Three low loaders came racing through the gap. They drove over to the pad and stopped just short.

Marr looked at Dukk.

"They are waiting for us to authorise the lift," Dukk said as he turned and headed towards the rig.

Annee and Bazzer were standing at the bottom of the ramp waiting for them.

"The security detail searched the rig, then just left without saying anything. What's going on?" Annee asked when they reached her.

"Lots," Dukk replied flippantly. "I'm going to do the external inspection and then raise the ramp. Marr, will you get into the cockpit and start the checklist. The launch plan should be on the message queue too. Bazzer, let's get this bird hot. We are leaving."

Bazzer stood there and stared at Dukk.

Dukk noticed the stare and took a deep breath. He counted to ten in his head.

With better clarity he spoke again.

"I am sorry Ann, excuse my tone. It is going to be fine. We'll debrief in the cockpit as we taxi."

Bazzer nodded, turned, and headed up the ramp. Marr was right behind him.

"The girls aren't fit enough for a launch?" Annee stated as they passed her.

"We aren't going far. Just moving the rig. Where are the girls?"

"In the lounge on the middle level. Suzzona is with them."

"Get them into their seats up top."

"Do they need g-suits," Annee asked.

"Nope, we'll take it nice and handy."

"I'll help," Mentor said.

5

Marr made her way upstairs and into the crew mess. She went over to Luna's cabin and knocked gently.

After a moment, the door swung open.

Bognath had opened it. He was looking worse for wear. His face was heavily bruised. He smiled slightly and held the door open for Marr to enter. He closed the door as he left.

Luna was lying on her back, loosely wearing a dressing gown. Her hands were behind her head, and she was looking up at the ceiling.

"Did the shower help?" Marr asked softly.

"A little," Luna answered.

Marr sat on the end of the bed. She didn't look directly at Luna. Instead, she just looked forward and cleared her mind. She waited.

After a minute of silence, Luna spoke again.

"I failed. In the crucial moment, I couldn't do it. I couldn't control my anger. I messed up. Now we won't have the information we need."

"It is a bridge we all must cross. It will stand to you next time when the choices are harder."

"How could they be harder?"

"When the evidence of the evil isn't as clear."

"That doesn't help with the pain."

"Only time can help with that."

"But what of uncovering what happened in Mayfield?"

"Things have moved forward; it will be fine."

"What things?"

"Get dressed and join us in the cockpit and we'll share what happened."

Luna didn't move.

"These girls are going to need your help. They will look up to you more than before."

"Is that a good thing or a bad thing?"

"Neither. Coming?" Marr asked as she stood up.

"Yep," Luna said softly as she swung her body off the bed.

As Marr left Luna's cabin, she found Bognath leaning against the table looking towards her. He took an ice pack off his cheek and put it on the table next to him.

"Is she okay?" Bognath asked.

Marr shrugged her shoulders.

"Are you okay?" she asked.

"I'll survive," Bognath answered.

"What happened?"

"They came in fast. By the time I put Zarra's body on the hanger floor, they were on top of me. I had no chance. They were jamming my comms too. Looked like a set up."

"It was. We are debriefing in the cockpit. Glad you are okay."

"Thanks."

Fifteen minutes later the rig was sitting in the middle of one of the launch pits.

The debrief was done. Bognath and Suzzona had taken their seats in the passenger seating area.

Dukk sat quietly as he watched the external cameras. He watched the low loaders as they left the pit. Then he watched the huge doors as they closed behind the low loaders.

"We have clearance," Marr said, breaking the silence.

Dukk reached over and authorised the next step in the launch plan.

The rig started to tremble as the vertical thrusters engaged and the rig started to lift into the air. As the rig gained height the main engines engaged to push the rig forward.

Their trajectory took them on an arc. Initially they travelled away from the settlement. Then they came back on it via another valley.

No sooner had they reached cruising speed when the vertical thrusters engaged again as the rig prepared for landing.

They had a clear view of the resort as they slowed.

The resort consisted of a large multi-story building built into the hill side. There was lots of glass and white stone. Surrounding the building was opens spaces. The entire complex was covered in a huge glass dome. The daylight emulation wasn't due for another thirty minutes, so their view was enabled by large spotlights in the grounds.

Further down the hillside was a hanger. The doors were open.

The rig slowed as it approached the platform outside the hanger. Instead of touching down, the autopilot navigated the rig into the hanger and set it down inside. The huge doors started to close the moment the rig came to rest on its jacks.

The short trip and unfamiliar sights had been a nice distraction.

The touch down brought them back to focus.

"Ann, what did you find out?" Dukk asked as he started the post landing checklist.

Before the launch, Dukk had shared the resort access and instructions with Annee. She had been going over them.

"It is pretty straightforward," Annee answered. "Once inside there is no security. We can move about freely. There aren't even any comms receivers in most rooms. Only the entrance hall, study, service areas and the main corridors."

"Having to physically find someone if you want to talk to them. That will be odd," Bazzer commented.

"How do we get inside?" Marr asked.

"There are a couple of lifts at the back of the hanger. A guest lift and a service lift. The guest lift opens into the entrance hall. I suggest we take that lift and I'll do an orientation briefing up there."

"Sounds good to me," Bazzer announced.

"What will we take with us?" Marr asked.

"Why don't some of us go up first and check it out?" Annee said.

"Do you know what?" Dukk said as he stood up. "This looks safe. I think we should all go up together. Why don't we shut down the rig and then all go? We can have a look around and then come get anything we feel we might need. I for one think we've done enough double checking everything for today."

Marr grinned.

Mentor nodded.

The others smiled too.

"Initiating shutdown," Bazzer announced.

Chapter 12 – Timeout

1

Ten minutes later everyone was standing in the entrance hall.

It had taken the lift three trips to bring everyone up.

Those that got up first had no issue waiting and gawking at the magnificence of the setting.

The entrance hall was three stories high.

A huge glass chandelier hung in the middle of the circular space. One side of the hall was glass from floor to ceiling. The view was of the grounds with the settlement in the distance in the base of the valley. The other side of the hall had a magnificent dark wood staircase that linked the three levels.

"Right," Annee said to get everyone's attention. "The ground floor has the living spaces. The kitchen, staff quarters and other services are towards the back. There are lounging and dining spaces to the right. The recreation area with pools, the gym, and games rooms, is to the left. As are the equipment rooms for venturing into the grounds and beyond."

"Multiple pools?" Luna said with interest. The others looked over. It was the first word she'd uttered since leaving the port. She suddenly looked self-conscious.

"Yes," Annee said quickly to draw the attention away from Luna. "Accommodation is on the two floors above us. The first level has twelve normal suites. The upper level has the master suite and three large, deluxe suites. The girls will double up on the first level. As captain, Dukk gets the master suite. Kimince and Trence get one of the large suites too. That leaves two large and six normal suites."

"I'm good with a normal suite," Bazzer said. "If it is anything like this hall, it will be the most luxury I'll have ever seen."

"Me too," Mentor added.

"Same," Suzzona said.

"Yep," Bognath nodded.

"Great. So, Luna and Marr, you each get a large suite on the upper level."

"This way, Kimi, let's find our room," Trence said taking Kimince's hand.

"Before you go," Dukk interrupted, "I'd like us to have a meal together. Given the time of the day, I'd suggest breakfast if everyone is happy with that. Perhaps in about an hour?"

"At seven a.m.?" Annee asked.

"Yep. That good with everyone?" Dukk asked.

Everyone nodded.

"Great," Annee said. "I understand you will find everything we will need for the next seven nights. Bedding, clothing, towels, food, and drink. However, after you've had a look around, if you want anything from the rig, let me know. I've put it in lock down so only Dukk and I can open it now. Grab me if you have any questions about using the facilities."

That was the signal Trence and Kimince were waiting for. The others watched and smiled as the two observers staggered and tripped their way up the stairs.

"Should I have told them there is a lift?" Annee giggled as the observers stumbled onto the first landing.

Everyone laughed including the girls. They had been huddled together slightly away from the crew.

The crew turned around to face the girls.

"Do you want to head up and pick your rooms?" Annee said gently. "You could take a shower? Freshen up before breakfast. And you can use the lift if you like. Over there."

The girls didn't move.

Marr looked at their faces. The giggle over the observers had lightened them a little, but their expressions still held utter terror. Most were looking at the floor.

Marr looked at Luna. She was staring at them too.

Marr knew what she needed to do.

"Girls, look at me," Marr said firmly.

The girls all looked up.

"Look at me. Look at Luna. Look at Annee. Look at Suzzona. Look at these men. Dukk, Mentor, Bazzer and Bognath. We are not the same as those we left behind on the Blue Weekender. We are here to help you. We are not here to harm you or save you for that matter. Only you can make that choice. However, be rest assured that from this moment forth we will see that no further harm comes to you."

While speaking the last sentence, Marr put her hand on the hilt of her knife.

She paused to allow that to sink in. Then she continued.

"Now, make your way up the stairs. Select a room in twos or threes, whatever you feel comfortable with. Close the door. Shower and wait. Luna will collect you when breakfast is ready."

Marr then turned and pointed towards the stairs. Partly because she could see the tears welling up in their eyes, but also because she was finding it hard to keep it together too.

The girls immediately started to move. They headed towards the stairs and lift.

Marr stepped over to Luna.

"Are you okay with that?"

Luna nodded and smiled. A tear was in the corner of her eye too.

When the girls disappeared into the corridor on the first level. Dukk turned to them all.

"Can we truly protect them here?" he asked.

Annee looked over at him.

"I asked our head of security to look into that very question."

She then turned to look at Bognath.

"I had a quick look at the security details during the flight over," he said. "I plan to take a closer look at things soon and then inspect the dome, outer grounds, and fences as soon as feasible. From what I could gather, access is only via the hanger which requires authorisation codes which must be shared via a flight plan. The glass dome is very strong and protected by automated ground to air missiles. The outer grounds are accessed via mantraps. There are three of them spread around the base of the dome. The mantraps are managed via the console in the utility room near the kitchen. There are two layers of fencing surrounding the outer grounds beyond the dome. There are motion detectors in the no-man's land in between. Several automated CDL turrets are located on the inner fence. They provide cover for the no-man's land. Air filtration systems provide quality air to the dome and for about the first two hundred metres into the outer grounds. Also, alarms go off in all rooms, if anything enters the no-man's land or if the hanger doors are activated."

"Sounds like you had more than a quick look," Bazzer laughed. "Must take a fine bit of juice to keep all that going."

"Yes, the resort has its own power supply. Dual hybrid solid fuel reactors. With two layers of redundancy across all components."

"I gather the short answer is yes," Dukk laughed.

Bognath nodded and smiled.

"Are there medical facilities here?" Mentor asked Annee.

"Yes, down to the left," Annee replied. "With the gym and pools and all that."

"I'll go and see what's there now. After breakfast, I'd suggest the girls get checked out. Perhaps in pairs. Annee you might organise it and accompany them. Luna you might want to help too."

Luna nodded.

"Yep, I'll organise it," Annee replied.

2

With that Bazzer, Luna and Bognath headed up the stairs. Mentor disappeared towards the left. Suzzona disappeared behind the stairs in the direction of the kitchen.

Dukk smiled at Marr and nodded in the direction of the stairs.

Marr nodded back but indicated that he should go ahead.

Marr then turned to Annee.

"I am going to share with Dukk if you want to take the other large suite?"

"Thanks, Marr," Annee said with a grin.

At that moment there was a scream from the direction of the kitchen.

Marr reacted immediately and dashed towards the door behind the stairs.

Annee did the same.

Dukk came down the stairs and followed them.

Marr rushed through the labyrinth of passageways and burst into the kitchen.

Suzzona was standing in the middle of a huge space. The space had multiple benches, sinks, grills, hobs, and ovens. Along three walls were stainless steel storage units. The final wall had floor to ceiling windows and sliding doors. Beyond the doors was a patio with garden furniture and a big stretch of a grass like surface. In the distance the edge of the dome could be seen where it met the ground. Beyond it were the fences and then hills. Several large doors to pantries and refrigeration units were open as were many of the storage unit doors.

"What happened?" Marr shouted as she tried to find the source of the alarm.

"A miracle," Suzzona shouted back in a hysterical manner.

"What?" Marr said in a confused tone.

"This place is unbelievable," Suzzona replied. "The best kitchen I've ever seen. And it is stocked to the brim with fresh amazing foods."

Marr burst into laughter as Annee and Dukk arrived. They looked confused.

"I need my knife set," Suzzona said as she headed for the door. "Ann, I need access to the rig. Coming?"

They could hear Suzzona still talking as her and Annee headed back towards the hall.

"What do you think we cook for breakfast, Ann. Perhaps eggs benedict. I saw fresh salmon too."

Dukk and Marr looked at each other and giggled, before falling into each other's arms.

"Don't go too far, Marr and Dukk," Suzzona shouted from the hall. "I'll need help cooking for this many."

After a deep kiss, Marr pulled back and whispered.

"You know I heard these elite mansions have multiple stairs and lifts. I am sure there is a quicker way to the master suite than going back via the entrance hall."

"Let's find it," Dukk replied.

A little later Marr and Dukk sat up after remembering Suzzona was expecting their help to make breakfast.

They both stopped and took stock of their surrounds. They had hardly noticed as they rushed into the room and leapt onto the bed.

After a giggle at each other, they got up and explored the huge space.

The double king size bed was in a separate large room off a large lounge and entertaining area. There was a separate reading room and a huge bathroom accessible via the bedroom. The bedroom also had a separate dressing room.

All rooms, including the bathroom, had floor to ceiling windows that gave a magnificent view of the valley.

After the quick inspection Dukk and Marr found each other again in front of the bedroom window. The view was mind blowing. The reddish glow of the sky was slowly being replaced by a white glow as the artificial daylight came into effect.

Marr snuggled into him as they watched.

"Shower?" Dukk suggested after a gentle kiss.

"Lead the way," Marr replied as he turned and led her towards the bathroom.

"Any ideas?" he asked Marr as they stood on the edge of a large space in the bathroom that appeared to be the shower.

"Warm tropical rain mode," Marr said firmly.

Instantly water started streaming from the ceiling.

Dukk laughed as he ventured into the watery space.

"Did you see what was in the dressing room?" Marr said as she enjoyed the sensation of the warm water.

"Nope," Dukk answered as he danced around.

"There are shelves full of new clothing. Casual and formal. All still in the printer packaging."

"I recall hearing Craig said we are to use and take what we need," Dukk said with a smile.

"He did indeed," Marr answered.

3

After the shower, Dukk and Marr raided the dressing room. They each found a fitted t-shirt, sweatpants, and sliders. The colours were earthly and warm. They felt a little odd.

"Wow, even in elite comfortable clothing you look hot," Dukk said with a grin as they stood together looking at the mirror.

"Thanks. Come on, we've got a job to do," Marr said with a chuckle.

They used the same lift they had used earlier. It put them into the service corridors on the ground floor.

The smells of food being cooked met them as they entered the kitchen.

"Be gentle. Don't shake the trays," Suzzona could be heard saying from a central counter as she took muffins off a large baking tray and placed them on plates.

The subject of her instruction was Bazzer. He was retrieving a large tray of poached eggs from an oven.

Suzzona and Bazzer looked showered and fresh. They were dressed in a similar fashion to Marr and Dukk. Except for the addition of black aprons.

"Oh, here they are," Bazzer laughed on seeing Marr and Dukk. "Showing up when it is ready to be eaten. And look what she is making me do."

"There is plenty to do still," Suzzona said as she stirred white sauce in a large pot.

"The table needs cutlery, mugs, glasses, and juices. The juices are in the fridges behind me. The table is through those double doors. Everything else is in the cupboards near the table."

"And Coffee?" Dukk asked cheekily.

"In there already. Large pots ready to pour."

Marr and Dukk went to the fridge, and each took two large jugs of juice. They carried them through the double doors. Beyond was a large banqueting hall with a long table. There were thirty chairs. The double height room had floor to ceiling glass windows on two adjacent sides. One view was of the garden. The other was the same as that of the entrance hall.

The table already had a white tablecloth and place mats.

They put the jugs in the middle of the table and went looking for the cutlery, mugs, and glasses.

As they started to set the table, Suzzona burst into the room with a large tray. On it were pots of yogurt and fruit.

"When that is done, come help bring out the plates. We are nearly ready," she said as she put the tray on a side table and disappeared back into the kitchen.

"That should do it," Marr said as they stood back to look at their handy work.

"This is surreal," Dukk said as he put his arm around her.

"It truly is," Marr answered.

They were looking at the table with the view of the garden behind it.

"What is?" came a voice from behind them. It was Luna.

She was standing between two large doors. She opened the doors fully and joined them.

"Oh, yes," she said as she too noticed the view.

Behind her came the girls. Followed by Annee, Bognath and then Mentor. They were all wearing the warm and earthly coloured t-shirts and sweatpants.

"Observers?" Marr asked on seeing that Mentor was alone.

"They are out cold," he replied. "Best let them sleep it off."

"Take a seat," Suzzona announced as she entered the space.

She was carrying three plates. Each contained two scrumptious looking eggs with slices of thick ham on muffins. They were covered with a creamy yellow sauce and garnished with fresh dill and parsley.

She placed the plates on the place mats and return to the kitchen.

Marr nudged Dukk and gave him a grin.

"Come on," she said as she turned and followed Suzzona.

With the food on the table everyone took their seats.

"Who wants to give thanks?" Dukk asked to get everyone's attention.

"Can I?" Luna asked.

"Of course," Dukk replied in a delighted but also surprised tone.

"Before we give thanks," Annee interrupted. "Can I suggest we take a moment of silent reflection in honour of Zarra?"

229

They all nodded and bowed their heads.

After about a minute, Luna cleared her throat.

Everyone looked up.

Luna then lifted her head and pulled her shoulders back.

"I express gratitude for all that was, is and yet to be. May Zarra find peace. May the days before us here in these surreal surrounds provide what we truly need. Focus on that which is real in the heart. Create the space so that the process can emerge. Honour that which serves you well. Engage in the journey as it unfolds. Thanks, I give."

"Thanks, I give," Dukk and the crew all replied.

The girls stared in dismay. Their expressions were somewhere between destress and awe. On top of the grief, it was clear that it was the first time they had witnessed the ritual of giving thanks or so many complete strangers acting in such a kind manner.

"Now we eat," Bazzer stated to lighten the mood, as he stuck a fork into the food before him.

The discussion during the meal mostly related to what they found in their rooms or the exploring they planned to do after eating.

At one stage one of the girls asked if the crew always ate like this. Suzzona answered the question bluntly by stating that the ingredients on that plate alone would take a week to earn in her old job in Mayfield. Having realised Suzzona had mis-interpreted the question, Annee said that yes, they try to eat together once a day, but what was on the table was typically rehydratable food boxes.

A little later the meal was done.

Volunteers were a plenty to help clear the table and pack the dishwashing machines. The girls were eager to lend a hand too. They saw how the crew all helped.

With the table clear, Marr had outlined the plan for the next day. It was decided the rest of today would be about rest and exploration.

Annee also outlined the chores rota, however she took Marr's lead and made it all voluntary. It was clear that a voluntary basis wasn't going to be an issue because of how they all responded to clearing the table.

4

"Time for rest before hitting the pool for the afternoon," Bazzer announced when it was clear the debriefing was done.

"Definitely," Suzzona said. "But before that, I am going to prepare the meal plan for the rest of the day. At this stage I am thinking about something light that is self-service for one p.m. That is for those that want it. Dinner at seven thirty p.m. I'll start preparation at five p.m. and a few volunteers to help would be appreciated."

"I'll help again. I'd say after my brilliance this morning you'd be hard pressed to find better help," Bazzer said as he chuckled.

Suzzona laughed hard and nearly fell off her chair.

Two of the girls piped up and added their names to the list.

Luna was next to offer direction.

"Girls, as mentioned before breakfast, Mentor has setup a clinic. Annee and I will accompany you. We'll go there now together. There is plenty to explore in the recreation rooms while you wait your turn. Mentor, do you want to lead the way."

With that Luna stood up. As did Mentor, Annee and the girls.

They all filed out of the room behind Mentor.

Bazzer gave them a moment before following. Suzzona headed towards the kitchen.

Marr turned to Bognath.

"Bognath, you said that you were going to walk the perimeter. I'd like to come along too."

"Me too," Dukk added.

"Sure," Bognath replied. "There are fatigues and the related paraphernalia in the utility room behind the kitchen. I plan to get changed down there and head out. And I wasn't planning on walking. I understand there are air scooters in the equipment sheds."

"Excellent, meet you down there," Marr replied.

"In about twenty minutes," Bognath added. "Before that, I'm going to check in with Luna and then brush my teeth."

Marr and Dukk followed Bognath out of the banquet hall.

The double doors took them into a wide corridor. At the far end they could see the entrance hall. The corridor had three further sets of double doors down the left side.

"Will we explore a bit on our way?" Dukk suggested.

Marr nodded as they arrived at the first set of doors.

Within they found a space three times the size of the banquet hall. The room was double height and had floor to ceiling glass windows with views of the valley as per the entrance hall.

The three other walls were shelved. The shelves were filled with books. Free standing bookshelves also stood in the middle of the room. There was furniture too. All made of dark wood. There were comfortable chairs and a few tables. A spiral staircase, also made of dark wood, served the narrow balcony that ran around the room and gave access to the higher shelves.

Marr stumbled as she came to terms with what she was seeing.

"Books!" she uttered in complete disbelief.

"Books!" Dukk echoed. He was also confused.

Marr walked over to the nearest shelf and started reading some of the spines. She held her finger close to the spines as she read but she dared not touch them for fear that it was an illusion.

Dukk walked a little ahead of her. He pulled a thick box from a shelf. Within the box was a book. He pulled out the worn looking book. It had a light blue cover and nearly fell apart as he opened it.

"They are real!" Dukk uttered. "Ulysses by James Joyce. First edition and signed no less."

Marr came up behind him and put her hands around him. She hugged him.

He lifted the book above their heads as he turned in her arms to face her.

"We were led to believe that they were all destroyed," she said quietly. "How many more lies have we been living with."

She started to cry as she buried her head into his neck.

Dukk did his best to hug her. He still had the thick and heavy book in his hands above their heads.

After a moment she pulled back a little and looked up at him.

"Let's come back later when we are rested and certain this resort is secure."

"Good idea," Dukk replied as he reached over for the box.

With the book back in its box and back on the shelf, they left the room and inspected the next double doors.

The middle room was a study. It was narrower than the library and had a kidney shaped mezzanine floating in the middle of the room. A spiral staircase served it on one side. On the mezzanine was a large desk. The floor level had two sets of leather sofas. One just inside the door and the other near the floor to ceiling glass windows. The walls were covered with painted portraits.

"The study," Marr stated rhetorically.

"Yep," Dukk said as they closed the doors.

Beyond the last set of doors was a large room. A lounge. It too had huge windows and magnificent views. The walls were covered with paintings. The furniture was arranged into four separate areas. Each space had three or four four-seater sofas. A glass enclosed fireplace sat in the middle of the room.

"How will we ever go back to the Imhullu", Dukk laughed as they gazed at the luxurious space.

Marr laughed too.

Ten minutes later, Marr, Dukk and Bognath were together in a change room adjacent to the utility room behind the kitchen.

"Do we need these?" Marr asked as she lifted a respirator from a shelf.

"Yes, if we want to go as far as the fence," Bognath answered as he buttoned up his shirt.

"What about guns?" she said as she pulled off her t-shirt and picked up a fatigue shirt.

"Unlikely, I'll have mine, and there is a gun cabinet in the utility room if we want to take further precautions," Bognath answered.

"These fatigues look light. Will we be warm enough?" Dukk asked.

Bognath laughed.

"What?" Dukk said.

"You haven't worn these types of fatigues before?" Bognath prompted.

"Nope. Not a lot of cause to in my designation."

"Nor mine, officially," Bognath said. "This material is highly specialised. Practically undetectable by most means. Super strong. Super light but plenty warm."

"How else do you think Luna and I got about without observers noticing us?" Marr added.

"Right, more that I didn't know. With every waking moment I feel less and less knowledgeable," Dukk laughed.

Marr grinned as she buttoned up her shirt.

5

With fatigues on, Marr, Dukk and Bognath made their way out of the building.

They followed a path away from the door at the back of the utility room. It wound around the back of the building towards the recreation area.

To their right was a green open space that stretched to the dome wall, some two hundred metres away.

"Synthetic grass?" Dukk commented as he ventured off the path.

"I guess it would be purple if it was the natural grass," Marr commented.

"It would be toxic too," Bognath added.

"Is this a running track?" Dukk asked as he bent down and felt the texture of the grass.

Marr came over and walked beside Dukk.

"It feels very realistic," Marr commented.

"Wow!?" Dukk said as they came around a corner.

Before them was a series of spaces separated by low hedges.

"Tennis courts?" Marr observed.

"And an outdoor pool?" Dukk noted. "I need to take a closer look at that!"

The three made their way around the tennis courts and entered the outdoor pool area.

The large radius pool was surrounded by plush cushioned sunbeds. Dotted in between were ten-metre-high poles. On the top of each pole were large lamps.

Two girls were standing beside a sunbed. They were wearing bikinis and looking up at the lamps. They were shivering.

"What is going on?" Marr asked as they made their way around the pool.

"These are supposed to give off heat and provide tanning at the same time," one of the girls answered.

"Are they turned on?" Bognath asked.

The girls looked at each other and laughed. With that they dashed back towards glass doors in the side of the building.

"They won't be back for a while," Bognath said. "I heard these yokes take about three hours before they give off sufficient heat for sunbathing."

They all laughed as they looked towards the windows. More girls were standing there staring out. They were all wearing bikinis.

"Did they bring those bikinis with them?" Dukk asked.

"I guess they found them in the rec area like the sweats we found in our rooms, and these fatigues. Everything appears to be provided in this sort of place," Marr noted.

From there they walked to a series of large doors in the wall beyond the pool.

Bognath pulled open the large doors.

The space beyond the doors was large and contained all manner of equipment.

Bognath went over to a row of air scooters. Each was about a metre long by one metre wide. Each had a low seat sitting in the middle of the scooter. The base was fifteen centimetres tall and the whole thing was resting on four small wheels.

Bognath unplugged the first scooter and wheeled it out of the doors. He then sat into the seat, put his right hand into the controller and pulled the trigger gently. The scooter came to life as the blades in the base pushed against the ground. The scooter lifted slightly. Bognath then twisted the controller and the scooter yawed to the left. He then yawed right, and finally came back down facing them.

"Show off," Marr said.

Bognath laughed, "Hey, I am just a hired gun. You two are the flyers."

"Will we join him?" Marr said looking over at Dukk.

"Absolutely!"

Over the next sixty minutes the three of them used the scooters to inspect the grounds. They flew the entire base of the dome. And from the utility, Suzzona helped them pass through the mantraps so they could get a sense of the outer grounds and reach the closest part of the inner fence line.

"That all looks pretty secure for now," Bognath said as they walked back to the utility door.

"It does," Marr agreed. "Though, I'd like to get back out to the outer grounds and see what else is out there. Perhaps tomorrow."

"Why?" Dukk asked.

"I saw tracks. Not human. Some sort of small creature."

"Take your gun," Bognath joked.

"I will."

With the fatigues off and into a washing machine, Marr and Dukk headed back upstairs. They enjoyed a quick shower and crashed into bed.

Near two p.m. they were sitting in the kitchen picking at the meat and cheese platter Suzzona had prepared.

"There appears to be lots to do here," Marr said casually.

"There has to be," Dukk said.

"Why?"

"Elites need something to occupy their time between drinks," Dukk laughed.

Marr smiled.

"You had enough?" she said pointing at the platter. "I want to have a look at the pool and gym. Perhaps work up a sweat and take a swim."

"I could help with some off that," Dukk said with a grin.

"Definitely, but later," Marr smiled.

The indoor recreation area was immense. There was a large gym. Massage rooms. A large sauna and wet space. Multiple indoor pools. Meditation and yoga rooms. A boxing rink. A dojo. Billiard and pool tables and rooms with various games and activities. It was so large in fact that they hardly saw any sign of the others.

Near five p.m., Dukk was waiting for Marr in the corridor just outside a restroom. They were planning on heading back upstairs to rest and then change for dinner.

Dukk's comms squawked. It took him by surprise as the comms hadn't been working in most areas.

He didn't even think of checking the caller ID. He just accepted the call.

The face of an attractive woman appeared in the air before him. She looked to be in her mid-twenties.

"Hello captain, my name is Emeelie. I am one of Mr Atesoughtons assistants. Mr Atesoughton has some information for you. He wants to deliver it in person. He will be landing in Emerald Valley at seven p.m."

"That's interesting," Dukk answered. "Please tell Mr Atesoughton we have dinner plans at seven thirty which I do not wish to change. He is welcome to join us."

"Give me a moment," Emeelie said as she put the call on hold.

A moment later she came back on the call.

"Mr Atesoughton has accepted your invitation. There will be four in his party, including himself. He is assuming the dress code will be formal. Please expect him at seven p.m. Where will I send the dietary requirements?"

"Send them to me," Dukk answered.

"Done. Goodbye."

"Oh, shit," Dukk said before bending over in laughter.

Chapter 13 – Temptation

1

"What is going on? What is so funny?" Marr asked as she joined Dukk in the corridor.

"You know those formal clothes you found in the dressing room upstairs?" Dukk replied as he composed himself.

"Yes. What about them?"

"Fancy giving them an outing this evening?"

"Why?"

"I just invited Craig Atesoughton to dinner, and he accepted."

"Oh!" Marr exclaimed.

"Let's see who is coming," Dukk said as he opened his wrist wraps and projected the message from Emeelie.

Four profiles appeared in the air.

"Craig, a man and two women," Marr commented. "Quite a party."

"That woman is the executive assistant I was just talking to. Her name is Emeelie," Dukk said as he pointed at one of the profiles.

"She looks like the person Craig was talking to this morning in his office. Who are the other two?"

"No idea."

"Personal security?"

"Perhaps. We'd better tell the others and Suzzona," Dukk said as he started walking towards the entrance hall.

"And the girls. We need to reassure them they are still safe."

"Let's divide and conquer. I'll find Suzzona, and you focus on briefing the girls. And we give the others the heads up as we see them."

"That sounds like a good plan. What shall we tell them?"

"Let's just say dress is formal and we have a surprise."

"The surprise idea might not work for the girls."

"Oh. Of course. They may see Craig's father in him. They may link him with their abusers. What do you suggest?"

"I'll just tell them we have other guests coming and they aren't a threat and we'll be with them the whole time as well."

"Will that work?" Dukk asked as they stepped into the entrance hall.

"I think so. I might run it by Mentor first."

"Great. I'm going towards the kitchen."

"And I am going to the library. Mentor mentioned he was going there after the pool."

"I can understand for most of us, but I would have thought Mentor wouldn't be overawed by the existence of books."

"I thought that too. I asked him. He said he knew of the private collections but had never seen one in person."

"It looks like we won't have time to go back there now today."

"If you can't find me anytime tomorrow, that is where I'll be."

"You are assuming I will let you get beyond arms reach anytime soon."

Marr came in close for a gentle kiss.

"Best get moving so we have time for a rest," Marr said with a grin.

"Absolutely. Oh, and show Mentor the profiles," Dukk said as he flicked the images towards her. "See if he knows who the other two are."

"Cool," Marr said as she headed towards the library.

Suzzona was already in the kitchen. She was pulling things out of one of the larder fridges.

"Suzzona," Dukk said as he approached the centre counter.

"Come to help too?" she answered without stopping what she was doing.

"Maybe. We have some additional guests for dinner this evening."

"How many?"

"Four."

"No issue. I would have had that covered as a matter of course."

"I have been sent dietary requirements."

"Not my issue. This isn't a restaurant. The food is as it comes. Take it or leave it," she said as she closed the door and disappeared into a larder cupboard.

"Hi," Bazzer announced as he joined them.

"Hi Bazzer. Suzzona, there is something else."

"What?" Suzzona said as she popped her head out of the larder. "Hi Bazzer," she added.

"Dress code will be formal. I understand there are clothes in each of our rooms."

"Formal?" Suzzona said with a quizzical expression. "No bother, we just need to factor in time to get dressed. That also means extra hands. Let's prep until six p.m. Get changed and then return at six forty-five to finish things. That will work fine."

With that she disappeared back into the larder. She appeared a moment later carrying jars.

"You said it will need extra hands?" Dukk asked reluctantly.

"Yes, you are washing and cutting green beans," Suzzona said as she picked up a large bag of beans and shoved it in Dukk's direction.

"Find a colander and wash them over there. Then cut the ends off."

"Colander?"

"A metal bowl with holes in it."

"Oh," Dukk said as he put down the beans and went looking for said item.

"Bazzer, you are cutting cheese and meats for the platter. Come over here. And both of you wash your hands and get on aprons."

"Right," Bazzer answered.

"Formal dress?" he then asked Dukk who was opening cupboards at random.

"We have some guests," Dukk answered as he inspected a large metal bowl with holes in it.

"Hi," came the chirpy young voices of two of the girls.

"Lilaho and Kayila. Great," Suzzona said. "You are washing and cutting fruit for our dessert. Come over here and I'll get you started. Dukk also tells me we are getting into some frocks for the meal. We'll break between six and six forty-five to dress."

"Yes, we know," said Lilaho. "Marr just told us. She said it is some big wig, but we aren't to be concerned."

"Perfect," Suzzona said dismissively as she moved the bags of fruit to a sink.

"Need any help?" Marr asked from the doorway.

"Yes. Help Dukk workout how to wash beans," Suzzona said with a laugh.

She was looking at Dukk. He was standing back from the counter with the bag of beans in one hand and the colander in the other.

"How did it go?" Dukk asked quietly as he and Marr stood at a sink washing the beans.

"Fine," Marr answered. "Mentor offered some suggestions but basically agreed with the plan and the girls took the news well."

"It didn't take you long."

"I only spoke with Lilaho and Kayila. I ran into them on the way in here. Ann, Luna and Bognath were in the library too. They will tell the rest of the girls."

"What else did he suggest?"

"Two things. In terms of the girls, he suggests we use the meeting of Craig as the foundation to help them move away from thinking in terms of generalisations. It will be a starting place to help them move back to seeing others as individuals."

"What do you mean by moving away from generalisations?"

"That we do what we do because of who we are as individuals, not because of our identity. We should want to be judged by the strength of our character, not our immutable characteristics."

"Yes, that makes sense. And the other thing?"

"That we carry weapons. He suggested that Bognath and Luna accompany us to welcome them at seven p.m. He says it will be important to demonstrate strength, especially if the other two are personal security."

"Perfect."

"I see we've been roped in," Marr said as she lifted a bunch of beans out of the colander. "Will we still have time to rest and get changed?"

"Rest, unlikely. Get changed, yes. The slave driver over there is giving us time off between six and six forty-five to get changed."

"I heard that," came the retort from Suzzona on the other side of the kitchen as she flung two large whole salmon onto the centre counter.

2

Near six forty-five, Marr and Dukk were standing in front of a wall mirror in their suite.

Marr was wearing a dark green halter dress. Her dark brown hair was loosely clipped back to accentuate her neck.

Dukk was dressed in a tuxedo. He had the jacket on, but the shirt was open; he wasn't wearing a bow tie.

"How do I look?" Marr asked.

"Stunning," Dukk replied. "I don't often see your hair like that. I love it."

"Excellent. But the credit must be given to the girls. They did the hair and make-up. They also helped Luna, Annee and Suzzona. Otherwise, it wouldn't have happened in forty-five minutes."

"Well, whatever you all did, it works for me."

"That is great to hear. I was concerned that the dresses here were all made for taller and petite frames."

"The kind of frames that would snap with even the slightest gust of breeze."

"Yep, that kind," Marr laughed.

She then added, "But then I found this halter dress."

"Well, that dress fits you like a glove. It leaves little to the imagination," Dukk said with a grin.

Marr looked over at him with a provocative expression.

"I am going to struggle to keep my hands off you," Dukk added.

"Who said I want you to keep your hands off me," Marr giggled.

"Well not while in the company of others," Dukk said with a laugh.

Marr smiled as she turned to face Dukk.

Dukk stepped in and put his arms around her.

"You are taller," Dukk observed.

"Stilettos."

"High heels."

"Yep."

"Are you okay with getting about in them? What if things get crazy and you need to do your thing?"

"The ability to move seamlessly in all kinds of circles and still be as effective at killing, is part of my training."

"I am not sure that is something I wanted to know," Dukk laughed.

"Tying a bow tie is also part of my training. Need help?"

"Yep, moving seamlessly within elite circles was never part of my training," Dukk laughed.

With the bow tie in place, Marr went over to the side table.

"Take your jacket off," she demanded.

"We don't have time. We are due back downstairs to help finish the meal preparation."

"Not for that," She giggled. "I need you to wear this."

Marr brought over a shoulder holster. It had a gun in it. She held it up for Dukk to put on.

"You want me to carry a gun?"

"Yes," Marr said. "Mentor said we are to make some of our weapons obvious to see how they react when they arrive."

"By that you mean I am to wear a gun that is clearly holstered under my jacket."

"Yes."

244

"What do you mean by some of our weapons?"

Marr leant down and hoisted her dress. She exposed her calves and the matching green Stilettos. Attached to her right calf was a small holster with a gun.

Then she hoisted her dress to her waist. On her inner thigh was a garter fitted with four small knives.

"Oh," Dukk said with a nervous grin.

He then added, "You'd better put that dress back down. We need to stay focused."

"Let's go," Marr laughed as she pushed the dress back down.

Marr and Dukk made their way to the kitchen.

They found Annee, Suzzona, Bazzer, Lilaho and Kayila working away.

Annee and Suzzona were each wearing a full-length fitted dress with a plunging neckline. Suzzona in black and Annee in gold. Their hair was shaped, and their make-up was subtle but stylish. Even with the aprons they looked stunning.

The girls were wearing straight cut, full-length, black dresses. Their hair and make-up were modestly done.

Marr reflected on the first time they met some of these girls in Maple Tower. They didn't have the same spark. That was clearly something Marr would be working on.

Bazzer was in a tuxedo. He was tieless. They were all wearing aprons too.

"Wow," Annee said as she saw Marr.

"You are stunning. I am suddenly quite jealous of Dukk," She added with a cheeky chuckle.

"Thank you, Ann. You are looking pretty good too," Marr said with a grin while emphasising the word 'good'.

Annee giggled.

"Have you started drinking already?" Dukk asked on seeing the three wine glasses on the centre counter.

"I needed to open a bottle for the marinade. No point in letting it go to waste", Suzzona said with a laugh.

A few minutes later, Marr, Dukk, Luna and Bognath were standing in the entrance hall. They had been alerted that the hanger doors had opened. The lift to the hanger was active. It was ascending.

Bognath was dressed in a tuxedo.

Luna was wearing a ruby plunging neckline velvet dress with matching stilettos. Her hair hung loosely on her shoulders. Her make-up was bright and fancy.

"Wow, you ladies look smashing," Bazzer said as he rushed down the stairs. "And you lads. But no, the ladies take the prize."

"Everything ok?" Dukk asked as Bazzer reached the bottom of the stairs and turned towards the kitchen.

"Yep, I just forgot my bow tie."

"Do you need a hand with it," Luna called out.

"Nope, Lilaho and Kayila, said they'll help me with it."

The lift doors opened as Bazzer disappeared.

Craig, Emeelie, a woman and a man stepped out of the lift.

Craig was wearing a tuxedo.

Emeelie was wearing a full-length, pale rose dress with plunging neckline that barely covered her breasts. Her black hair was loosely tied back. Her make-up was subtle and stylish against her creamy skin and light green eyes. She was tall, thin, and simply stunning. That didn't stop her from looking Marr and Luna up and down and frowning. It was clear she was not used to being shown up.

The other woman wore a black full-length dress with spaghetti straps. She had black hair pulled back in a high ponytail. She had pale skin tones and blue eyes. She looked to be in her early forties, and she was more like Marr in stature, than Emeelie.

The final new arrival was a tall man with dark brown skin tones and short black hair. His manner and physique were like that of Bognath.

3

Craig walked directly over to Dukk and put out his hand.

"Not often that I am welcomed into one of my own properties by another," he said.

Dukk took his hand and shook it firmly.

"Welcome, Mr Atesoughton," Dukk said confidently.

"Call me Craig," Craig laughed. "It is Dukk, isn't it?"

Dukk paused. He felt something wasn't right. He wasn't using his new alias.

Craig grinned.

"After learning that Septemo, I mean Mentor, was on that G5 rig, I did a little more research. Imagine my surprise when I saw a picture of the registered captain. The same face as was sitting in my office this morning. But under a different name. I gather the rest of the crew from that G5 rig are here somewhere too."

Dukk smiled sheepishly.

"It is Marr, isn't it?" Craig said as he released Dukk's grip, turned and put his hand towards Marr.

"It is, Craig," Marr said confidently as she took his hand and shook it firmly.

"You look stunning, by the way," Craig added before saying in a dismissive tone, "This is Emeelie, my second brain and, Eleettra and Alessano, two of my personal security detail."

He was still holding Marr's hand and holding her stare.

Marr checked her emotions. She realised she was starting to blush.

Craig smiled subtly.

Dukk stepped around Craig so he could shake hands with Emeelie, Eleettra, and Alessano.

Emeelie held on a little as Dukk shook her hand.

"Shall we?" Craig said as he gently released the hold with Marr. "I am dying to learn exactly what Septemo meant when he said that he had cooking real food covered. And I'd love a drink before we dine."

"What about the information we requested?" Dukk asked.

"Emeelie has it. But, after dinner," Craig said dismissively as he turned to look out over the valley.

"What a magnificent view," he added.

"It is," Marr answered absently as she gazed at Craig.

Dukk didn't quite manage to look at the view of the valley, either. His gaze had returned to Emeelie.

"Who is taking my order?" Craig said after a moment, as he turned towards the corridor to the right.

"No one," Dukk said in an empathetic tone.

Craig stopped, turn to Dukk, and stared. He looked confused.

Dukk smiled and continued.

"There are no staff here and there will be no one serving anyone else. You are of course welcome to help yourself. One of my crew is preparing the meal with help from some others, who too volunteered. The menu is fixed. Take it or leave it. I will happily prepare you a drink as I prepare one for myself. I suggest we move to the banquet hall as the others will be gathering there too and they might need help getting the meal on the table."

"Brilliant," Craig laughed genuinely. "Tieanna warned me that one day I would be put in my place. I guess that day has come. Splitting bread with hauliers no less. Please lead the way and I will have whatever you are having."

Dukk nodded, then stepped back slightly and turned so that Luna and Bognath were part of the group.

Craig followed his lead and looked over at Luna and Bognath.

"You have already met my co-pilot, Marr," Dukk said. "Let me introduce you to further members of my crew. This is Bognath our head of security. And Luna our long-range weapons expert."

"Pleasure to meet you both," Craig said as he approached them and shook hands.

"Travelling with specialised military skills," Craig added as he stood back and looked at Luna and Bognath. "I am not surprised from what I've heard of the exploits of Septemo's alter-ego. Are you all carrying weapons or just you lads?"

Craig grinned as he turned back to Dukk.

Marr grinned too. Mentor was right.

"Never can be too sure these days," Dukk answered.

"Perhaps we can at least leave our holsters out here and not have them in the dining room?" Craig suggested.

"Agreed," Dukk answered as he removed his jacket and then removed the shoulder holster.

Bognath did the same as did Alessano.

They put them on a table just near the stairs.

"Shall we," Dukk said as he returned to the others in the middle of the hall.

"After you," Craig said.

Dukk looked at Marr. She smiled at him and nodded towards the corridor. Together they led the guests down the corridor towards the banquet hall.

Luna and Bognath remained in the hall.

Marr and Dukk pushed open the banquet hall doors. They stood aside to allow the others to enter.

"Where is everyone?" Craig asked as they entered the room.

"Getting ready or cooking," Marr answered.

"Can we see what we will be eating?" Craig said as he marched towards the kitchen doors.

Craig opened the doors and stepped into the middle of the kitchen. Marr, Dukk and Emeelie followed. Eleettra and Alessano stayed in the doorway. Suzzona, Annee, Bazzer and two of the girls were at the central counter. They stopped and looked up.

Bazzer smiled as he confirmed the two and two, he had put together.

Suzzona stumbled and her mouth dropped open. While she knew who she was looking at, her expression show that she had clearly not given much thought to the identity of the surprise guests.

Annee grinned with amusement having also had suspicions about the mystery guest's identity.

The two girls looked a little nervous. They looked at Marr.

Marr smiled genuinely at the girls and mouthed, "It is okay."

"Who do we have here?" Craig announced as he looked around.

"Our chief engineer, Bazzer. Annee, our chief mate and head of house. Our chef, Suzzona. And." Dukk said and then stopped as he realised that he couldn't remember the girls' names.

"Lilaho and Kayila," Marr said quickly to cover Dukk's blunder.

"Pleasure to meet you. Please call me Craig. This is Emeelie, Eleettra, and Alessano."

"What is cooking?" Craig asked as he reached out to shake hands.

Suzzona stuttered a few words before finding her feet.

"For starters we have a Greek meze platter. Main course is baked salmon with roasted parmesan rosemary potatoes and skillet green beans. And dessert is simply ice cream and fresh fruit. In my mind, the simpler things are often the best. Unfortunately, I've been too busy preparing the food to think about wine. And the table needs to be set."

"Wine, yippy," yelped one of the girls.

Annee frowned and shook her head.

"I know the wines. Allow me to do that," Craig said.

"Thank you, Craig," Suzzona said as she started to relax again.

"Perhaps someone can help me. Marr?" Craig added in a quizzical tone.

"Oh, of course," Marr said with a slight stumble.

"You'll need more than just the two of you to get enough wine for us all," Dukk suggested as he sensed Marr's nervousness.

"Of course. But let Marr and I pick them first. Wine choice doesn't need a committee. And don't worry, in my absence, Emeelie will be good company and is super helpful."

Dukk grinned nervously.

"After you," Craig said as he pointed towards the door that led back to the entrance hall.

Eleettra and Alessano went to follow, but Craig waved them off.

Dukk watched as Marr and Craig disappeared out of the kitchen and into the service corridors.

"The table settings are back in here, aren't they?" Emeelie said politely.

Dukk turned to her.

"Ah, yes," he said with a stutter. He struggled to keep his eyes raised.

She appeared to sense his gaze and she leant forward a little and tilted her head. The deep plunging neckline of her dress now left even less for the imagination.

4

"What is your story, Marr?" Craig asked as he walked beside her. "You don't have the same mannerisms of Dukk and the others."

"Mannerisms?" Marr asked in reply.

"Like that of a haulier."

"What does that mean?"

"There is something else about you. I can't place it. Perhaps you weren't always a haulier?"

"That is right. Six weeks ago, I wasn't," Marr answered before realizing she had broken one of the golden rules. Not to share too much.

"What were you then?"

"I was a keeper," Marr said quickly and in a dismissive tone. She hoped that the tone would encourage him to probe no further.

"Ah, I see," he said as they reached a door just behind the entrance hall stairs.

Craig opened the door. There was a staircase. It led down.

"Does this go to the hanger?" Marr asked cautiously.

"It does, but two flights down, is the cellar," Craig said as he entered the stairs.

Marr followed.

"What drew you to hauling?" Craig asked as they descended.

"The desire for a new adventure."

"Sounds like you found it," Craig said as he opened a door on a landing two flights down.

Marr said nothing.

The cellar was a long room with glass cabinets. The cabinets were filled with wine bottles.

On the floor just inside the door were several six bottle wine carriers. Craig grabbed one and headed into the cellar. Marr took the hint and collected one too.

"That woman said that the starter is a meze platter, so a classic rosé would be in order."

"Her name is Suzzona."

"Of course, sorry," Craig said as he scanned his hand along the cabinets and read the labels of the bottles within.

"This will work," Craig said as he opened the door and started extracting bottles from the chilled cabinet.

With four bottles in the carrier, he lifted it and continued further into the cellar.

"Pinot Noir is next, given salmon is for main," Craig said absently.

After further scanning, he stopped, opened a cabinet, and extracted further bottles. With his carrier full, he passed six bottles over to Marr.

He then closed the cabinet and stood back to look at Marr.

He was smiling.

Marr looked back. She felt awkward, but excited at the same time.

"Shall we," he said after a moment.

"Of course," she blurted as she bent down and lifted the carrier.

When Marr and Craig re-entered the banquet hall through the main double doors, they found everyone had arrived. The rest of the girls, Luna, Bognath, and Mentor. Dukk and Emeelie were there too. Alessano was standing near the kitchen doors. Eleettra came into the room just after Marr and Craig. Marr had noticed her following them when they came up from the cellar.

Mentor smiled. The girls looked a little anxious.

"You are back," Dukk said nervously.

He pulled away from Emeelie and walked towards the door. When the table was set, she had become quite clingy. Even when the others arrived, she still clung to him as he introduced her.

"Let me help you with that," Dukk said as he reached for the wine bottle carriers. He took them and walked towards a side table.

"Mentor," Craig said as he put his hand out. "Good to see you again."

"Welcome, Craig," Mentor said as he shook his hand.

"Hello everyone," Craig said as he looked around at the girls. "Please call me Craig as you introduce yourselves."

Marr followed Dukk as Craig shook hands with the girls.

"Are you okay?" Marr asked quietly. "You look flushed."

"Emeelie has been a bit too super helpful," Dukk laughed.

"Really?"

"And very friendly," Dukk added as he put down the wine.

"She is looking pretty good. Your type?"

Dukk laughed nervously.

"You took your time selecting wine," Dukk said in a tone that had a touch of annoyance.

Marr looked at him unsure about how to respond.

"I'd better get these open, I need a drink," Dukk said.

Marr stood back. She was now annoyed as well.

With the bottles opened Dukk and Marr joined the others.

It wasn't long before Bazzer, Suzzona, Annee, Lilaho and Kayila carried out trays and placed them on the side table.

"Is anyone hungry?" Suzzona asked as she removed her apron. "Grab a plate and help yourselves."

"Don't you have two observers with you?" Emeelie asked.

"They are sleeping," Mentor answered. "They are taking the edge off a bender."

"Oh," Emeelie said.

"Jackets on or off?" Craig asked.

Dukk wasn't sure how to respond. The others looked confused too.

"Off," Mentor said. "We are all friends here."

"Excellent," Craig said as he removed his jacket. Initially he started moving towards the head of the table.

The girls had already gathered around the far end of the table. That left twelve seats free.

Dukk noticed Craig's hesitation. He removed his jacket. He walked around the table to the third seat along and hung his jacket on the back of it.

"You aren't sitting at the head of the table?" Craig asked in surprise.

"There is no one more or less than me in this room. I am no more deserving of the head than anyone else here."

"Well, that goes for me too," Craig said as he put his jacket on the seat opposite Dukk.

Craig then looked up. "Surely, such a momentous evening like this one, we should mix things up. Boy, then girl. Emeelie perhaps you over there next to Dukk. Marr over here next to me.

Emeelie was already moving around the table.

"Great idea," Bazzer said as he followed Emeelie around.

Marr grinned nervously as she moved to the table. She gave Luna a slight nudge as she passed by her. Luna took the hint and followed her to the seat on the other side of Craig.

The others filed in around them.

Suzzona waved Eleettra and Alessano over from the doors. She insisted they too take seats.

When they had all taken their seats after selecting items from the platters, Craig cleared his throat.

"Could I be so bold as to ask to be the one who gives thanks?" Craig asked aloud.

"You give thanks at meals?" Marr asked in a surprised tone.

"No, well, not usually. Only in the company of one other," Craig answered in a solemn tone.

"Oh," Marr replied.

"Please do," Dukk said in an empathetic tone.

"Can I make a suggestion before Craig does the honours?" Annee asked.

Dukk looked over and nodded.

"As we did this morning, can we include a moment of silent reflection in honour of Zarra? Perhaps we can make a habit of it while she is with us. Until we get her back to Earth for a proper burial?"

"Yes, I think that is a great idea," Dukk answered.

Craig looked confused. He then looked down the table. His face indicated a light bulb moment as he looked at the melancholy expressions of the girls.

"Oh," Craig said solemnly. "I am truly sorry. I have stumbled into what is a very sad occasion with my merriment. Girls, please accept my apology and sincere condolences for your loss."

They nodded and lowered their heads.

Silence fell.

Marr paused too. She realised in all the excitement she too had completely forgotten the tragedy that befell the girls during the early hours. She looked down at her emerald colour dress and then at the girls, all in black."

Similar realizations were in the faces of the others at the table.

Then one of the girls spoke.

"Zarra would have loved that we are dining in style in her honour."

That brought a smile to the faces of most of the girls.

Marr did a mental sigh of relief.

"Well said, young lady," Dukk said.

He then added, "A moment of silent reflection is still in order and then we will dine in style in her honour."

Dukk bowed his head. Everyone followed.

After a minute, Dukk said, "Rest in peace."

The others followed suit.

Dukk then looked over at Craig and nodded.

Craig nodded, then lifted his head and pulled his shoulders back.

"I express gratitude for all that was, is and yet to be. Zarra, may you rest in peace. And may you all find what we seek and may no one come to any harm. Thanks, I give."

"Thanks, I give," They all replied.

Marr turned in her seat to look at Craig. She was seeing a completely different side to him. She liked it.

"We are all individuals and not guilty by association," She reflected to herself.

Dukk was looking on. He noticed how Marr's expression changed.

5

Within no time, the mood lightened. The food was enjoyed, and the wine flowed.

The conversation bounced around various light topics.

Craig was keen to learn about what the life of a keeper was like. Marr and Luna relaxed and competed for Craig's attention in sharing stories.

On the other side of the table, Dukk and Bazzer competed to share stories of hauling. Emeelie gave them both plenty of encouragement.

On both sides, the stories got more outrageous as the wine flowed.

The others joined in at times and chatted amongst themselves too.

The girls listened in and occasionally whispered and giggled.

Marr and Dukk avoided eye contact for much of the meal. The tension created earlier increased. So much so that if Emeelie leant into Dukk or touched his hand or face, Marr would mirror the behaviour with Craig. Or if Craig leant into Marr, Dukk would do the same with Emeelie.

After dessert, Emeelie stood up abruptly and went to the corridor. Moments later she returned and whispered into Craig's ear.

"My cruiser is due to return soon," Craig said after hearing the message. "It feels way too early to be turning in. Besides there must be a bed or two free in this big place."

Craig said the last sentence while looking at Marr.

Dukk looked over at Marr. She noticed him looking and then made a point of smiling provocatively at Craig.

"Yes, absolutely," Dukk blurted. "It is too early to end the fun. The night is young."

He made a point of saying the last sentence while looking at Emeelie.

"Yes, and there are a couple of normal suites spare. And we aren't using any of the rooms in the staff quarters," Annee said with sincerity. She was clearly having too much fun to notice the little war Marr and Dukk were having.

"Excellent, we'll make a night of it if that is okay with you all?" Craig asked.

He glanced around the table looking for acknowledgement. He also made the point of looking at Emeelie, Eleettra and Alessano. They nodded too.

"That's settled then," Dukk said.

Craig smiled.

"Will we clear the table and move somewhere more comfortable?" Suzzona suggested as she stood up.

"We will clear the table," said several of the girls as they stood.

"Thank you," Suzzona said as she smiled towards them.

The others acknowledged their offer too.

"We are out of wine!" Bazzer announced. He was standing at the side table.

"I'll go," Emeelie said. "I am thinking we need a medium red now."

"I'd like to stay on the Pinot Noir," Suzzona said.

"No problem, I'll get some of that too. I might need some help. Dukk?"

"Of course," Dukk blurted. Lead the way.

"Me too," Bazzer added.

Emeelie smiled half-heartedly at Bazzer for a moment. Then she took them both in her arms and headed for the door.

With more wine opened and the table cleared, everyone gathered in the lounge. The girls took one of the groups of seats near the windows and everyone else took the other.

The conversation was had as a group, more so than at dinner. The stories were largely about hauling. Marr and Luna still did their best to offer counter stories when they could.

Even as the wine flowed and the shoes and bow ties were discarded, the conversation managed to stay clear of the more difficult topics. Like the vast differences between the life of the elites and themselves. They also avoided talking about the truths they had learnt from Mentor about the observers, concubines, incubators, and Tieanna's relationship to Dukk.

The game being played by Marr and Dukk also continued. Dukk, Bazzer, Emeelie and Eleettra occupied one of the couches. Marr, Luna, Craig and Bognath had another. The final long sofa was occupied by Mentor, Annee and Suzanne. Alessano sat on the floor against the window.

There was lots of laughter and rubbing off on one another as the conversation got more and more animated. That was especially true for both Marr and Craig, and Dukk and Emeelie.

Near midnight, Annee noticed the girls were mostly asleep on the adjacent sofas. She got up and suggested she help them get upstairs. Suzzona also offered to help.

The movement reminded Dukk that he hadn't yet got the information from Craig.

On mentioning it, Emeelie suggested they go to the study, so she could show him how to access it. Dukk accepted eagerly. They both jumped up and made their way to the door. They had a skip in their step.

Marr watched them disappear.

Craig was watching Marr.

"You mentioned your interest in books earlier. Can I show you some of my favourite books?" He asked.

Marr turned to look at Craig. The wine had her head spinning.

"Absolutely, lead the way," she said enthusiastically.

Craig stood up and offered his hand to help Marr up.

Marr took his hand and then linked her arm in his as they departed the lounge.

Within the library, Craig escorted Marr to a table with a wide seat.

"Can I ask you something?" Marr asked as she watched Craig open a glass cabinet and extract a large box.

"Sure," he said as he placed the box on the table.

"Who is Tieanna to you?"

Craig paused and looked at Marr.

"She raised me like I was her own child."

"What about your birth mother?"

"A flake."

"Where is she now?"

"On Earth in one of her villas. Probably smashed off her head as usual."

"You don't seem bothered?"

"I am not. She was never around," Craig said as he extracted a large book from the box and placed it on the table.

"The Book of Kells?" Marr uttered in astonishment as she looked at the book.

"Yep," Craig said as he eased himself into the seat next to her.

"The original?"

"No just a very good replica. Even made with vellum and similar ink. It has the rust and stains too. Open it. Touch it. It has the same look and feel as the original."

"You've seen the original?"

"Yes, we keep it on Earth in one of our villas in Citadel Genda."

"This is amazing."

"Yes, it is amazing what moving in certain circles awards you." He said as he moved closer to look at the book with her.

His left arm was on the back of the wide chair they shared. His chest came to rest gently against the back of her bare shoulder. The fine fabric of his shirt touching her skin sent a shiver through her body. She was feeling intoxicated by not only the wine but also by Craig's presence. She was finding it challenging to manage her emotions. She could sense he was looking at her. She turned to look at him. He drew closer.

Meanwhile Dukk was in a predicament of his own.

He and Emeelie had found their way to the study. On Emeelie's suggestion they had gone up to the mezzanine. She had got Dukk to sit in the desk chair. Emeelie had then leant over the desk and showed him how to access the video feeds and records of the men's movements in Mayfield and New Montana. There were also records of interviews of their staff, in and around the assassination and arrival into New Montana.

With the content shared, Emeelie had turned and then leant back against the desk as Dukk stood up.

"We don't have to re-join the others right away," she said looking at him. "We could have some fun."

Dukk stood there unable to find the best way to respond. The wine was clouding his judgement.

Then Emeelie stood up. She stepped over to him. She then pushed the dress straps off her shoulders. Her dress dropped to the ground. She stepped out of it. Now naked, she leant in and whispered.

"Take me."

Chapter 14 – Redemption

1

After a moment of staring at each other, Dukk took a half step backwards. He then crouched down while still holding her gaze. He collected the dress off the floor and stood up.

"Very tempting, Emeelie. But my mind and body are wanting for another."

Emeelie Smiled.

"She is a lucky woman," Emeelie said after a moment of holding his gaze.

She then took the dress from is hand, stepped back and put it back on.

Back in the library, Marr pulled her head back as Craig leaned in. She smiled.

"No," she said in a gentle tone. "I don't think this is a good idea."

Craig smiled kindly as he pulled back.

"Let's get back to the others," Marr said as she got up.

"Absolutely, the night is still young," Craig said as he followed her to the door.

Marr and Craig found Dukk and Emeelie in the corridor just about to re-enter the lounge. Dukk was holding the door open for Emeelie.

"All sorted?" Craig said provocatively as he reached the door.

Dukk paused for a moment and then smiled before saying, "for now."

Dukk held the door for Craig too.

"Who's got the wine?" Craig roared as he caught up with Emeelie and took her arm.

Marr paused at the door and smiled awkwardly at Dukk.

Dukk smiled back awkwardly too.

After a moment, Dukk stood back into the corridor and let the door close without them.

He and Marr looked at each other.

Then at the same time they blurted, "I need to."

"You first," Dukk then said.

Marr looked in both directions, up and down the corridor.

She then grabbed Dukk's hand and dashed to the study.

She pulled the doors open and pushed him in. Then she closed the doors behind them and spun around to face Dukk.

"I was going to say, I need you right now," Marr said as she pushed him against the back of the doors.

She undid the top of her dress and let it fall to the floor. She then kissed him passionately while she pulled at his shirt and pants.

A little while later, they crashed back onto the sofa near the door. Marr draped herself across Dukk's chest. They were both breathing hard.

"What were you going to say in the corridor?" Marr asked after a moment of enjoying the feeling of his chest rising and falling.

"I was going to say I needed to apologise for being an idiot."

"What happened earlier?" Marr asked.

"When?" Dukk answered in a half-hearted tone. He knew what she meant but wasn't sure how to admit his mistake.

"When you were opening the wine and I commented on how pretty Emeelie was."

"I was taken aback. I was hurt by the suggestion I'd want to be with someone else."

"I guess I was feeling confused. I tried to make light of her flirting. I made a joke. A poor one, but I didn't mean to suggest you wanted to be with her."

"Yes, I realise that now. I wanted to punish you for making me feel I could not be trusted. So, I barked back. I see now how that was just stupid and had nothing to do with you."

"The bark threw me off balance even further. I see now how playing along made things worse."

"I guess I got caught up in my own insecurities," Dukk said sincerely.

"We both did," Marr admitted. "At least we found a way back."

"Yes, we did," Dukk said as he squeezed her gently.

Dukk then relaxed and looked up at the artwork above the doors.

"Do you think most children look the same?" Dukk asked.

Marr looked up at him and then turned to follow his gaze.

Above the door was a painting. It was of a man and a boy. The boy looked about ten years old. The man looked in his seventies.

"Not at all," Marr answered as she took in the painting.

"Craig and his grandfather," she added.

"Yes, I guess. You can see the resemblance."

Marr paused. It wasn't the only resemblance she was sensing as she turned back to look at Dukk.

"What?" Dukk said having noticed Marr's curious expression.

Before Marr could answer, the doors were flung open.

"Marr?" Luna shouted as she came through the doors.

"Aha! There you are. Wo!" Luna added as she processed what she was looking at and spun around so that her back was to them.

Dukk and Marr cracked up.

"Dukk, at least we are now even," Luna said with a giggle. "Anyway, I was going to the cellar for more wine. I wasn't sure if we needed two or three bottles. Are you coming back to join us?"

"Yes, absolutely," Marr said.

"You sure you don't want to take yourselves upstairs?" Luna asked.

"Nope, not yet. The night is still young," Marr said with a laugh.

"Well, you'd better put some clothes back on before you do. We don't want to give Craig and Emeelie any more ideas. They are already quite animated."

With that Luna departed. She closed the doors behind her.

"What did she mean by 'we are now even?'" Marr asked.

"I guess she is talking about when I saw her naked last month. The time I had to resuscitate her after the DMD bounce. She was sleeping in the buff."

"I guess Bazzer owes me too so," Marr laughed.

2

When Marr and Dukk re-entered the lounge, the girls were gone but the others were back.

Alessano was laying on a sofa near the door. He had his eyes closed but didn't look asleep.

The remainder were sitting together in a section near the window.

Bazzer was sharing a sofa with Mentor. Eleettra was sitting between them. She was looking quite relaxed and happy with herself.

Bognath was sitting alone on another sofa.

Annee and Suzzona were sitting together, arm in arm at one end of the third sofa. Craig and Emeelie were at the other end of the same sofa. Emeelie was snuggled into Craig's arms with her legs on the sofa between them and Annee and Suzzona. Her dress was doing a poor job of covering her body. She didn't seem bothered about it.

Emeelie smiled warmly at Marr and Dukk as they sat on the sofa with Bognath.

No sooner had they taken their seats when Luna came bouncing into the room with four bottles in a wine carrier. She came over to them.

"Fresh glasses, as this is a Malbec," Luna said as she lifted a bottle.

"Luna, you have an eye for quality," Craig said. "That is one of my favourites. There aren't many bottles left. It was part of a palette given to me by my grandfather for my tenth birthday. He said I couldn't drink it until I was twenty-one. Let's get it opened."

"Excellent idea. Who wants to sort that? I want to change the music. We need something a little more upbeat."

With the glasses full again, the conversation shifted a little.

Craig was interested in how companionship worked in the haulier world. He was intrigued by the idea of spending so much time in a confined space with the same people.

The conversation moved into ideas and some stories of experiences.

Then Craig asked a question about things getting stale.

"I know what works with that," Luna blurted.

She had been dancing by herself near the windows. As she spoke, she spun around and slipped. Her legs went in opposite directions, and she ended up doing the splits as she landed on the floor.

She stopped for a moment in shock and then broke into laughter as she toppled over to one side.

The fall had ripped her dress. The tear ran up from the hemline and well into the bodice.

"Luna, your dress!" Annee called out.

Luna lifted herself up with an elbow and sat up to inspect her dress.

"Oh, I appear to have fallen out of my clothes," she said before breaking into laughter again and laying on her back.

The others could not but laugh too as Luna lay sprawled practically naked on the floor in front of them.

"Hey," Luna called out. "Stop the room spinning. I want to get off."

That brought more laughter.

Then she slurred, "Better me bed get."

The laughter erupted to uncontrollable levels for all.

When Bognath regained some degree of composure, he got off the sofa and walked over to her. He stepped over her, crouched down. He then lifted her arms and put them around his neck. Then he lifted her up with him. She dangled off him still giggling.

"Need a hand?" Mentor asked as he stood up.

Marr and Dukk had got up too.

"No, I got this," Bognath said as Luna slipped down his body.

She laughed even harder.

"Maybe a little help," Bognath conceded.

Mentor stepped over to help Bognath. Between them they helped get Luna to her feet.

"We'll help. This day is done for us too," Annee said.

"Yep, I am ready for bed also," Bazzer said in between coughs of laughter.

Craig sat up and looked at Eleettra. She was yawning between giggles.

He then said, "Eleettra, please find a bed if you wish too. I am sure I am in safe hands here. Collect Alessano as you go."

Eleettra nodded towards Craig and then stood up. She smiled at Bazzer as she did.

Bognath nodded towards Craig and Emeelie, then Marr and Dukk. They nodded back.

"Goodnight, all," Mentor said.

"Goodnight, Mentor. You will find her, right?" Craig added.

Mentor nodded.

"Night, night," Luna slurred between giggles as Mentor and Bognath helped her towards the door.

3

Silence drifted in with just the four of them left. Emeelie had changed the music. It was more mallow than when Luna had been playing DJ. Marr was lying against Dukk. Both their legs were on the sofa. His arms were around her. They were in a similar position to Craig and Emeelie on the sofa opposite them.

"You may not think it, but you have it easy, all things considered," Craig said out of the blue.

"What do we have easy?" Dukk asked.

268

"Choosing companions. Even with the long hours of being out there moving through the galaxy."

"How so?"

"At least you aren't expected to get your potential companions vetted."

"Since when have you had to get companions vetted?" Emeelie challenged as she turned to look up at Craig.

"Ok, good point, I am the exception," Craig laughed.

"But I am supposed to," he added.

"What do you mean by supposed to?" Marr asked.

"Those with significant inheritance, like me, are supposed to have all companions vetted by the Veneficans."

Dukk and Marr both stiffened slightly. The Veneficans had come up again.

"Really?" Marr asked in a tone that was as relaxed as she could muster. She wanted to hide her interest.

"Yea, but granddad wasn't into that crap. He prohibited them from coming anywhere near me. Tieanna wasn't keen on them being anywhere near me either, for that matter. That is why they were in Mayfield, the day before the assassination. They had been trying to contact me independently of my grandfather. Their messages said something about me reaching the age where I was to participate in some sort of initiation ceremony. The messages said that I had to meet with the Venefica Magnum Reginae in person to be tested ahead of the ceremony.

"If I am truly honest, I am mildly interested. I've heard some odd things about them. I'd like to find out what they are about. Anyway, I didn't want to go against my Granddad or Tieanna's wishes, so I ignored their requests. Failing direct engagement, they took another path. They got my father involved. He was keen to help them. It was glaringly obvious that he was under some sort of pressure. He even tried to convince me that it wasn't a big deal. He said he participated in their initiation ceremony when he was my age as did most of the men he knew. He said it wasn't for me it was initiation for the future

Veneficans. I am off track again. So, anyway, my father had organised for me to meet him in Mayfield. However, when we arrived out of traverse and saw the Mammoth ring, I put two and two together. I ordered my flotilla to about face and get out of there."

Craig then chuckled.

"What's funny?" Emeelie asked.

"Can you imagine the queen turning up, with her huge entourage, only to find that she'd been stood up. She must have been really pissed."

He laughed again.

"Did Tieanna know that you were meeting your father?" Dukk asked.

"No. She sided with Granddad. Neither wanted me to have anything to do with him."

Craig stopped talking abruptly. Then added, "That's interesting."

"What?" Emeelie asked. She looked up again. Her expression was showing curiosity. It was as if she was sensing something new to a story that she already knew.

"I wonder if they knew about the assassination?" Craig asked rhetorically.

He paused and looked over towards the windows.

After a minute he continued but in a manner that was almost like he was talking to himself.

"Why did he start getting keener for me to meet them after the accident with the cruiser I was lending him? That is interesting."

With that Craig smiled and looked back at Marr and Dukk.

"Anyway, who needs Veneficans vetting your companions when you have a Tieanna looking over your shoulder. She would ask fifty questions about every woman that I showed an interest in."

He started laughing again.

Emeelie tensed a little and showed clear signs of discomfort.

Craig's last words hung in the air.

Marr's mind was racing. This new information was important. She couldn't put her finger on why. The wine was clearly in the way. Figuring it out would have to wait.

Dukk was going through a similar process in his mind. However, one question kept jumping ahead of the attempts to rein in the confusion.

"What is she like?" Dukk blurted.

"Who?" Emeelie replied.

"Tieanna."

Marr tensed a little. She squeezed Dukk's arm gently.

Dukk gave her a tender hug in return. He knew what her signal was about. He wasn't to share too much.

Craig looked up at the ceiling.

"She is unique," Craig answered. "She is like no other. Intelligent. Caring. A great listener. Able to ask the right question at the right time. And strong willed. Get on the wrong side of her and you'd better run."

"And she loves hunting," he added after a moment of silence.

"Hunting?" Dukk asked.

"Yes. Hunting. We used to go out beyond the dome at this very villa. We'd ride air scooters and take air guns. We'd chase the little critters that run rampant out there."

"That sounds like fun," Marr said eagerly.

Marr sensed this new direction in the conversation was what they needed to avoid getting themselves into trouble by sharing too much.

"We should go hunting together," Emeelie blurted. Her manner also suggested that she wasn't interested in any further deep reflection.

"Yes, tomorrow, all four of us," Craig said cheerfully.

Marr grinned. They were through the difficult moment.

"Excellent idea," Dukk said as he caught a big yawn.

"Speaking of tomorrow," Emeelie said quietly.

"Yes, perhaps today is done," Craig said.

"Did you figure out which rooms are free?" Marr asked.

271

"Yes, Annee sorted it," Emeelie answered.

"It will be odd not being on the upper level," Craig added.

"Not always getting our way opens the door to other opportunities," Marr laughed.

"Yes, it does, Marr," Craig said with a smile.

With that, Marr sat up and swung her legs off the sofa. Dukk untangled himself too.

"Goodnight, Craig. Goodnight, Emeelie," Marr said as she stood up.

"Goodnight, Marr, Dukk," Craig said smiling up at them.

Dukk nodded at them both as he stood and linked arms with Marr.

As they passed through the door, they noticed the lounge lights dim and the music change. It had a softer and rhythmic beat to it.

4

Marr stopped Dukk in the corridor and leant into kiss him.

"Are you okay?" she asked as she pulled back realising that he wasn't engaging.

"Something is bothering me about what we just heard."

"What is that?"

"I want to hear that message again."

"What message?"

"The message Mentor received from Tieanna the night before the assassination."

"Why?"

"I think we may be making a connection that might not exist."

"What do you mean?"

"We are assuming that the 'they' the men talk about is the same 'they' that Tieanna mentioned. Craig's update tells us why the Veneficans where in Mayfield around the time of the assassination. It is unrelated to anything we already knew. Which has me thinking about the other events. The attack on Craig's cruiser by an interceptor.

Perhaps it wasn't the Ukendt. Perhaps the girls being moved, and the last piece of Tieanna's message are unrelated. Perhaps also all these events are completely independent of Kimince being framed for the assassination, the replacement observer and the Ukendt coming after us. It does point to multiple motivations. Multiple motivations could mean different players. What if the 'theys' aren't the same 'they'? What if there are more multiple mystery players in this game?"

"But that is what a hydra means. Multiple heads. Multiple motivations."

"Yes, but what if we are talking about multiple hydra?"

"Oh," Marr said in shock as she too realised the potential mistake.

"I was there with the men before Luna executed them," Dukk said. "I heard the way they talked about 'they'. It wasn't the same as the way I recall Tieanna talking about 'they'. I want to see the video message again to confirm my suspicion."

"We would have to ask Mentor."

"There might be another way."

"How?"

"While in the study with Emeelie, she gave me access to their central processing system here in this resort. She had loaded all the video surveillance into it. The system is very powerful. More than we'd have on the rig. We might be able to use it to get at the Imhullu's video projection systems. Mentor used the projection system to share the message."

"Wow, you are really getting into this sleuthing stuff. Are you sure getting at Mentor's messages is a good idea?"

"We aren't prying into Mentor's messages. We are just replaying a message he already shared with us. And I'll struggle to rest with this question hanging."

"Ok, let's do it."

A little while later Marr and Dukk were squashed into the big office chair at the desk on the mezzanine. Several panels filled the air above the desk.

"There," Marr interrupted. "We are all sitting around the table debriefing after we traversed away from the explosion."

"I'll fast forward to the end and reverse it," Dukk said.

Moments later they were looking at the right spot in the play back.

In the air before them was an image of a middle-aged woman. Her expression showed warmth with a touch of sadness. Her long hair was light brown with wisps of silver. She had fair complexion and she had dark brown hazel eyes.

Dukk pressed play.

Tieanna started to speak. "The party is still going ahead. It is a hydra. We just cut off one of the heads. We've worked too hard to have another group of girls come to harm." She paused. A tear fell down her cheek. "There is something else." She paused again. "They know!" The video then froze.

Dukk teared up. Marr did too. They nudged into each other to acknowledge the moment.

It was then that they spotted it.

"He stopped the recording!" they blurted together.

The footage clearly showed Mentor pausing the projection.

"Wait," Marr said. "The system is showing the video message is buffered. There is more to the message."

"Can we access it?" Dukk asked.

Marr reached into the air and interacted with the system.

"Look, the system here is truly powerful. It can extract the message from the buffer. But Mentor didn't share the rest of the message. Should we really be watching it?"

They looked at each other in silence for a moment. They were both still teary from the initial replay. The wine was messing with their cognitive functions too.

"We must," Dukk said. "No more secrets!"

"Ok," Marr said reluctantly.

Marr pressed play.

The message played back as before. Then at the end there was a pause before Tieanna spoke again. She said, "Septemo, they are coming for him. Let go of me. Don't look for me. Keep him safe."

Marr and Dukk sat in silence.

"This is about you!" Marr said eventually as she turned to look at Dukk.

"Maybe," Dukk answered. He was thinking the same.

"It must be. Who else would she be talking about?"

"Craig?"

"No, that isn't what I feel. This is about you."

Dukk said nothing. He felt she was right.

Marr continued.

"It might explain why Mentor is seemingly relaxed about finding Tieanna. He is in conflict. If he searches too hard, he puts you in the frame. He wants to take his time getting back to Earth. He wants to find out everything he can without getting noticed."

"He wasn't bothered about returning to rescue Kimince and the girls. And then following the girls here."

"I think that was unrelated. I think that was because he didn't want their harm on his hands."

"What do we do?"

"We sit on it. We must know more before we say anything to Mentor."

"More about what?"

"Who Tieanna is talking about. We need to know who is coming for you. We're exposed without that."

"That is what Mentor wants too. Isn't it?" Dukk thought out loud.

Dukk was in turmoil. If there was more than one bad actor it would be harder to know if what Dukk and his team were doing was working into the hands of one or another, or all.

Marr was having a similar thought. In addition, she was questioning the motivations of her mentor of thirteen years. This wasn't going to get solved with a head full of wine and after forty-eight hours of broken sleep.

"Exactly," Marr said with a big yawn.

"Sleep?" Dukk suggested having come to the same conclusion independently of the yawn.

"Absolutely," Marr said as she swiped away the panels and stood up.

5

Near one p.m. the next day, Marr and Emeelie were standing next to some air scooters. They were on the hard surface outside the equipment building near the outdoor pool and tennis courts. They were watching Dukk and Craig race around on the air scooters. Bazzer and Eleettra were still in the equipment room getting their air scooters. They had all followed the same routine as per the day earlier with Bognath. They got changed together in the room off the utility.

Before crashing into bed in the early hours, Marr had set an alarm. She was keen to honour her promise to start the program. She was glad of it now, even with the heavy head at the time. The early start had helped her get her head together.

Marr had been joined by Dukk, Luna, Mentor, Bognath, Annee, Suzzona and half the girls. Marr considered the turnout was a great start.

The first morning involved some quiet reflection time, followed by Tai chi and a swim. However, the story circle was skipped in favour of brunch as no one was up for breakfast after the reflection time.

This plan worked out well because Bazzer had figured that might be the case. He, with help from Eleettra, and a couple of the girls, had put out a spread of cereals and breads, yoghurts, poached eggs, and bacon. Craig and Emeelie had also joined them. The banter during the casual gathering had been about comparing hangovers. Luna was the worse for wear and had gone back to bed after they had eaten.

"Do you think this display is for your benefit or mine?" Emeelie asked casually as they watched Dukk perform a stunt with the air scooter.

"Neither! It is for each other," Marr answered. "It is a display of dominance. They are competing to see who the alpha is. We all do it, just men more so."

"You speak is if there is a difference between men and women. We were taught that we are the same and we can choose."

"What does your experience tell you? Are men and women the same?"

"Well not physically, obviously, that is something that never sat well with me against what we were taught in school."

"What about behaviour, talents, and tendencies?"

"Well, I guess we do behave differently, and we do certainly compete."

"For dominance?"

"No, more like influence."

"Yes, and do we do it in the same manner?"

"No, we do it differently. I see your point. So why were we taught that we are the same?"

"Good question, however, perhaps the answer is for another time."

"When there is wine," Emeelie suggested.

"Exactly," Marr replied.

"Right, we are ready," Bazzer announced as he and Eleettra pushed scooters onto the hard surface.

"Need any tips?" Marr joked.

"I'll have you know, young one, that I was flying well before you started using a training bra."

Marr laughed as Dukk, and Craig arrived back from their racing.

"I'll concede you win in terms of the air scooters skills," Craig said loudly as the scooters spun down.

Dukk grinned widely as he got off his scooter.

Craig stepped off his scooter and put his hand out towards Dukk.

277

Dukk took his hand and shook it firmly.

"But I think being a flyer gives you an unfair advantage," Craig said cheekily.

Dukk laughed.

"Let's see how you get on with hunting," Craig added.

"What are the teams?" Emeelie asked.

While they got changed earlier, Craig had explained what they were hunting. He explained that the creatures that roamed the outer grounds were like Earth's armadillos. Just twice the size and with leathery armour that was nearly impenetrable. Craig shared that they moved quickly. He said they folded into a ball while running if hit by a projectile. The air rifles were used for this purpose. The ball rolling only happened when they were moving fast. They also were known to charge if threatened so staying out of their path was important. The aim of the hunting game was to take turns in teams to find a creature, get it moving and then take your shot. Each team would have ten minutes to cause a ball roll. They would fire a flare on success or when their time was up. The other team would join them to verify the hit and take their turn. The winners were the team that was first to get five hits.

"How about men verses women?" Marr said to the group as they stood around the scooters.

"Interesting," Craig replied.

"Keep me out of this," Bazzer said looking at the scooter. "I'm here to enjoy the freedom this yoke offers."

"Yes, keep us out of it," Eleettra added. "My job here is to keep you all safe, not rush around like crazy idiots chasing those creatures."

"Great, you'll be the umpires and keep the score," Craig said with a smile.

Dukk looked over at Marr. She was grinning. He knew this wasn't going to go the direction Craig wanted.

"I am up for it," Dukk laughed.

"Right, brother! Let's do this," Craig said as he put his arm around Dukk's shoulders.

Marr stopped and looked. The affectionate and casual use of the term 'brother' had spooked her once more. She was spooked in the same manner as when she saw Craig for the first time and when she saw the painting in the study. She knew from her reading that before the reset, the term was used both figuratively and literally. That was no longer the case, but it still gave her cause to pause.

Marr noticed Emeelie change her demeanour too. Something had caused her to pause as well.

Dukk stood there grinning. The use of the word didn't cause him to pause. To him it was simply a way to say close male friend. He was getting to like Craig and he liked the thought of having another close male friend. Bazzer was the only other close male friend he had.

Chapter 15 – Bonding

1

The hunting game went as Dukk had anticipated. Dukk and Craig did a reasonable job of getting hits. Dukk's flying skills complemented Craig's skill with the air rifle. However, Marr's shooting skills were far superior. She and Emeelie worked together to find a creature and get it moving. Then Marr simply pulled up, aimed, and took the shot. She didn't miss. The women won five to two.

During one of the men's turns, Marr and Emeelie were sitting on their scooters waiting for the flare.

"Last night we talked lots about keeping and hauling," Marr said. "We didn't talk much about anything else."
Emeelie nodded.
"I am curious about what your story is," Marr said.
"Not much to tell."
"Where did you start out?"
"I was a hostess and got noticed by Craig's family."
"What do you mean by got noticed?"
"Just before my sixteenth birthday I was selected for their fast-track program."
"What is the fast-track program?"
"It is a program where hostesses join training academies within elite households. We were moved out of the normal hostess training centres into private centres. These centres were located within the elite's villas on Earth or in large settlements like New Montana. We

spent an extra three years studying. It set us up for working within the elite's inner circles."

"I've never heard of this program."

"It is kept under the radar. Craig said Tieanna started it within the Atesoughton family and the other families followed suit. However, she denies being responsible for the proliferation of centres."

"Why is it kept under the radar?"

"I don't know why exactly. Craig thinks it is because the Veneficans don't like it. It gets in their way."

"Like what Craig was saying last night about Veneficans vetting companions."

"I guess so."

"What happened after the academy?"

"I started working for the Atesoughton family as a personal assistant. Mostly with Craig and Tieanna."

"Do you know Tieanna well?"

"Yes of course, she is my boss. Well, more than that really, I guess."

"What do you mean?"

"She supports me. She guides me."

Marr thought about that for a moment. She realised her impression and beliefs associated with elites and those around them, was changing. She was also wondering more and more about what Tieanna was up to.

"What is the situation with you and Craig?" Marr asked when the thoughts dissipated.

"I've been his personal assistant for five years."

"It appears you are more than just a personal assistant."

"By that you mean that I share his bed too."

"Yes."

"I guess that goes with the role."

"You seem close."

"I guess we are."

"Your relationship is open too."

"Of course."

"How do you feel about it being open?"

"It is fun."

"Fun?" Marr said in a questioning tone having noticed the disingenuous way Emeelie answered.

"OK, it pisses me off. But it is the only way that I know. It has always been this way. Also, Craig says it is necessary for building influence."

"What makes you so sure that it must be that way to work?"

"What do you mean?"

"Like Dukk and I. And Luna and Bognath."

"You and Dukk were open last night, granted it didn't go to completion."

Marr paused and gave that some thought. She knew Emeelie was right.

"We all make mistakes," Marr said after further reflection. "We get distracted. Do stupid things when we lose sight of what is important. The point is that it didn't go to completion."

"What stopped you?"

"I remembered what was at stake. Having sex with Craig last night would potentially destroy what I had already built with Dukk. I would be going backwards."

"What if it turned out better than what you have with Dukk?"

"Unlikely," Marr laughed. "But throwing away what you have, for the hope that what you get is better, doesn't work in the long term."

"Why?"

"Because you aren't building on what you have. You are starting over each time."

"Doesn't it get boring?"

"What is boring, really? What causes it?"

"The same old, day in, day out."

"Is everything you do new every time? Do you do the same things ever?"

283

"Of course, all the time."

"Why?"

"Sense of comfort in some level of stability."

"Are those activities boring?"

"No, not at all."

"And is the intimate time with Craig boring."

"Well, no, we have lots of mind-blowing sex."

"So, what is the problem?"

"It is hard at times being with Craig. He gets grumpy. I get grumpy too. You know how it goes. It gets difficult."

"Is what you are saying is that it is much easier just to avoid that? And instead to flirt and play?"

"Yes"

"So, you have gone through some tough moments together."

"Yep."

"What happened when you did?"

"It was great. Things got easier for a time. The sex that followed was great too."

"So perhaps boredom is just avoidance of what is hard, but worthwhile?"

"Interesting. You are starting to sound like Tieanna. Except I've never spoken about sex with her. It just felt weird to talk about Craig around her."

Marr gave that a moment then continued.

"What is needed here?"

"Stop having sex with others and see if that works?"

"Is that something you want?"

"Yes."

"What is in the way of you trying that?"

"I fear getting hurt even more. And Craig wouldn't do it."

"Are you sure of that?"

"No."

"What could you do?"

"I could suggest it to him."

Marr smiled.

Emeelie then looked over at Marr. Marr looked over too.

"Thank you," Emeelie said. "That has really helped."

"You are welcome," Marr said sincerely.

2

With the game complete they had made their way back through the mantraps and put away their scooters. Then they had returned to the change room to get out of the fatigues.

"You played me, Marr," Craig said as they got changed in the room off the utility. "And Dukk, why didn't you warm me she was one of Mentor's prodigies?"

"My friend, it is better to let them win out there, than lose in other places," Dukk laughed.

Craig grinned.

"Cheeky monkeys," Marr said as she pulled her t-shirt over her head.

"Perhaps a rematch is in order?" Emeelie said cautiously.

"Definitely," Craig answered before pausing to look at Emeelie.

"Maybe tomorrow," he added.

"Are we staying?" Emeelie asked.

"Another night away from my commitments wouldn't hurt. If of course, our hosts will be happy with our company for another evening?"

"Absolutely," Dukk replied without hesitation.

"Good, that's settled then. And I am cooking."

"Cooking?" Marr said in a curious manner.

"Yes, I am a master at the barbecue. The outdoor pool area is set up for it. We can eat out there too. Last night was formal. Tonight, should be casual. Swimmers and sliders. I see the girls have already got the heaters running. It gets quite warm when they are at full tilt. It will be just like a midsummers evening back on Earth."

"So, you will be cooking the meat?" Dukk asked Craig to confirm what he thought he heard.

"He might need a little help with preparing the meats for cooking and sides to go with it," Emeelie said with a laugh.

"Yes, true. Emeelie, you might see what can be done about that."

"Or you could ask Suzzona yourself. She is very accommodating," Marr said in a cheeky tone.

"Yes, Marr, that's a good idea. I'll have a word with Suzzona myself."

Marr looked over at Emeelie and winked. Emeelie smiled.

"Oh," Craig added, "I might need a hand getting the barbecue fired up. Guys?"

"I'll help," Dukk answered.

"Leave me out of it," Bazzer answered.

He then added, "I have work to do. By the way, why am I bothering to get dressed again, I need a shower after chasing you lot about."

"And a rest," Eleettra added.

Bazzer smiled as he left the change room.

"That works," Craig said. "Let's say, back in the kitchen near six p.m. to get started."

Dukk nodded.

"Great, I'm off to find Suzzona," Craig said as he headed out the door.

"What work does Bazzer have to do," Emeelie asked Marr as they prepared to leave the change room.

"He is making a coffin. He is converting a RoboCrate into a sealable casket."

"Who for?"

"Zarra. We are taking her back to Earth for a proper burial."

"Oh, of course."

Near six p.m. Dukk was approaching the kitchen. He and Marr had spent a few well needed hours resting in their suite. She had gone in search of a swimming costume.

A familiar voice met Dukk as he opened the kitchen door.

"Not bad for a first attempt," Suzzona said.

Craig and Suzzona were standing at the centre counter. In front of them on cutting boards, were large pieces of meat. Craig was wearing sliders, a t-shirt, and a very bright pair of boardshorts. Suzzona was wearing a yellow bikini, a white see-through cover up and sliders. Both had aprons over the top.

Three girls were also there on the other side of the counter. They were threading vegetables and chunks of chicken onto skewers. They were similarly attired in swimwear.

"Dukk, great timing," Craig said as he looked up. "Suzzona is showing me how to fillet a side of beef."

Suzzona laughed and then said, "But at this rate it will be sometime next week before we'd be ready to cook. How about you and Dukk go light the barbecues and let me, Alion, Lilaho and Kayila finish this off."

"Great idea," Craig said as he headed over to the sink to wash his hands.

"Nice shorts," Dukk laughed.

"And where are your pool side clothes?" Craig said back in jest.

"I didn't see any upstairs."

"No, they are in the change room near the indoor pools. Let's go there on our way to fire up the barbecues."

Ten minutes later, Craig led Dukk into the change room. They had got delayed slightly on the way there. Craig had insisted on doing a mini tour. Which he had assumed was needed without checking. Dukk found it amusing but went with it. He didn't feel it was necessary to point out that he and Marr had already explored the recreational area the day before.

The change room was a large open space with storage, lockers, benches, and shower cubicles with three quarter high, smoked glass doors.

Marr was already there looking through the storage. She was sifting through the swimwear options.

"Dukk and Craig, great," Marr said as she looked over. "I've found some options and I need a second opinion."

Marr then held up two packages. The packages had clear wrapping. Brightly coloured fabrics could be seen beneath the wrapping.

"They are very colourful. I would have thought you would be into white, or that fabulous emerald-green you had on last night," Craig said.

"These are shorts. They are for Dukk," Marr laughed.

"I am already ready," she added as she dropped the packages and pulled open her robe. Beneath the robe was a blush pink faux suede, high cut deep v thong one piece swimsuit.

"Wow, good choice," Craig said.

"Yes, wow indeed," Dukk said with a grin.

"I am glad you both approve," Marr said cheekily.

"Why don't you help Dukk get changed while I go find the barbecue coal," Craig said with a wink as he headed for the door.

With Craig gone, Dukk walked over to Marr and put his arms inside her robe. He pulled her towards him.

"It is getting harder and harder to get things done around you when you are looking this hot," Dukk giggled as he lent in for a kiss.

"Perhaps it is best then, that I let you get changed on your own," Marr said in a whisper after the kiss.

"Yes, that might be best," Dukk answered reluctantly as he let go of the embrace.

3

An hour later, Dukk and Craig were standing over two large barbecues.

The two men were shirtless beneath large black aprons. They had barbecue tongs in one hand and a brown bottle in the other. On the barbecue were an assortment of meats and vegetables. Their muscular upper bodies were glistening. They were sweating.

"I see what you mean by the heat of those overhead lamps," Dukk said as he poked at a chicken skewer. "One could easily forget one was not on Earth basking under the yellow dwarf but here on New Montana with its dull red sun."

"Absolutely. How's that beer?" Craig asked.

"Getting warm."

"You need to drink it faster!"

"Or use one of these?" Annee called from a sunbed nearby.

Annee held up her beer bottle. It was sitting in a white cup.

"I tried," Dukk said. "It didn't have the same feel as holding onto the bottle directly."

Dukk turned around as he answered Annee. He smiled at the scene.

Marr was sitting on the edge of the pool dangling her feet. She was chatting to a cluster of girls who were standing in the shallow water in front of her.

Luna, Bognath, Alessano and some of the girls were playing water polo at the other end of the large pool.

Bazzer and Eleettra were standing behind a fully stocked outdoor bar. They were making cocktails and having a great laugh by the look of it.

Kimince and Trence had finally made an appearance. Mentor had made a circle with sunbeds. The observers were sitting there sipping cocktails and listening intensely to what Mentor was saying. A cluster of girls were there also. They too were listening intensely.

Suzzona was laying out next to Annee. She was sipping a cocktail and watching the others.

Dukk's gaze returned to Marr. She was looking in his direction. She smiled.

Marr was enjoying the chat with the girls. They had lots of questions. Mostly about her time as a keeper.

She was also watching Dukk. The light from the head lamps kept bouncing off his muscular back. It moved as he lifted his beer and poked at the items on the barbecue. The butterfly feeling was washing over her again. She smiled when he gazed over.

"Speaking of Earth. That reminds me," Craig said as he put the tongs and beer on the flat surface near the grill. He then opened his wrist wraps.

After flicking through some panels in the air before him, he looked up and said, "here, catch."

Dukk put his tongs and beer down and opened his wrist wraps to catch the transfer.

"What is this?" Dukk said as he opened the message.

"An order," Craig answered as he picked up the tongs and beer again.

Dukk opened the message. It was a haulier purchase order docket. He read the instructions. The order was for transportation of eleven hostesses back to Earth. It also included the transportation of the body of a child back to Earth for burial. It was stamped with an Atesoughton family executive order seal. The seal would enable him to take the rig through Atesoughton family-controlled systems and those systems where trade agreements were in place. Which didn't exclude many routes. The order also included a significant payment.

Dukk gasped. He looked over at Craig and got a little emotional as he realised what he had just been given. Payment aside, the order would legitimise his movements. There would be no more need for sneaking about.

Craig smiled on observing the emotion.

"I can't take the credit. It was Emeelie's idea," he said. "The girls told her that Zarra wanted to see the stars. Perhaps you can take them all on the scenic route back and honour that wish."

"Thank you," Dukk managed to say as he put his hand out.

"Pleasure man," Craig said as he put down the tongs and beer. "You, Marr, and your crew are an inspiration. You have completely changed my world view."

Craig then pushed aside Dukk's attempt at shaking his hand. Instead, he leant in for a hug.

Marr was watching the exchange with intrigue. Curiosity overcame her and she excused herself from the girls.

She stood up and started to walk around the pool to see what was going on. Then she noticed Emeelie coming through the glass doors from the indoor pool. Emeelie was wearing a similar swimsuit to Marr, just in white.

Marr paused. Emeelie was looking fabulous but tired.

Emeelie started walking towards Dukk and Craig at the barbecue.

Marr changed direction and headed towards her.

"Are you okay," Marr asked Emeelie when she reached her.

"Yes, just tired," she answered. "After the hunting, Craig and I had a long talk. I had work to do after that. I was interviewing for my replacement."

Marr paused. She was confused.

"Ah, here she is," came a booming voice from the barbecue. It was Craig.

Everyone stopped and looked over.

Craig put down his barbecue tongs and beer once more and marched over to meet Emeelie and Marr.

When he got there, he took Emeelie's hand and leant in for a deep kiss. Then he turned to face everyone.

"I want to make it official in front of my new friends," he said as he looked around.

He then turned back to Emeelie. She smiled and nodded.

"I am delighted to announce that Emeelie and I have agreed to be companioned. I will miss her as my personal assistant, but I am sure she will have her replacement whipped into shape in no time at all."

Emeelie beamed. She made a point of looking over at Marr and smiling.

Marr smiled back as a tear formed in the corner of her eye.

Dukk had followed Craig over. He was the first to offer them congratulations. He took Craig's lead and gave them a big hug.

Marr was next.

The others all came around to offer there well wishes too.

Marr and Dukk stood back a little. Marr put her hand around Dukk's waist. He followed suit.

"Is this your doing?" Dukk asked as they watched.

"Maybe," Marr said with a giggle.

"Or perhaps it was a miracle," she added.

Dukk turned to her. He reached his other hand over and drew her in for a kiss.

"What was all that about with you and Craig a moment ago?" Marr asked after the kiss.

"Another miracle," Dukk answered with a chuckle.

4

A little over twenty-four hours later, Marr and Dukk were in bed. They, like most, had decided on an early night after the madness of the last week.

The previous evening, around the pool, had turned into a little party following Craig and Emeelie's announcement. While not going as late as the previous evening, it was still near midnight before everyone found their beds. The latter part of the evening involved Mentor sharing stories around a firepit that sat alongside the pool area. Everyone stayed on as long as they could stay awake. The reason was not just because of Mentor's skill as a storyteller. It was also because of the novelty of the firepit. Except for Craig, Emeelie, Eleettra and Alessano, none had experienced anything like it. The experience was even more unique as the wood for the firepit had been hauled from Earth.

The next day started off in a manner like the day before. However, everyone, including all the girls and the guests got up for Marr's reflection and structured training. The slightly earlier night gave Marr the confidence to do the Wu Style Tai Chi for a change of pace.

After a swim and showers, they all helped organise brunch. It was a joyous time with laughs and sharing of thoughts coming from the events of the previous days and Mentor's stories.

With brunch done, Craig and Emeelie said they had to rain-check the hunting rematch. With their companionship announcement and Emeelie's change of status, they had things to do and people to tell.

A boisterous and perhaps tad teary send-off was had in the entrance hall. Then, Marr, Dukk and Bazzer escorted the guests down the lift and onto the shuttle that was parked waiting on the platform outside the hanger.

The remainder of the day was casual and easy. It was concluded with a simple shared meal prepared by Suzzona with help from Luna and Bognath.

"I just realised it is a week since we lost the Dinatha," Dukk said as he ran his fingers through Marr's hair.

"I know," she replied. "It is hard to believe it has only been a week. So much has happened."

"I don't think I have ever had a week as eventful and life changing as this."

"Well, I would be very happy if nothing at all happened for the next week, and I was able to just stay here in this massive bed and sleep."

"Just sleep?" Dukk asked in a provocative tone.

"Well, perhaps not just sleep," Marr giggled.

After a pause she added, "Perhaps some food will be needed. And perhaps a swim or two. Oh, and maybe some wine. And, of course, lots of time in the library."

Dukk chuckled.

Marr pretty much got her wishes.

During free time after lunch on the seventh day since arriving, Dukk and Bazzer had gone down to the rig to monitor the refuelling, cycle up the reactors and warm up the systems ahead of the evening launch.

Dukk was in the cockpit interacting with the controls. He was excited about the thought of getting underway again. The week had been wonderful, but it wasn't the life he knew. He felt rested but unsettled. He was ready to get back to the way of life that he loved.

Bazzer entered the cockpit and came up beside him.

Dukk looked up.

"Did I see Eleettra with the security detail on that fuel tanker?" He asked.

"Yep," Bazzer said sheepishly.

"She is a great gal."

Bazzer laughed and then said, "Don't start to think you are all wise and knowledgeable about companionship just because things are going so well with Marr. Believe me, you have a long way to go before you have something wise to offer me with respect to companionship."

Dukk laughed, then asked, "How are we looking?"

"Diagnostics are running. We should have a full set of results in twenty minutes. But at first glance we are in good shape."

"Great," Dukk answered as he turned back towards the windshield.

As Dukk turned, he noticed Suzzona leaving the service elevator with a bunch of girls. They were wheeling food laden trolleys.

"Do you think she will leave even a coffee bean for the next users of this villa?" Dukk asked.

Bazzer looked down. He laughed.

"I thought she was just replacing the fresh food she used from the stuff we brought from Mayfield," Dukk said.

"That was before you told her that we would take nearly three weeks to reach Earth. She went back to the fridges and larders again. I told her to leave the wine behind."

"Good move," Dukk laughed. "I could do with a dry spell."

After a moment of watching, Dukk added, "I gather that is why the hold platform has been lowered?"

"Yes and no," Bazzer answered. "We are going to turn the container around. Once in orbit, between traverses, we want to be able to get at it from the front of the hold. We are going to integrate the crates, fridges, and freezers into the storage space forward of the hold. Suzzona said the container is traceable and we might want to dump it somewhere on route. Perhaps have it burn up on re-entry to some useless rock. Besides, with twenty-one on board, we are going to need the space for exercise."

"Something Luna said now makes sense."

"What was that?"

"I said I'd like her and I to get simulation time together to get proficient at evasive manoeuvres alongside weapon usage. And she said Suzzona gave her an idea for target practice and test firing."

Bazzer laughed deeply.

He then said, "Well we'd better make sure we are alone in orbit before we do that."

The next arrival was Marr and Luna. They stepped out of the main elevator lift. They were carrying large bags stuffed with what appeared to be clothing.

Dukk grinned. He was thinking it was good that this rig was designed to haul heavy metals. Otherwise, they'd never get airborne with what was being put on board.

"What is the story there?" Bazzer asked.

"Emeelie told Marr that Craig meant what he said about using and taking what we needed. Emeelie also said that lots of the clothing never gets used and is thrown out. The fashion changes and their guests don't want to be seen in last year's styles. They don't even recycle. It just gets incinerated. She said it is more cost effective to just reprint."

"Yes, I heard that too. It's crazy. I was just wondering what they are going to do with that stuff. The casual clothes are impractical on the rig. And, it isn't like we'll have the opportunity to go fine dining or hanging by a pool any time soon."

"Never say never, Bazzer. Besides, we have friends in high places now."

Bazzer laughed and then said, "I guess you are right. All the things I have seen, couldn't have prepared me for what has happened over the last two weeks."

Dukk turned and said, "I'd better go and supervise where that lot gets stored. I don't want my favourite red shirt binned to make room for a spare tuxedo. "

"Good idea," Bazzer said with a laugh.

"There you are!" Marr said as she met Dukk at the top of the stairs.

"What did you do with those bags of clothes?" Dukk asked.

"Luna is putting them into the storage lockers in the nose section."

"Do I want to go down and see exactly how much extra stuff we have on board?"

"Nope," Marr laughed as she put her arms around his neck and leant in for a kiss.

Dukk laughed as he accepted her lips.

"But I have something else to show you?" Marr said after the kiss.

Dukk raised his eyebrows.

"I have the ideas for the flight plan. Shall we look at them?" Marr grinned cheekily.

"Of course," Dukk said with a laugh, as he let go of the embrace.

Marr took Dukk's hand and turned towards the lounge. She sat them into the middle of the long sofa and then enabled the projector in the air before them.

"So, we want to track towards the edge of the Atesoughton cluster. I suggest we get there via New Katoomba."

"You want to see a blue giant star?"

"Yep. I see that there is a research station and resort on a moon orbiting a large planet in the outer regions of the system."

"Have you checked that it is still there?"

"Yes! The sun hasn't gone supernova yet," Marr said before making a rude face at Dukk.

"Besides, we'd know about it even this far off in New Montana," she added.

Dukk grinned. He loved that Marr engaged with his dry sense of humour.

"After that?"

"Then we move across to the Asimov cluster," Marr answered. "Mentor wants us to visit Newterratwo. I'd like our path there to track via IACL2. Then after Newterratwo, I'd suggest we take in Utah's Twin and Tau Ceti 1 on the way to Earth."

"IACL2 sounds familiar. Why that system?"

"Isaac's nebula."

"Oh yes, it has a good view of the brightest nebula in this sector."

"Are there others?"

"Not that I know of."

"Why is it the brightest then?"

"I made that part up. It sounds better than just saying nebula."

Marr gave him a gentle nudge in the ribs, then said, "You are in a giddy mood."

"I guess I am excited about getting moving again."

"Me too," Marr said as she put her arms around him again.

When they pulled apart from the kiss, Dukk said, "That all sounds good with me. Will we work it into a flight plan so we can load it up?"

"I already have the plan ready," Marr said with a smile.

"Great, let's load it up," Dukk said as he got up, took Marr's hand, and headed towards the cockpit.

Near five p.m., Dukk and his crew were seated around the crew mess table. They were there for the pre-departure circle-up.

"This feels all very tight compared to the banquet hall," Luna said as they sat down. "It is time to go back to fighting over showers, stumbling all over each other again and near zero privacy."

Then after a pause and a giggle, she added, "Mind you, none of that ever got in the way of having a bit of fun."

"Very true, Luna. And I am glad it appears you have your mojo again," Dukk said to control the room.

"Me too," Luna replied.

Dukk smiled and then continued.

"First, let's check where we are at with housekeeping. Ann?"

"We are in good shape, captain," Annee replied. "The supplies are all loaded. The girls are settled into their dorms. We have done the safety briefing. And we are ready to do an evacuation drill."

"Excellent. And the villa?"

"Suzzona?" Annee responded.

"Cleared out. Sorry, I mean everything is in good order. All that is left is a final walk around before locking it down. We can depart at any time after that."

"Any chance of using the showers before we launch?" Bazzer asked.

"Absolutely, that won't change anything," Suzzona replied.

"Good. I've been busy getting this bird ready for launch and could do with a long shower. And I'm not quite ready to be fighting Luna again for the shower rose."

"That joke is getting very old, Bazzer," Luna laughed.

Bazzer chuckled. He looked to be enjoying having the fun version of Luna back too.

"Great, and Bazzer, seeing as you've taken the floor, how are our systems looking?" Dukk said to keep things on track.

"The system diagnostics all checked out. Everything is in good order. We are in slow running ready to power up for launch."

"Excellent, Bazzer," Dukk replied. "Marr has the flight plan sorted and we are ready to request launch permission. Let's aim for near six-thirty p.m. That will give us time to do whatever else is needed. Pre-launch circle up at six p.m. Anything else?"

"What is our path?" Luna asked.

"Marr, do you want to run us through it?" Dukk asked.

"Sure," Marr said as she enabled the projection in the air above the table. "Our first stopover on the way back to Earth is WZX4, also known as New Katoomba. To get there we traverse via WZV6 and WZV9."

"The blue giant?" Annee asked.

"Yes. We'll spend twenty-four hours at the resort and take in the view."

"You can moon walk there too," Suzzona added.

"Excellent. So, from there we track to the edge of the Atesoughton cluster via WZX7 before crossing over to the Asimov cluster. Our first destination in that cluster is IACF2. We'll dock at a research station that offers fabulous views of Isaac's nebula. To get there we traverse via IACF8. We'll stay for twenty-four hours before continuing onto Newterratwo and the yellow dwarf sun. Getting to The Shipyard, as most know it, will only require traversing through IACE7. We'll make that a longer stay of three days. After Newterratwo we have a longer leg to get to Utah's Twin. Which is a hub in IACB5, a twin red dwarf system. We get there via IACE1, IACD3, IACC9 and IACC4. We'll stay for at least thirty-six hours so we can see the shifting of the two suns. Our last stopover will be the hub at New Earth in the Tau Ceti 1 system. We get there via ICAB9, IACB2 and IACA6. After that we are pretty much in bound to Earth. Our path will take us via Tau Ceti 13, 9, 8 and 5."

"Marr, that sounds like a fabulous track. A once in a lifetime excursion," Annee said.

"Thanks, Ann," Marr said with a smile.

"How long until we are back on Earth?" Luna asked.

"Using estimated traverse wait times, it should be about three weeks," Marr replied.

"So," Luna said before pausing to do the math. "That would be about two months since we first left Earth on the Dinatha."

"Yes, I think it would, Luna," Marr replied.

"Wow," Annee blurted. "It feels like a lifetime ago since we were all sitting around the crew table for the first time. Dukk as a new captain, and Marr, Luna, and Mentor in their sparkling new crew uniforms with matching Dinatha branded jackets."

"It does," Marr laughed.

"That reminds me," Dukk said. "How exactly did you get those branded jackets so quickly?"

He then continued talking and answered his own question. "Let me guess. Mentor had them printed already, because joining the Dinatha was part of his plan."

Mentor smiled.

After a chuckle, Dukk then stood up.

"Well, if there isn't anything else, let's finish it there. We have just under an hour until the commencement of the launch sequence. And I need a shower too."

"The reactors are running again, so we can't leave the rig unattended. Suzzona and I need to complete the resort lockdown. After the showers of course," Annee said as a reminder.

"Yes, of course," Dukk replied.

"I can take the conn if you like," Mentor said. "I'm already showered and ready to go."

"Excellent. That means one last luxury shower," Dukk said as he smiled. He looked over at Marr.

Marr was already looking at him. She was smiling too.

Chapter 16 – Touring

1

A little before half six, Dukk stood at the top of the ramp. He had just completed the external sanity check. He was waiting for the ramp to retract so he could seal up the rig.

He smiled as he recalled the time with Marr after the pre-departure circle-up. The shower had been more like two showers. The second one was in cold water so they could cool down.

At six p.m. the crew had locked the villa, and everyone had got settled into the rig.

A brief pre-launch circle-up was followed by the evacuation drill. Dukk had caught everyone by surprise. As the circle-up finished, he walked over to the console and activated the drill. Dukk was pleased that he did it that way. It caught them off guard and showed they all needed practice if they were to survive a real emergency.

When the chime sounded to indicate the ramp was up and sealed, Dukk opened the crew comms.

"We are sealed. Starting the integrity checks. Bazzer, let's go hot. Marr, we can get those hanger doors open now and submit the launch go request."

"On it," was the reply from Bazzer.

"Will do," was the reply from Marr.

He then sealed the inner airlock door and made for the stairs.

When he reached the stairs, he put his hand on the stair rail and paused. He tuned into the vibrations and waited for the change as the other two reactors spun up. He was keen to learn the rig's moods. Knowing the Dinatha's moods had saved him on several occasions.

He wasn't planning on things being any different with this new rig. When he was satisfied that he could tell the difference, he enabled the broadcast mode on his comms and continued up the stairs.

"Good evening, everyone. The doors are sealed, and we are now making final preparations for launch. After leaving this hanger we have a fifteen-minute journey to clear the settlement. We'll then engage a hard burn of just under nine minutes. We should be safely in orbit near seven p.m. preparing for our first traverse. Sit back and enjoy the ride."

When Dukk reached the passenger area he was met by noise and chaos.

The girls were all dressed in blue g-suits. They had their hair tied back in low ponytails. Each wore a black arm band in honour of Zarra. Most were seated. They filled the first three rows. Some had their belts on. A few had their helmets on already. Those that did were messing with their comms and trying to chat with each other. Annee and Suzzona were in among them trying to get them all sorted.

Kimince and Trence were seated against the window, in the fourth row. They had their helmets on and appeared to be chatting casually to each other.

Dukk didn't see Bognath. That didn't surprise him. If he was Bognath, he would be hanging back until all the helmets were on and quietness had been restored. He would then quietly take a seat at the back.

Dukk grinned at Annee as he stood at the top of the stairs. Annee rolled her eyes and smiled back.

Even with the mayhem, Dukk was glad. He was pleased to see the girls had their spark back. It wasn't the same as when he first met four of the girls in Maple Tower. It was different. It still had energy, just a different kind.

"What is New Katoomba like? Is it a big planet like Earth?" one of the girls could be heard asking.

"Not sure, I've never been," Annee answered. "Supplies out there are usually sourced from larger settlements in the cluster. Hauling out that far is not usual for Earth based rigs."

"I've been there," Suzzona said.

"Really," one of the girls said in an enthusiastic tone.

"Yep. Firstly, New Katoomba is not a planet. It is the name for a research station and resort on the moon orbiting one of the largest planets in the system. The moon is large in comparison to Earth's moon, but still has limited gravity. The settlement is solely based on artificial habitats. The port is surface based but there are passenger boarding bridges and tunnel systems to move about. The resort won't be for the likes of us, however there is a viewing platform and a reasonable eatery and bar within the staff habitats."

"What can we do there?"

"Stare at the sun through viewing goggles?"

"Oh. Anything a little more exciting?"

"We can do a moon walk. We can hire equipment and a guide."

"That's sounds better," the girl answered in a gleeful tone.

2

Dukk was about to move through to the cockpit when he got reason to pause longer.

"I hope we meet the girls from Norline," one girl piped.

"What do you mean, Nabiel?" Annee asked.

"Some of the older girls went to New Katoomba last year," Nabiel replied.

"What do you mean by went there?" Annee asked.

"They talked about going there and then one day they were gone."

"Did you hear from them since?"

"Nope, I guess they went to one of those elite schools like Emeelie," Nabiel added a little reluctantly.

"Yes, that is it," another said before adding, "Emeelie is super cool isn't she."

"Absolutely," said yet another before adding. "And how brilliant is it that she and Craig are now companioned. When I am older, that is what I want too."

Dukk looked over at Annee. She was going white. She looked over at Dukk. Dukk frowned.

"Now is not the moment to destroy their hopes further," he thought to himself as he resumed his journey towards the cockpit.

Inside the cockpit things were a little calmer. But there was still lots of activity.

Marr was working through the pre-launch checklists.

Mentor was flicking through passenger med pages making sure all the girls would get the correct sedative dose on launch.

Dukk paused and watched for a moment.

"I am home again," he thought to himself. "It still feels comforting to enter the cockpit just before launch. Will that ever change?"

With no answer to his question, he smiled and walked to the front of the cockpit. He took his seat on the left.

He looked over at Marr. She looked up and smiled.

"What?" Marr asked sensing his odd mood.

"Mixed emotions."

"How so?"

"On one hand, I am excited to be moving again. On the other hand, I just overheard the girls talking about other girls from Norline going to New Katoomba."

"Yes, I heard that too earlier when I was briefing them about the flight plan."

"What did you say about it?"

"I just said that we might try and meet with them."

"You think they are there?"

"No, I don't. From what Emeelie told me, I am pretty sure there are no elite schools out that far. But they aren't ready to hear more hard truths."

"Yes, that is what I thought too," Dukk added.

Marr gave it a moment then shifted direction.

"I am ready when you are to do the cross checks," she said.

"Great, let's do it," Dukk answered as he grabbed his helmet and stood up again.

Marr did the same but before putting the helmet on, she used her free hand to reach for Dukk and pull him in for a kiss.

"Leave it out, you two!" Luna announced as she entered the cockpit.

Bazzer was right behind her.

Marr and Dukk laughed as they pulled apart.

"Are we all set?" Dukk said to them both as they took their places in the second row.

"Yep, everything is humming beautifully," Bazzer replied.

Annee was the last to enter. She closed the door, leant back against it, and sighed.

Dukk laughed.

"We are going to have to take turns doing that," Annee said with a laugh.

"I am sure it will get easier," Mentor said.

"I hope so," she replied.

Marr and Dukk put their helmets on and took their seats.

Dukk then enabled the crew comms again.

"Check-in please. Passengers and vitals, Mentor?"

"All hooked up and stable. Med lines are primed," Mentor answered.

"Engines, integrity and biosystems?"

"The reactors are hot. The burners are priming. The coolers are running well. Integrity is at one hundred percent. All systems are green," Bazzer replied.

"Stealth tech, weapons and defences?" Dukk asked.

"Online, Diagnostics are clear," Luna replied.

"External comms, scanners, Ann?"

"We have just the usual evening activity. Nothing to concern us," Annee replied.

"Good to know," Dukk replied. "Marr, flight control?"

"Hanger doors are open. We have clearance. The autopilot just needs your approval, captain," Marr answered smiling over at Dukk.

"Anything else, anyone?" Dukk asked as he turned and looked back. He was met with smiling faces.

"Well then, let's go," Dukk said with glee as he authorised the autopilot.

The rig trembled as the vertical thrusters engaged to lift the rig gently and back it out of the hanger. The vibrations and noise increased as the thrusters and then main engines engaged. The rig lifted away from the hillside dome and then moved into the reddish darkness beyond. After fifteen minutes of gradual lift, the hard burners engaged. The rig turned skywards and shot towards the upper atmosphere.

3

Twenty-four hours later the rig had just completed the second traverse since leaving New Montana. Everyone was conscious again and stable. The first twenty-four hours of their return journey had passed quickly. The crew returned to their rig operating routines. The program continued for the girls. The others joined in when they could. It took everyone a little time to get used to the confined spaces again. This was especially true of the girls.

"How are we looking, Ann?" Dukk asked.

"The radar is clear, and the relay isn't showing any activity. We are alone," Annee answered.

"Great, let's do some target practice."

Dukk then enabled the broadcast.

"Welcome to WZV9, a featureless system by the look of it. As we hoped, the system is empty but for us. This gives us the opportunity to offload the container and test fire our weapons. The DMD will remain off for about an hour as we complete this activity. You are free to move around, but take care in the zero-g."

Dukk then removed his helmet and turned around.

"Bazzer, you and Bognath are up. Let's get the platform down and the container out."

Thirty minutes later the container was slowly moving away from the rig. Bazzer had used a transport pod to extract the container and push it out in front of them. Bognath had helped get the towing arm connected and disconnected.

Marr, Dukk, Luna and Annee had remained in the cockpit helping with airlock doors and operating the hold bay platform. They had also spent time going back over the procedures for firing weapons.

With the transport pod and E.V.A. packs stowed, Bazzer, Mentor, Suzzona and Bognath had joined the others in the cockpit as it promised to have the best view of proceedings.

Dukk had already shared a message with the girls and the observers. He had suggested they take their seats and belt up during the test firing.

Annee had also shared a broadcast for the benefit of the relay. The message mentioned ordinance testing. They were keen not to have a suggestion of conflict echoed to adjacent systems.

"Weapons control authorised," Dukk said when everyone was ready.

"Check, captain," Luna replied as she interacted with the controls at her console.

"Charging the CDL while we test the rail guns," she added.

"Good idea," Dukk replied. "Fire away when ready."

Luna smiled, then said, "Static rail guns firing in three. Three. Two. One."

The rig shook and there was a rattling sound as Luna engaged the weapon.

The rapid-fire projectiles were hardly visible to the naked eye. However, a zoomed video feed of the container showed a series of holes cut in the container's side.

"Shit," Annee exclaimed. "That is nasty."

"Right, Dukk, let's try them while doing a corkscrew," Luna said as she adjusted her aim.

"Check," Dukk said as he disengaged the autopilot.

"Brace," he then said on the rig's broadcast, before pulling at the joystick on his right side.

The rig started to turn on its lengthways axis.

The container wobbled in their view. The rock planet racing below them now appeared to orbit them as they spun.

"Moving rail gun firing in three. Three. Two. One," Luna said.

The rig shook again. The rattling was slightly different. As before the projectiles weren't easy to spot but the video feed showed the container getting another hammering.

"Brilliant, Luna," Marr said with a touch of pride in her voice.

"You are a very dangerous woman, Luna," Bazzer said in jest.

Luna grinned but stayed focused on the task at hand.

"The CDL is charged," Luna said.

"Authorised," Dukk added.

"Moving CDL firing in three. Three. Two. One."

The rig vibrated violently as the laser sent a burst in the direction of the container.

The naked eye had no issue seeing the hit. The video feed showed a large hole that went straight through the middle of the container.

"That is badass!" Suzzona said.

"Let's put some distance between us for the final test," Luna said.

"Check", Dukk said as he interacted with the controls to bring the rig out of the spin.

"Brace", he then said into the broadcast as he pushed the joy sticks forward.

The rig shot forward and quickly overtook the container.

"That should do it," Dukk said after a few minutes.

He was about to pull back on the joystick when Luna interrupted him.

"Dukk, let's do this while accelerating. It will be more realistic."

"Whatever you like, you are the one in the hotseat with a fine audience."

Luna grinned again as she interacted with the controls.

A sharp noise rang out in the cockpit and in their comms. It was a similar sound to the missile lock warning they got when the patrol accosted them on the way back to Mayfield. But it was slightly deeper in tone. It indicated that Luna had acquired missile lock on the container.

"Missile authorised," Dukk said as he turned to watch the video feed from the tail camera.

"Firing missile in three. Three. Two. One."

A thud was felt in the rig as the missile shot out in front of them. It then did a tight turn to rush past them.

Thirty seconds later the rear camera video feed showed a sharp explosion.

"Bye, bye," Suzzona laughed.

"Well done, Luna," Marr said as she stood and started to clap.

The others joined in.

"Thanks," Luna said with a big grin.

"Yes, well done, Luna," Bazzer said when the clapping stopped. "Now we know we'll be safe if we come into contact with a hostile RoboContainer."

Luna turned to Bazzer in the seat next to her and bluffed a right hook.

"You'll keep," she added with a laugh.

The others laughed too.

"Right," Dukk said to regain the room. "Let's get the DMD online again and get ourselves over to New Katoomba. We have a date with a blue giant."

4

A little before eleven a.m. the next morning, Dukk and Annee were standing in the passenger boarding bridge at the port door. The rig was sitting on a pad in the port of New Katoomba.

The last traverse had proceeded as expected as had the approach and landing.

Dukk and Annee were waiting for the security personnel to arrive to do their inspection.

Next to them was a port worker. He looked old and worn out.

The bridge had clear Perspex walls. That gave Dukk, Annee and the port worker a good view of the port and habitats.

"This looks all very grand," Annee said to make conversation. "I guess this is the resort. Where are the research station and staff habitats?"

"You are looking at them. The resort is over that ridge," answered the port worker.

He pointed in the opposite direction to the habitats in front of them.

"Why do these habitats look like a resort?"

"It is the old resort. A new resort was built five years ago near the old staff areas. They were mostly demolished to make way."

"Mostly?"

"Some of the services like backup generators and the original incinerators were kept in place."

The mention of incinerators got the attention of both Dukk and Annee.

"What do you mean by original incinerators?" Annee asked.

"They built new incinerators when they built the first resort. They are all we use now."

"It doesn't look like much is going on?" Dukk said as he looked around the port.

Theirs was the only rig. The other nineteen pads were empty.

"Nope. Our business comes in peaks and troughs. The resort is block booked for perhaps a week. They come and then they go."

"What do you mean by they?"

"Elites and their entourage. They even bring their own staff and supplies."

"So, no workers from here go over there?"

"No, we go there to clean and do maintenance. Just not when it is occupied."

"So, you have seen the place?"

"Of course. I've been here since the very beginning. Mind you, there are parts of the resort we aren't allowed near."

"What do you mean?"

The worker paused. He held a blank expression.

Dukk paused too. Then it hit him.

"Annee, will we take a selfie," Dukk said in a slightly contrived tone. "Perhaps a nice shot with the habitats in the background?"

Annee looked at Dukk with a 'What the!' expression.

"Would you like to join us?" Dukk said to the worker.

"Sure," the worker said with a smile.

Dukk took the selfie. Then he used the Antiw picture app to add some crypto. He then flicked the selfie over to the port worker.

The port worker inspected the selfie and then smiled.

"If one was allowed into the restricted parts of the resort, what would one most likely see?" Dukk asked.

The worker looked behind them and then back down the bridge.

He then said, "You might see some rooms with odd equipment. Some call them red rooms."

"And the original incinerators. Are they ever used?"

Once more, the worker looked behind them and then back down the bridge.

"Yes. But not often. Just after some of the parties."

"Would it be possible to inspect the rooms or incinerators?"

"Rooms, no. Incinerators, perhaps. They are outside. One could go for a little moon walk."

Movement on the airbridge disrupted their oiled conversation.

"IDs please," said a voice as two security personnel made their way towards them.

The port worker grinned as he stood aside to allow the party through. He then nodded at Dukk and Annee, before turning and disappearing back down the airbridge.

"Looks like another location," Annee said after her and Dukk were scanned.

She then turned to follow the security detail.

"Yes, it does. Very interesting," Dukk answered as he looked out towards the ridge.

"What is interesting?" came a voice from the port airlock. It was Marr.

She came up to Dukk, put her arm around his waist and looked out too.

"Rock and dust. What is interesting about that?" Marr asked casually.

Dukk turned to Marr.

"We just had a very interesting conversation with a port worker. We will have to take a little walk this afternoon."

Marr looked up at Dukk. Her expression showed curiosity.

Later that afternoon, Marr, Dukk, Annee, and Mentor were in their E.V.A. suits. They were standing outside large incinerators at the back of the new resort. Luna, Bognath and Suzzona had gone with the girls and observers on a guided moon walk. Bazzer was watching the rig.

"Why are the doors all opened?" Annee asked into their comms.

"To allow the contents to drift out," Mentor said.

"To leave no trace of what it was used for?" Annee suggested.

"Yep. But we might still find something," Mentor said as he climbed into the body of the contraption.

Moments later he reappeared.

He held something in his glove.

"What is it?" Marr asked.

"Looks like part of a strap. Much like what we found in the old incinerator in Mayfield."

"Oh", Annee said.

"Well at least we know," Dukk said. "Nothing more can be achieved out here. Shall we go?"

The others nodded.

5

Marr and Dukk took a little longer to get back to the rig. They had let Annee, and Mentor go ahead. There wasn't much to say after their discovery and Marr wanted some space to think. Dukk stayed to keep her company.

They had just finished putting their E.V.A. suits in the starboard suit locker on the middle level.

A scream met them as they entered the corridor from the suit locker.

Lilaho, one of the girls, was standing just outside the lounge. The door was closed.

She was looking very angry.

"Lilaho, what is going on?" Marr asked as she ran over to her.

"Marr, someone needs to stop Nabiel from saying those things."

With the rant over, Lilaho clenched her fist, tilted her head back and screamed again.

"Lilaho! Stop! Look at me!" Marr shouted above the scream.

The scream stopped. Lilaho dropped her arms and her head.

Marr waited. After a full minute, Lilaho looked up at Marr.

"Thank you," Marr said calmly. "Now, can I ask you something?"

"Yes," Lilaho said quietly after another minute of silence.

"How do you feel right now?" Marr asked.

"I feel small, useless and unimportant."

"Who is it that you want to be responsible for what you do or don't do, feel or don't feel, think or don't think?"

"Me," Lilaho answered reluctantly but in a slightly more engaging tone.

"What happens when it is someone else taking responsibility for what you do, feel or think?"

"I give up my autonomy."

"You give away your ability to choose?"

"Yes."

"What happens then?"

"I am powerless. I am at the mercy of someone else's will. I am at risk at having to feel, think and act in a manner that serves their best interests, not mine. I open myself up to being taken advantage of. I open myself up to being abused. I am willingly putting myself into the role of a victim."

"Is that what you want?"

"No!"

"And what are we learning about what happens when society adopts this?"

"People self-censor. Open and honest conversation becomes impossible. Innovation is non-existent."

"Yes, and what does that do?"

"It creates fertile grounds for victimhood trojan horses like psychological safety, micro aggression theory and related practices."

"Yes, and what is the impact of that?" Marr asked calmly.

"It makes it worthwhile to virtue signal victimhood."

"What happens then to the real victims of abuse?"

"Their voices get drowned out."

"And what happens to the perpetrators of the real abuse?"

"They go unchecked and get bolder."

"What happens then when most are in a victim mindset and perpetrators get bolder?"

"The perpetrators are the only ones left to take the lead. They move into positions of authority. They orchestrate the conditions so they can continue their abuse. They usher in authoritarian control over everyone else."

"Right. So, who is responsible for how you feel about and react to Nabiel's behaviour?"

"Me," Lilaho answered.

"And what happens when you don't do that?"

"I give up my ability to choose."

"Okay, so what is the effect of someone else telling others how they need to behave to protect how you feel?"

"I am giving away responsibility for how I feel. I am giving up making my own choices."

"Right. So, what is needed here?"

"I need to punch Nabiel in the face," Lilaho said with a chuckle.

Dukk laughed.

Marr smiled. She knew humour was a signal that there had been a shift.

"And when it isn't appropriate to do that, what is needed?" Marr said in an empathetic tone.

"I need to name my emotions, quieten my amygdala and look for a more rational way forward that leaves me in control of my choices."

Lilaho said this in a calm tone.

Marr said nothing.

"Thank you, Marr," Lilaho said after a moment of further reflection. "I hope one day I am as wise as you."

"Wait! What did you just do there?" Marr said sharply.

"I moved back into a victim mindset," Lilaho replied. Her tone was slightly insecure.

"Right. And?"

"I already have everything and am everything I need for the moment before me."

"Good!" Marr answered in a quieter and calmer tone. "So, what are your choices here?"

"Ignore her. Stay away from her."

"Is that realistic?"

"No."

"What then?"

"I must confront her."

"What is the first step we talked about when confronting this type of behaviour?"

"Determine if the behaviour is intentional or not."

"What could you do if it was intentional?"

"I could try the Mark Goulston, 'I Know What You're Hiding' approach."

"OK, and if not intentional?"

"Give her time to calm down and for her amygdala to release its control. Then try something like the Mark Goulston, 'Shock Absorber'."

"Right. Do you think her behaviour was intentional?"

"No."

"What makes you think that?"

"She is upset about the girls from Norline not being here."

"So, what are you going to do?"

"Give her some space then try the 'Shock Absorber'."

"OK. Come and find me if you want to practice that before you speak to her."

"Thanks, I will."

"Are you good now?"

"Yes, Marr," Lilaho said with a smile.

Marr smiled warmly.

Lilaho turned and headed for the stairs to the lower level.

Marr and Dukk stood and watched Lilaho disappear.

"That was hard," Marr said with a sigh.

"It was brilliant," Dukk said. "You are a total natural at moving someone from a victim to growth mindset."

"Thank you. But now I am exhausted."

"Well, we have an hour before we are due to take over the conn."

"Lead the way, captain," Marr said with a smile.

Chapter 17 – Bridging

1

Four days later, Dukk, his crew and their passengers had just arrived out of traverse. They were now in orbit of a planet of similar size to Earth in the glow of a sun just like Earth's. Officially this place was called Newterratwo. Those that called it home refer to it as The Shipyard.

The rest of the time in New Katoomba had been sobering. The discovery had put a cloud over their visit. They still went for a meal and did their best to make the most of the unique viewing opportunity.

From New Katoomba they headed to IACF2 to see Isaac's nebula. The facilities were even more limited than New Katoomba. So, they only left the rig to use the viewing platform at the research station they had docked with. They had departed that system twenty-four hours earlier.

The view before them, as they regained consciousness after the traverse, was like that when they arrived back at Earth each time. The light from the yellow dwarf sun, danced off the atmosphere.

Dukk's idle gaze, as he regained his senses, noticed a difference between what he was seeing and what he knew of Earth.

Unlike Earth where the cloud systems were varied. All that he could see here, were huge circular formations. Massive cyclones. With some up to twice the size of others. There was no other formation of clouds. Just these massive circular cloud structures pinned against each other and moving slowly.

Dukk had been nearly as excited as everyone else to reach The Shipyard and experience another yellow dwarf. He had heard of it but never been. There wasn't a lot of cause for hauliers like himself to visit any parts of the Asimov cluster. There wasn't a lot of buyers for fine foods and wine.

The odd cloud formations reminded him that he really knew very little of this place.

"What new adventure awaited them here," Dukk thought as he turned to look at Marr.

Marr was having a similar conversation with herself. It had just dawned on her that as well as not knowing why Mentor had insisted on this stop over, she knew little about it.

Since rescuing the girls, she had been around Mentor at times. However, it had mostly been during shared meals or during the story circle. She now realised that she hadn't spoken to him properly in nearly two weeks.

Equally, her focus had been on the program for the girls and enjoying time with Dukk. She hadn't had the usual downtime to do research.

She checked her decisions as she looked over at Dukk. She was sure she had used her time well. He was looking down at the planet. The time with Dukk had been wonderful. They had barely been apart as they operated the rig, enjoyed the stop overs, and worked with the girls. And they had found plenty of time alone too. She had also spent plenty of time with Luna and other members of the crew. Granted, she conceded, that time had been largely about what they were doing with the girls. But she hadn't spent time with Mentor. She knew he had been busy working with the observers. Marr was also wondering if she was avoiding him after what her and Dukk had discovered about his last message from Tieanna.

And she was tired. More tired than she could ever remember. She craved rest and steak. Which she also reflected on as being odd. Then there was her body. She wasn't feeling herself. Also, she could swear that her breasts were larger. The g-suit and her tops felt tighter. Her mind pointed her towards what she'd read about pregnancy in the hidden archives. However, that wasn't adding up Sure, her menstrual cycle was all over the place again. But the lack of regularity was a known side effect of the traverse drugs. "Surely, that is why I am late," she reflected to herself. She also reminded herself that, like other deprivileged, she had been sterilised during the test.

She could see Dukk's expression change just as he turned towards her.

She smiled as they met each other's gaze.

"Now I know why it is called 'The Shipyard'," Luna blurted.

Marr and Dukk look back together to see Luna. She was floating on her back peering out of the top part of the windshield.

They both looked up with her.

Above the rig, orbiting the planet was a chaotic scene.

All manner of space craft, in various stages of assembly, could be seen attached to multiple large disc shaped structures. The central structures looked like small hubs. Some of it was rotating slowly. Other clusters were static. There were huge arrays of airbridges, scaffolding and smaller craft zooming between them all.

"Hold on to your hats," Bazzer said gleefully.

Marr and Dukk looked down. Bazzer was nodding towards the surface of the planet.

A rocket could be seen emerging from the centre of one of the cyclones.

They watched in awe as it zoomed towards them.

It got larger and larger as it approached. Then it changed direction and passed behind them.

"What was that?" Luna asked.

"An old-style rocket," Bazzer said. "It is bringing processed ores to the ship builders up here."

Suddenly there was an alarm.

"Missile lock!" Annee blurted. "And we are being hailed."

"Any details?" Dukk asked as he returned his focus to his controls.

"There are too many signals on the scanners," Annee replied. "I have no idea where it is coming from."

"I do," Marr said.

Dukk looked up. Orbiting just in front of them were two arrows.

"I guess stealth measures are out of the question then," Bazzer joked.

2

"Let's accept the hail," Dukk said.

"Ok", Annee answered.

Instantly an image appeared in the air above the front console. Four people dressed in grey g-suits came into view.

"Imhullu, state your business!" said a woman.

"We are carrying out an executive order on behalf of the Atesoughton family," Dukk answered.

"Please send over the order."

Dukk turned to Annee and nodded.

The video showed the woman interacting with something in front of her. Then she looked up.

"This is a transportation order. Your destination is Earth. Are you lost?" the woman asked in a rude and sarcastic manner.

With that the three others on the call broke into laughter.

"No, we are not lost," Dukk answered. "We are looking for resupply and some downtime."

"Well, executive order or not, you are not welcome here. This is a secure area. It is invitation only. Make ready for boarding. We are going to make sure you are disarmed and then send you on your way."

At that moment Mentor stood up so that he would be front and centre in the video call.

"You will do no such thing!" Mentor said firmly.

"Oh, would you rather we launch our missiles?" the woman said snidely.

"I have just sent a message to your boss," Mentor said calmly. "I suggest you check-in with him before you utter another word!"

The woman looked annoyed. She muted the call. The video feed continued. She could be seen uttering something to one of her colleagues in the seats behind her.

Dukk and the others waited for a full five minutes. During this time, the video feed showed the accosting party arguing. Then it all stopped. They appeared to be listening intensely to something. Their faces went red and then the woman unmuted the video call.

"Sending you over docking permission and instructions," the woman said. "Please proceed at your leisure."

With that the video call disconnected.

The two arrows immediately turned and disappeared from view.

"Missile lock gone," Annee said.

Dukk removed his helmet and turned around to look at Mentor.

"What in the world, Mentor?" Dukk asked.

"Dukk, by now you should not be surprised by the reach of my influence," Mentor said with a grin.

"True," Dukk said with a laugh.

"We've received the flight plan," Marr then said.

"What does it look like?" Dukk asked as he turned back to the console.

"We are docking in a hanger in the largest of the structures. It will take us about ninety minutes to get around to it and then dock."

"Let's load it up."

"What do you think the scene is like here?" Luna asked as she continued to float and stare out the windshield.

"The main hub is lively," Bazzer said. "There are a few bars. It is rough, but that's half the fun."

"Excellent. We should be docked by half eight and we aren't on watch until two a.m. I'm off to shower and get a frock on."

"Sounds like a plan."

"What about the girls?" Annee asked.

"We'll bring those that want to come," Luna answered.

"We might need some extra muscle," Bazzer said.

"Why, are you afraid of some hub dwellers?" Luna taunted.

"Hub dwellers aren't what you will find here."

"Who will we find here in the bars then?"

"Ship builders and miners."

"Interesting," Luna said as she did a horizontal spin.

"We'll have to keep the rig secure too," Annee said.

"Right, that's the docking plan loaded and checked," Dukk said to get everyone's attention. "How about we focus on getting docked? We can have a circle-up after that to work things out. We plan to stay here for about three days. There should be plenty of time to explore the bars."

"Yes, that is a good idea," Mentor added. "Besides, we may need to speak with Bartiamos before we do anything."

"Who is Bartiamos?" Luna asked.

"The boss," Mentor replied.

"Fine, but I am still going to have a shower and put a frock on," Luna replied.

"You might want to hold on to something first," Dukk said as he authorised the autopilot.

The rig vibrated gently as the autopilot adjusted the orbit to put it on course towards the main structure.

"Everything ok?" Marr asked Dukk when the others had left the cockpit.

"Yes, I guess. Why?"

"I noticed your expression change just before the patrol hailed us."

326

"Yes, good catch. I realised how little I know of this place or why Mentor had insisted we spend three days here. What about you? I also noticed your smile wasn't as brilliant and bright as usual."

Marr smiled fully and pushed herself out of her seat. She floated over and sat into Dukk's arms. She then lent in for a kiss.

"Yes, I realised that too," Marr said after the deep kiss.

"Is that all?"

"Why?"

"I don't know. You seem a little distracted at times. Tired too."

"I guess things have been crazy with the program for the girls."

"Are you sure there isn't anything else bothering you?"

"Yeah, of course," she lied.

Dukk looked at her now. He saw the lie. He held her gaze.

"Ok," she said eventually. "I've been feeling a little odd."

"Perhaps you should have Mentor check you out?"

"I don't know if I can do that right now."

"What are you concerned about?"

"I think I am avoiding him because of the last part of Tieanna's message."

"Yes, I think I've been doing that too."

"Perhaps we should talk to him together," Marr suggested.

"Yes, that is a good idea. Maybe after we get docked and sorted with Bartiamos."

3

Just under ninety minutes later the rig touched down inside a medium size hanger.

"This is a strange sort of hanger," Luna said. "Why is it shaped like a half sphere and what are those things on the walls?"

"Directional EMP," Dukk answered.

"What for?"

"I'd say we aren't out of the woods yet," Bazzer replied.

With that the orange depressurisation lights stopped flashing. Two doors opened on either side of the hanger. Armed personnel rushed in.

"Dukk, we are being hailed," Annee said.

"Put it through," Dukk answered.

The video call showed a small room with two operators at a console. One of the operators looked up and spoke.

"All persons on the Imhullu, you are to disembark immediately. Line up in front of the rig. No weapons. Arms where we can see them. You have five minutes. The EMP is armed, and we will not hesitate to use it."

The call then disconnected.

"What the!" Luna exclaimed.

Dukk unbelted and stood up so he could take a better look.

"I count twenty-four-armed security," he said. "This doesn't look good."

"It should be okay," Mentor said as he unbelted. "I suspect this is just optics."

"I hope so," Dukk replied before opening his comms to alert the others.

Five minutes later the crew and passengers were assembled in a line in front of the rig.

The leader of the security contingent stepped forward.

"The captain and chief mate, please accompany my colleagues to search the rig."

Dukk nodded at Annee, and they both stepped forward.

"Lead the way," said one of the guards.

Dukk and Annee escorted the group of guards through every part of the rig.

When they arrived at the storage room, the guards insisted on them opening each of the crates.

"And that one," the guard said to Dukk as she pointed at Zarra's makeshift casket.

"Not a good idea in here," Dukk replied.

"Why?"

"It contains a decomposing body."

"Fine. Move it to the platform and we'll open it on the hanger floor."

Dukk and Annee worked together to get the crate onto the hold platform.

With the inspection complete, the platform was lowered, and the group returned to the others on the hanger floor.

Meanwhile the leader had scanned all their IDs. She completed the job when Dukk and Annee returned.

No sooner had she completed the scan when one of the doors opened in the side of the hanger. Two people came through the door and marched towards Dukk and the others. They stopped halfway. They were dressed in a manner like the security detail, however their uniforms looked newer. On seeing the newcomers, the first group of security guards all stood to attention. The leader rushed over to the new pair and spoke briefly. She then came back to the others and spoke in a firm tone.

"Who sent the message when our patrol intercepted you?"

Mentor stepped forward.

"Follow me," the leader said.

She escorted Mentor over to the pair and then stood back.

After a short exchange with Mentor, one of the new pair nodded at the leader. She joined them again. A moment later she marched back over to Dukk and the others.

"Captain, Dellington and co-pilot Maldana, follow me," the leader said in a formal tone.

"What about my crew and passengers," Dukk demanded.

"They are to remain with the rig for now. My colleagues must ask each of them a few questions," the leader replied.

Marr and Dukk followed the leader towards Mentor and the two.

"My name is Vilemia," one of the pair said when Marr and Dukk reached them. "I am the head of security. You have a meeting with the station owner. Please follow me."

Vilemia and her colleague escorted the three of them through the door.

On the other side was a wide corridor. Sitting in the middle of the corridor was a six-seater hover cart. It was floating just off the floor.

Dukk crouched as he approached to verify it had no wheels.

"Levitation using magnets," Vilemia said having noticed where Dukk's attention was.

"Please take a seat," she added as she got into the first seat of the front row of three.

Dukk looked at Marr.

He nodded at her to indicate she should go first.

Marr climbed in next to Vilemia. Dukk followed and took the remaining seat in the front row.

Mentor sat into the back row with Vilemia's colleague.

The cart immediately began to move.

The cart brought them past large windows as they moved through the station.

The windows showed the planet and other parts of the space craft building operation.

"Great view," Marr said to make conversation.

"It is," Vilemia replied.

"From here it looks a lot like Earth."

"It may look it, but it is nothing like Earth. Yes, it has an atmosphere, and the gravity is similar, however it isn't stable. The air is toxic, and storms ravage the place. Life is not easy down there."

"What are the rockets for?"

"They bring processed ore from our mining."

"How are you mining in those storms?"

"By being innovative. We have mining machines that largely work below the surface. They come to the surface in the eye of the storm to meet the rockets and transfer their ore."

"That must be challenging."

"It is at the best of times. Then every ten years or so a super storm develops. It roams the planet for six months. Smashes everything in its path."

"What do you do?"

"In the early days we would lift what we could and bury the rest. The mining crews would sit it out up here."

"That must have been expensive."

"This planet has plenty of natural resources. The potential outweighs the costs and risks."

"What do they do now when a super storm develops?"

"The operation is run from self-contained, mobile habitats. They can survive the worst the planet can fling at them."

At that moment, the cart came to a stop outside some large doors.

"We've arrived," Vilemia said as she got out.

4

Vilemia led them into a large room. She closed the doors behind them and then stood to attention just inside the doors. Her colleague did the same. Their manner indicated to Marr, Dukk and Mentor that they should line up as well.

At one end of the large room was a large desk. At the other end was a lounge setting. In the middle of the room was a large digital table. One whole side of the room was glass. It overlooked the operation. In the view, were the other disc shaped structures with a multitude of space crafts in various stages of assembly. The planet could be seen racing below.

Standing on the far side of the table looking out of the windows was a man. He looked to be in his sixties. He was tall, bald, heavy set and of dark brown complexion.

"Hello, Bartiamos," Mentor said.

"Back from the dead. Twice," Bartiamos replied as he turned around.

"Twice?" Mentor asked.

"There were rumours circulating about a well-known assassin being on a G5 called the Dinatha. The one that exploded at the same time as a bunch of mercenaries went missing. Their rig was called the Ukendt. It all happened just after the assassination of Craig Atesoughton the second. Both rigs were known to have left Mayfield the morning after the assassination. It seemed unlikely that this well-known assassin would run into that sort of trouble. But also, one could reasonably assume if that said assassin was on the Dinatha he would have escaped the explosion. It happened before. Then a few days ago rumours started circulating about this same assassin having gone down with the Dinatha. That connected him to the assassination. The assassination connection added up but not going down. Then a new rumour appeared and then there was the thing that went up on the bounty board yesterday."

"What new rumour? And why the rig search?"

Bartiamos smiled as he walked over to the table.

"So, this is where the Ukendt ended up," Bartiamos said casually as he flicked an image into the middle of the table.

The image showed the hanger with the Imhullu. The crew and passengers were still there with security guards among them. One was separated from the group being questioned.

"You know this is the Ukendt?" Dukk asked as he walked to the table to get a better look.

Marr and Mentor followed. Vilemia and her colleague stayed near the door.

"Of course! A creator always knows their creations," Bartiamos answered. "Even if they get a new name. Now let me guess. It is true that you were on the Dinatha. Someone sent the Ukendt and its crew to take you out. Unfortunately, they bit off more than they could chew. The hunter became the hunted."

"Something like that," Mentor laughed.

"I like the new name! What evil are you banishing?"

"For starters, whoever sent the Ukendt," Mentor grinned.

Bartiamos then flicked away the image and a new image appeared. It was a different view of the space station than they could see out the windows. The image included the station that they were currently floating in. It also had a view of the planet. Another rocket was making its way into orbit.

"The rockets look odd," Marr said absently.

"This is old school rocket tech," Bartiamos replied. "They predate DMD usage. They were used in colonising Mars. When the DMD came into use these rockets basically became redundant for day-to-day use on Earth. For efficiency, the DMD requires a completely different platform."

"However, when war broke out there was an urgent need to get as much heavy machinery off the surface. The rockets found a purpose again. They then sat idle as our ancestors searched for suitable Earth like planets to colonise. Newterratwo was seen as the most promising, so they strapped DMDs to the rockets and brought it all here. Then when it was realised the weather systems didn't dissipate like on Earth, the rockets and equipment were left idle again. It basically got forgotten about as the families abandoned the search for planets in yellow dwarf systems.

"It all sat idle until my great grandfather stumbled across it. He was a miner looking to lay a claim. He cannibalized the plant and equipment floating out here in space. He made a huge mining machine. He put it on the surface and then used the rockets to bring the processed ore to orbit. It was then shipped all over the galaxy. The abundance of raw resources and the efficiency of his approach made him very rich. Eventually he built orbit-based refineries and made even more wealth. The metals produced here were sort after far and wide. Most rigs you see today are made from those raw materials."

"Is this planet lifeless because of the storms?" Marr asked.

"Not at all. There are signs that life is returning. The oceans for sure. But also, on land."

"How are your activities impacting that?"

"Minimally. We have failed to get close to areas that we suspect are new habitats for indigenous land users. Attempts to go beyond where we find ore deposits doesn't ever succeed."

"What has stopped you?"

"Your guess is as good as mine."

"Watchers?"

"Watchers!" Bartiamos laughed.

"You don't believe in them?"

"Nope. Been around too long. I think it is more incompetence or simply bad luck."

"What about the mining? Doesn't that destroy the potential for other land users?"

"Kind of, but something stops us going too far. After a time, our machinery starts to break. We know it is time to move out and blow up the site."

"Seriously!"

"Yes, we collapse the tunnels on themselves."

"That must destroy everything above it and create craters?"

"Yes. However, we've looked back at sites closed fifty years ago. There is water and even signs of new growth. Sure, the place is still toxic to us but the whole planet is and will be for thousands of years. So, it makes no difference."

"What brings the life back?"

"I think it is the super storms. They clean it up. Turn the holes into new eco systems. Repairs and rebuilds."

"You make it sound like the planet is repairing itself and your efforts are helping it."

Bartiamos grinned.

"Could that have happened to Earth too?"

"What?"

"Another species strip mining it for a time?"

"Perhaps."

5

"But there is more than just mining going on here," Dukk noted.

"Yes, captain, there is," Bartiamos answered.

He then continued.

"My father took things a step further. He used the wealth to get into the space craft building business. He took contracts to build existing designs. He quickly became one of TLMs main producers. The G5 was the first of those he took on. He also took on the massive and heavily fortified, mammoth space stations. I was there when the Veneficans took receipt of their fifth and final mammoth, with its unique customisations. I stood by my father's side. I was five at the time. They were terrifying in their white full-face masks, and their blood red, hooded cloaks."

"Anyway, then it was my turn. I have taken it to another level. I got us into designing. We now design, produce and then sell our designs under the big brands. The Interceptor and the Arrow are perfect examples. We also do customisations. Military upgrades and that type of thing. We are now by a country mile the biggest producer of new vessels. We are also one of the biggest players in the customisation and upgrade business. No other producer can match our scale and efficiency. Hence the slightly unfriendly welcome. We have a significant operation to protect."

"So, you produce and sell all manner of craft across the galaxy?" Marr asked.

"That is correct."

"And, therefore, you would know who is building up their military capacity too?"

Bartiamos paused and looked at Marr.

"Very astute of you," he said. "Yes, I would have the inside track on which of the families is expanding their fleet."

"So, Bartiamos, who is building up their military capacity?" Mentor asked in a firm tone.

Marr and Dukk looked at each other. At the same moment they figured that they knew the reason Mentor was insistent on visiting this system.

Bartiamos smiled.

He then said, "My friend, that is the wrong question."

Mentor paused and looked back at the table.

Silence fell. For a full minute no one spoke.

Dukk looked at Bartiamos, then at Mentor and then Bartiamos again.

"I know what the right question is," Dukk then said.

The others turned to look at Dukk.

"The right question is who isn't. Who isn't strengthening their arsenal?"

Bartiamos smiled.

"Correct, young captain."

They all then looked at Bartiamos. He had returned his gaze to the table and the image of his operation.

After a moment he spoke again.

"All the families, including us are strengthening. It is another reason for your frosty welcoming party. Things are destabilising. The peace that has prevailed for nearly one hundred years is waning. There are signs of distrust. Trade agreements are coming under pressure. There are more and more small skirmishes. Inter family gatherings are being cancelled. There is a restlessness in those that I speak with."

"What is causing that?" Marr asked.

"I think we have reached the limits of what we can realistically do with our galaxy. Innovation has nearly stalled. Most of the labourers are just too busy staying alive. The families are bored. Worst still, and if I am honest even with myself, the families lack the drive and traits necessary to build momentum again."

"So, who isn't strengthening their arsenal?" Marr asked.

Bartiamos interacted with the image. It showed a clear picture of the vessel assembly zone.

"Look here. What do you see?" he asked Marr.

"Many vessels in various stages of assembly."

"Notice any patterns?"

Marr looked harder. Then she saw it.

"Clusters of emblems and colours. Aligned to the various elite families," she answered.

"Correct. And then what aren't you seeing?"

Marr looked harder. Dukk looked harder too. Then it hit him.

"There is no blood red," Dukk blurted.

Bartiamos smiled.

"Are they using another builder?" Marr asked.

"Not to my knowledge."

"Interesting," Mentor noted.

"Yes, it is interesting that while everyone is strengthening, the Veneficans are holding onto their coin."

"Why is that?" Marr asked.

Bartiamos shrugged his shoulders.

Marr thought she was now certain that she was at the answer as to why Mentor chose to visit Bartiamos. Then Mentor confused her again.

"Bartiamos, so do you still have the training centre?" Mentor asked.

"Yes, sir," Bartiamos answered. "We've made a few improvements. But it is basically as per your original design. First class zero-g and near zero-g hand to hand combat facilities. We also now have one of the best pilot combat training centres. Far superior to anything you would find in the simulation programs on the rigs."

Marr and Dukk took a moment to process all that.

"You said something about a new rumour," Mentor stated after a moment of silence.

Bartiamos change the image again back to the hanger with the Imhullu. He zoomed in on the crew on the hanger floor.

"Yes, I did. The rumour is that you had been compromised. You slipped up. Your assassination of Craig went bad. You were double crossed by the crew with the help of some mercenaries. You see they didn't find enough evidence in the Dinatha wreckage to suggest lots of bodies went up with it. And there is evidence of bodies being on board a transport pod that disintegrated on re-entry to the planet. The relay in that system is pretty good. One of my own. Anyway, the new rumour didn't have any sway with me because I know you. Now before me I see a couple of mercenaries but mostly a bunch of hauliers masquerading as mercenaries in a rig, they have no business being in. It is all very intriguing."

"Yes, it is," Mentor said. "You also mentioned something about the bounty board?"

"Ah yes, bounties have been put on the Dinatha's last crew. Twenty thousand credits for the captain and ten thousand each for the crew. Not enough to bother with, but for the most desperate bounty hunters. However, it is enough to put the crew on Earth's most wanted list. I guess the lease holders of the rig want reparations for their loss."

"Who issued the bounty?"

"That isn't clear. It is a Citadel decree. Out of Kuedia."

"Can I see them?"

"Sure," Bartiamos said as he flicked an image into the air.

The image had a series of names with last known whereabouts. The list also included the bounty figure.

They all stared at the board.

Mentor stood back. He was clearly shocked. Dukk and Marr could understand why.

On the board were their own names. Right at the top of the list was the name of a level seven observer. The name was Thosmas. The bounty was two million credits.

At that moment, an incoming call alert sounded. Bartiamos accepted it. In the air before them appeared the face of the leader of the security detail in the hanger.

"Well?" Bartiamos asked.

"The rumour checks out. We got a consistent story from the crew and observers. The passengers have no knowledge of it. They joined the rig in New Montana."

"Please share what we know."

"That Thosmas didn't leave Mayfield with the Imhullu. That Thosmas was last seen escorting the freed observer back to the rig. But Thosmas didn't join them for the trip to New Montana. The crew were very consistent on that. The observers' recollection ends shortly after leaving the lock-up."

"And the body?"

"As they said. The body is that of a young female."

"Thank you. Tell the crew they can go back onto the rig and wait for their captain to return. You can withdraw your team."

With that Bartiamos waved the call away.

After a moment, Bartiamos said, "It is convenient that the video feeds in the Mayfield hanger were playing up that morning. Thosmas was able to slip away. Some say the level seven boarded another rig. However, none has any record or knowledge of that. The observer simply disappeared."

Marr, Dukk and Mentor said nothing.

"So, Thosmas is in the wind. No reward for anyone here," Bartiamos said quietly.

"So, it would seem," Mentor replied. "You'd hardly need that reward."

"True."

"So, why the rig search rigmarole?"

"I am keeping up appearances. I suggest you keep your real identities well-hidden while you are here. I have influence but this is a big facility. Others have spies here, just as I have spies everywhere else."

"We will."

"So, why are you really here?"

"Training."

"That is all?" Bartiamos asked.

"And to shore up old friendships."

Bartiamos smiled as he looked up at Mentor. It was the first time he had made eye contact with Mentor since they entered the room.

Chapter 18 – Remembering

1

"What are the chances of a surface tour happening while we are here?" Mentor asked Bartiamos now that he finally got eye contact.

"You've been there," Bartiamos answered. "What reason would you have to go again?"

"It isn't for me. I'd like Dukk and Marr and some of the others to see it for themselves."

Bartiamos looked over at Marr and Dukk. He looked at them intently for a few moments before turning back to Mentor.

"I don't know. This is my livelihood. There are those that wouldn't approve of what is going on down there."

"I trust them with my life," Mentor said. "They won't be a threat to your choices."

"And what of the others that you speak of? Can they be trusted too."

"They can."

"What's wrong with a pass over? You could drop out of orbit in your interceptor. Have a look around and then hard burn back before you get caught in a storm?"

"I'd like them to experience it fully. The old tech. The way of life. All of that."

"As you know, the only way in and out is on the supply rockets. Are they up for a ride on the rocket?"

"They are."

Bartiamos looked back at the projection of the Imhullu. The hanger floor was now empty. The security guards had gone, and the rest of the crew, the observers and the girls were back inside.

After a few minutes of silence, Bartiamos looked up again. He looked at Mentor and nodded.

Bartiamos then looked over at Vilemia.

"Will you look into it," Bartiamos said.

Vilemia nodded.

"Also," he added, "Please escort the captain and his co-pilot back to their rig. Have hanger operations move them to a normal hanger and help them get settled in. My old friend and I have some catching up to do."

"This way, please," Vilemia said as she opened the door and looked over at Marr and Dukk.

"Dukk and Marr," Mentor said before they left. "Encourage all the girls to join you on the surface tour. However, don't mention it to Kimince and Trence. They aren't ready for what they will see or the rocket ride, for that matter."

Dukk nodded as he followed Marr towards the door.

Thirty minutes later, Dukk and his crew were gathered in the cockpit. They had been debriefing what had occurred in Bartiamos's boardroom. They were also watching the surrounds change as the rig was moved to a new pad within the station.

They had discovered that the initial hanger was simply an outer security gateway. When they were all back on board, large doors opened, exposing a much larger hanger. Low loaders were now bringing them through the hanger. These machines were much like the self-lifting kind they had experienced in New Montana.

"So, who's up for an excursion to the surface?" Dukk asked when the questions had died down.

"Wouldn't miss it for the world," Marr said.

"Definitely," Luna added.

Annee, Suzzona and Bognath gave similar responses.

"I'm good," Bazzer said. "I have had my fill of crazy happenings recently."

"Great," Dukk said. "That means you and Mentor will keep an eye on the observers and the rig. Vilemia said it will likely be around midday tomorrow before we can get a ride. She said we should expect to be away for about twenty-four hours. The ride is supposedly rough. We are to pack light. We will share backpacks with only one change of clothes and basic toiletries."

"Will we wear our normal g-suits?" Annee asked.

"No, Vilemia said we'll be given suits and helmets. The bio systems on the rockets are different to what we'd be used to."

"I am having second thoughts after hearing all of that," Suzzona said.

"It will be fine," Marr added. "Vilemia mentioned that she loves visiting the surface. She said it will be a trip we won't be forgetting anytime soon."

"So," Luna said. "We still have time to see some of the station and have some fun."

"Absolutely, and we aren't back on watch for another five hours," Bazzer replied.

"Just remember we must use our aliases," Marr said. "We have bounties on our heads now. So, we must be extra cautious not to share our real identities."

At that moment, the rig came to a stop. The low loaders put the rig onto the hanger floor and withdrew.

"Dukk we are being hailed," Annee said. "It is operations again."

"Put it through," Dukk replied.

Two operators appeared in the video call.

"Captain," said one of the operators. "Your identification signals have been registered with the station. You are free to move about common spaces. Your access will be revoked should you attempt to go into operational or restricted areas. Also, I have a message from head of security. Passage to the surface has been arranged for one p.m. tomorrow. Please share the IDs of all those who will make the journey.

A preparation briefing will be held at eleven a.m. I am sending you the directions to the briefing room. Enjoy your stay. Good evening."

"Thank you," Dukk said as the operator disconnected the call.

"There you have it," he then added to his crew. "Let's power down."

With that the others started to make their way out of the cockpit.

"Before you go," Marr said as they started to move. "I want to brief the girls now about the surface trip. Does anyone want to help me do that."

"I will," Annee replied.

"Thank you, Ann. Dukk, do you have it under control if I do that now?"

Dukk laughed and then said, "Yep, I think I'll be okay to manage the post set down protocols. I've done it once or twice before."

2

The rest of the evening and the following morning had been typical for a hub visit. From eleven a.m. in the morning, things got a little different.

The briefing had been straight-forward. It was a typical safety briefing not that dissimilar to the one that Dukk gave new crew or passengers. Then they got a shuttled to another space station to board the rocket.

Dukk and Marr had been invited to sit in the cockpit. The others were strapped into a very confined space just behind the cockpit.

The cockpit wasn't very spacious either. There was no actual windshield. Instead, there were several small portal windows. The cockpit had a row of four seats flush up against the forward bulkhead. The two middle seats were sat slightly forward from the outer two. In front of the middle seats were digital console panels. Clustered around the panels and every other wall were nobs and dials. The two front seats also had control columns and rudder pedals. All of which surprised Dukk as he had never seen one in any space craft that he had been in.

"Manual override," the pilot said to Dukk having noticed his fascination with the control column.

"Do you ever use it?" Dukk asked.

"Of course. The conditions down there play havoc with the digital and electrical systems. This rocket has been modified from its original design. It is now largely controlled with hydraulics. The digital and electrical systems give the manual controls some assistance. We can't land without the precise capabilities of the digital systems, but we can do rudimentary adjustments with the manual controls."

"What is that?" Dukk asked.

In front of him was a pedestal with grinding handles.

"Our jump starter. It puts pressure into a hydraulic pump."

Dukk looked closer. A black tube ran out of the grinder up to a large breaker switch above their heads.

The pilot was watching Dukk.

"A big lightning strike causes this main breaker to trip," the pilot said as she pointed to the large breaker Dukk was looking at. "In these sitting positions we can't get leverage on it to reset it. The switch is too big. The hydraulic makes light work of it."

"That sounds a little antiquated."

"Yes, but it is very reliable in the conditions we operate."

"We have release clearance," the co-pilot announced suddenly, interrupting Dukk's informal tour.

"Going for release," the pilot said as she started interacting with the controls.

Thirty minutes later, the rocket had broken orbit and was descending towards the cloud line.

Both Dukk and Marr were doing their best to see what was going on. Which wasn't easy on account of the small portal windows. But also, because they had to look over the shoulders of the pilot and co-pilot to see the images on the panels. It wasn't helped by them not having access to what the pilot and co-pilot were saying to each other. They were using a closed-circuit radio link as the rocket had no implant receivers.

Everything until that point had been relatively smooth. It had been what Dukk would have expected. That changed as they dropped into the clouds. The rocket started to shake, the noise increased, and rain could be seen smashing against the portal windows and the video feeds.

Then the flashes started.

Dukk twisted to see if he could get a glimpse of the lightning. It wasn't easy. One moment it was grey then there was a bright blinding flash.

Then suddenly there was a colossal bang. The controls, panels and lights all went out.

Further cracks of lightning lit up the cockpit periodically and the rocket shook even more violently than before.

Beside him the pilots were frantically flicking switches to the off position.

Then the pilot turned to Dukk. She had lifted her helmet visor and started to speak. He couldn't hear her properly.

Dukk stalled for a moment before realising that he could open his helmet visor too. He wasn't accustomed to helmets that had visors that could be opened.

He stumbled for the latches and opened his visor.

"Dellington, you're up," the pilot yelled again when she saw his visor was up.

"What?" Dukk yelled back.

The pilot pointed towards the grinding handles.

"Oh, shit," Dukk replied as the storm raged, and the rocket continued to shake violently.

He reached over and grabbed the handles. He started to move them. It was like a weights machine.

There was another tap on his shoulder.

He looked over.

"Faster!" the pilot yelled as she made a gesture to suggest Dukk speed up.

Dukk spun his arms faster.

A dial on the top of the grinder showed how much pressure he was creating. Not much. He spun his arms even faster. The pilot was now watching the dial too. She was also gesturing for Dukk to spin even faster.

The pilot had her hand on an in-line lever in the ceiling. She moved the lever. As she did, the grinding got much harder.

The large circuit breaker moved a little. But it didn't flip.

Both the pilot and co-pilot now shouted and gestured to encourage Dukk to grind even harder. This time there was considerable panic in their expressions.

Dukk put everything into it. He pushed his upper body to its limits as he spun the handles.

The pressure pushed the breaker to centre position. Then with a loud crack, it flipped.

The panels started to pop back into life. At the same time ear-piercing alarms echoed in the cockpit. Red lights started flashing across the walls.

"Well done, Dellington," the pilot yelled as she started flicking switches. "You've just done your first jump start. Now let's bring her around."

The noises and vibrations sung a different tune as the rocket came back to life and corrected its descent.

Then it all suddenly changed again. The clouds, rain and lightning were gone. The wind noise was reduced but now the roar of the engines could be heard as they brought the rocket into the eye of the storm and started inducing a climb.

Dukk caught glimpses of the blue sky as the rocket went vertical.

For a moment they were weightless again as they dropped back towards the surface. Then the engines engaged, and they were pushed hard into their seats.

Dukk could see parts of the video feeds from the rear cameras. A small circular target was coming into view. It was at one end of a long and wide platform. The platform appeared to be moving slowly against the rugged and barren surface.

Dukk closed his eyes at this point to ride out the g-forces being exerted on his body.

Dukk opened his eyes moments later as the noise dissipated. They had landed.

"Hold on," the pilot said as Dukk went to unbelt. "We aren't done yet."

Dukk looked over at the panels.

External camera feeds showed they had been caught between two huge arms. These arms were now pivoting the rocket.

Dukk felt the rocket swing forward. He went from lying in his seat to basically being upright.

There was a loud bang as the arms locked the rocket into the surface of the platform they had just landed on.

"Take care as you unbelt," the pilot said. "The gravity here is as it is on Earth."

Once unbelted, Marr and Dukk climbed through the cockpit and joined the others. They made their way back out of the tight space and down a narrow passageway. The co-pilot was ahead of them and opened the door in the side of the rocket. The door opened into an airbridge.

Two people were standing in the airbridge. They looked to be in their sixties. They had olive skin tones and well-kept grey hair. They were fit and healthy looking. They were both wearing grey fitted shirts and slacks. Their outfits had fluorescent yellow strips running down the lengths of the shirt arms and pant legs.

Dukk and the others filed into the dull and tight space.

The rumble of the machine they felt in the rocket was even more noticeable now.

"Welcome to mobile habitat H9, more fondly referred to as Neo Jordan, or just Jordan," said the man. "My name is Stephen or Steve if you like. This is my coniunx. Sorry! You don't use that term. Let me start over. This lovely lady is my primary companion, Meredith. We are the leaders of this community."

"Thank you, I am pleased to meet you," Dukk said. "My name is Dellington, though I prefer going by Dukk. This is some of my crew, Maldana, Cabley, Viredd, Joncolt and Suzzona. And these young ladies are our passengers."

"Welcome," said Meredith. "And please call me Mary."

"Thank you," Marr said. "And please call me Marr."

Stephen nodded at the co-pilot, who then closed the door behind them.

"Now, if you will please follow me," Stephen said to the group. "We will have to continue the pleasantries elsewhere as loading is about to start. We must disconnect the airbridge for that."

Stephen led the group along the airbridge, through another door and then down two flights of rusty stairs. At the bottom they passed through a door into another dimly lit and grungy corridor.

With everyone through, Stephen swung the very heavy door to close it. He turned a large wheel in the door to seal it.

He then pulled a device off his belt and spoke into it.

"All clear. You can commence loading."

"Copy," came a crackled response.

Dukk looked on with curiosity.

Stephen noticed Dukk's expression.

"We don't have implants or med lines, for that matter," he then said with a grin.

"Oh," Dukk said.

"And now we are going to split up," Stephen said. "Ladies, Mary will be showing you around. Gentlemen, you will accompany me to the bridge as you've arrived at a busy time. And men please give your things to the ladies."

Marr looked over at Dukk and shrugged her shoulders. Dukk did the same.

"Ladies, this way please," Meredith said as she headed off down the corridor towards the middle of the machine.

Dukk, Bognath and Stephen watched them go.

"Right, men, this way," Stephen said as he headed down the corridor in the direction of the front of the machine.

Stephen led Dukk and Bognath down some stairs and then opened another large door like the door after leaving the airbridge.

Beyond was a well-lit corridor with dark green walls. It was clean and looked well kept.

Stephen turned and led them forward a short distance. They then passed through a door into a wide space that looked to be some sort of control room. An array of consoles ran along the length of the far wall. The console showed video projections of the surrounds. There were various gauges that Dukk guessed were engine controls. The consoles also had other projections that looked to be satellite images of the weather patterns. There was also radar and related navigational information being displayed. And the consoles had joysticks.

Above the consoles were heavy glass windows. The view out the windows was of the bleak path ahead with the wall of the storm in the distance.

Two operators sat at the consoles. A man and a woman. They were dressed the same as Stephen and Meredith.

"This is our drive control room," Stephen said as they stood in the centre of the room looking over the shoulders of the operators.

"Hello," one of the operators said without taking her attention away from the console.

"This control room manages our drive and navigation functions," Stephen offered.

"There are other control rooms?" Dukk asked absently and to make conversation.

"Yes, we have a separate control room for mining operations. We have a radio room that looks after inter-habitat communications. Then there are eco-system control rooms. We have various plant and machinery. They have their own control rooms too. Also, we have air traffic control and communications for extra-terrestrial activity."

"Extra-terrestrial?" Bognath asked.

"Anyone that isn't from here," Stephen replied.

"Oh."

"It is a big operation," Dukk stated as he looked around.

"Yes, it is," Stephen answered. "In these conditions and with just under six hundred and fifty people to support, it must be. Here, let me show you."

Stephen brought them over to a free console. He interacted with it and projected a three-dimensional image of the habitat.

"Jordan is typical for a modern habitat. It is three hundred and sixty metres long, by one hundred metres wide by thirty-five metres high.

As you can see the bottom quarter of the habitat is all caterpillar-based track drives. We have eighteen independent sets of track drives. Three rows of six. They can be raised or lowered as we drive up and down inclines, across streams and over uneven ground. This helps keep the habitat stable and relatively level. On relatively flat terrain we can operate on less tracks. That allows us to do maintenance while still underway. Which is important as the storms are constant. And we need to stay in the eye as much as possible so we can catch and load rockets."

"What happens when you reach a mountain range, or wide rivers and stuff like that?" Dukk asked.

"We turn around. Go back into the storm and find another eye."

"Does that happen a lot?"

"By that do you mean what percentage of the time is spent in eyes verses in the storm?"

"Yes."

"We generally stay inside an eye for around forty-eight hours. We are now moving slowly to stay in the eye. But we can reach up to seventy kilometres per hour on flat terrain. So, we usually don't spend more than twelve hours tracking through a storm to re-align with the eye. Also, we have pretty good weather forecasting data. And the storms generally follow the same path. We often spend months going back and forth on the same tract of land."

"When does the mining get done?"

"What do you mean?"

"It sounds like you are continually moving. How do you do the mining?"

"We have separate, self-contained mining machines. We call them drills. There are habitats, drills, and primary crushers all in the one machine. They have a crew of six and they work the resource beds adjacent to the habitat's path. They can move quickly over the surface through the storms to reach the underground mining sites. It might take them a day or two to reach the site and then a day or two to get back to us. They would drill for about five days straight or until their hold is full. They are generally away for ten-day cycles. They come along side. We pick them up. They unload, resupply, change crew, and then head off again. That generally takes about two hours. It can be done in the eye or when we are travelling in the storm if needed. But generally, we try to avoid that as it is more hassle."

4

Meanwhile, Meredith had led the women and girls through a series of corridors and doors. Everything was rusty and dimly lit. They had to stop at times to open and close large doors like the door after leaving the airbridge from the rocket.

Apart from when Meredith was opening and closing the doors, she and Marr walked together. They spoke as they walked. The others listened in.

"Do men and women always split up?" Marr asked at one point.

"Not at all," Meredith replied. "Once in conjugium, sorry, I mean companioned, men and women work alongside each other. Everyone does their share. Some work on the mining drills. Some are more suited to keeping the habitat functioning. Those in conjugium work the same rotation."

"This concept of conjugium sounds very like being companioned. Is it the same?" Marr asked.

"Similar, except, conjugium is for life. You swear an oath before the creator, your friends and family to stand by each other, throughout this life and the next. You take an oath to be with no other."

"You commit to the same person for sex, forever, from that moment on?" Luna asked.

"Yes, but not only that. It is our way that sex does not happen until in conjugium." Meredith answered.

"What happens if it does?" Marr asked.

"Much disgrace comes down on the family."

"That must create some challenges."

353

"Yes, it does. Before conjugium, boys and girls work in same sex pairs, alongside those couples in conjugium. Those couples are often their relatives. Things change a little when couples start their families."

"What do you mean by 'start their families'?"

"When couples start having children, they focus on that."

"You raise your own children?"

"Yes, there are no incubation centres here."

"How do men and women work at the same time as raising their children?"

"Children are raised within families with help from the community. Miners stop the drill rotation once they start having children and until the couple's oldest child reaches twelve. During that time, they help run and maintain the habitat."

"And what happens when their oldest reaches twelve?"

"The couple return to their rotation on the drill."

"Then, what happens to the children?"

"When parents are away from the habitat, their children are cared for by their grandparents, siblings, cousins, aunties and uncles with help from the community."

"Why not separate the parents. One goes on the drill while the other stays here?"

"It is dangerous work on the drills. Accidents happen. When they do it isn't typical for a crew to return. The conditions are just too difficult. It is best that a conjugium pair go out together than leave one behind."

"Oh," Marr replied.

"We have arrived," Meredith said as she opened a door at the end of their short journey.

The cohort filed through the door. After the dimness of the corridors, they had to squint and put their hands up. Before them was a three-story high atrium. They stood on a balcony looking out over the central space of the atrium. Around the entire space, were windows and doors, serviced by balconies and stairways. The space was filled with green plants. Sunshine streamed through thick glass windows in the ceiling and walls. It was a truly beautiful sight.

The floor of the atrium had a labyrinth of circular and rectangular spaces of various sizes. They were divided by bushes and small trees. Some spaces had tables. Some had just seats. There were also some open spaces.

In one of the spaces, a large group of teenage children were sitting on the floor listening intently to an elderly man seated on a stool. Some small children were sitting in the dirt between some plants playing with toys. Another group of children were running along the balcony laughing. Several women with very small children were sitting in a group talking.

Their clothes drew their attention also. The odd person was wearing a uniform like Meredith, but most were in colourful clothes. The styles and arrangements weren't chaotic like the observers, but cleaner and simpler. One girl was wearing a dress with three different shades of blue. Another was wearing a white shirt with navy shorts. Yet another wore a green loosely fitting tracksuit.

Marr and the others looked on in awe.

"This is our living quarters," Meredith said as she escorted Marr and the others to a set of stairs. "We all live in apartments of varying sizes. The size depends on the size of your family and what you can afford to maintain. The apartments generally have a shared living space surrounded by two or more bedrooms. Each apartment has its own bathrooms and kitchen. Other facilities are shared between multiple apartments. There are lots of common spaces used for all sorts of gatherings from shared meals to schooling to community meetings.

As a child we will live with our parents and one set of grandparents. Typically, on our mother's side. Men generally move in with their coniunx's family. Children under twelve share one room. Boys and girls are then separated after that into shared same sex rooms. Couples have a room of their own. When a couple's children become grandparents, they too will move into their own apartment with all their children and grandchildren. A family moves to larger apartments as the family grows and their means accumulates. Then it reverses as our children's children start their own families. We move into smaller apartments until eventually it is just the grandparents left. Then they join other elders in apartments dedicated to great grandparents."

"We don't get a lot of visitors," Meredith said as they reached the atrium floor. "Especially a group of teenage girls. I see from the information we received from the Shipyard that you girls are between fifteen and sixteen."

"Yes," Marr replied on their behalf.

"So, you will have to be billeted out in twos or threes. You will stay the night with a family that also has teenage girls. We will meet them now. And ladies, we will accommodate you in the single dorms in the elder's accommodation."

"What do you mean by single?" Luna asked.

"Those not in conjugium," Meredith said.

"What if we aren't single, but companioned?" Suzzona asked.

"I see only two men in your visiting party. You can't all be companioned."

"What has the number of men got to do with it?" Suzzona asked.

Meredith smiled.

"Oh, I see my mistake now. I apologise for appearing to judge your customs. That is not my desire or intention."

"You don't have any same sex couples here?" Suzzona asked.

"No, that wouldn't make sense."

"Why?"

"We survive only because we have children. Without children we have no future. Childbirth requires a man and a woman."

"Oh," Suzzona replied.

"Don't worry. We understand our customs aren't yours. We will simply adjust our accommodation plans for you."

356

"Thank you," Marr said.

"Girls let's meet your billeted families," Meredith said as she led them all to the group of teenagers.

"May I interrupt please," Meredith said to the group. "Our visitors have arrived."

"Of course," the elderly man answered.

The group all turned and looked in fascination at the visitors in their grey g-suits.

"Those girls who are hosting the visitors, please come over here," Meredith said.

Five girls stood and came over to Meredith.

Meredith then turned to Marr and the girls.

"Will I choose, or do you want to pick your partners for your stay?"

"We'll choose," Nabiel said confidently.

The Earth girls then organised themselves into pairs and one triple.

"Excellent," Meredith said. "Now hosts, please bring your guests over to the circle. You can finish the lesson then you might all want to freshen up and change for tonight's celebration. Your hosts will help you find what you need."

Meredith, Marr, Luna, Annee and Suzzona watched as the Earth girls joined the others. They immediately started introducing themselves.

"Will we continue the tour?" Meredith asked after a moment of enjoying watching the interactions.

"Yes, absolutely," Marr answered.

5

"Mary, can I ask you something?" Marr asked as Meredith led the way through the garden.

"Of course, anything," Meredith replied.

"I see children, young women, and older people, both men and women. However, I don't see many young men here. Why is that?"

"The young women you see are mothers with small children. Their coniunx are here somewhere. Some do help with running the habitat. But most are here. Look closer."

Marr stopped and looked around. Then she saw it.

The bushes and trees they saw from the balcony weren't simply for aesthetic value. They were in an orchard. Then she noticed rows of vegetables. In amongst it all were young men. They were working.

"I see them now," Marr said in surprise.

"We also have animals. They are kept separately owing to the smell. Some couples work there, but most of the heavy work is done by fathers of young children. We recognise that at times division of labour is best done in a manner aligned with nature."

"This is very enlightening," Marr concluded.

At this point they passed into another small clearing. A group of women were seated in the space. There were some toddlers playing nearby.

As Meredith escorted them into the space, the seated women stopped talking and turned towards them.

Marr gulped and put her hand over her mouth. Luna, Annee and Suzzona had a similar reaction.

Meredith smiled as she watched the scene. The women were in various stages of pregnancy. Some looked to be nearly due.

"They are pregnant?" Luna blurted.

"Yes," Meredith said as she brought the newcomers into the circle of women.

As Marr and the others entered the circle, one of the very heavily pregnant women let out a squeal. Marr was looking at her bulging stomach at the time. The woman was wearing a tight top which clearly showed the baby kicking.

Marr stopped and stared.

"Oh! Earth children are born in incubators. So, you have never seen a pregnant woman?" the woman suggested on noticing Marr staring.

Marr nodded. She was feeling very uncomfortable. More so than at any time that she could remember.

"Do you want to feel it?" the woman asked.

Marr looked up at the woman.

"Ok," Marr answered reluctantly.

"Put your hand here," the woman said as she brought Marr's hand and placed it on her belly.

Marr didn't have to wait long before the baby kicked again.

Marr burst into tears. The emotion brought on by what she was witnessing was overwhelming.

"Are you okay?" Luna asked.

"Yes, I am fine. Just feeling oddly emotional of late," Marr answered.

Meredith and the woman looked at each other. Their expressions where that of confusion.

Marr and the others spent another couple of hours sitting and chatting with the women. They all had lots of questions. On both sides. They also had a light meal of cold meats, cheese, and bread.

"Well, ladies, it is time to get ready for the celebrations," Meredith said when she felt they had spent enough time together.

"Celebrations?" Luna asked.

"Yes," Meredith answered. "Tonight, we have several couples undergoing the conjugium ceremony. Two other habitats are coming along side. Everyone will be gathering in our garden for the celebration. It will be a sight to see. Something that doesn't happen but once or twice a year."

"Is it a fancy sort of affair?"

"By that do you mean that we dress up, share good food and wine?"

"Yes."

"Then yes, it is a fancy sort of affair."

"We don't have fancy clothes with us. Just our haulier uniforms and these g-suits."

"We have plenty of clothes we can lend you. Shall we?"

"Yes, thank you once more for your generosity and hospitality," Marr answered.

Meredith brought the party to a large apartment on the third level of the atrium.

Stephen, Dukk and Bognath arrived around the same time.

Meredith then addressed them all as they sat in the common space inside the apartment.

"I think it is best, given what we now know of your circumstances, that you all stay here with us."

"Is this your apartment?" Marr asked.

"Yes, it has been our home for nearly thirty years."

"It is quite big. Does no one else live with you? Did you not have children of your own?"

"Yes, we did have children," Meredith answered warmly. "We have children and they had children and now their children are having children. Marr, the baby you felt kicking in the womb earlier will be our first grandchild of our youngest child. Their whole family have now moved into their own home. We are soon to relocate to an apartment to share with other elders."

"Oh," Marr answered as she tried to figure that out.

Meredith smiled and then continued.

"Stephen, we need to find these visitors some suitable clothes for the celebration."

"Why don't we let our visitors get showered while we go to the stores?" Stephen answered.

"Yes, good idea."

"I have so much to tell you," Dukk said to Marr as they inspected the small double room they had been given.

"Really," Marr said with a smile knowing she too had much to share.

"Yes," Dukk continued as he inspected the bed and small cupboard. "We saw the reactors, dual fuel backups, bio-systems and much more. Did you know they have capped oil and gas wells they visit every so often to top up their tanks. Their systems can consume and process raw materials. They have lots of redundancy and are self-sufficient. They don't need to sell their ore outputs if they don't want to. They basically do it in return for protection from aliens. Sorry, I mean those not born on this planet. Which basically means us and everyone we know. Bartiamos guarantees their security and privacy. Anyway, we saw a drill come alongside. It got lifted onto the side of the habitat. Did you know that a group of families co-own a drill. They basically operate as independent businesses. The families compete, in a way to get a little ahead. That affords them a little more comforts. But they are also interdependent. They rely on each other for their survival. Imagine that! This is basically a co-op. And can you believe that they raise their own children. Big families too. Couples generally have five children, but some have more. They say the children are their future. The more the better. Some spend six months or a little more in the Shipyard around the age of eighteen. However, few ever remain up there. Most end up living their entire lives in a habitat like this one. We also saw one of the other habitats come along side. They connected a passenger bridge. There is a celebration tonight. Did you hear?"

"Yes, I did," Marr said with a laugh.

"What?"

"You are like a boy who has found a new toy?"

Dukk laughed as he put his arms around her and drew her in for a kiss.

Chapter 19 – Walking

1

Near eleven p.m. two days later, Marr and Dukk were in bed, back on the rig. They were undocked from the station and waiting for the first traverse.

The rest of the evening on the surface had been a wonderful experience. They had eaten, drank, talked, and danced. The celebration had gone into the small hours. Then they were woken at eight a.m. the following morning for a simple breakfast before boarding a rocket for the return trip.

The rest of the time in the main hub had flown by also. They had made good use of the training facilities and simulators. They had socialised in the bars. They had spent time sharing stories about the celebrations on the surface.

Marr and Dukk had found themselves always with others. The time in bed felt short and they slept solidly. It was only now with the rig in slow running and the normal watch roster back in play, that they finally took time to be with each other again.

"The Newterratwoians were welcoming," Marr reflected aloud as she snuggled into Dukk's chest.

"Yes, and very open about their way of life," Dukk answered.

"Absolutely. Their way of life is so foreign to most and even a threat one could say. They were very trusting."

"I suspect Bartiamos said something to them. Perhaps Mentor was involved too."

"Yes, we have secrets too that we don't want shared. It is in all parties' interest to speak little of this."

"Notwithstanding the hardships, it felt like a pretty satisfactory life," Marr added.

"There were certainly some good things going on," Dukk acknowledged.

"You sound a little hesitant."

"It wasn't all rosy down there. They have conflict, substance abuse and social problems from time to time. They have a disciplinary process and even a lock-up."

"Of course, there can't be growth without conflict and problems to overcome. The pretence of the absence of that in the Rule of Twelve is telling in how it stifles the potential for learning and therefore, growth."

"Interesting," Dukk commented.

After a moment, Dukk asked, "What did you make of their division of labour?"

"Do you mean when they have young children?"

"Yes, but also roles at other times too. The men and women might share the same shift, but they don't do the same tasks."

"I think it works. It keeps the balance. They are taking advantage of typical natural abilities specific to each."

"What do you mean?"

"On average women are into the details, but men are more about the gist. Women see the trees. Men see the forest. On average women have better command of linguistics, but men are better at mathematical comprehension."

"This is contrary to the teaching under the Rule of Twelve."

"It is."

"You mentioned balance. We have balance. How is what we have different?" Dukk asked.

"Perhaps we are talking about different ideas of what balance is."

"Balance is about safety. Compliance. Calmness. That type of thing."

"That is what the Rule of Twelve teaches. But that is not balance as I see it," Marr replied.

"How do you see it?"

"I mean the balance between order and chaos. The right balance brings stability but with sustainable growth."

"Are you saying that balance isn't there under the Rule of Twelve?" Marr laughed.

She then added, "Do you think there is stability and growth under the Rule of Twelve?"

"Yes, well there is definitely stability."

"Disappearing someone who doesn't go along with the party line isn't stability for that individual."

"No. Good point. Why don't we have your version of stability?"

"The balance between the masculine and the feminine ego broke."

"Is this answer going to involve another child's story? A story like the explanation of where the war is at and the take on the Hansel and Gretel story?"

"No, I will lay it out straight," Marr said laughing.

Marr then continued.

"The masculine ego is concerned with leading from the front. Being at the top of the pile. The top dog in the hierarchy. As such masculine ego is upfront, bullish, confrontational. Physical strength is key here. That physical strength is utilised to get to the front and to stay there. Success for the masculine ego is measured by the height of the structure they are on top of. Control for the masculine is about maintaining the top position. The masculine ego also looks for the spoils of that position."

"What do you mean by spoils?"

"Unquestioned authority, but also comforts, luxuries, and finery."

"Women?"

"Yes, concubines. An unlimited supply."

365

"And the feminine ego?"

"The feminine ego is concerned about being in the centre. The feminine ego desires dependency. Sociability and influence are key strengths here. Success for the feminine ego is about the breath of the network around them. The larger the sphere the better. Control for the feminine is about staying in the centre. The feminine ego also looks for spoils."

"Like what?"

"Some material in nature, but mostly reassurance that all others are totally helpless without them."

"So, what is broken?"

"The Rule of Twelve has the extremes of both. The Rule of Twelve drives high dependency and enforces it via an iron fist."

"So, for it to work must one have the opposite?"

"No. Not really the opposite. Just balance."

"What do you mean?"

"A masculine ego driven leader charges out to battle and in doing so gets disconnected from those at the back or those supporting the endeavours of the leader. Those supporting the leader need their concerns to be heard and addressed too. The feminine ego thrives on that aspect. The innovative and bullish notions of the masculine ego can stretch the resources of the leader too thin or cause instability. The whole structure is susceptible to being smashed from outside. The feminine ego brings stability to the structure, through listening, compassion, and influence."

"So, the masculine ego has the best chance of succeeding when there is a feminine ego behind the scenes?"

"Well, in front or behind is a matter of perspective."

"Good point. But isn't it still a subservient relationship?"

"Let me paint another picture. So, a feminine ego driven leader builds out from themselves. The feminine ego brings all decisions back to the centre. This makes followers overly dependent. Innovation and growth get stifled in the absence of independent thought or autonomy. The structure becomes overly dependent on the centre and implodes. The masculine ego brings that strong need for autonomy. It drives the independent thought. It enables the feminine ego to see what should be let go of. This facilitates autonomy."

"I see. Neither approach works in isolation. Each cancels out the failings of the other."

"Yes, but they also complement each other too," Marr added with a smile.

Dukk yawned.

"Am I boring you?" Marr asked in jest.

Dukk laughed.

"Rest time," Marr suggested as she turned towards Dukk for a kiss.

"Yes, goodnight, Marr," Dukk said after the kiss.

2

The next evening the crew had just completed their daily meal together. While it was still a full week before they would reach Earth, Dukk felt they had turned the corner. He wanted to know more about what was instore when they got there.

"We now have bounties on our heads," Dukk said to get everyone's attention. "On top of that, we are transporting a bunch of girls. Even with the Atesoughton seal we will still turn heads. We will hardly be able to just waltz into a citadel. Also, what happens to the girls now. They are hardly ready to assume labour roles. They will stand out like sore thumbs."

"We won't be going to a citadel," Mentor commented. "Nor will the girls be reintegrated, yet. We will make other arrangements. We will get them to the resistance base south of Utopiam. They will sort it."

"How do we get in there?"

"There are man-made caves south of the base. Big enough for a rig this size."

"Show me," Dukk said as he interacted with the table projector.

A three-dimensional image appeared in the air above the table. It showed the hills and fields of Utopiam. At the centre was the citadel.

Mentor reached in. He manipulated the image. He zoomed in on a hilly area thirty kilometres south of the citadel.

"The caves are here," Mentor said as he pointed to a hill just north of a cluster of tall eucalyptus trees. "You approach from the ocean at this point. Turn north here and it is pretty much a straight line through the valley into the caves. It would require staying low to avoid detection."

"Wait! Crossing the shoreline there would mean navigating that area. Is that a wind turbine graveyard?"

"Yes, it is the remnants of a wind farm. Many of the masts are still standing. Even some of the heads and blades."

"And by staying low, you mean just above sea level through the wind farm graveyard, and then just above the surface through the valley and trees?"

"Yep."

"Impossible."

"No, it isn't," Marr interrupted. "I've flown it loads of times. You just need to know the track."

"You've flown a rig this size, through there?" Dukk asked in a sceptical tone.

"Well, no, not a rig."

"What then?"

"A four-seater quadcopter. But the clearance is plenty big enough for a rig this size. I think."

Dukk laughed. "Right, this is going to be exciting. Bazzer, you'd better make sure we have a spare can or two of paint, should we get a scratch."

Bazzer laughed now too.

"Marr knows the track," Mentor said calmly. "And, you have got plenty of time between now and when we get there, to practice the approach using the simulator."

Marr grinned at Dukk.

Dukk smiled. He was up for anything at this stage. Nothing felt beyond them.

Eight days after leaving the Shipyard, the rig was in descent into Earth, having broken orbit three hours earlier.

They had made two further hub stops, over the intervening days. Most had been an anti-climax after the adventures prior.

They were now near the end of their descent. It was night-time on this side of the planet. They had broken orbit in the wake of another rig to hide their arrival. Then the stealth capabilities had been used to keep the rest of their descent hidden. The rig was now flying low over the ocean.

It was almost two months to the day since Dukk had got his first captaincy. For Dukk it felt like a lifetime ago. It was at a time when he knew little of the truth about the world, he called home.

"Switching over to manual," Dukk said as he interacted with the controls.

"Speed is a little fast," Marr observed.

Marr was tracking the rig's progress against a map she and Mentor had prepared. She and Dukk had practiced this approach many times in simulation.

"Adjusting now," Dukk answered.

"Now we get to see just how good a team you two are," Bazzer commented from behind them.

The rig bounced a little as the vertical thrusters took up the challenge of keeping the rig airborne. That was needed now that it was flying slower than the speed needed to generate lift.

"We are coming up on the windfarm," Marr said.

"Preparing to hit the brakes," Dukk replied.

He then opened the broadcast.

"Hello again. This is going to get a little bumpy. Hold on everyone."

"Now!" Marr said loudly.

Dukk pulled the joysticks.

The rig shook as the forward thrusters slowed the velocity just as the rig entered the wind farm graveyard.

"OH!" Annee exclaimed.

Even in the dark, the since abandoned wind turbines still loomed large into the distance on either side.

"Speed is good. Left ten degrees on my mark," Marr said ignoring the commentary from behind her.

"Now," she then added.

Dukk adjusted the trajectory.

For another fifteen minutes, Marr and Dukk continued to work together to bring the rig safely through the wind farm graveyard, over the shoreline, through the trees and up the valley towards the caves.

Dukk slowed the rig to a crawl as they approached the caves.

"It looks mighty tight. These are big caves, but this is a monster compared to a quadcopter," Dukk said as he looked into the mouth of the cave.

Even with the rig's spotlights it was still hard to make out the inside of the cave.

"As we practiced, Dukk. Mentor got confirmation during our descent. Just hold it steady and the doors will open for us," Marr said.

Sure enough, as they passed into the body of the cave, large doors in the opposite wall began to slide out of the way.

Within was a circular landing pad. It was illuminated by green lights.

Dukk manoeuvred the rig into the tight space and brought the rig down onto the pad.

"What now?" Dukk asked as he and the others stood at the bottom of the ramp.

The pad door had closed just after they touched down. The cave they now occupied was empty but for the Imhullu. It was dark. The green pad lights had gone out once the pad doors closed. Dukk had left the rig lights on. They illuminated the walls. That gave them some sense to the overall size of the cave. The ramp also had lights. Those lights allowed them to see each other as they contemplated their next steps.

"We wait," Mentor answered.

"No sign of any other doors," Bognath said as he approached them. He had done a quick scout the moment that they had dropped the ramp.

"They will come," Mentor said as he sat down on the ground near the ramp and closed his eyes.

"I am going to the gym," Bazzer said as he turned to go back up the ramp.

At that moment, a crack got their attention. It was the sound of a door opening. At the same moment, a bright light appeared in the cave wall.

A group of armed people emerged from the light and walked swiftly towards the ramp.

Marr, Luna and Bognath drew their weapons.

Mentor stood up and waited for the group to reach them.

"Mentor, it is you!" their leader said on reaching Mentor. "We got your coded message to give you access to this pad. We found it hard to believe. We heard you were dead. Twice."

"Yes, so the rumours got here too," Mentor replied.

"Yes, and we assumed the worst for Marr and Luna. It is good to see that you are safe. Did you also hear that the crew that you left Earth with, all have bounties on their heads?"

"Yes, we heard that too."

"Wait! Is this the Dinatha's crew?"

"Yes, it is."

"Right, you'd better come inside immediately. You, the captain, Marr, and Luna."

"Hello, Ricardi. What is going on?" Marr asked the man.

"Marr, you will see," Ricardi said as he turned.

"What about everyone else?" Dukk asked.

"They should wait here. This will only take a few minutes."

Marr, Dukk, Mentor and Luna followed Ricardi towards the light.

Beyond the door was a wide and tall corridor. A short distance down the corridor Ricardi led them into a small room. It was some sort of control room. An operator was sitting at a console. On the panels above the console were infrared video feeds of the hill they had just flown through. There were also video feeds of the inside of the cave. It showed the Imhullu and everyone standing around the ramp.

"Can we have the room please," Ricardi said to the operator.

Ricardi closed the door as the operator left.

"Where is teacher?" Marr blurted.

Speaking with Teacher had been on her mind the moment they had reached orbit. Reaching orbit of Earth had triggered the memory of the conversation she had with Mentor and Dukk just after the Dinatha disaster. She felt it was time to get some answers. She wanted to know about the grander plans that Mentor had spoken of. Now that they were back in the bases south of Utopiam the desire to speak with Teacher was overwhelming. In her mind Teacher was the first person she thought they would meet on their return.

"She is not here," Ricardi answered.

"What do you mean?"

"She left the very day we started to hear reports of a pirate attack on the Dinatha."

"Where did she go?"

"Walkabout."

"What does that mean?" Dukk asked.

"It means she went into the wild," Marr answered. "We won't find her unless she wants to be found."

"We need to speak with her!" Marr then added in an angry tone.

"That is why I brought you here to this control room," Ricardi said. "Before she left, she recorded a message. Her instructions were very specific. The message was to be shown to Mentor, Marr, Luna and the Dinatha's captain. She said it was to be shared with you the moment you returned. We dismissed it as some crazy rambling. The reports were that you were all dead."

"What!" Marr said angrily. She was losing her patience with all this.

"Let's see it," Mentor said calmly.

Moments later the image of Teacher appeared in the air above the desk.

"Hello, welcome back my dear people. You must have questions. However, I can't answer them right now as I must go into hiding. Things are at a critical point. You must find Tieanna. She will reveal to you what you need to know. Luna knows where she is. But when you find her, only Dukk must enter octet one. No-one else must go. Goodbye for now. I will see you again near the end."

The message finished.

"Me? What is she talking about?" Luna blurted.

"Is that it?" Marr asked in a calmer tone, having regained control of her emotions. A process that she was finding increasingly difficult of late.

"Pretty much. Apart from the second message," Ricardi answered.

"Second message?" Mentor asked in a shaky tone.

Marr noticed the tone. It took her by surprise.

"Three weeks ago, we got another message. It simply said to send the girls and observers into the wild for a time. She said it would do them good. There was also mention of a deceased girl. We have made provisions for her too. You will take her with you. She will be buried properly in the wild."

"Is that organised?" Mentor asked.

"Yes, we've been on standby since we got the second message. The group taking them have been checking the known meeting places every few days. The girls and observers just need to be taken there and they will be met."

"When can we leave?"

"Right now. Everything is ready."

"Which meeting place is our best option?" Marr asked.

"What pace?" Ricardi asked.

"Medium."

"Then I would suggest heading for Bobtail gorge."

"If I remember correctly, at medium pace that is about two days walk from here."

"Yep, that sounds right."

"Can you show us the gear?"

"Follow me."

"What are we going to do?" Marr asked Mentor as they followed Ricardi out of the control room.

"First, you get the girls and observers to where they need to be," Mentor answered.

"What about Tieanna?"

"Teacher has planted some information with Luna. Luna needs to remember what it is."

"She is crazy. I have no memory of anything of the sort," Luna said shaking her head.

"Some time walking might help bring clarity," Mentor said.

"You said, 'you' just now. What do you mean? Aren't you coming with us?" Marr asked.

"No, I have some investigating to do. We need to find out who raised the bounties."

"You think it is connected to the sabotage on the assassination plans?"

"I am not sure yet."

4

An hour later Marr, Dukk, Luna, Bognath, Annee, Suzzona, the eleven girls and the two observers were standing outside the cave. It was dark. They could sense the cave behind them and the valley walls on either side.

Bazzer had stayed behind to watch the rig. Mentor had left for the citadel.

The gang had been given fatigues, boots and small backpacks with water and protein bars. Marr, Luna and Bognath also carried their weapons.

They also had several ponies with them. One carried Zarra's body. The remainder carried bed rolls, water, food, and camping equipment.

"You've done this before?" Dukk asked Marr as they waited for their eyes to adjust to the darkness.

"Yes, many times," Marr answered.

"I can't see a thing. Are you sure we can't use torches?"

"Yes, it shows up on satellite imagery. Your eyes will adjust in a moment. We'll be following well-trodden paths. And the moon is rising so we'll be fine."

"If it is well-trodden, why do we need to move at night."

"We only need to clear the caves. There is a place about ten kilometres south of here. We should be there by midnight. We can camp there and then resume walking in daylight after that."

"Two hours of walking!" Dukk observed.

"Yes, you have to put to use all that training at some point," Marr said with a laugh.

The voices of Kimince and Trence rose gently into the night.

"I am afraid," one said.

"Me too. But Mentor insists we have what we need. We just need to stick together. We just need to help each other figure it all out," the other replied.

Marr put her arm around Dukk's waist and leaned in.

"That's good advice," she whispered.

"It is," Dukk replied.

A little before midnight, the gang arrived at the place Marr had mentioned. Their stopping place for the night was a eucalyptus tree grove in the shadow of a rocky outcrop.

The walk had been as easy as Marr had suggested. The path they followed had been relatively flat and easy going.

While an easy walk, Marr had kept them moving at a good pace. She was mindful that the excitement of this latest adventure was only going to last so long. So, she was keen to get as far as she could. She also knew the past three weeks of mental and physical training would stand to them. And it did.

Working together they made light work of unloading and securing the ponies. With watch allocations agreed, they each took a bed roll and settled down for some rest.

"Remember, don't put your swag in the path. Bush pigs often use them. Just find a flat place on the side," Marr said aloud as she unrolled her bed.

"Swag?" Dukk asked as he put his roll next to Marr's.

"That is what these bed rolls used to be called in this part of the world," Marr answered.

"Do they make them for two?" Dukk said quietly with a chuckle as he sat into and then inspected the inch thick mattress in its green canvas cover.

"I'm not sure. It might be worth investigating," Marr said as she reached over to him for a kiss.

Sunlight woke Dukk. It streamed in through the eucalyptus trees. He had fallen into a deep sleep the moment he closed his eyes. For a moment he was confused. Then he pushed away the flap of the bed roll and looked around.

Marr was sitting against a nearby tree smiling at him.

Then he remembered that they were supposed to take the last two hours of watch together.

He climbed out of the bed roll, walked over to Marr, and sat down next to her.

"You didn't wake me," he said quietly as he looked out over the sea of bed rolls in amongst the trees.

"No, you were out cold. I decided to let you sleep. I also needed time to think."

"What about?"

"Teacher's disappearance. I really thought I would get to the bottom of the question I asked Mentor."

"About the grander plans for you."

"Yes."

"I am sure we will see her soon enough."

"I don't know. Something feels very odd."

"What do you mean?"

"She knew the girls were with us," Marr answered.

"Mentor must have messaged her," Dukk suggested.

"I tried to ask him before we left the caves. He basically said he hadn't had any interactions with her since we were on Earth last. He also said the thing with the trafficking wasn't anything to do with her. And therefore, neither the rescue."

"What do you mean by 'tried'?"

"It took a lot of effort to just get that information. He was distracted and dismissive."

"Okay, so something is odd."

"Yes, it is odd," Marr replied.

"Who are we going to meet out there? Wild people?" Dukk asked after further reflection.

"Well no. Well, maybe. We are going to meet a squad of robin hood raiders."

"Like those who attacked us on the last return with the Dinatha?"

"Somewhat. These will be more ground based. They steal and then graze livestock. They help keep the resistance food stores well stocked."

"What do you mean by maybe?"

"We might come across some of the wild people."

"Have you?"

"Met any wild people. No."

"Will they be ok out there?" Dukk said as they watched the others start to wake up.

"The girls or observers?"

"Both."

"The girls, yes. I am pretty sure we have prepared them well enough. As for the observers, I am not sure. But I guess Mentor wouldn't have let them come if he didn't feel they were ready."

"Will we see them again?"

"Maybe. In about six weeks they will be given a choice. They may choose to stay on or come back to the base. Mentor is confident they can also be re-integrated into labour roles if they choose."

Dukk nodded.

"What is the plan for today?" Dukk asked after a moment of enjoying the coolness and quiet of the morning.

"We have something to eat, pack up and continue walking."

"How far do we have to walk?"

"We must cover seventy kilometres over the next two days. It will be too hot to walk in the middle of the day. We will walk four hours now. Rest for the middle part of the day and then do another four in the late afternoon. We'll repeat the process tomorrow and we'll be at Bobtail gorge tomorrow evening."

"It feels a long way to walk just to meet others. It would be much quicker to use the rig!"

"But nowhere near as much fun," Marr added with a laugh.

"This is fun?"

"You'll see."

5

The next two days was a surreal experience for Dukk and most of the others. They had spent much of the time in quietness. Whether it was while walking along the dusty tracks or sitting beneath the shade of a tree.

Dukk had taken Marr's advice and practiced clearing his mind. He had put aside all the questions and immersed himself in the sounds around him. Those sounds were so different to the hum of the rig's engines, even during the long hours of slow running. He had found a different form of inner quietness.

By the time they reached the camp at Bobtail gorge, Dukk was feeling calmer and more connected to himself than he could ever remember.

As they worked together to unpack the ponies and raise the camouflage nets, he observed the general calmness in the others too. It occurred to him that they all had undergone a similar transformation.

Marr too had reconnected with herself. She had returned to a level of calmness that she hadn't been able to achieve since leaving Earth two months prior.

Their first evening at Bobtail gorge was spent enjoying stories around a campfire. Marr was confident the fire was okay as the location was well hidden. They had then spent the day resting and swimming in the stream that ran through the gorge.

Night had just engulfed the camp. Marr looked over at Luna. They both stood up and put their hands to their weapons.

"Relax, Marr," came a voice from the darkness.

"Trevor! I should have guessed that you would be leading the meeting party," Marr replied.

"There weren't a lot of volunteers to lead a party to walk in circles for weeks. When I heard you were involved, I couldn't say no," Trevor replied as he appeared out of the dark.

Marr smiled and put her arms out for a deep hug.

"What have you got yourself into this time?" Trevor asked as he stood back from the hug.

"More trouble than you can ever imagine," Marr laughed as she looked around.

Two others appeared from the shadows. They were dressed in fatigues too.

"Nothing wild about these people!" Suzzona blurted.

Trevor tilted his head with a curious expression.

"What were you expecting?" Luna laughed. "Half naked bodies, spears and war paint?"

Suzzona laughed.

"Let me introduce you," Marr said to move things along. "This is Dukk, our captain. His chief mate, Annee. Luna, you know. Bognath is our head of security. This is Suzzona the rig's chef. And over there we have Kimince, Trence, Lilaho, Kayila, Liyl, Yeara, Alion, Zire, Mella, Nabiel, Samie, Jaine and Habili."

Trevor repeated a similar process with his squad.

"And is that the girl?" Trevor asked as he looked at the wrapped-up body of Zarra, which was resting in a hammock between two trees.

Marr nodded.

"Tonight, we will share stories in her honour. There is an ancient burial ground very close to here. Tomorrow we will go there and lay her to rest using the old ways. Then tomorrow night we will dance and sing and help her friends celebrate her memory."

"Thank you. That means a lot to us all," Lilaho said on behalf of the others.

After a moment of reflection, Marr continued.

"Are there only three of you?"

"No. We are just the scouting party," Trevor replied. "Come, look."

Trevor led them up to a small mound just above the camp.

They were able to see more of the gorge. The moonlight was just starting to bounce off the trees and bushes.

"The bushes are moving," Annee commented.

"Look closer," Trevor replied.

As their eyes adjusted to the darkness, the picture became clearer.

People, horses, and cattle were moving in the shadows up the gorge towards them.

"Oh!" Annee replied.

"How many?" Marr asked.

"There are twenty-eight in this cohort. Plus, animals."

"That's a lot to be walking in circles."

"It is what we do."

The next thirty-six hours passed very quickly. The gathering at Bobtail gorge was the celebration Trevor had promised. The burial had taken place in the cool of the afternoon. Then the dancing and singing started. When everyone was exhausted, stories were shared, and reunion plans were made. Then just after dawn on the fifth day, since they set the Imhullu down in the cave, the girls and observers headed further into the wild with their new friends. While Dukk and his crew retraced their steps.

As they approached the cave, late in the evening on the seventh day since arriving back to Earth, Luna stopped suddenly.

"I remember!" she said loudly.

Marr, Dukk, Annee, Bognath and Suzzona all stopped and looked at Luna. They waited for a moment as a huge grin appeared on Luna's face.

"Teacher says lots of odd things. Some more odd than others. Remember when we were jogging? The last time we returned to Earth. Just before our final haul with the Dinatha."

"Yes, Teacher was at the hut in the orchards. She spoke to us briefly and then fell asleep," Marr replied.

"Exactly. I was the last to exit the hut. You, Dukk and Annee were outside already. She suddenly sat up, said my name, and uttered the oddest message. Which I promptly ignored until now!"

"What was the message?"

"She said, 'She will be found with those that cut with a knife, swish right, swish left, and swish right again'."

"So?"

"Don't you see. When we arrived at orbit of Mayfield, just before the assassination, the mammoth ring was there. I thought the emblem on the mammoth was a blade cut not an eel. Teacher had already put the image in my head."

"The Veneficans!" Dukk exclaimed.

"Yes, Tieanna is with the Veneficans on their mammoths," Luna replied.

An hour later and the crew were all back on the Imhullu. Mentor was back from his investigation. He had failed to find the source of the bounties. The others had just brought Mentor and Bazzer up to speed on the week in the wild and on the message that Teacher had given Luna.

"But we've been through this," Dukk said after the story was shared. "We discounted the Veneficans from any involvement in Tieanna's disappearance. They had a legitimate reason to be in Mayfield at the time. They thought they would be meeting with Craig. His father had arranged it."

"We've missed something important," Mentor said quietly.

"What do you mean?"

"Just because they had one clear reason to be there, it doesn't mean that they didn't have others. And there is something else."

"What?" Marr asked.

"I also spoke with Teacher when we were last on Earth. She made a point of saying I should visit Bartiamos on the way back to Earth. She kept saying visiting him was key to the success of the grander plans."

"So?"

"I thought her cryptic message was related to you seeing what was happening on the surface. It was clearly about something else."

"What do you mean?"

"Those mammoths were built at the shipyard. Bartiamos would know them inside and out. He would know how to get into one if one was ever needing to rescue someone."

"Oh, shit," Luna said. "Looks like we need to return to the Shipyard."

"It does, Luna," Mentor answered.

"Are we ready to launch?" Dukk asked.

"Yep," Bazzer answered. "While you've been gallivanting in the wild, I've been working hard to keep this rig in tip top shape. The fresh food stores are replenished, and we are fully fuelled too. This complex is surprisingly well resourced for an underground operation."

"Excellent. Let's get this bird fired up."

Chapter 20 – Backtracking

1

Near midnight that evening, Marr and Dukk were lying in bed. The rig was orbiting Earth on the countdown to the first traverse on their journey back to Newterratwo.

"We need to come clean with Mentor," Marr said. "Today, it was more evident than ever that we need to come together now. I even felt I couldn't ask him about what happen when he went to the citadel this week. And there was something odd about him after we heard the messages from Teacher."

"Yes, I agree, it is time to clear the air," Dukk replied.

He then yawned and added, "but, not right now."

"Yep, goodnight," Marr said as she snuggled into his chest.

The next afternoon, Marr and Dukk found Mentor alone in his seat in the cockpit. He and Annee were on watch. She was on a walkaround, doing a routine inspection of the rig.

"Mentor, can we talk to you?" Marr asked as they entered the cockpit.

"Of course," Mentor said as he turned around.

Marr sat in Luna's seat, adjacent to Mentor. Dukk walked between them and then turned and leant against the forward console.

Marr took a couple of deep breaths and then just said it.

"While in the resort at Emerald Valley, we listened to the rest of the message from Tieanna. The part of the message that said they are coming for him, to keep him safe and not look for her."

"I know," Mentor answered.

"What! How?" Marr asked.

"You've been distant since then. I knew the message was buffered and you'd eventually find it. I didn't feel up to sharing it, but I wanted you to know."

"Oh!" Marr replied.

Dukk gulped. He then spoke.

"Why did you feel we needed to know?"

"Because the weight of it has been hard to carry. I am sure Tieanna was talking about you, Dukk. Which caused me much conflict. I want to find her but fear by searching for her, I would put you in danger."

"Oh!" Dukk then said.

"I am glad you finally came to me. Now we can talk openly about what we must do now."

"What is that?"

"We must find her."

"But that puts Dukk at risk," Marr stated.

"Teacher's instructions have changed my mind. I think that perhaps there is something that Tieanna doesn't know. Something crucially important. Something that only Teacher knows. She has made it clear that Dukk alone must go into rescue Tieanna. Teacher might be a tad bonkers, but everything she does is intentional."

"But would she put Dukk at risk intentionally?"

"No, not from what I know of the grander plans."

"Which are?"

Mentor smiled.

"For another time?"

"Yes."

"Well, I hope Teacher is right about all of this. It does sound majorly perilous," Dukk added.

"Yes, we are going to need to be very prepared," Mentor answered.

Marr looked on. She had another question. She wasn't sure if it was the time for it.

Mentor noticed her hesitation.

"Is there something else?"

"Yes, Mentor," Marr replied. "When we heard Teacher's message, you weren't yourself. You sounded shaken."

"Yes, I was taken aback."

"Why?"

"Teacher instructed us to find Tieanna."

"So?"

"I have never spoken to Teacher about Tieanna. Or Tieanna about Teacher. Tieanna would have some knowledge of some of my activities because I shared pieces. However, I never shared the source of those activities. Tieanna wouldn't know who has been giving me my instructions. It is safer that way. Equally, Teacher would have some knowledge of the work that I was doing with Tieanna. Things like stopping trafficking. However, I never spoke about who I was working with. And yet, clearly Teacher knows about Tieanna and even where she is. This is seemingly impossible."

"Oh!" Marr exclaimed. She felt she now understood what had troubled Mentor. It was now troubling her too.

"Are you sure Teacher can be trusted?" Dukk asked. He felt it was the obvious question.

"Yes," Marr and Mentor both said firmly, at the same time.

Dukk was shaken a little. He was not expecting such a strong reaction. He paused as he felt now wasn't the time to question her or her motives.

Marr was aware of her defensive reaction to Dukk's question. His question was reasonable. She collected her emotions and spoke.

"That was a fair question. It requires a better answer."

Dukk smiled.

"Yes, Marr is right," Mentor added.

Marr then continued.

"She has never done anything to suggest she can't be trusted. Her behaviour is odd at times; however, she has never lied to me or misled me. Her actions speak for themselves in the many hours she has devoted to sharing stories and giving time to those that want to learn. It is for these reasons that I feel we can, and perhaps must, trust her."

"I couldn't have said it any better," Mentor added.

"That's sounds like a fair answer," Dukk said. "However, I suggest that just because it hasn't happened before doesn't mean it won't happen. I suggest we take no chances with this endeavour and plan this meticulously."

"Agreed," Marr replied.

Mentor nodded.

"And, by that, I also mean we don't rush in. We are agreed we need to rescue Tieanna, but we take it one step at a time. That in my mind means we proceed carefully. That includes making proper stopovers to resupply. It means taking time for intermediary inspections and generally running this rig to the best of our abilities."

Both Marr and Mentor nodded.

"One final thing," Dukk said.

Marr and Mentor waited.

"We share all of this with the others."

"Agreed," Marr and Mentor said in unison.

2

Even though they took a slightly more direct route, and only had one hub stop at IACB5, it still took six days to reach Newterratwo. It then took another thirty-six hours to get an audience with Bartiamos. They didn't want to raise an alarm, so they indicated that their visit was social. That put them low on the priority list.

"What reason would you have to learn more about mammoths?" Bartiamos said bluntly after he heard the request.

Marr, Dukk and Mentor were standing just inside the doors of the office as per the first time. Bartiamos had his back to them. He was looking out of the windows.

"We have business to break into one," Marr answered.

"Impossible!" Bartiamos answered without turning around.

"Will you tell us what you know of them?" Mentor asked politely.

"That would take days. There are many variations. You need to be more specific."

"We are interested in the mammoth ring," Dukk said bluntly.

Bartiamos turned around. He looked at Dukk.

"That would be more than impossible. It would be suicide," he answered.

On observing the seriousness of the question from the expressions in the faces of Marr, Dukk and Mentor, Bartiamos continued.

"What business do you have with the new puritans?"

"They have imprisoned someone we need to talk with," Mentor answered.

Bartiamos laughed as he walked over to the digital table. He waved them over.

"Always on some hero mission is Mentor," he then added.

Marr, Dukk and Mentor approached the table.

"Well, if you want to die, who am I to get in the way," Bartiamos said as he interacted with the digital table.

A mammoth space station appeared in the air above the table.

Bartiamos then interacted with the station as he spoke.

"The mammoth is like most DMD enabled stations. It is disc shaped. The DMD is woven into the underside, and it has a multitude of services spread across several sections. You have the rig capable hangers. There are stores. You have the accommodation and living areas. There is the control centre, and you have the biosystems. In addition, mammoths are heavily fortified. Missile silos dot the upper surface. Railgun turrets are found on top, below and on the sides. They also have CDLs. They usually carry a fleet of arrows and interceptors. You won't get anywhere near one, let alone dock with it. The Venefican mammoths have something even more special. In the centre of each is an ultra-secure section. Very few know these even exist. Access is only via a single entrance. Within there are two spaces. There is a common area and then separately, there is an apartment. They call these centre sections the octets."

The mention of the octet brought Marr, Dukk and Mentor to attention. Teacher had mentioned it in her message.

"So, there are five octets? One per mammoth?" Marr asked bluntly.

"Yes," Bartiamos answered cautiously. He then looked up with a curious expression.

"Are they all the same?"

"The octets?"

"Yes."

"No. The octet in the first mammoth is different. Why do you ask?"

"We need to get into octet one," Mentor said in a firm tone.

"You are serious about getting yourselves killed! Fine, whatever," Bartiamos said as he changed the display to show a blueprint.

He then continued.

"The octet in mammoth one, has these odd small rooms, in addition to the common space and apartment. We speculate that these small rooms are prison cells. The apartment is also different. Inside it is some sort of computer room. An ultra-secure data centre is our best guess. It even has its own power supply via a dual reactor."

"Speculate?" Marr asked.

"We've never been in there. Nor has anyone we know. Even the original builders mysteriously disappeared."

"You mentioned access was via a single entrance. What is hard about that?" Marr asked.

"Yes, each octet is accessed via a special type of mantrap. But it isn't straight-forward. The mantrap self-seals on entering. It has some sort of air sampling DNA based security system. There is a single door, accessed from a service corridor. It is like an airlock. Once in the room, the air is cycled three times. Oxygen is removed. If you don't have the right DNA, the oxygen isn't added back. You suffocate. The floor opens and you are shot into space. Wearing a g-suit and having your own air supply won't help you either. The mantrap also has targeted EMP. So, if you fail the test your suit and all electronics will be rendered useless."

"How do you know this?"

"Some of my crews have been a little too ambitious with their activities to repatriate the Venefican's ill-gotten gains. The odd individual has thought they might chance their luck at entering the octets. They have ended up dead."

"Oh."

"But listen," Bartiamos said in a frustrated tone. "Even if you find a way to get into it, the octet isn't somewhere you want to be."

"Why?"

"Because of this!"

Bartiamos was pointing to an oddly shaped room in the middle of the data centre.

"What is it?"

"We suspect it is a dark matter containment unit."

"Oh shit!" Dukk blurted.

"Yes sir! Oh, shit indeed!" Bartiamos stated.

"Clearly, I am missing something. Can someone fill me in?" Marr asked.

"If the dark matter has been activated, it must be contained," Dukk replied.

"Why?"

"Because if it isn't contained it will fold everything around it into itself."

"Yes, if the containment unit was breached the dark matter would collapse the middle of the mammoth. At best, in an instant, you'd see a doughnut not a disc," Bartiamos added.

Silence fell on the room.

"What do you mean by ill-gotten gains?" Dukk asked after feeling it was time to move on.

Bartiamos laughed before continuing.

"I guess if you go ahead with this madness, you'll be dead soon, so it won't hurt speaking out of school. We have the service contracts on those mammoths, like most of the larger vessels we've made. We regularly visit them for repairs and routine maintenance. Of late the Veneficans haven't' done themselves any favours. They been taking produce and supplies from others without paying. They claim this unpaid appropriation of goods and services is payment for their wisdom. Superstition is rampant. Most think it is bad luck to stand up to them. They don't even pay us. However, our reputation is built on quality. We can't afford to have one drop out of the sky. Anyway, we have found a way to compensate ourselves. We repatriate their ill-gotten gains. We have tool trolleys that have hidden compartments. We do our repairs and leave a little heavier than when we arrived. The fine foods and wines are easily moved on the black market. I even hear from my friend at Maple Tower that you have sampled some of the French vodka we sourced for him."

Dukk laughed, which brought a smile to Bartiamos too.

"Could you get us on to mammoth one?" Marr blurted.

"Maybe. But it is complicated," Bartiamos answered.

"In what way?"

"We don't know where they are."

"What do you mean?"

"The Venefica are always on the move. They don't stay in major systems from more than twelve hours, and they don't publicise their movements. They are ultra-secretive. I'd probably do the same if I was disliked like they are."

"How do you do your repairs if you don't know where they are."

"We have service centres all over the place. We maintain lists of jobs. When they appear in orbit near a service centre, we dispatch crews to do the repairs before they traverse again."

"So, to get us on to one, you'd need us to be waiting in a service centre for the off chance that they show up?"

"Yes, or if you had some way to draw them in. That might work too."

"What do you mean by draw them in?"

"If they had some reason to be somewhere and you knew where they'd be, you could be waiting ready to be smuggled on board."

At that moment, the door opened. Vilemia stuck her head in.

Before she could speak, Bartiamos swiped away the mammoth and spoke.

"I am afraid that I must end our chat now. A very important client has arrived to go over the plans to refit his family's mammoth."

"I tried to stop him," Vilemia said, interrupting Bartiamos.

3

Vilemia stepped out of the way as both doors were flung open.

In the doorway was Craig Atesoughton. Emeelie was there too.

They entered and came directly over to them.

A two-person security detail stepped in behind them.

Vilemia swiftly closed the doors and looked over.

"My friends!" Craig shouted joyfully, as he went to hug and kiss them all.

Emeelie too got in on the greeting ritual.

"When I saw the Imhullu, I came right up here," he added.

Bartiamos stared at them all. As did Vilemia.

"You know each other?" he said to regain the room.

"Of course," Craig answered. "We've broken bread and even had a barbecue together."

"Oh, right," Bartiamos answered in a confused tone.

"What has you in the company of this master builder?" Craig asked as he looked between Marr, Dukk and Mentor.

Mentor looked at Craig and then the two security guards.

Craig followed his glance. He then flicked his head at the two security guards. They turned and left.

When the door was closed behind them, Mentor spoke.

"We know where Tieanna is."

Craig's expression went from delight to concern.

"Where is she?" he asked.

"On the mammoth ring."

"Oh! But! Wait. How?"

"It is a long story and perhaps better for another time. The bottom line is that we are certain she is being held prisoner on mammoth one."

Craig then looked between them all.

"You are here picking Bartiamos' brain for knowledge of how to get into that mammoth?" he asked.

Mentor nodded.

"And is there a plan?"

"We haven't got that far yet. We are just exploring the obstacles."

"Which are?"

"We need to find them. Bartiamos suggests we could draw them in if they have a reason to be somewhere."

Craig paused for a moment. He then looked at Emeelie. She nodded.

"I could invite them under the cloak of getting their approval for our companionship?" he said reluctantly.

Silence filled the room.

"You'd have to insist on meeting the queen if you want the mammoth ring," Bartiamos eventually said.

"Yes, clearly, and I wouldn't expect it to be any other way," Craig added.

"Well, that would definitely draw them in."

"Bartiamos, you said if we could draw in the mammoth ring, you could get us on board" Marr stated.

"Yep. But you would have to pretend you are looking for a joy ride."

"Joy ride?"

"Joy rides are another side-line we do. The overly curious who have accumulated too much crypto, pay a pretty penny to get a first-hand glimpse of the mammoth ring. It wouldn't be hard."

"Earlier, you said it was suicide."

"It would be suicide to approach one or go wandering about within one for that matter. Not to stay hidden on a repair shuttle."

"What about the system relays. Can they not track joy riders?"

"Yes, relays could be used to highlight the joy ride. A good data analyst could not only determine if there were extra passengers, but they could determine when occupants were swapped between craft."

"That will be a problem for us."

"Well, maybe not. You see, we made all the relays that are capable of scanning for occupancy levels on vessels in orbit. We have back doors. It isn't uncommon for a relay to be playing up when we are hosting joy rides."

Bartiamos said 'playing up' while making quote marks in the air with his hands and fingers.

Marr smiled.

"How would the invitation work?" Dukk asked as he looked at Craig.

Craig looked at Emeelie.

"We put a message into their official channel. We give some suggested dates and locations. They then just arrive, unannounced," Emeelie answered.

"So, we'd have to be on standby," Dukk observed.

"Yes, you would need to be wherever we are."

"We could just follow you. That would put us wherever you are."

"They have spies, just like us. They might see the trap if you are simply following Craig's flotilla," Bartiamos observed.

"We'd have to hide our movements," Dukk said.

"Or hide in plain sight," Craig added.

"What do you mean?"

"I am leaving an interceptor here for upgrades. That leaves me down one escort. You could step into that role. And if you've delivered the girls back to Earth, you have capacity to carry one of my armed squads."

"That could work. And yes, the girls are on Earth again so we can accommodate a squad."

"We must celebrate this step forward and enjoy some good food and wine together," Craig then said to shift the direction.

"Not here," Bartiamos stated firmly. "They have spies here. I suggest you keep all this behind closed doors. Hauliers and mercenaries don't socialise with future heads of families. It would draw unnecessary attention to you all."

"Agreed," Mentor added.

"Well, that is something we are going to have to change," Craig said. "But, yes, until Tieanna is safe, we'd better keep things under the radar. My new chief of staff will initiate the flotilla escort arrangements."

Craig looked over at Emeelie as he finished talking.

"She will," Emeelie said with a smile.

"I will have our head of security put a formal request through when we leave this meeting," she then added.

"Speaking of meeting. We must get on with the review of your mammoth refit," Bartiamos said.

"Yes, we will leave you to it," Mentor said to acknowledge the hint.

"We'll rain check our gathering until we are at the beach," Craig said.

"The beach?" Dukk asked.

"Yes, from here we are going to Earth. We have a complex that is one thousand clicks south of Citadel Inquis. It is on the beach. There is awesome surfing there."

"I've flown that area plenty. There isn't anything south of Inquis."

"Have you passed directly over all of it?"

"No, we are restricted to certain flight paths."

"And those restrictions are there for a reason. We don't want others knowing about it. We had to reclaim a good chunk of the ruins of a once thriving beach suburb of a large city in that region. We also left a good buffer of poison lands to hide it from the wild people. And we control the satellites and flight paths, so it is hard to know it is there."

"Intriguing," Dukk said.

"Yes, it is. We built a space port there too. There is plenty of room."

"Great, sounds good," Dukk answered.

After more hugging and hand shaking, Marr, Dukk and Mentor left Bartiamos' boardroom and returned to the rig to brief the others.

4

"The emphasis on orbit transfers was odd. But I guess we'll know why in a moment or two," Marr said.

Marr and Dukk were sitting in the lounge of another interceptor. One of the existing escort ships. They had been summonsed there ahead of the captains briefing. With flotillas, the captains briefing took place just prior to departing a location.

The past twenty-four hours had been very busy. They had barely slept. On top of getting more details from Bartiamos about mammoths, they had their new role within Craig's flotilla to prepare for. Everyone had agreed that their induction into the flotilla should be done by the book. It would avoid attracting unnecessary attention. The induction process had included a thorough inspection of the rig and all its systems. Bazzer had been mildly insulted by the need. The induction had also involved interviews and tests. Dukk and his crew had been thoroughly tested in their ability to handle the rig in challenging circumstances. They were also put through various simulations should the flotilla come under attack. They had come through all tests with flying colours. They had also been given a new set of clothes to wear. Both g-suits and shirts and slacks. All in the customary grey of elite staffers.

"Yes, I guess we will," Dukk replied before adding, "Can I ask you something?"

Marr looked over and nodded.

"During yesterday's meeting with Bartiamos, he referred to the Veneficans as new puritans. You flinched. Had you heard of that label before?"

"Yes," Marr answered. "It is a lesser-known term that was used to describe the group of people who were responsible for the reset."

"Those that established the citadels."

"Yes."

"So, the Veneficans are the original founders of the citadels?"

"I have no idea, but it is an interesting thought."

"Is it another question for Teacher?"

"Yes, I think so."

"You know, it is a pity we can't stay any longer," Marr said sensing it was time to change subject.

"Why?"

"I'd like to visit Stephen and Meredith again. I feel as if I still have lots of questions about their way of life."

"Like what?"

"Well, it is a working example of how things were before the Reset. When family was the normal for everyone, not just elites. A time when it was normal to be in a lifetime union with the same person."

"Yes, I've been giving that some thought too."

"What occurred to you?" Marr asked.

"A singular commitment with no get out clause puts a different emphasis on nearly every part of the relationship."

"Yes, it does. When one must make it work no matter what, things play out differently."

After a moment of reflection, Dukk spoke again.

"Do you think that is something we might entertain?"

"Dukk, are you asking me to be your primary companion, for ever?" Marr said with a slight stumble.

"Yes, Marr, I guess I am," Dukk said with a gulp.

"Well, I accept," Marr said with a stutter, as she reached to hug him.

At that moment, the door to the lounge opened.

Dukk and Marr pulled apart and looked up.

Emeelie, Eleettra and two security guards entered. The latter two stood just inside the door. Eleettra and the guards were wearing grey uniforms. Emeelie was dressed in a fitted shirt, mid-length skirt and half jacket. All in the Atesoughton blue.

Emeelie shook her head gently to indicate this wasn't a social occasion.

"Good evening, Captain Dellington and co-pilot Maldana," Emeelie said in a stilted tone. She was playing along with the masquerade nicely.

Marr and Dukk stood up. They sensed it was appropriate.

Emeelie then continued.

"I am Mr Atesoughton's Chief of Staff. You can call me COS or Ma'am. This is Eleettra, our head of security."

"Ma'am, Eleettra," Dukk and Marr said in union as they all shook hands.

Emeelie then sat on the couch opposite. Eleettra sat next to her. Marr and Dukk sat also.

Eleettra flicked open some documents in the air above the coffee table between them.

"I see everything is in order," Emeelie said after interacting with the documents for a moment.

"You passed all the tests with zero mistakes. That is impressive," She added.

"Thank you, Ma'am, we aim to please," Dukk said in a slightly provocative tone.

Emeelie grinned briefly before returning to a serious expression. She then continued.

"Welcome to the flotilla. Eleettra will now run through our protocols. Please ensure you fully understand them before the captain's briefing in one hour. We operate to a tight schedule and want no unnecessary delays as you come up to speed."

"Understood, Ma'am," Dukk answered in a serious tone.

With that Emeelie stood, turned, and left. The two security guards followed her.

After an awkward moment of looking at each other, Eleettra checked the door was closed properly.

"That was odd. Emeelie is playing optics for the security guards. How are you?" she said in a friendly tone as she came over to give them both a hug.

"Yes, we understand. We are good, thank you, Eleettra. How are you?" Marr replied as they hugged.

"Couldn't be better. Emeelie cleaned house when she started as chief of staff. Lots of changes. She made me head of security. Which has been a blessing and a curse."

"How so?"

"Lots more paperwork. Much less making cocktails by the pool," she replied with a laugh.

"They were certainly good times."

"They were. Anyway, we have a lot to get through before the briefing. So, I suggest we get started."

"Absolutely."

Eleettra flicked away the test documents and replaced them with a depiction of two cruisers four arrows and two interceptors.

"Since this is your first experience of travelling in a flotilla, I will start with the basics. If that is ok," Eleettra asked.

"Yep, that works," Dukk answered.

"Craig likes to travel light and fast. So, he travels with only two cruisers. Each cruiser is accompanied by two arrows and an interceptor. We also have two arrows operating as scouts. That also enables some leap frogging. The interceptors usually carry an armed squad of six persons. Only Emeelie and I know in advance which cruiser Craig and his inner circle will use for any specific part of the journey. We also change things at times if we sense trouble. We may also use one of the interceptors from time to time. And we keep the flight plan hidden. You'll get instructions for the next traverse just after exit of the previous one. For the traverse, we operate a staggered protocol. Two arrows go first, then at two-minute intervals, an interceptor, the first cruiser, then the second cruiser, second interceptor and finally, the last two arrows. Your place in that sequence will also change. Generally, only half the flotilla will dock at hubs or deorbit when we reach planets. The half that remains, run DMD countdowns to enable a fast exit should circumstances require it. We mix things up to enable resupply, repairs, and downtime. Any questions?"

"Is all the switching around the reason we had to do hatch transfers in the simulation test?" Dukk asked.

"Yes. And don't worry, Craig and his entourage have become quite skilled at moving across the near zero-g barrier."

"Good. What about communications?"

"Traverse details will be shared via an encrypted channel. I will share the details with you in a moment. Communications with outsiders is forbidden while we are in transit. Also, any communications with others when in port must not include specifics of any flight path taken."

"That's fine."

"Fuel and resupply?"

"We will resupply at stopover locations. Paid on account. That also goes for rehydratable supplies."

"Fresh food?"

"Side hustles are strongly discouraged, but we won't be concern with what you have in your onboard stores," Eleettra said with a grin.

Dukk nodded.

"Any other questions?"

"Yes, I have a question," Marr said.

"Shoot," Eleettra answered.

"What is leap frogging?"

Eleettra laughed.

"Sorry, I keep forgetting that you are new to this," she answered. "Leap frogging is where the scouting craft go ahead. They then start the traverse countdown in the next system. When the flotilla arrives, the scouting craft are near traverse. If we need a quick exit for Craig and his inner circle, they can transfer to the scouting craft."

"Wouldn't that then put them ahead of the flotilla?"

"Exactly. So, the approach is rarely used. Mostly, when we are close to the destination."

"Cool."

"Any final questions?"

Marr and Dukk shook their heads.

"Oh, I nearly forgot. As this is your first transit, as head of security I will be mostly on your rig. I assume I can make use of the double bunk room of the lower level as my base?"

"Yes, of course," Dukk answered.

"Great. I must leave you as I need to prepare for the briefing. Let me share the protocol documents and encryption codes. Read over them while you wait for the briefing. Someone will fetch you when the briefing is ready to start. It will be held upstairs in the crew mess."

"Perfect," Dukk answered.

"Thank you," Marr added.

The moment the door closed, Marr and Dukk fell into each other's arms and kissed deeply.

"How and when will we tell the others?" Marr said when they pulled apart.

"Why don't we keep it between ourselves until we reach Earth and Craig's resort on the beach?"

"Yes, great idea. It will be fitting given how Craig and Emeelie announced," Marr replied with delight.

5

Ninety minutes later, Marr and Dukk were walking across the hanger. They were on their way back to the Imhullu.

"They aren't messing about?" Marr noted.

Supply crews were swarming Craig's cruisers and escort ships.

"No, they aren't. I guess when they decide to move, it happens fast. They don't want to alert enemies."

"I hope the others are ready."

"Let's check," Dukk answered as he opened the comms channel to his crew.

"Good evening gang," Dukk said on the comms. "We passed the test and the captains briefing went smoothly. We are to prepare for departure. Let's have a circle-up in ten minutes."

Ten minutes later, Dukk and his crew were sitting around the crew table on the Imhullu. There was a tension in the room. The colour of the new uniforms was adding to the change of mood.

"I think I cut a fine shape in this grey," Luna said to break the tension.

"Blue is more my colour," Bazzer said with a chuckle.

"Yep, that's for sure," Luna replied.

Bazzer blew a raspberry in her direction.

"When you are ready?" Dukk said with a smile.

Silence fell.

"Ok! This pre-departure briefing isn't quite typical in that we don't have a flight plan. We know unofficially that our eventual destination is Earth. But officially we are running blind. We'll get each traverse instruction as we progress."

"Very hush, hush, hey?" Suzzona stated.

"Yes, it is. So, we are lifting off in about forty-five minutes. The station will be sharing the departure instructions soon. Meanwhile, we need to check fuel and resupply and get warmed up. The resupply vehicles should be alongside at any moment. We just need to go out and give them our order. We should restock our rehydratable stocks, just in case."

"Yes, good idea. We are down to three weeks of fresh food," Suzzona replied.

"And, we are going to have further extras. That is in addition to the squad, who, I am told will be self-sufficient."

"Extras?" Annee asked.

"Yes, head of security and her assistant will be joining us for most of this run. She will take over the double bunk cabin on the lower level. We need to clear it out. Bognath? Suzzona?"

"Yep, not much of my stuff is still there. Most is up here in Ann's cabin," Suzzona answered.

"Yep, me too," Bognath added.

They looked at Bognath.

"No, not Annee's. Shit, you know what I mean," Bognath said as he shook his head and laughed.

That brought a laugh from all.

"I'll go down and give it a once-over," Annee said.

"Thanks, Ann. Any questions?" Dukk asked.

"Any changes to how we run the rig?"

"Not really, Ann. We'll continue to run watches and our typical routines. We will be doing the occasional hatch to hatch transfer while running the DMD. But, otherwise, it will be business as usual."

"What do you mean by hatch-to-hatch transfers?" Luna asked.

"When the DMDs are running we can't use the port door and airbridge. The gravitational field generated by the DMD make it too dangerous. Instead, we dock belly to belly. The gravitational fields cancel each other out. We use the hatch in the underside to move people between the ships."

"Is that hard to do?"

"Docking is straightforward, with practice. However, moving through the hatch is a little unsettling. The gravitation field flips as you go through."

"Cool. And who will be moving through the hatch?"

"Some of their people. Perhaps Craig, Emeelie and a security detail."

"Will Craig and Emeelie be traveling with us?"

"From time to time. They mix things up to reduce the risk of attack."

"Interesting."

"Anything else?" Dukk asked.

There were no replies.

"Great. Normal stations. Let's get to it."

At that moment there was an alert on Dukk's comms. It was the ramp sensor.

"It looks like our guests have arrived," Dukk said. "Marr let's go and give them our sermon. Ann, I will escort them to the lounge for your briefing."

"Let's do it in the downstairs dining area. I'll be down there anyway. I will be checking that cabin for the head of security and the assistant," Annee added.

"Bazzer, you might want to come with us," Marr said with a grin.

Bazzer looked up with a curious expression.

Chapter 21 – Momentum

1

Dukk led Marr and Bazzer to the door at the top of the ramp.

Eleettra was peering through the portal window in the door.

Dukk unlocked the door and waited for it to swing open.

"Welcome to the Imhullu," Dukk said as he stepped into the opening.

"Hello, captain," Eleettra replied. "This is my second, Jaani."

Directly behind her was a female in the same grey uniform as Eleettra. Behind them on the ramp were two sets of lockers. They were the ones on wheels that Dukk recommended to his crew. Dukk smiled.

"Welcome, Jaani," Dukk said. "I want to have a quick chat with you all before you enter. Can we join the squad on the hanger floor?"

"Of course," Eleettra replied as she gazed down the passageway and spotted Bazzer. She smiled before turning and heading back down the ramp.

"After you," Dukk said with a chuckle as he turned to Bazzer.

Bazzer rolled his eyes and shook his head at Dukk.

Dukk laughed.

At the foot of the ramp was a squad of six security guards. All dressed in grey uniforms. Each too had a locker on wheels.

Once all assembled on the hanger floor near the ramp, Dukk addressed them.

"Welcome all, my name is Dellington, the Captain of this rig. This is my co-pilot, Maldana. And this is my chief engineer, Chebaker. While you have been allocated to this rig, you are still subject to my conditions of entry. You are to stay within the designated accommodation area and not attempt to enter any areas marked otherwise. You fend for and clean up after yourself. The kitchen and service docks will be kept fully stocked. The bathrooms and living spaces will be cleaned when the opportunity arises, so it is in your interest to keep on top of it. There are washers and dryers if you need them. Fighting of any kind will not be tolerated and result in confinement. Weapons are to remain in your lockers. If there is an emergency, you are to do exactly what you are told by me and my crew."

Dukk paused to let that sink in.

"These conditions are non-negotiable. Of course, you have the right to refuse them. You can exercise that right by requesting a transfer which I will happily accommodate. Continuing up this ramp is indication of acceptance."

Dukk paused once more. No one flinched.

"Excellent, I'll scan your IDs now and then bring you on board. My chief mate will be conducting a housekeeping and safety briefing in the dining area in a moment."

Dukk then turned and led the squad up the stairs.

Marr waited for them to pass.

"Go ahead," Eleettra said to Jaani and Marr.

Marr smiled and followed Jaani and the squad up the ramp.

Fifty minutes later the rig was sitting in an airlock ready for departure. Everyone was in their seats. Dukk opened the broadcast to those on board.

"Hello again, thank you all for your help in getting us underway and participating in the evacuation drill. We are expecting undocking permission at any moment. From there we have a little manoeuvring to do before we start the traverse countdown. You will be free to move about once we have engaged the DMD. Current estimates put the first traverse at ten tomorrow morning. However, before that, near eight a.m., we will be doing some hatch-to-hatch docking. Please expect the rig to move about somewhat. It is advised to stay in your bunk or stay seated during this time. Otherwise, enjoy your evening and I will be back on the broadcast just ahead of the traverse. Goodnight."

Dukk disabled the comms and then turned to Marr.

"Are we all good?" he asked.

"Yep," Marr answered. "We are waiting on the craft in airlock three. Then traffic control said we are good to go."

"Any heads up on what the hatch-to-hatch docking is for?" Luna asked.

"Not at this stage," Dukk answered. "Although Eleettra said it is unlikely Craig and Emeelie will use our rig initially. So, it will just be for optics."

"The shell game!" Bazzer stated.

"What are you talking about?" Luna asked.

"Also known as thimblerig, the shell and a pea or the old arm game. It is a gambling game using three identical containers, like cups or shells, and a ball. The aim is to guess which cup has the ball. The hatch-to-hatch docking in a flotilla is like that. Onlookers must guess which cruiser or escort has the prize."

"We've got the go signal," Marr Interrupted.

"Right, off we go," Dukk said as he interacted with the autopilot.

Before long, the rig was in the orbit of Newterratwo. The DMD was loaded with the traverse details and the countdown had begun.

"Ann and Mentor, the conn is yours. Rest awaits as it is going to be a busy morning," Dukk said as he unbelted.

"Absolutely. I am bombed," Marr added.

"Roger, captain. Bazzer and Luna, see you at two a.m.," Annee said.

"Copy that," Bazzer answered as he headed towards the cockpit door.

"Where will I call for you if you aren't around at two a.m.?" Annee said with a giggle.

"You'll keep!" Bazzer laughed.

2

A little later, Marr and Dukk were together in their cabin.

"I am in turmoil," Marr said.

"What about?" Dukk answered.

"I really enjoyed seeing Craig and Emelie. My heart sung when they rushed into Bartiamos' boardroom yesterday."

"Me too. I felt the same way. So where is the turmoil?"

"Up until six weeks ago, Craig represented everything I stand against. He is the heir apparent to an elite family. The same group of people that oppresses us. The same group that caused the dismantling of what I understand as to be truly amazing accomplishments of humans. I am struggling to see him as that. I know it would be naive to think he hasn't had a hand in breaking the human spirit and propagating or propping up the lies. Still, and with all that, I now see him as a fellow human, struggling to make sense of it all. That is the turmoil."

"Yes, I've been giving that some thought too."

"Any success?"

"Some, but nothing concrete."

"What have you got to?"

"Well, I've been placing that question within the stories and frameworks you and Mentor have been sharing. And, from what I gather, the things that I heard somewhat from Tieanna when I was a toddler."

"And what has that process produced?"

"Nothing yet?"

"What do you mean?" Marr asked in a surprised tone.

"Well," Dukk laughed. "The idea of using the stories and frameworks was where I got to. Not actually applying them. Perhaps we could do that together?"

"I like the sound of that. Where will we start?"

"Perhaps the creed."

"Ok, let's start with the first line, 'Focus on that which is real in the heart'. What applies with that?"

"For me that says I should focus on the bonds that are forming through spending time together. The joy of exchanging ideas. The mutual respect. The kindness. Those types of things."

"And not the preconceptions of what he represents."

"Exactly."

"Ok, that works for me too. Now, what of the second line, 'Create the space so that the process can emerge.'?"

"Well, that is easy. I must take action that enables spending more time together."

"Yep, I can see that too. And, the third line, 'Honour that which serves you well.'?"

"This is where caution comes into my mind."

"How so?"

"He moves in different circles for which he must honour. Some of the needs of those circles might not be aligned with everything we are doing. So, we must keep some degree of separation."

"Do you mean that we don't share everything we know or the sources of our knowledge?"

"Exactly."

"So that works for me too. And then what of the final part of the creed, 'Engage in the journey as it unfolds.'?"

"For me, that talks to being fully present when in his company. I must not let my mind be distracted by other commitments. I must not rush into the next thing."

"I like it," Marr said. "However, that doesn't fully answer my quandary."

"What is the question that is holding you up?"

"If I no longer stand against him, do I no longer stand against what he represents?"

"What is stopping you answering that question?"

"Oh! You are getting good at this coaching stuff!"

"You must be rubbing off on me. So, what is stopping you?"

"I am seeing him as part of the collective, not as an individual."

"What do you want?"

"To see him as an individual."

"And?"

"So, I can honour him as an individual whilst still standing against the collective he is part of."

"Ok. And that works for me too."

"Oh, so you were with me on this too?"

"Of course. Thank you for helping me rationalise it in my head too."

"You played me," Marr said as she jumped on top of him and started a soft wrestling match that quickly became something else.

3

"Brace everyone, this is going to get a little bumpy," Dukk announced on the comms.

It was near eight a.m. the following morning. The rig was about to complete the first of two planned hatch-to-hatch docking manoeuvres. This first manoeuvre would be with one of the cruisers.

Dukk was closely monitoring the approach. The autopilot was doing the work. However, Dukk had to be ready to take the controls if the autopilot failed or if something unexpected happened.

The rig shook as the combined gravitational forces of both their rig and the cruiser came into contact with each other. The thrusters worked hard to bring the craft closer without them crashing into each other.

A video call and two video feeds were being displayed above the forward console. The video call was a link with the cockpit on the cruiser. They had been exchanging basic safety information as they prepared for the docking. The video call was currently muted. One of the video feeds showed the view from the underside of the rig. The underside of the cruiser was quickly filling that view. The other feed showed the lower hatch airlock. Bognath and Eleettra could be seen bracing themselves against the walls of the narrow space. They were suited up. Helmets and all.

Moments later a series of alarms sounded as the rig and the cruiser came together.

Dukk verified that the rig was holding steady, then spoke into the comms.

"Bognath, we have connection. I am engaging the hatch interlocking mechanism. You can open the hatch when the lights go green."

"On it," Bognath replied.

The video feed showed Bognath bending over the hatch, monitoring the interlocking process. He then stood up and interacted with a panel on the wall above the hatch. The hatch door lifted open.

With the hatch open, Bognath knelt again. Bognath could be then seen waving towards the hatch. After a moment, he made the shape of a zero with his hand.

With that, he stood up and looked towards the camera in the ceiling.

"Captain, no one to come across," he said into the comms.

"Roger. Close the hatch and we'll give it two minutes to complete the charade before undocking," Dukk replied.

After two minutes, Dukk unmuted the video call with the cruiser.

"Sapphire IV, it looks like we are all done, initiating undocking. Have a good morning."

"You too, Imhullu. Over and out," came the reply.

Apart from the shell game, moving with the flotilla was no different than any other passage. Dukk and his crew ran the rig, used the gym, rested, and enjoyed a meal together once a day. The presence of Eleettra and her assistant made the meals a little more entertaining. There was a new audience for the well told stories. Even the two-day layover at the hub at IACB5, had been very typical with rig maintenance and downtime in the hub bars.

413

They had also used the time to progress their plan for raiding the mammoth. It was determined that Marr and Dukk would go in alone. A larger team would attract too much attention and not fit in with what Bartiamos could arrange. The instruction from Teacher had made Dukk's involvement clear. It was also decided that Marr was the best to accompany him owing to her fighting skills, but also technical capabilities should they need to hot-wire a door or shutdown some surveillance.

Shortly after reaching Earth, they got a nice surprise. Eleettra had already informed them that they would be deorbiting with half the flotilla. She also said there was to be one final hatch-to-hatch docking sequence. The squad they'd been transporting would be crossing over. When the hatch opened, Craig and Emeelie were there ready to be pulled through. Because of the short notice, Dukk and Marr stayed at their seats in the cockpit and commenced deorbit protocols. Only after the rig was safely into the three-hour slow descent did they all get the chance to say hello.

"Welcome on board, Craig and Emeelie," Dukk said as he left the cockpit and entered the passenger seating area. Mentor, Luna, Bazzer and Annee followed.

Craig and Emeelie were sitting in the first row of seats.

"Thank you, brother!" Craig said with glee as he unbelted and got up for a bear hug.

Emeelie also stood and engaged in a warm embrace.

"Hi all," Marr called from her seat in the front of the cockpit. "I'll have to wait here until Dukk is back at his station before I can say hello properly."

"Hello, Marr," Craig called from the doorway.

"Can I enter?" Emeelie asked Dukk.

"Yes, of course," he replied as he stood out of the way.

Emeelie brushed past him and went over to greet Marr.

Marr stood up and gave Emeelie a hug as she reached her.

"Sorry for all the formalities and distance since we left the Shipyard. We had to keep up appearances. Especially now that I am officially part of the family and not staff."

"That is totally understandable, Emeelie," Marr replied. "How have you been?"

"It has been a crazy six weeks since announcing the primary companionship and me resigning from Craig's staff."

"But isn't chief of staff a staff position?"

"It was," Emeelie said with a grin. "With Tieanna missing there was a void in his team. I wasn't interested in being a shadow or a subordinate. So, I suggested that we change things. I suggested we make it more of a partnership arrangement. Craig is great at driving forward but lacks the finesse to keep all the relationships in check. It is also a great way to stay close to each other."

"Interesting," Marr said with a smile.

4

"What's interesting"?" Dukk said as he and Craig entered the cockpit.

"Just women's stuff," Marr said with a wink.

Dukk smiled.

"It is good to see you both," Marr said as Craig came over for a hug.

"Yes, and I can't wait to show you the beach," Craig answered.

"Speaking of which," Emeelie interrupted. "I have new descent instructions for you. Marr?"

Marr nodded as Emeelie interacted with her wrist wraps. She then flicked a message over to Marr. Marr caught it and projected it to the cockpit projector.

A satellite image appeared in the air around them. Emeelie, Craig and Dukk stood back so they weren't interfering with the image. The rest of the crew had also crowded into the back of the cockpit or were hovering in the doorway.

The projection showed the west coastline of the large continent in the northern hemisphere. Citadel Inquis was clear in the image as a green space with the unmistakable circular structure at its centre. A waypoint marker was flashing to the south of the citadel.

"This is our beach complex," Emeelie said as she pointed towards an area near the coast that was covered by bushes and trees. It was just north of the waypoint marker.

"There is nothing there?" Marr said.

"The complex is integrated into the hillsides. The roof tops are made to appear just like the surrounding vegetation."

"The waypoint marker isn't where you pointed."

"No, we aren't going to the main complex. The rest of the deorbiting half of the flotilla is going there. Our destination is a smaller, more private beach house. Very similar to Emerald Valley. We have had it stocked and cleared of staff. It will be private, but we'll have to fend for ourselves. I assume that won't be an issue."

"Absolutely not, this is wonderful," Marr said with a big smile.

A general sense of delight could be felt moving through the cockpit.

"Right then," Dukk said to regain the room. "Marr, do you want to feed that into the autopilot, and I'll authorise it so we can get this plan into action."

"Absolutely," Marr replied as she sat back down and started interacting with her console.

"What's our arrival time look like?" Craig asked.

"Three thirty p.m." Marr said a moment later.

"Great, we'll have just enough time for a quick swim before firing up the barbecue!" Craig stated.

"Right, I'd better get my knife set into a bag," Suzzona said as she pulled her head out from the jam in the cockpit door.

"So, Dukk, I won the bet!" Luna laughed.

"Bet?" Marr asked.

"Dukk challenged me for keeping the bikinis as we left Emerald Valley."

"Yes, Luna, you'll be making use of the bikini again!" Dukk replied.

"And you have to go skinny dipping!"

"What?" Marr said as she looked up.

"That was the bet. If we reached water again suitable for swimming before the bikinis went out of style, Dukk had to take a dip in his birthday suit," Luna laughed.

"That's great, entertainment already sorted for the evening," Craig added.

The room erupted into laughter.

Dukk shook his head.

Just under two and a half hours later, Dukk and Marr were at their seats in the front of the cockpit. The rig was on the final approach. Ahead of them was the coastline. It was fast approaching. From their angle of descent, they could only see green vegetation. There was still no sign of buildings or anything resembling a space port.

"There!" Marr stated as she pointed towards a flat area of vegetation a short distance in land from the beach.

The vegetation was moving. The roof of an underground hanger was opening.

"Got it," Dukk said as he interacted with the controls to bring the rig to and then through the opening.

"Wow!" Luna said out loud as the rig descended into the hidden hanger.

With the rig on the hanger floor, the roof closed again. Darkness engulfed them.

"Let's initiate shutdown protocols," Dukk said as he took his hands off the controls.

"On it," Bazzer replied.

"We are down, welcome back to Earth," Dukk said on the broadcast.

"Time for a swim, Dukk! I hope it is warm out," Marr said with a laugh.

Dukk rolled his eyes as he smiled over at Marr.

417

Leaving the rig was straight-forward. The crew were already quite comfortable with what was needed after the time in Emerald Valley. After a quick tour of the beach house, which was similar in many ways to Emerald Valley, they all headed to the beach for a swim and to witness Dukk honouring the bet.

"I don't think I should be doing this alone!" Dukk said in protest.

The others were standing around him. Everyone was in swimsuits. They were looking out at the ocean. Rolling waves came up the white sand to gently wash their toes. The water was warm. The sky was clear. The sun was shining. They were alone in the two-kilometre-wide cove.

"Why not? Reneging?" Luna said in jest.

"No, I am not reneging. I just think this wasn't something I could have anticipated. These events are beyond my realm of knowledge."

"A bet is a bet!" Luna said.

Dukk rolled his eyes as he went to drop his boardshorts.

"I'll join you, seeing as you are here because of me," Craig said as he stepped over to Dukk.

"Yeah!" heckled Luna with delight. The others joined in the jeering.

"Brilliant," Dukk said with a smile.

"Right then, on three," Craig said with a laugh.

On three, both Dukk and Craig dropped their boardshorts and then bolted for the water. The others cheered, clapped, and whistled.

Eight days later, Marr and Dukk were standing in the hidden hanger. They were watching a quadcopter passing through the ceiling doors. They had just said goodbye to Craig and Emeelie. They were going back to the main complex to board a cruiser for the launch. The flotilla was on the move again.

Their time at the beach house had been bliss.

They had swum, learnt to surf, played games, used the library, had quiet time, enjoyed many meals together, and at times too much wine.

Dukk and Craig were almost inseparable. Marr had also enjoyed strengthening her bond with Emeelie.

The crew had tagged along at times. They had also found their own space.

The group had ended most evenings on the beach, around an open fire, sharing stories.

They had also done some planning and touched a few edgy topics.

They had shared a version of how they came into knowing the whereabouts of Tieanna.

They had talked about ways of living. They had explored balance. They had touched on old ways and possibilities, without sharing their knowledge of the resistance or the reality of the Rule of Twelve.

Craig had also shared more about what Tieanna was up to. In addition to knowledge of trafficking, they were also aware of the existence of unauthorised incubation centres and the risk they posed for children. Tieanna had been actively trying to identify the ring leaders. Mercenaries had been used occasionally to intervene and attempt rescues. It hadn't made much of a dent. Craig mostly had his hands tied. He had to keep the peace between families.

They learnt more about the cruiser that Craig had lent to his father, and the events surrounding it getting blown-up. Craig was as surprised as everyone but didn't think there was foul play. He was sure it was an equipment failure. He had no reason to think otherwise. Also, he had suspected that his father was using it for his wayward activities but wasn't sure how to intervene.

And Marr and Dukk had shared their decision to become primary companions. A piece of news which was the catalyst for one of the evenings where perhaps a little too much wine was shared.

"Do you think there will be a time when we can openly socialise with Craig and Emeelie," Marr asked Dukk.

"One day, surely, but for now I guess we'll have to make do with sneaking around."

As he answered, Dukk gave Marr a gentle squeeze with his right arm.

"What is your take on Craig's request to see Tieanna the moment we get her off the mammoth?"

"He feels it is very doable."

"He is taking a huge risk by being the bait in this plan. He puts his whole family on a potential war footing with the Veneficans. Coming near us just after we grab Tieanna puts him in the frame."

"It does. However, I like his plan of using the shell game to hide his movements after the meeting. It will give him an alibi and hide his involvement. When the Veneficans show up, he puts his flotilla on the move. He states he has urgent business elsewhere. He shares the destination. He then has his meeting with the queen on the surface. After that he boards an arrow. The arrow is to deliver him to the flotilla. Once in orbit, the flotilla does the shell game. In that process he docks with us. The Imhullu will be running a traverse count down. After meeting with Tieanna briefly, he transfers back. The flotilla then heads off and we go a separate direction. It will look all very normal from the outside. And if they follow him, they won't find Tieanna."

"As long as he doesn't get caught with us and Tieanna."

"Yes, that is something we are going to have to stay on top of."

"It is."

"Will we go?"

"Yep," Marr answered.

Dukk then opened the comms to his crew, "they are clear. Let's fire the old bird up."

"Copy, captain," came the reply from Bazzer.

420

Chapter 22 – Raiding

1

"I decoded the traverse instructions sent over by Eleettra."

Marr and Dukk were alone in the cockpit. They were waiting for the others to join them ahead of leaving the beach house hanger.

"What is the destination?" Dukk asked.

"A planet in the Innes system. Isn't that in the direction of the Carina constellation?"

"Yes, which makes sense."

"Why?"

"Craig mentioned that the holiday was over, and he needed to get back to doing the rounds."

"Now that he and Emeelie are official?"

"Yep. He said they are using it as a good excuse to sure up relations with other families and strengthen trade agreements."

"Which family is out that direction?"

"The Hintaught family."

"Are we going to Drafuse?" Annee interrupted having just entered the cockpit.

"I gather," Dukk answered.

"Drafuse?" Marr asked.

"It is the most likely hub stop on the way to Abrolhos," Dukk replied.

"What is at Abrolhos?" Luna asked having followed Annee in and taken her seat.

"The Hintaught's largest settlement," Annee replied.

"Hintaughts! We haven't had dealings with them since Dukk became captain," Bazzer announced as he landed into his seat.

"Hintaughts! Sounds like we have received the flight plan," Mentor stated as he joined them.

"Nope, just the first traverse, the rest is speculation," Marr answered.

"Will we get going or do you want to sit here and discuss elite family specifics for the rest of the evening?" Dukk said with a chuckle.

He was met with cheeky smiles from his crew.

The speculation was indeed correct. Over the course of six days, the flotilla made its way towards Abrolhos, a planet in the HDK85 system in the general vicinity of Canopus. The rig had just arrived out of traverse. Marr and Dukk were alone in the cockpit. The crew members had either gone looking for breakfast or gone back to bed. Marr and Dukk were waiting for the coded message from Eleettra. It would contain the next traverse timing.

"I am looking at the path we've just taken. Is it typical?" Marr asked.

"Remind me what course we took."

"From Innes, we traversed to IK56, IK91, Tapecue, Drafuse 3 and then the Midway hub in the Drafuse 1 system. Pity we didn't find any trace of your old crew member, Chuk."

"I suspect that was a good thing. He was too fond of the bottle. We couldn't have left him behind and his presence now would only complicate things."

"Good point. Anyway, after that we traversed through Drafuse 5, Drafuse 7, Drafuse 9, HDK145 and HDK216. That puts us here, in HD 95086."

"Yes, that is a typical route to HDK85, where we'll find Hintaught's settlement on Abrolhos."

"Do you think Abrolhos will have one of Bartiamos' service centres?"

"Should do. The Hintaughts have a fleet nearly as big as the Atesoughtons. There aren't many ship builders big enough to service a large fleet."

"I've been thinking about Bartiamos' suggested plan."

"What improvements have you made to it?" Dukk asked with a smirk.

Marr made a rude face and then continued.

"I think we need to take Bartiamos' repair crew out of the equation. Make sure they can't be implicated in any way."

"What do you suggest?"

"We drug them."

"How do we do that if they are flying the repair shuttle?"

"Ok. So, we get smuggled on board as Bartiamos has suggested. Then once we set down in the hanger of the mammoth, we sedate the repair crew. We then raid the octet, get Tieanna, and return to the shuttle. We then wake them and get them to fly out and commence the deorbit. We then sedate them again before the Imhullu picks us up. The shuttle autopilot will deorbit and bring them down safely. Even if the Veneficans grab them before they get back to the ground, they won't have a story to tell. They won't be lying when they say they have no knowledge of what happened."

"They will have mighty sore heads after."

"Yes, but that will be better than what they'd get if they are suspected of involvement."

"True."

A message alert interrupted their raid planning.

"Yep, HDK85," Marr said after decoding the message.

"Excellent, let's load it up."

"Will do. What kind of activities will we find at Abrolhos?"

"Lots! It is a big settlement. The Hintaught family prefer to operate a smaller number of larger settlements. The staff and labour district has the usual bars, restaurants, and recreational activities. There is also a lot of trade and some crafts."

"Shopping!" Marr exclaimed as she looked up from the console.

"Yes, you'll have many ways to spend the crypto we've been accumulating."

"Nice."

"Mind you, I guess it will be the Imhullu's turn to stay in orbit."

"So?"

"You and I will have to hitch a ride to the surface. We will need to be there just in case the Veneficans show up and we need to get smuggled on board a repair shuttle."

"How does that change the shopping plan?" Marr asked as she looked back at the console.

"We'll need to pay for some sort of accommodation."

"That's fine. You spend your crypto on the accommodation and I'll spend mine on some local crafts."

Dukk laughed, then added, "you've got this all worked out."

Marr grinned.

"That flight plan update is ready for your authorisation."

Dukk smiled as he turned back towards the DMD controls.

2

A little over twenty-four hours later, Marr and Dukk were wandering through busy streets. They were in the labourer quarters in the main settlement on Abrolhos. It was near midday. The previous evening, they had reached orbit, packed a very small overnight bag, handed over the rig to Annee as second in command, and hitched a ride on an arrow about to deorbit. Once on the surface, they had found a double h-pod in a hotel.

"Do you think all these people are actually born on Earth and then brought here?"

"Why do you ask?" Dukk asked.

"There is a lot of them. A lot more people than you'd think were needed to service the elites."

"Where else would they come from?"

"Illegal incubation centres or places like Newterratwo?"

"Yes, maybe."

"Do you want a coffee?" Marr asked as they stopped outside a small coffee shop.

Dukk nodded as he followed Marr to a table just inside the door.

"Do you know what I've been thinking," Marr stated after they placed their order.

"Nope, I gave up that frivolous pursuit long ago," Dukk said with a laugh.

Marr grinned.

"Anyway, the magnitude of this challenge worries me."

"How so?"

"If Craig can hide the beach resort on Earth from most on the planet, observers and even other elite families, how will we ever find and shutdown the trafficking and unauthorised incubation centres."

"Yes, that has occurred to me too. Craig also acknowledged the existence of the unauthorized incubation centres and their potential for abuse of children."

"Even just considering Earth, the challenge is enormous. They could be anywhere. In hidden places like the beach house. Even within the citadels themselves. Families have their own protected spaces. Craig admits he doesn't have access to all areas of the Citadels or parts of the planet. Then you have the activities outside of Earth. It is hard to fathom how we can make the slightest of difference."

"We made a difference to the lives of the eleven girls."

"Yes, that is true. But that has me wondering where we should go next."

"Mentor and Tieanna were making progress. Surely, we just follow their lead?"

"I guess so."

The rest of the day and the next were much the same. Marr and Dukk spent time exploring the settlement. They played the role of cashed up mercenaries. They also made sure they knew the location of and how to connect with the crews in Bartiamos' service centres.

"How was it?" Bazzer asked as he greeted Marr and Dukk on their return from the surface.

"Like a well-earned holiday," Dukk answered with a grin.

"Well-earned? Six days in space after the beach and you needed a holiday?"

Dukk laughed as he closed the port door.

"Welcome back, captain," Annee said into the comms. "Do you want to complete the undocking process, or will I continue?"

"I'll come up, Ann. The launch on the arrow was fine, all things considered, but I am done being a passenger."

"Right, see you up here. There is also a coded message from Eleettra with our next traverse instructions."

Marr and Dukk made their way back up to the cockpit. Annee was sitting in the captain's seat. Mentor was next to her. They got up as Marr and Dukk entered.

"The airbridge has been withdrawn. We are ready to go," Annee said as she made way.

"Thanks Ann. Any issues while we were gone?" Dukk asked as he took his seat.

"Nope, just a stir-crazy crew."

"Well, at least for the next planet, we should all be able to explore the settlement."

"Yep, here is hoping."

"Carina X3. That is further away from Earth!" Marr stated a little later after decoding the message from Eleettra.

"Sounds like we are off to Southern Cross."

"As in the settlement on a planet in the Acrux system?"

"Yep."

"So, looking at the charts, and if that was our next destination, after Carina X3, we'd traverse to Carina Z2, Mimosa 3, Mimosa 1, and then Acrux."

"Yep, that would be the typical route."

"So, two and a half days. And no hub stops?"

"It wouldn't be needed."

"The traverse details for Carina X3 are in the flight plan," Marr said as she looked up from the controls.

Dukk authorised the update and the DMD accepted the instructions.

A tingle ran through them as the DMD came online and started the countdown to the traverse.

Marr felt very odd. Like the first time she had experienced the traverse. She felt like she needed to vomit. She excused herself and headed to the bathroom.

"Are you ok," Dukk asked when she returned.

"Yes, I am fine. It must have been that street food we ate before launch," Marr said hesitantly.

"Odd that I don't feel unwell. Are you sure that you are ok? Should Mentor run some tests?"

"I'll be fine," Marr said as she focused on taking deep breaths.

"Do you two have a minute?" a voice came from the doorway. It was Mentor.

"Are your ears burning?" Dukk asked.

"No, why?" Mentor answered in a puzzled tone.

Marr looked at Dukk and shook her head gently. She tried to communicate that she didn't want Mentor looking at her. Dukk shrugged his shoulders.

"Sure, what's up?" Dukk asked as Mentor came to the front of the cockpit and leant against the forward console.

"I was going back over the raid plans and the information Bartiamos shared. I think we need to take further precautions."

"Like what?" Marr asked in a tone that she hoped would hide her current state.

"While I don't see any surveillance equipment near the mantrap to the octet, I suspect there must be some in the hangers and other places. Even if you don't use your comms, the implants will still admit a signal to find receivers. Even with a false digital ID, the device still has a unique signature. I think it best that we completely disable them. We completely mask your presence on the mammoth."

"That makes sense. But how will Dukk and I communicate when Dukk is in the octet?"

"Good question. I hadn't thought about that yet."

"We could use two-way radios. Like the ones they use on the surface on Newterratwo. Stephen said that the tech is so old that modern systems can't even detect it being used," Dukk stated.

"Do we have some?"

"No, but we can print them."

"Great. So, before you head off next time, I'll disable the comms."

"And I'll talk to Bazzer about printing the radios."

3

Three and a half days later, Marr and Dukk were making their way through the side streets of the main settlement in Southern Cross. It was near one p.m. They were wearing full-length grey cloaks. These were covering the grey service staff g-suits that Bartiamos had leant them. They had the hoods over their heads, and each had their helmet in a carry bag.

During the afternoon of the day before, they had reached the planet and landed with half of the flotilla. After a typical planet side evening, the crew got word that the mammoth ring had arrived in orbit. A coded message from Eleettra arrived a short time later. It said a meeting was scheduled for four-thirty p.m.

Mentor had operated on Marr and Dukk's implants and then the Imhullu had made ready for departure. After a quick goodbye, Dukk had passed control over to Annee. Then, he and Marr had watched them return to orbit to start the traverse countdown.

The instructions they got from Bartiamos' people was to find a restaurant in the labourer district.

"That has to be it," Marr said to Dukk as they tried their best to look casual.

"Yep, looks right. What's the time?"

"Twelve fifty."

"A little early, but it should be ok. Let's go."

Dukk opened the door of the rough looking street food restaurant. He held it for Marr.

Inside were a dozen or so tables. Some were occupied.

Marr went over to the food counter.

A dowdy looking server mumbled, "yep?"

Marr ordered a specific set of items in a specific order. It was as Bartiamos had instructed.

The server took the order and then asked for payment for the items they all knew they wouldn't be eating or drinking.

Marr took a selfie and shared the required amount of crypto.

The server then nodded towards a door at the back of the small restaurant.

Marr led the way.

Beyond the door was a waiting room. There were a half dozen seats. Marr shrugged at Dukk, and they sat down to wait.

Two hours later, the wall at the end of the room opened.

A man nodded to them to enter the room beyond. The back room was some sort of storeroom. There was a shutter door at the far end. It was closed. In the middle of the room were two robotic crates. They were the types that Dukk was familiar with for carrying food supplies. They were both open.

"Get in," the man said.

Marr and Dukk looked at each other. They observed each other's concern, nodded, and went over to the crates.

The journey in the crate took about thirty minutes. Dukk speculated that, the crates were moved to the port via a service hyperloop.

When the crates opened, Marr and Dukk found themselves in another storeroom. There was a shutter door. It was down. There was a small door to the side of the shutter. The same man from the back of the restaurant greeted them as they climbed out of the crates.

"Leave your cloaks on the bench over there. Put your helmets on. Lower the sunshield. Leave this room and go to shuttle SYCX5. Climb on board," the man said before disappearing out of the door.

The small door opened into a medium size hanger.

Three small shuttles were sitting on pads in the hanger. Marr and Dukk walked towards the shuttles and found SYCX5. A ramp was lowered from the belly of the shuttle.

The ramp brought them to a storage hold. It contained a robotic tool trolley. It was as long and as wide as two robotic crates and a little taller. At the forward end of the hold was a doorway. It was open. The cockpit could be seen beyond.

"Welcome, intrepid adventurers, the ride of a lifetime awaits," said one of the pilots as he peered towards them from his seat.

Marr and Dukk approached and stepped through the doorway. The cockpit had four seats. The pilot and the co-pilot occupied the two front seats.

"Take a seat but keep your sunshield down. Unless you want your mugs on file. We are preparing for launch."

From the cockpit they had a great view as they left the port, blasted into orbit, and entered a hanger on mammoth one. It took about forty-five minutes. The hanger they had landed in, was exactly as pre-arranged with Bartiamos. He had organised that the repair crew would take on a service job that was close to the octet entrance.

"Now, we are going to leave you for a bit and take our trolley for a walk," the pilot said as he removed his helmet and reached for his service crew cap.

That was the signal that Marr was waiting for.

In a single and smooth movement, she leant forward and jabbed both pilot and co-pilot in the back of the neck. Instantly their heads dropped forward.

Marr then leant over the pilots and interacted with the controls. A panel that had been showing a video of the cockpit suddenly went blank.

She nodded at Dukk. Both then grabbed the service crew caps and left the cockpit. In the storage hold, they removed their helmets and put on the caps.

Dukk activated the ramp, while Marr checked that the lower compartment of the trolley had sufficient room for Tieanna.

4

Keeping their faces hidden as much as possible, Marr and Dukk escorted their trolley out of the hanger. It didn't take them long to reach the entrance to the octet. It was an ordinary looking door on a short passage that linked two main artery corridors. On the way, they passed a few sentinels, but none gave them any cause for concern. It was clear that the appearance of Bartiamos' repair crews was very normal.

On reaching the entrance to the mantrap, Marr and Dukk stopped to look at each other.

It was a tense moment. They had agreed they should avoid speaking in case their voices got picked up and analysed. They both wanted to express how much they meant to each other, should this be their last moment together.

After what felt like an age to both, but was more likely twenty seconds, they smiled and nodded.

Dukk then activated the door to the mantrap and walked in. The door closed behind him.

Marr looked through the small portal window. She could see Dukk standing in the middle of the small space. There were two doors at the other end of the mantrap. One on the left and one on the right.

Dukk looked around. The room looked seamless. He could see no sign of air vents or a false floor.

Then there was a noise of rushing air. The oxygen was being removed.

He felt lightheaded.

Then the noise changed. The oxygen was being restored.

He felt the process repeat twice more.

Then the door on the left swung open.

The sense of relief was intoxicating.

He turned back towards Marr and waved.

Marr watched as Dukk turned and walked through the door on the left. It closed immediately behind him. She breathed again.

At that moment she heard movement. There was someone moving on the main corridor. They had planned for this eventuality. There was a storeroom opposite the octet entrance.

Marr spun around, opened the doors, and pushed the trolley into the storeroom.

However, the room was small, and the trolley just fitted. There was no room for herself. She shut the doors and stepped back. She looked left and right. She could see the shadows of sentinels in both main artery corridors.

She was stuck. She was exposed. She stumbled back once more and bumped into the door control panel. The mantrap door sprung open, and Marr tumbled in. The door swung closed immediately.

Marr looked around. There was no panel to reopen the door.

Then there was a noise of rushing air.

She felt lightheaded. She was certain she was going to pass out. Sitting on the floor, she thought she could feel motors activating as if the floor was about to open and jettison her into space.

She reached for the two-way radio and tried to click it three times. A series of three clicks was the way that they had agreed to call for help.

Meanwhile, Dukk had found the cell. The space beyond the left door indeed included a prison.

Immediately inside the door was a large lounge area with a kitchenet. It looked to be well supplied with rehydratable packages. Beyond was a long corridor. He walked down the corridor and found a series of cells. Each contained a bench, a toilet, and a sink. The first eleven were empty. The last was occupied.

Dukk put his hand on the door control panel. It activated. The door opened.

A woman was inside sitting on the bed.

She looked up at Dukk standing in the doorway.

She stalled for a moment and then stood up.

"My boy! You came!" she blurted.

She was trembling. She then burst into tears.

Dukk burst into tears too. The emotions were overwhelming. The memories. Here she was after all this time. The wonderful mother he knew for such a short time so many years ago.

Tieanna rushed over to him and collapsed into his arms.

They cried openly together.

Eventually, Dukk managed to pull himself together enough to ask if she was hurt. He also thought he heard the two-way radio click. Marr must be encouraging him to hurry up.

"No," she sobbed as she stood back a little. "I am fine, just overcome with seeing you again in person after so long. Seeing the strong and beautiful man that my little happy boy has become."

She sobbed again. He joined her.

"I have so many questions," Dukk said when the emotions abated a little.

"I am sure you have. But my darling boy you should not have come. It is what they wanted. You are too important. Why didn't Mentor listen!"

"It wasn't his choice."

"Didn't he get my message."

"He did. Look, we don't have much time. We must go."

"Go?"

"Yes, together now. We are here to rescue you!"

"We?"

"Not important right now. Let's go."

Dukk grabbed the two-way, held the talk button and whispered, "We are on our way."

"Wait, I need to leave a note."

"What? Why?"

"Just because. Do you have a knife?"

"Yes," Dukk answered as he extracted a small knife from his belt.

Tieanna took the knife and made a small cut in her finger. She then wrote on the wall. The message read, 'You will not prevail!'

Dukk stared. He wasn't sure what to make of that.

"Ok, let's go," Tieanna said as she handed him the knife.

Meanwhile, Marr hadn't passed out or been jettisoned into space. Instead, the oxygen had returned, and both the left and right doors had swung open.

"Why aren't I dead?" she thought as she looked over her shoulder at the two open doors.

Curiosity overtook her. She jumped up and bolted for the door on the right.

Within was the apartment that Bartiamos had speculated about. It looked fresh and recently occupied.

There was a door on her right. The door had a small window. She went over and looked in. It was a computer room as Bartiamos had suggested. In front of a series of computer cabinets was a desk and a single chair. It looked dusty.

There was a hand panel near the door. She felt an intense need to put her hand on it. The cautionary message from Bartiamos about the dark matter containment unit echoed in her mind. Before she thought better of testing fate, a claw emerged from the panel and trapped her hand. She felt a prick in her finger. The claw released. She looked at her finger. Blood. Then the door clicked. It was open.

Marr entered the room and cautiously went over to the desk.

Sitting in the middle of the desk was a small note. It wasn't visible from the window in the door. It simply read, 'My dear child, if I am dead, you know what you must do. If you are here before my death, and you are still free, cover your tracks and run. Make it look like you were never here. Love, Helenal.'

Marr was confused. This was very odd. She looked around at the desk. On the left was a cradle. It was dusty as if what rested in it was long since removed. Next to it was another cradle. Resting in it was a palm size disc. She reached for it and accidentally knocked it from the cradle. As it came to rest on the desk it came to life. A holographic image appeared in the air above the disc. In the image were Craig and Emeelie. Craig was speaking.

Marr reached into the image and interacted with some controls. She turned the volume up.

"With all due respect, I really would appreciate not having to converse with a mask," he said.

"As you wish," said an unseen speaker.

Hands appeared in the view. It was now clear to Marr that she was seeing Craig and Emeelie through the eyes of another. Marr could see a mask being removed. The view showed the mask being put on the table in front of the person. The person now looked up. Marr now had a wider view of the scene. She could see in the periphery that someone else was there. But Marr couldn't see her face. She could see that the other person also removed their mask.

The image clearly showed Craig and Emeelie. Their expressions were now of shock as they looked between the two that were in front of them.

"You look like you've seen a ghost," a female's voice could be heard saying.

Marr assumed it was the person whose eyes she was borrowing.

"We are on our way," squawked the two-way radio.

Dukk's message snapped Marr to attention. She grabbed the disc and stuffed it into a pocket. She pulled her cap off and whooshed the dust as she retracted her steps. She then bolted for the mantrap. This time the outer door opened the moment the inner door closed. She then spun around and peered through the portal window. The left door opened. Dukk came through. A woman was with him.

Without speaking Marr and Dukk helped Tieanna into the lower compartment of the trolley. They then returned to the shuttle.

"I will wake the pilots," Marr said once the ramp was raised.

"You can climb out now, but keep your face hidden inside your cloak," Dukk said to Tieanna as he opened the lower compartment of the trolley.

"We are in great danger. You shouldn't have come," Tieanna said as she climbed out.

"I know. I think we have that under control."

"I hope so."

"Come and sit over here," Dukk said as he walked over towards the bulkhead. "The shuttle might move about a bit but there are no other seats, so this corner will have to do for now."

"That's fine," Tieanna said as she sat down.

"Once we get on board the rig we can talk," Dukk said from a crouching position.

"Is Septemo with you? Sorry! I mean, is Mentor with you?"

"He is, and it's okay because I know what you call him."

"He told you?"

"No, Craig did."

"Which Craig?"

"The Craig you raised?"

"You've met him?"

"Yes. He is coming to meet you too."

"Does he know that I am your mother?"

"No, we kept away from that topic. There is so much to tell. And I have a lot of questions."

"Yes, so much to tell. First, I must speak with Septemo. Alone."

"There will be time when we get picked up."

"They are coming around," Marr called through the hatch.

"Sit tight. I need to take my seat," Dukk said as he headed towards the cockpit.

Meanwhile, Marr had stuck an antidote into the necks of the pilot and co-pilot. As Dukk took his seat, she started shouting at them.

"Quick, wake up! You two passed out, we were scared shitless that we'd be stuck here. Get us out of this hanger. They might traverse any minute."

"Oh, right," stuttered the pilot. "But the repair?"

"Stuff the repair. There is no way you will explain your way out of this if we are caught on board."

"Yes, you are right," he said.

Ten minutes later and after more manic demands from Marr, the shuttle was clear of the Mammoth and tracking towards the deorbit point.

With calm restored, the pilot turned to look at Marr and Dukk.

"What the hell just happened there?" he asked.

"We drugged you," Marr said as she slammed another sedative hit into the necks of both the pilot and co-pilot.

When they both collapsed forward, Dukk pushed himself out of his seat and returned to the hold.

"You can come up the front now, there is someone I want you to meet properly," Dukk said as he put his hand out to help Tieanna.

"Marr, this is Tieanna, my mother," Dukk said as they all floated together in the cockpit.

He said the last part with a gulp. A tear formed in the corner of his eye. He collected himself and continued.

"And, Tieanna, this is Marr, my primary companion."

The last part of the sentence was said with a stutter. More tears welled in his eyes.

Marr welled up too.

Tieanna approached Marr with her arms open. They embraced and hugged. Tieanna then opened one arm and beckoned Dukk to join the embrace.

"Right," Dukk said after a moment. "We'd better get organised."

"Marr, what an interesting name you have," Tieanna stated as she pushed back.

"Thanks," Marr answered with caution.

"How did you come to choose that name?"

"I am not sure."

Marr stuttered the reply. She was looking at Tieanna looking at her. Tieanna was showing a curious expression.

"I can see them," Dukk said a moment later. "They are coming in fast. You'd better hold onto something."

Dukk was floating between the two front seats. He had been looking up. The Imhullu hadn't been visible on the shuttle's radar. But the stealth tech didn't hide it from the naked eye. Dukk could clearly see it now as it swooped in above them.

Dukk turned and reached over the pilot to access the thruster controls. He pulled the controls to counter the gravitational effects of the Imhullu's DMD.

There was a bang and a crunch as the Imhullu's lower hatch connected with the shuttle's upper hatch.

Dukk then interacted with the hatch mechanism to enable a seal.

"We're connected," he said as the hatch opened. "Tieanna, you go first."

On the Imhullu side, the hatch was lifting.

Mentor leant in, once the opening was clear.

"Septemo!" Tieanna called before bursting into tears.

"Hello Tieanna. Reach up and we will pull you through."

Mentor and Bognath helped them all through the hatch. Then Bognath leant back in and hit the close button on the inside of the shuttle ceiling. He then withdrew himself and closed the Imhullu's hatch."

"Suzzona, we are clear," he then said into the comms.

The rig shook as they put distance between them and the shuttle.

"Welcome back, captain," Suzzona's voice could be heard echoing out of the airlock speaker.

"Thank you, Suzzona. That was some impressive flying," Dukk replied looking up at the green dot in the ceiling.

"Well, the next challenge is all yours. Get your arse up here."

"Med-bay first. I want my comms back on. Besides, it looks like you have it covered. And I gather Luna is sedated somewhere if you are driving."

"This stunt needed a special type of crazy. I wasn't up for it," Annee added.

Twenty minutes later, Marr and Dukk were on their way upstairs. Mentor had re-enabled their implants and then closed the med-bay door so he could talk privately with Tieanna. Before leaving, Dukk had got Tieanna's med details and loaded them into the system ready for the traverse.

Chapter 23 – Awakening

1

"Right, we are all set to dock with Craig's arrow," Dukk said as he sat back from the controls. "They should be with us soon. Someone needs to go and invite Mentor and Tieanna to take seats for the docking."

"I'll go," Marr blurted as she stood up. Sitting down for too long wasn't helping with the nausea she'd been feeling since passing through the hatch.

"Great. And we need someone to accompany Bognath to the lower hatch and prepare to welcome our guests?"

"My turn," Luna said.

Marr had just reached the middle level when she stopped short of the med-bay. The door was opening. She stood back to wait.

"We need to get you a suit and a helmet," Mentor could be heard saying.

"Wait, I need to clarify something else," Tieanna then added.

"What is that?"

"Dukk and Marr, and this rig name. This is a fantasy story I created from an ancient Mesopotamian origin story. It was where Marduk defeats Tiamat and her warlord, Kingu, using Imhullu, the wind weapon. I fantasised that Marduk could be reformed by joining the best of the masculine with the best of the feminine. That union would then defeat evil and bring back balance. It drew on the foreshadowing already established in the labels used by the resistance for the five citadels. I theorised that you'd just need to interrupt the sterilisation process for a key and well-placed man and woman. You would then name them and then let the mythology carry it forward. But it was just the silly musings of an overly imaginative teenager."

"Really! Well, I never! So, your fantasy is now taught to resistance leaders as the path forward."

"What? How can this be? I only shared this fantasy with one other. And I haven't heard or spoken with her in nearly thirty years. She disappeared."

"But you had me intervene with Dukk and ensure that he take that name when he came of age."

"I did, but I was just a foolish dreamer. How did Marr come to her name?"

"She said she picked it herself, just like Dukk thought until recently."

"Did someone implant the name, like you did with Dukk?

"I don't know, but I have my suspicions."

"What about the intervention? Marr too?"

"I am not sure, but I think it must be so."

"Who do you suspect was behind it?"

"Teacher."

"Who is Teacher?"

"She is a mentor, storyteller, and other things. She is part of the resistance movement in Utopiam."

"Other things?"

"She knows things that she has no business knowing."

"And the name of this rig?"

"Teacher's idea."

"What else is she behind?"

"My efforts to bring Marr and Dukk together, as companions."

"Interesting. How old is she?"

"Mid-nineties. I think."

"What does Teacher look like?"

"Dark brown complexion, black eyes, wild grey hair, and her ears are disfigured. And she has scars that run down the side of her neck."

"The age works. But not the looks."

"Marr, they are in range," Dukk said into Marr's comms.

The message startled Marr. She stumbled in shock and banged into the door as she did.

Mentor and Tieanna emerged.

"Are you ok, dear?" Tieanna asked.

"Yes, sorry, I was just rushing down here and ran into the door. The rig is about to maneuver so it can dock with Craig's arrow. You might want to take a seat."

"We don't have a lot of time before the traverse. We'll come up after I get a g-suit and helmet for Tieanna," Mentor said.

Marr nodded and headed back up the stairs.

The new information was exploding in Marr's brain. The nausea wasn't helping.

Instead of returning to the cockpit she went to her and Dukk's cabin. She braced herself against the window and took several deep breaths.

As she straightened back up and adjusted her g-suit, the disc she took from the octet, tumbled out on to the shelf below the window.

A new scene appeared in the air.

The scene was that of the inside of a shuttle or leisure craft. A woman in uniform was standing next to a door. It looked like a cockpit door. From the movement of the woman's arms and clothing, it looked as if the craft was in orbit.

"That was a complete waste of time," said an unseen speaker.

Marr recognised it as the same voice as before when she saw Craig and Emeelie in the projection.

"Something is wrong. Change of plan. Inform the captain to take us immediately to mammoth one. Right now!"

The woman in view immediately turned. She opened, and then disappeared through the door.

It was then that Marr noticed a message below the image. It read, 'Buffered. 20 Minutes remaining'.

Marr snapped herself back to attention. She grabbed the disc and shoved it into a drawer. She then headed back to the cockpit.

"Yep, got something," Annee could be heard saying as Marr re-entered the cockpit.

"What have you got?" Dukk asked.

"There were three Venefican vessels. A cruiser and two interceptors. They launched just after Craig's arrow. Once in orbit they started a track towards mammoth four. Then they abruptly changed trajectory. That was about twenty minutes ago."

"Where would the change in trajectory put them?"

"Mammoth one."

"Oh. That is interesting."

An alarm sounded. They were coming up on Craig's arrow.

Ten minutes later, Luna was escorting Craig, Emeelie and Eleettra, to the crew mess. Bognath was bringing up Tieanna's travel lockers. They had been passed through the hatch.

"Let's move the conn to the crew mess. I am sure we will all want to hear what Tieanna has to say," Dukk said as he stood up.

2

When Dukk and the others reached the crew mess, Craig and Emeelie were already there. As was Tieanna. They were hugging.

"What happened?" Craig blurted as he stood back from the embrace.

"Your questions will be answered, my boy," Tieanna said. "I understand we don't have much time. So, I want to share a story that is well overdue. Come."

444

Tieanna walked over to the head of the crew table.

"Sit, please everyone," she beckoned as she sat down.

She then added, "Craig here on my left with Emeelie after him. And Dukk, please sit on my right. Marr after, then Mentor please. Everyone else, please find a seat."

"First, I have some questions of my own," Tieanna said as she looked around at all those on the table.

"I understand, Craig, that you lured the mammoth ring here on the promise to meet with Magnum Reginae?"

"Yes, that's correct."

"Did you meet with her?"

"Yes, the queen and her daughter."

"What was it like?"

"Eerie."

"Did she unmask?"

"Yes, and the resemblance is uncanny," Craig said.

As he said 'uncanny', his gaze drifted towards Marr.

Marr felt the gaze just as another wave of nausea hit her. She clenched her hands. She had forgotten that she was holding Dukk's hand under the table.

Dukk felt the squeeze and looked at her. She had gone green.

Tieanna had followed Craig's gaze too. She looked puzzled.

"Craig," Tieanna said bluntly to bring everyone's focus back to herself. "What did she say to you?"

"That I would be summonsed in about six months. I would have to come to Earth to help with an initiation ceremony."

"How did you respond?"

"I said nothing. I felt a response wasn't required."

"Good. And what will you do when you are summonsed?"

"I will tell those new puritans to take a hike."

"Excellent," Tieanna laughed.

445

Tieanna then closed her eyes and took three deep breaths.

Everyone wasn't sure what to do, so they just stared.

Tieanna started to speak as she opened her eyes.

"This is the first and last time I will share this story in its entirety. Please hold your questions. I want to share this story in a specific order for reasons that will be clear only at the end."

She then paused to look around the room at everyone seated. She looked at each person for a moment and smiled before moving her gaze back to the centre of the table.

Then she started to speak. As she did, she looked directly at each for a moment. It was as if she was speaking to each person on an individual level.

"I started out in Utopiam. Like all children, I was raised in the incubation centres. After the test I was put into the hostess track. That you already know. What you don't know, is that shortly after my sixteenth birthday, I was put through the Venefican's initiation ceremony. Yes, I am of Venefican descent."

Mentor sat up. He looked shocked. He went to speak.

Tieanna held up her hand and said, "Wait Septemo, allow me to finish the story."

Mentor sat back and nodded.

"To understand what happened to me, I need to talk about the ceremony. The initiation ceremony is not what you think. It is a ghastly ritual that I am sorry you need to hear about. However, it is important for context.

"The ceremony is endured by all those born to Venefica. It has been that way for over one hundred and fifty years. All daughters of the Venefica are subject to this brutal and unthinkable ceremony. It is considered a crucial step in becoming a Venefican. Like all daughters of the Venefica, I didn't know my birth mother was a Venefican and she didn't know where I was. In the months prior to the ceremony, I was taught an ever-intensifying curriculum that suggested all men were evil. That the evil was built-in to men. That they were born that way. This didn't align with what I already knew of the great men in history, from all the reading I was doing since the test. Yes, I also read of evil, but it was far more often the opposite. My closest friend was also an intelligent boy with a huge heart. I just couldn't believe he was or would become evil. It didn't sit well with me. Then the ceremony came. I prepared as I had been trained as a hostess. I knew it would involve performing some of the things I had been taught about sex. However, I wasn't prepared for what happened. Over the course of several hours, I was beaten and repeatedly raped."

Gasps filled the room. Tieanna held up her hand and continued.

"I was battered and bruised. The swelling lasted for days. For much of it I was restrained and blindfolded. Only at the very end did I see my abuser. A man. I was devastated. I couldn't fathom what had happened. After the initiation, I was isolated from everyone else. During the isolation I became angry. As my body recovered my mind slipped into darkness. I started to believe in the suggestion that, all men were evil. I started to replace the love and respect I had for Septemo with hatred and disgust."

Tieanna then paused to take a breath. Once more she held up her hand to prevent any questions.

"You see, the founding members of the movement had legitimate cause to hate men. They had been brutally abused by some truly evil human beings. The founders committed to preventing this from ever happening to another. And they were willing to do whatever was necessary to make sure no man had power over women like this ever again. Nothing was off the table. They desired above all else to control all to prevent what they felt was the evil above all other evils. This singular focused enabled them to rationalise all manner of means to achieve their ends. The willingness to do evil of all sorts drew incredible power to them. However, over time only the memory of their abuse was present. Those that followed, found it harder and harder to convince other women of their belief in the evil of man and the need to hate them deeply. So, they created the initiation ceremony to instil that hatred. They manufactured the hatred in their daughters to keep the movement alive. They lost sight of why they were founded. They ended up creating fertile grounds for the very thing they sort to prevent."

3

Tieanna paused again. She was struggling emotionally. It was evident in the expressions around the table that everyone else was too.

"Weekly, after the ceremony, I was inspected by a physician. I later came to understand that I was being tested for pregnancy. I later discovered that if I didn't fall pregnant, I would be subject to the abuse again until I did. Also, if the unborn child was male, the pregnancy would be aborted, and I would have to endure the abuse once more. This is because Venefica can only be women. So only daughters can be born to them. That is when the miracle happened. I was shown the light again. I stepped back from the brink. You see, I did get pregnant straight away. However, it was a boy. That is when a Venefican called Helenal intervened."

Marr felt her system shutter. The name Helenal. "What in the world?" she thought. She felt like vomiting again. She squeezed Dukk's hand once more.

He looked at her. She did her best to smile.

Tieanna hadn't noticed and continued.

"Helenal got me away from Utopiam and the Veneficans. She saved my unborn child. She made it look like I died. I got a new identity and went to work in an incubation centre in Kuedia. She put me in the care of others who I later discovered were part of the resistance. With their help, I was able to carry the child to full term and give birth. Giving birth to my son and holding him in my arms restored my hope. It gave me a new purpose."

Dukk was struggling. Tears welled up. Marr was struggling too. It was all very overwhelming.

Craig went to speak. He too was showing emotions on top of an expression of confusion. As were the others.

"Wait, my dear, let me finish the story," Tieanna said as she raised her hand once more.

"So, for the next four years I worked in the incubation centre and raised my boy. With the help of Helenal and the resistance, I stayed hidden. Unfortunately, Helenal was finding it more and more challenging to hide my existence from the other Venefica. They weren't convinced that I had died. They were looking for me. They are very protective of their bloodlines."

"Helenal convinced me that I must go somewhere that the Venefica had less influence. I was to get myself into an elite family and build a new life. We conceived a way that my boy could be protected and helped on his journey. Then we got wind of a girl getting pregnant to an elite heir and a rift within that family. Yes, Craig, this is where your story starts. The rift was that which was between your father and your grandfather. With Helenal's help, introductions were made. I was put forward to be your nanny. Unknowns to most, I also did a deal with your grandfather. He didn't want his son inheriting the family fortune, nor did he want his son raising you. He didn't see him as fit for either role. In return for getting what I needed, I promised to help shape you into the heir your grandfather wanted. The conditions in that deal included that I was to be free to raise you as I see fit. What I said went, no matter what. A major requirement was that the Venefica were not to be allowed near us under any circumstances.

"Perhaps you might be asking yourself at this point as to the identity of Helenal. Where is she now? Perhaps you are wondering what happened to this amazing woman who saved me? All I can tell you is that she took incredible risks to save me and others. It cost her dearly. I am sworn to say no more and to never utter her name again. It was telling this story and within this story alone that she said that I could mention her real name. I ask too that you honour that wish and never mention this name to another. She told me that she will reveal herself at the right time."

Tieanna paused again. The faces of all showed a combination of shock and amazement.

"Now, I know there are questions hanging. You are thinking about the identity of my abuser and some of you are wondering about what happened to my boy. I will now answer these questions. Let me clarify first the details of the deal I did with your grandfather, Craig. The deal was that only after I raise you to be worthy of taking your grandfather's place, would I be free to seek retribution for the abuse I suffered. That time came finally, with some unforeseen consequences and chance encounters which put us here in the shadow of the mammoth ring. Now for the truth which I have not shared with any other. The abuser, Craig, was your father. And the boy I spoke of is Dukk. Yes, Craig, Dukk is my son. And Dukk, yes, Craig is your half-brother. I have finished my story."

With that Tieanna burst into tears. The years of hiding the truth overwhelmed her.

Dukk sat stunned. Marr too.

Craig and Emeelie stared, gob smacked.

Tieanna leant forward and reached out for both Dukk and Craig.

At the same instant, both men rose and went over to hug her.

Mentor went white and teared up.

The others were also in total shock. Emotions overwhelmed them all.

A chime rang out. It was the fifteen-minute traverse warning.

"Oh, shit!" Annee blurted. "We are about to traverse. And we are upside down."

"Shit indeed!" Emeelie yelped as she stood up. "Craig, we need to get out right now! We won't want to be caught here. That will take a lot of explaining."

Dukk stood up. The traverse warning snapped him back to reality. He dragged the water from his eyes.

"Yes, Ann," Dukk blurted. "We need to move. Bazzer, system prep. Marr, cockpit. Start the traverse checklist. Annee and Mentor, help get Tieanna seated and hooked up. Craig, Emeelie and Eleettra, let's get you to the hatch."

Craig stood up. He nodded.

Tieanna was on her feet too. She hugged Craig quickly and then pushed him back.

"Go, we will meet again soon," she said turning to Emeelie to give her a hug.

"Take care of each other," she added as she did her best to wipe the tears from her eyes.

Dukk turned and headed for the crew mess door. Craig, Emeelie and Eleettra followed. Bognath went along too.

4

Moments later they were at the hatch. Emeelie went through first.

"Dukk, my brother," Craig said with an emotional gulp. "Keep Tieanna safe. Take her to the beach. She will be safe there. The Imhullu is already authorised. Just use the same codes as last time."

"I will, my brother," Dukk said with tears.

A final hug, and Craig disappeared through the hatch.

Only Eleettra remained.

"Aren't you going?" Dukk asked.

"Nope. New assignment. Administration wasn't for me. Too much paperwork."

"What is the new assignment?"

"Personal bodyguard for Tieanna," Eleettra said as she hovered over the hatch.

"Does she know this?"

"Nope, she doesn't think she needs it," she answered as she reached in and pulled up the first of her two travel lockers. Bognath helped her.

"Does Bazzer know?"

"Nope," Eleettra said with a chuckle as she retrieved the last locker.

Dukk smiled as he clicked the hatch close button.

Meanwhile, Marr hadn't gone directly to the cockpit. She had ducked back into her cabin. Her emotions were all over the place. She needed a moment alone. Then, she remembered the disc. She retrieved it from the drawer.

When the disc activated, the image was that of the view of the desk in the computer room of the octet. It was the same view she saw when she peered through the door's portal window, before opening it.

"She has been in here! Look the second disc is gone now too. Look at the attempts to cover her tracks."

The voice was the same as heard during the two previous projections.

"But how? There are no signs of anyone attacking us or breaking in?"

The second voice was younger sounding.

"She probably got help from Bartiamos' dim-witted repair crews. Nothing we can do about that. We need to keep him onside for now! Anyway, the how is not important at this moment."

"Why?"

"Because she has just made a huge mistake. Taking that second disc out of here is the opportunity that we've been waiting for. It is time to get rid of her and those discs."

"But without the discs, we can't access this data centre. We will still be locked out of our funds, the weapons systems on these mammoths, and the incubation databases."

"If the discs stop connecting to the network, the locks on this door will automatically reset. We'll have access again. We won't need the discs."

"But the reset waits for six months after it receives the last signal."

"We have made do for over thirty years. We can wait another six months. It must be done. She is somewhere here now. In orbit on one of the craft up here."

"If she is here, we can get the mammoth ring back to earth!"

"Unless we can get into this data centre, we can't be assured that the defences won't fire on the ring."

"What if it was a lie?"

"We've been through this before. We can't take the chance that she was lying when she said Earth defences would attack the mammoth ring if it ever came near it. No, we need to get into the data centre and take back control of the citadels. This needs to be done before we bring the mammoth ring anywhere close to Earth. She must go! We must take her out now!"

"We can't just have our arrows and interceptors fire missiles at them all."

"No, we can't. Not with Craig's flotilla up here. That would surely put us at war with the Atesoughton family. We can't afford a war with them. They are our biggest contributor."

"What do we do?"

"Here is what I see. Craig would be foolish to be directly involved in this. Clearly, he is complicit in enticing the mammoth ring here with that bogus meeting. He had his reasons. But he knows that entering our mammoth and interfering directly to retrieve that woman, would be no different than firing a missile. No! Others are supporting her.

She got help like before. Perhaps they are part of his flotilla. On one of the arrows or interceptors. The flotilla mobilised the moment we reached orbit this morning. That was nearly nine hours ago. However, the flotilla will use normal routes, so it won't traverse for another three hours. The scoundrels that are helping her will go somewhere unmonitored. They will traverse soon. Perhaps any moment."

"We don't have much time."

"No, we don't. But our scouts and leapfrog arrows are still counting down. The first wave will traverse any moment. We'll message the captains. If they see a single arrow or interceptor when they arrive in the unmonitored system, they are to fire. No quarter."

"What if we are wrong?"

"No one will know."

"What if they manage to get missiles away too and take out our arrows? How will we know it is done?"

"Let's mobilise further scouts to check. Now put your mask back on. You remind me of her."

Suddenly, the words 'Where are you? We are about to traverse!' echoed in Marr's comms. Dukk's panicked interruption snapped her back to attention. She dropped the disc into a pocket and dashed for the door.

Dukk was confused that Marr wasn't in her seat when he reached the cockpit. He squawked a message to her as he landed into his seat.

He then interacted with the controls and updated the autopilot.

"Sorry," Marr said as she landed into her seat next to him. "Nature called."

"Ok," Dukk said as he scrambled to get his console ready.

"Dukk, we have multiple vessels exiting the mammoths," Annee said.

"They must know. Let's get out of here," Dukk replied. "Prepare for traverse."

Five minutes later they were out of the traverse and orbiting an unmonitored system.

"Let's load up the DMD again, go to slow running and catch our breath," Dukk said once the post traverse checks were complete.

"Oh shit," Marr exclaimed. She had managed to hold it together after the traverse but the minute she stood up, a new wave of nausea hit her.

She bolted out of the cockpit, went straight through the passenger seating, and launched herself into the bathroom.

When Marr emerged from the toilet, she was met by Dukk, Mentor, Luna, and Tieanna. They were all standing in the corridor waiting for her.

"Are you sure that you are ok?" Dukk asked.

"It is just a bit of nausea," Marr stated unconvincingly and then stumbled.

Dukk stepped in to support her.

"How long have you been experiencing these waves of nausea?" Tieanna asked.

"The last few days or so," Marr answered softly.

"I think I need to have a look at you. Men, bring her to the sofa I saw in here. I noticed my travel lockers where there too."

Tieanna headed off towards the crew mess.

A moment later, Marr was lying on the sofa. Tieanna was leaning over her. Dukk was sitting on the edge, holding Marr's hand. Mentor were standing behind Tieanna. Luna was sitting at the console. The rest of the crew were gathered around the table.

"What is that?" Marr asked as she looked at a device in Tieanna's hands.

"It is a foetal doppler."

"What is it for?"

"You will see."

Tieanna used the device and then looked up with a smile.

"An extra heart beat?" Mentor prompted.

"Nope, two extras! Twins! Dukk and Marr, you are about to be parents. Mentor, your mission is complete," Tieanna answered.

Marr looked up at Dukk. At the same moment they both burst into tears as they leant into each other for a messy kiss and warm embrace. The room around them was awash with emotion.

A familiar but unwanted alarm interrupted the joyous moment. It sounded on the console behind them.

"Dukk, we have company," Luna said as she spun around and started flicking panels into the air.

"What does it look like?" Dukk said as he sat up.

"We have another vessel. It just came out of traverse. I got a crude signature and then it disappeared. I guess stealth."

"Stations everyone. Not a drill. Let's take no chances," Dukk said before giving Marr one long kiss and dashing for the crew mess door.

Luna was hot on his tail as he ran through the passenger seating area.

He had only just reached the cockpit when a new alarm sounded. The sound indicated that they had been missile locked.

"Stopping the DMD. I need countermeasures and stealth, ASAP," Dukk shouted as he landed into his seat.

Luna was right behind him.

A new alarm sounded. It was loud.

"Incoming missile," Annee yelled as she joined them.

"Dukk, I need a corkscrew with a hook," Luna said calmly.

"Brace," Dukk yelled into the comms as he flicked off the autopilot.

He then swivelled the joysticks in unison. The rig reacted instantly. Those that were seated were pushed into the sides of their seats as the rig spiralled. Bazzer was thrown into the side of the cockpit. He hadn't got to his seat in time. Mentor tumbled back into the passenger area. He had only managed to reach the cockpit door before the manoeuvre.

Luna gave the rail guns a burst. The rig shook as the projectiles shot out of the back of the rig.

When the burst stopped. Dukk pulled back on the joysticks. The rig arched up.

The missile ran into the rail gun trail and exploded.

The blast took the rig with it. The rig shook violently and then spiralled into a higher orbit.

New alarms sounded.

"Mentor, vitals! Bazzer, rig status ASAP," Dukk said in quick succession as he silenced the alarms.

"I'd think plenty of raised heart rates. Give me a second," Mentor replied as he took his seat.

"We've got a problem,", Bazzer said as he went to leave.

"Wait, Bazzer," Mentor interrupted before opening the comms to all on the rig.

"Everyone, take a seat," he said. "Let me fire in some meds just in case we took a radiation hit in that blast."

Dukk counted his breath as the cocktail hit is system.

"Ugh, what the hell!" Luna exclaimed as she tasted the chemicals.

Marr landed into her seat beside Dukk.

"You up for it?" Dukk asked.

She nodded as she grabbed at the seatbelts.

Dukk smiled.

"Excellent! Charts! Find the coordinates of another planet in this system."

"On it," Marr replied.

"Ann, I want to know who fired at us. See what you can find."

"Right," Annee replied instantly.

"Bazzer?"

"Bloody chemicals. No fun," Bazzer replied. "Hull integrity appears compromised. I need to get it sorted before we bring the DMD back online."

"Go for it, Bazzer. Luna, I give you permission to fire back."

"Copy," Luna replied in a gleeful tone.

"I've got the coordinates," Marr said.

"Great. Load the autopilot and let's get the rig stable again and adjust orbit ready for the traverse."

"Wait," Mentor interrupted. "Stay dead stick for now. A thruster burst will put us back on the map. We don't know who is hunting us or if they can fire again."

"Good point," Dukk acknowledged. "Best not look out the window then."

The rig was tumbling. The planet was flicking in and out of view.

Silence fell on the cockpit.

"Dukk, I can't find anything," Annee announced after what felt like an age, but was more like two minutes.

"Looks like we aren't the only ones up here with stealth tech," Luna added. "No chance of me getting a missile lock if they aren't detectable."

Marr gasped.

"What now?" Dukk asked as he looked over.

"I saw something spin past. Or more accurately. It spun into view briefly. Look, there it is again."

"There isn't anything in that direction on the scanners," Annee added.

"Shit," Dukk said as he caught a glimpse of what Marr had seen. It was a good way off, but it was clear what it was.

"What?" Annee asked.

"The colour. Blood red!"

"A Venefican arrow," Marr said quietly as she got a better look.

"We're in trouble," Annee noted. "They always travel in pairs. Perhaps it is the scouting or leap frogging craft. They must have traversed just after us. We appear to have inadvertently taken the same path."

"Bazzer, I need an update!" Dukk said into the comms.

"I'm patching up a small rupture in the belly," Bazzer replied. "The foam is going hard now. Needs another few minutes before we can test it."

"I have an idea," Marr said as she pushed herself out of her seat.

She propelled herself to the back of the cockpit. She then turned and held up her wrists. She took a photo. Then she pushed off the back wall and landed back in her seat. After a few moments of interacting with her console, an image appeared in the air between them. It showed the planet, their location, and the photo she had just taken.

"We can go old school," Marr said as she pointed to the image and looked at Luna.

"Charging the CDL," Luna said with a giggle.

"What are you two talking about?" Dukk asked.

"We can triangulate the Venefican's position using the photo with the frame of the windshield and our position. We hit them with a laser," Marr answered.

"At this range they won't see it coming or be able to do anything about it," Luna added.

"The two of you are truly terrifying," Dukk stated.

"What is stopping them doing that to us?" Annee asked.

"If they had the skills of Marr and Luna, we wouldn't be having this conversation," Mentor commented.

"Integrity is back to normal. Looks like the repair will hold up for now," Bazzer announced into the comms.

"Great, let's load the DMD and get out of here," Dukk said.

A moment later, Marr looked up.

"The DMD is refusing to take the coordinates. With the autopilot off and dead stick, it can't match the required orbit speed safely."

"Okay, we are going to have to get creative," Dukk replied. "At the right orbit, one that is comparable to both planets, and given how close we are, relatively, the traverse should happen almost instantly. So, we are going to estimate the needed orbit height and initiate a hard burn. As we approach the correct altitude, we'll send the instructions to the DMD. It should take them and traverse shortly after."

"The hard burn will light us up," Marr said. "They will get missile lock."

"So, let's shift things in our favour. Just before we hit the hard burn, we go with your CDL plan. We give them something else to worry about."

"And you think 'we', are terrifying!" Luna said and then laughed deeply.

Dukk smiled.

"Do you want to do the orbit estimation and I'll help Luna with the triangulation," Marr suggested.

"Yes, I was thinking the same. Ann, keep a sharp eye out. We want to know where the other Venefican arrow is."

"Yep, on it," Annee replied.

Five minutes later, Bazzer was back in the cockpit. Everything was ready. They had their helmets on and were plugged into the med lines. Luna was ready to fire the laser. Dukk was ready to initiate the hard burn. Marr was ready to send the traverse instructions. There was an eerie silence.

Dukk slowed his breathing. He cleared his mind.

Marr glanced over. She smiled.

"Ok, on three," Dukk said into the comms. He paused.

"One, two, three, FIRE!"

The rig shook as the cannon fired and the hard burn was initiated.

A glimpse of an explosion flashed passed as the hard burn kicked in.

The crew were pushed back into their seats as the autopilot corrected the tumble and shot the rig towards the required orbit.

A new alarm.

"We've been missile locked again," Luna yelped.

"I've got the other arrow," Annee added. "It was tracking towards us. Shit! It has disappeared again, and I have got a missile heading our way."

"How long?" Dukk asked.

"It is nearly on us," Annee exclaimed.

"Luna?" Dukk stated.

"Give me a corkscrew."

"No can do. Not while in hard burn."

"Side-step!"

"Call it," Dukk commanded as he disabled the autopilot.

"NOW," Luna shouted as the rig's rail guns rattled projectiles ahead of them.

Dukk pushed the joysticks. The thrusters fired. The rig shifted slightly but kept moving fast in the same direction.

The missile shot past them and immediately started to arc back around.

"It is reacquiring," Annee stated.

"Marr, try the DMD."

"It took the instructions. Twelve minutes. No, wait, eight minutes."

"Great, it is adjusting as we get closer to a more compatible orbit."

"It just changed to six minutes."

"This is going to be tight. Let's get ready to load up the juice. Ready!"

"Now it is saying two minutes."

"Missile is coming around," Annee added.

"Now it says twenty seconds."

"Mentor, run the juice!" Dukk shouted.

Dukk closed his eyes as the cocktail hit his blood stream and his consciousness faded.

The End

Continue your awakening at <u>RuleOfTwelve.com</u>.

The Rule of Twelve trilogy:

Book 1, Double Take

Book 2, Convergence

Book 3, Regeneration